Church Folk

MICHELE ANDREA BOWEN

Walk Worthy Press

West Bloomfield, Michigan

WARNER BOOKS

NEW YORK   BOSTON

Copyright © 2001 by Michele Andrea Bowen
Reading Group Guide copyright © 2002 by Warner Books, Inc., with Walk Worthy Press.
Excerpt from *Second Sunday* copyright © 2002 by Michele Andrea Bowen
All rights reserved. No part of this book may be reproduced in any form or by any electronic or mechanical means, including information storage and retrieval systems, without permission in writing from the publisher, except by a reviewer who may quote brief passages in a review.

Published by Warner Books, Inc., with Walk Worthy Press
Real Believers, Real Life, Real Answers in the Living God™
Walk Worthy Press
33290 West Fourteen Mile Road, #482, West Bloomfield, MI 48322

Cover design and illustration by Paul Davis

Warner Books

Time Warner Book Group
1271 Avenue of the Americas, New York, NY 10020
Visit our Web site at www.twbookmark.com

Printed in the United States of America

Originally published in hardcover by Warner Books with Walk Worthy Press
First Trade Paperback Printing: June 2002
First Mass Market Printing: March 2005

10 9 8 7 6 5 4

"My name is Theophilus—"

"I believe I know your name, Reverend. I thought you looked familiar. Ain't you that revival preacher who was in Jackson this week?"

Before Theophilus could answer her she said, "You sure are. And now you back up this way spending up their offering money and thinking you can talk up some little jook joint cook." She blew a puff of air out of her mouth in disgust, adding, "And I'd be surprised if you ain't a married man to boot."

"I realize that I haven't made much of an impression on you this evening," Theophilus began. "But you have to believe me when I say that I didn't come back here to be disrespectful. I just wanted to meet you ... You should also know that I am a single man, all by myself, just hoping to find a good woman."

CHURCH FOLK

"Charming . . . some very unexpected twists and turns . . . A joyful and enriching first novel."
—Bookreporter.com

❧

"Readers will enjoy the rich glimpses into the spirit-filled African-American church of the 1960s, complete with politicking, blackmail, [and] colorful dialogue."
—*Publishers Weekly*

❧

"Will please churchgoing readers."
—*Kirkus Reviews*

❧

"An entertaining, fast-paced story filled with colorful characters and dialogue . . . Explores the challenges and morality issues church folks face in their Christian walk."
—Irmines.com

❧

"Exceptional . . . CHURCH FOLK really tells it like it is!"
—*Salisbury Post* (NC)

SECOND SUNDAY

#1 *Essence* Bestseller

"Fresh, passionate, and laugh-out-loud funny."
—*Dallas Morning News*

❧

"Get ready for some Godly grit and gumption, served up hot and tasty. Readers won't regret meeting the spunky, hilarious members of Gethsemane Baptist."
—*Romantic Times*

❧

"Done with wit and intelligence. The cast is a delight."
—*Midwest Book Review*

❧

"Strong ... Humorous ... Conspiracies, drama, and political intrigue abound. Bowen deftly balances romance, church politics, and spirituality and offers lessons on a myriad of issues including the power of love and forgiveness and the strength of community. A funny, honest drama."
—*Greater Diversity News* (NC)

❧

"Bowen's writing humorously explores familiar terrain for anyone who has witnessed church politics. [This] book contains important messages about redemption and love—that we are imperfect people who serve a gracious and merciful God."
—*Black Issues Book Review*

❧

"Bowen [has] an astute sense of character and sharp, humorous dialogue."
—*Pathfinders Travel*

Also by Michele Andrea Bowen

Second Sunday

This book is dedicated to my mother, Minnie Bowen,
and in memory of my father, Wadell Bowen.
My parents didn't have a lot of money
but they were rich in spirit, love, and wisdom,
just like the folks in *Church Folk*.

Acknowledgments

WHEW! THIS HAS BEEN A LONG JOURNEY—A blessed one but a long journey nonetheless. This novel started out as a dream six years ago, with me sharing my hopes and scribbles with my friends and family, heart wide open, faith activated, and prayers going up to have the courage to write it, to be blessed with the story, to find an agent and get *Church Folk* to this point.

So many people have contributed to my being able to write this book through their prayers, words and notes of encouragement, and patience when I started talking about Essie and Theophilus 'nem like they were real folks sitting right in the kitchen with us. I know I will not be able to include everybody who blessed me with their love and support for this book but I will try to name a few. So here is my thank you note.

I want to start out by thanking a man named Mr. G. C. "Pete" Hendricks, who wrote a book called *The Second War* and taught a writing workshop in 1995 for the North

Carolina Writers' Network for beginning novelists. *Church Folk* was in its very early stages and Mr. Hendricks pulled me aside and told me that this project was a real novel and that I should pursue it to the end. And then there is Marita Golden, who took me on as a student and told me that I was definitely writing a novel, nurturing me at a time when I really benefitted from encouragement from a seasoned and well-respected author. Thank you, Marita.

Professor Daryl Dance for including a very early excerpt of *Church Folk* in your highly respected anthology, *Honey Hush!* You have been such a wonderful supporter. David Bradley, author of *The Chaneysville Incident*—my workshop teacher for the Hurston/Wright Foundation's Summer Writers' Workshop in July 1996. Ron James and his wife, Claudette. Ron, you were so kind and read every last page of *Church Folk*, discussing the characters with me, cheering me on when I felt discouraged, reading excerpts to Claudette, who laughed at us and said, "You all talk about them like they real people." My loving friends in Richmond, Virginia, and Durham, North Carolina. My girls, who call themselves club members on my behalf—yawl know who yawl are.

To the First Ladies and Ministers who have graced my path and taught me what it was like to be the First Lady, the Pastor, a Minister, and the Minister's wife. A special thank-you to my aunt, First Lady Bessie Nelson, and my uncle, Bishop James D. Nelson, Sr., at Greater Bethlehem Temple Apostolic Church in Baltimore, Maryland.

To my family and St. Louis folks. Thank you for believing in me. And thanks to my family and friends who laughed when they heard I was writing a book and said, "Well, she always made us read her stories when we were little." To my home church, Washington Metropolitan African Methodist Episcopal Zion Church in St.

Louis, Missouri—so much learned and blessed in so many ways when I was growing up there.

To my two beautiful daughters, Laura and Janina. My sweet babies have lived this novel for a big portion of their lives. Laura, you have cheered Mommy on and have been proud of me since you knew about the book and you helped me so much. And Janina, you sat in Mommy's lap, drinking from your bottle, playing writing and editing, while I worked. Thank you Pookiey and Nee Nee.

To my mother, Minnie Bowen, who told me to write my stories on paper when I was little and was prone to telling these long and detailed dreams and stories. My grandmother Anniebelle Bowen, who didn't live to see this book. But I know you would have liked it. My grandmother Jeffie Hicks, who always listened to my dreams, no matter how outrageous and funny. To my father, Wadell Bowen. Daddy, I sure do wish you were still here. It would be wonderful to hear your "hey now" when you read *Church Folk* and then took it around to show to your friends.

Thank you Elisa Petrini, my editor for Walk Worthy Press. I learned a lot from you and really appreciate your kindness, humor, and sensitivity.

And last, but not least, thank you Denise Stinson. Thank you for taking *Church Folk* on when it was still in its 'infancy.' Thank you for being patient with me through my life's challenges, like having a baby in the midst of rewriting an earlier draft, and for making me a member of the Walk Worthy Press family. Like I once told you, if you were a singer and Aretha Franklin were a publisher and literary agent, chile, yawl would be the same person!

Michele Andrea Bowen, January 3, 2001

P.S. Thank You, Lord!! Thank You. Thank You.

Church Folk

Prologue
1960

T THE AGE OF TWENTY-NINE, THE REVEREND Theophilus Henry Simmons had developed one unshakable conviction about God—that He loved women. If He didn't love women, how could He have created such a magnificent creature as a fine, deep, dark chocolate woman who looked real good in pinks and oranges, had big, sexy legs, and a stardust twinkle in her smile—the kind of exquisite Negro woman who compelled the Universe to praise every swing of her large, shapely hips?

But there was a time during his senior year at Blackwell College, before he entered The Interdenominational Theological Seminary in Atlanta to study for the ministry, when he had mistaken God's love of women as an excuse to become entangled with one Glodean Benson. Being a young, single, good-looking Negro man, the kind many a Negro woman wanted to make her own, he had constant opportunities to get in trouble but managed to fight off that particular temptation—until

. Her brand of loving was intoxicating but , like cheap corn liquor that numbs your brain before you have the sense to figure out it's no good for you. Then when you finally let it go, its bitter aftertaste lingers, along with the burning in your stomach and the aching in your head.

When Theophilus finally told her, plain and simple, "I'm leaving you, Glodean," she blinked back her tears, looked at him like he was crazy, and smiled as she said: "You poor man—walking around thinking I wanted you just for you. Just what is it you thought you could offer me—unless and if you ever do become a reverend— besides the seat in the front pew of your church reserved for the First Lady?"

Those words sliced through him right down to the bone, but she wasn't through: "And now that you're off to the seminary, Mr. Hope-to-Be-Reverend, believin' you're too high and mighty for Miss Glodean, don't think I can be dismissed like some silly little shouting churchwoman, shakin' all up in your face. I'm going to stick to you, 'Re-ve-rend'—and some day, some way, I'm going to get you . . ."

Theophilus couldn't imagine what she could do to him. But he was already so ashamed of what he had done, it didn't matter. What did matter were her words, which crushed him so until he thought he heard his heart shatter from the impact of them on his spirit.

He knew he was wrong to go with Glodean—"a gal with somethin' in her drawers that snapped," as he once heard an old man say about women like her. It was his curiosity about that "snappin'" that caused him to put Glodean's feelings, his reputation, and his relationship with God in jeopardy. He repented to God, and he knew God had forgiven him—but it was the kind of mistake that he never dreamed would dog him long after the affair ended. Glodean's words and his sense of remorse haunted him, even in his sleep, making him toss and turn, only to wake up tired and hurting in body and soul.

It was only the rigorous demands of his seminary training, along with a lot of prayer and meditation on God's word, that eased the disappointment he felt with himself. Then, to his dismay, just before his final ordination, he heard that Glodean was working in Atlanta, where she had family. She began turning up at seminary social functions, and with no more than a look she tormented him, filling him with fear and—he had to admit it—a still-glowing spark of his old desire. He managed to fend her off, but the war between his resentment at Glodean's obsession over him and those sparks she could still ignite, was an agony that made him feel like he was losing his mind.

And now, as graduation day approached, he had been assigned to take over the pastorship of Greater Hope Gospel United Church in Memphis, where Glodean and all of her family had gone for years.

Reverend Murcheson James, the pastor of Mount Nebo Gospel United Church in Charleston, Mississippi, raced over to Atlanta when Theophilus found out about his assignment and then got up enough courage to place a desperate call to his friend and mentor, asking for help with his dilemma. Rev. James knew Glodean's family— her aunt, Willie Mae Clayton, owned a big-time funeral home chain based in Memphis, with branches throughout the South—and he couldn't even fathom how this boy had gotten caught up with the likes of her. Where was the boy's good sense? But the more Rev. James listened, the less sympathy he felt, and the stronger his urge grew to whip Theophilus's tail until he couldn't see straight.

But maybe Theophilus would learn a powerful lesson from all of this. For some time, Rev. James had been feeling that Theophilus was a little too comfortable with his flirtations with women—conduct unacceptable for a godly man and especially one who was becoming a minister. This time, Theophilus had gone farther than he was sure the young preacher had ever gone before. Not that he didn't understand the boy's needs, because he did. Happily married himself to a wonderful woman, he couldn't imagine pastoring without the love, support, and comfort of a good woman like his wife, Susie. But to seek that kind of comfort outside of your marriage was unacceptable. And as for marriage and Glodean Benson? That went beyond unacceptable. It was a mess, plain and simple. To make matters worse, it sounded like the fool still had the scent of that heifer stuck in his nose. A man didn't need to have a woman's scent branded in him like that, unless it was the right woman, a woman who would stroke your heart, soothe your soul, comfort you, and make you laugh. A woman who is your wife.

Rev. James figured it was time Theophilus learned that pastoring was serious business. A lot of young seminarians never did learn that and they got blindsided by the temptations that came with the job—liquor, money, politicking, women. Though he loved Theophilus like a son, Rev. James decided not to spare the rod. "Look here, Theophilus," he said. "You smart on most counts, but you lost your doggone mind on this one. You are just a few months shy of getting your final ordination papers, and look at you—miserable, all tore up over what? It ain't God that has you all upset. You know He done forgot about what you did as soon as you told Him you were sorry. No, you tore up about a piece of tail so lethal it ought to be a military weapon. Boy, if I was your daddy, I'd knock you clean out your pastor's chair. 'Cause you know better. I *know* you know better."

Theophilus stared at the floor, having trouble looking Rev. James in the eye. He certainly didn't have anything worth hearing to say in his defense. He was searching his mind for words but Rev. James wasn't looking for answers. "Now, before you start up, just listen. Sometimes you need to be strong enough to stare evil down in the face. You know why you are getting sent to Greater Hope? You are going because Bishop Percy Jennings wants you there. Bishop Jennings is being reassigned to the Tennessee/Mississippi District. The Board of Bishops is doing some reshuffling after suspending Bishop Otis Caruthers for approaching that little seventeen-year-old girl."

Just thinking about it, Rev. James shook his head in disgust. "You remember that mess, don't you? Little girl so young, she still had milk and cookies on her breath."

Theophilus nodded, wondering himself what would possess a grown man to even think of looking at a little teenager. But men who believed women were beneath them often didn't feel bound by the rules of decency. Putting Bishop Otis Caruthers "on location"—taking away his district—would keep him out of commission for a while. But there was always a chance that a corrupt bishop would bounce back. A few wads of bills placed in the right palms, at the right time, and a bishop was back in power. It wasn't so easy to get rid of a bishop in the Gospel United Church.

"You don't know this, son," Rev. James was saying, "but Percy Jennings asked the Board of Bishops for special permission to take you with him to his new district. Greater Hope is the only open ministry there, and he personally assigned you the pastorship. He has been watching you. He believes that young pastors like you, who are godly men, who can preach the rafters out of the roof, and who can understand what this new civil rights movement is bringing, are the future of the Gospel United Church."

Theophilus could not believe what he was hearing. Why would Bishop Jennings take a personal interest in him? He started to ask, but Rev. James held up his hand. "I'm not finished, Theophilus," he said. "You are being tested. You are being tested because it needs to be known if you can handle yourself right when in the fiery furnace. Can you be like those three Hebrew boys, Shadrach, Meshach, and Abednego, and trust that the Lord will stand with you and guide you? Then will you be obedient to do what He tells you to do? 'Cause that the kind of faith and commitment you gone need, not only for pastoring Greater Hope but when you go even farther than that. If you can't pass this test, you can't handle this call God has on your life. Don't let your flesh lead you in another direction. You hear me, Theophilus? Can you accept this call?"

"Yes," said Theophilus. "I accepted God's call on my life a long time ago—and yes, Rev. James. Yes, I will go to Greater Hope."

Now, for the first time during the visit, Rev. James smiled. "Glad you still got some gumption in you, boy," he said. "Scared me for a minute there. Thought that gal took all your strength away, just like Delilah did that fool Sampson. Now, let's pray."

To ease Theophilus's passage at Greater Hope, Rev. James appealed to Mrs. Coral Thomas, his wife, Susie's, best friend and a longtime deaconess of the church, to keep an eye on the young pastor. Many a morning Theophilus would come to work and find Coral Thomas bustling around his office, setting out a pot of delicious-smelling coffee and a plate of fat ham biscuits, saying, "Sit down, Pastor, and get yourself some breakfast. Made up these biscuits 'specially for you."

During his first year, Coral became his right hand. It was she who encouraged him to make some much needed reassignments in the church, giving jobs to the most qualified members instead of those who gave the most money. There had been hurt feelings at first, but now folks acknowledged that the choir had improved a hundredfold and that the Usher Board, which visitors barely recognized before, conducted their duty with a new pride. Now, instead of regular church clothes, the men wore dark suits, white shirts, and blue ties, while the women wore white shoes and white dresses with blue lace handkerchiefs fixed to their shoulders with gold usher pins.

The church was growing, with new members joining every week, attracted by the new pastor's fiery preaching and his message of social justice. But every Sunday, Theophilus scanned the faces of his congregation with his heart pounding and sickness in his stomach, ready to break out in a cold sweat, should he glimpse the pale pink suit, pink lace gloves, and matching rose church hat that was the signature ensemble of Glodean Benson.

To honor his first anniversary as pastor, Bishop Jennings and Rev. James arranged for Theophilus to serve as the guest preacher for a week-long revival that was being held at St. Paul's Gospel United Church in Jackson, Mississippi. Usually more seasoned and well-known pastors worked revivals, for it was a way to gain visibility in the denomination. Theophilus recognized that choosing him was an expression of confidence and faith, and he fervently thanked God for granting him the strength to face the challenges of that first year. Every morning before he started working, he got down on his knees and prayed, saying, "Thank you, Lord. Thank you for forgiving me, Lord, and keeping me strong and steadfast. My trust is in you, Lord. Thank you for walking with me each day, lighting my path into the future you have set before me."

And the Lord, ever mindful of the most pure, sincere, and heartfelt desires of his children, now granted Theophilus a two-for-one prayer miracle. The first miracle was blessing him so that he preached with such power that it was as if he was trying to raise the dead. And the second miracle dealt strictly with matters of the heart.

His first revival sermon sent folks home feeling good about what God had said to their hearts, thinking about what Theophilus had prayed about, and looking over the scripture readings that accompanied his text. But with each passing day, his sermons became hotter and hotter, until on that last night, he walked up in the church so full of spiritual fire he felt like he had what his mother said was "fire all shut up in his bones." He had "gotten the spirit" before, but he had never felt anything so consuming as the power of God in that little church on that last night. All while he was preaching, he couldn't keep still, couldn't stay put in the pulpit, and before he knew it, he was taking one long-legged stride out from behind the podium, shouting, "Thank you, Jesus," and running right into the center aisle of the church.

When he ran into the aisle, folks started coming out of their seats, waving their hands in the air, fanning fans and programs in his direction, talking about, "Preach, boy, preach!" And when it was clear that just about everybody in the sanctuary was becoming lit up with the Holy Ghost, the organist hopped up from his seat and began to play *duum-duum, duum-duum*—that generic, deep-bass-sounding melody that always let everyone at a highly charged Negro church service know it was time to cut loose.

When the organist saw that folks were itching to shout, he started playing louder and with more intensity, looking around to see which one of the women would get the spirit first. But it was Theophilus, and not one of the women, who took up the cause and got everybody dancing and running through the aisles. And at that point, the *duum-duum, duum-duum* turned into a fast-paced *duum-duum-duum-duum, duum-duum-duum-duum* that set off a chain reaction of shouting, dancing, and praising God that tore up every pew in the sanctuary. When the congregation reached a peak that couldn't be surpassed and Theophilus started experiencing a climax of his own raging emotions, he looked over at the musicians and signaled for them to calm the music down.

At that point he walked back into the pulpit and said breathlessly, "I don't know about you but I'm sure glad that these musicians found some time to steal away from Hallowed Ground Church of God and Christ to play for us tonight. You know, church, I do believe that God likes that music about as much as we do. Who ever said that the Gospel United Church didn't know how to praise the Lord?"

"I don't know, Reverend!" the organist, a tall, thin, ebony-colored man, shouted out. " 'Cause y'all is sho' havin' some church tonight. The Holy Ghost ran by and touched every Saint in the house. Praise the Lord!"

"Thank you, Brother Organist. And if you will, sir, I would ask that you play 'At the cross, at the cross where I first saw the light, and the burdens of my heart rolled away . . .'"

As the organist started playing, Theophilus called the congregation to join him in a circle of fellowship that went around the entire sanctuary. Once the circle was in place, he said they needed to come together to cement the spiritual bond they had formed over the course of the revival week. And when everybody joined hands, he led them in a prayer petitioning for forgiveness of past transgressions—including his own—asked for healing of their sorrows, and thanked God for stopping on by St. Paul's Gospel United Church tonight, because they all knew He had His hands full with all that was happening to Negroes in the South. Then he pulled himself up off his knees, opened his arms in a symbolic embrace of the congregation, and with the permission of St. Paul's pastor, opened the doors of the church to everybody at the revival looking for a church home.

Part 1
1961

Chapter One

AFTER A WEEK OF EMOTIONALLY CHARGED RE-
vival preaching, Theophilus was too spent to
race straight back to the arms—and the demands—of his Memphis congregation. He
was tired and hungry, and he needed some time alone.
So he was glad to see 32 West off of Highway 55, the
exit for Charleston, Mississippi, where he knew of a
place to stay, Neese's Boarding House for Negroes. He
had also heard about a place there, Pompey's Rib Joint,
which had the best rib tip sandwiches around—not to
mention being known for hosting some of the best blues
artists in the region.

It was in Charleston, a tiny Delta town thirty minutes
west of Oxford, that the Lord's second and most important life-changing miracle for Theophilus occurred. It was
his second miracle, the one he prayed for deep in his heart,
not even aware of how intensely God was listening to him
and not aware that the Lord loved him so much— He
really did know the exact number of hairs on his head.

He drove to the "Smoky" section of the town and found the Negro boarding house. As he walked in, he took care not to let anyone sitting in the living room area catch a glimpse of his robe. His workday was over and he didn't want to have to explain if he happened to run into someone from the boarding house over at Pompey's. He felt a little twinge of guilt about going to Pompey's after preaching a revival, but he shrugged it off by telling himself that Pompey's was probably the best place he could go to have some peace. The last thing folks at Pompey's would be looking for was a preacher to tell their troubles to.

His room was simple, immaculate, and comfortable. The high double bed looked inviting with its starched white linens, and yellow and white cotton patch quilt. There was a large gray, yellow, and white rag rug in the middle of the worn but freshly waxed beige linoleum floor, and crisp white cotton curtains at the one window facing the bed across the room. There were even fresh daisies in a plain white pitcher with a yellow satin ribbon tied around it sitting on an embroidered linen runner on the dresser.

Theophilus put his things on the bed and unzipped his garment bag to get some fresh clothes. He had no intention of showing up at Pompey's in the navy chalk-striped suit, white shirt, and blue, black, and white tie he was now wearing. He selected a pair of silvery gray slacks and a pale gray silk knit sports shirt with silver buttons down the front, and matching pearl gray silk socks. He got his bathrobe, toiletry bag, fresh underwear, and left the room in search of towels and the bathroom so that he could take a quick bath and shave.

Thirty minutes later, he pulled into a dirt parking lot across the road from Pompey's Rib Joint. The smell of succulent ribs and the light from the hot pink neon sign that blinked POMPEY'S RIB JOINT—BEST RIBS IN THE DELTA led a straight path in the black night to the old brick building sitting off to itself on the other side of the road. Inside, where there was a rough wood floor, light purple walls, and unfinished wood tables and chairs, was packed. As soon as he walked in, Theophilus saw that the only seats left were at the bar.

He pressed his way over to the bar and put his hand on a stool just as a short, round woman wearing an orange print dress and holding a big white pocketbook on her arm was about to sit on it. He had begun to apologize when she spotted some friends and gave him the seat. Mouthing thanks, he squeezed through the narrow space and a thin, light-skinned man with freckles and a broad smile moved his stool to make more room for him. He lifted his shot glass in a neighborly fashion when Theophilus nodded a quick thank-you and settled his large, muscular frame on the shaky barstool.

He got more comfortable and started looking around the room, unintentionally making eye contact with two women who were dressed in identical lime green chiffon dresses. One of the women ran her tongue over the top of her lip and blew him a quick kiss when she was certain her man wasn't watching her. He nodded at her, taking great care not to get caught by her man. It was one of those no-win situations. If he ignored that redbone woman with "good" hair, chances are she would get mad at him and say something about him to her man. If he were too friendly with her, then her man, a small, wiry fellow with a process and dressed in a red suit, would get insulted and probably be inclined to fight. And the one thing he knew about little wiry-built men was that they were easily insulted, mean, and carried a serious weapon.

Theophilus was relieved when the waitress finally

came to take his order, making it possible for him to have a decent reason to stop the eye contact with that woman and her friend. But it took him aback when she walked up to him and right into the space between his legs as she rubbed his knee and whispered in his ear, "What you think you be wantin' tonight, baby?"

All he could do was smile at first. He was fully aware that he should know better than to respond to such outrageous flirtation. But the man in him, the part that loved getting attention from good-looking women, couldn't stand to let her get the best of him. He just had to give her back as good as he got. So Theophilus sat back on his stool and smiled, looking her up and down, admiring how good she looked with her sepia-colored skin in that skimpy black satin dress she was wearing. He stroked his chin and said, in a voice that sounded to her like midnight on a clear summer evening, "I don't need much, sweetheart. Just a tall glass of iced tea with a few sprigs of mint leaves and a rundown of what you have to eat. And make sure it is something succulent for a hungry man like me."

She grinned at Theophilus, moved closer to him and spoke into his ear, this time allowing her lips to brush the tip of his earlobe, sending a rush of warmth across his neck and shoulders.

"We has a rib tip sandwich special tonight. And baby, them ribs so good till they will make you want to do something real bad and nasty, if you know what I mean."

Theophilus gave her a sultry smile to let her know that he knew exactly what she meant. Then he winked at her and said, "So, tell me, sweetheart. What's on this sandwich that makes it so good it'll make me want to do something nassty?"

She felt a little quiver in her thighs and had to take

a few deep breaths before she said, "Them tips is just good, baby. They soaked in hot, homemade barbecue sauce, with potato salad on top, and Wonder Bread."

He smiled at her again. "I'm gonna trust you and take one of those sandwiches. But, sweetheart, if the sauce is real hot, bring me some ice water along with my order. I think I'll need more than a glass of tea to cool me down with a sandwich like that."

She leaned on him one more time, a big smile spreading across her face. She inhaled the scent of his cologne some more before saying in the sexiest voice she could, "I'll bring your tea real fast and then go get your order settled."

Theophilus smiled to himself as he watched the waitress walk away, deliberately giving him an eyeful of her fat, fine behind just swinging and swaying all for him. He thought to himself, "Boy, get yourself together, carrying on like that. Just a few hours ago you were all down on your knees at church and glad to be there, too. Shame on you, Rev. Simmons."

The waitress brought his tea just as the band performing tonight, Big Johnnie Mae Carter and the Fabulous Revues, finished setting up on stage. The Fabulous Revues was a good-sized band—bass player, lead guitarist, tenor saxophone player, trumpet player, pianist, and drummer. These men, who were anywhere from the ages of thirty to fifty, looked good in crisp black pants with razor-sharp creases, light purple silk shirts, shiny black Stacy Adams shoes, and slick black straw hats cocked on the side of their heads. When everybody was in place, the drummer raised his drumsticks high in the air, brought them down hard on the first beat, and Pompey's Rib Joint got to jumping.

Big Johnnie Mae Carter, a tall, husky, square-shaped

woman with big breasts and a headful of coarse, bleached blond hair piled high on top, was in rare form tonight. Decked out in a long light purple evening gown with splits up to the knee on each side and rhinestones glittering in her ears, she strutted her stuff to the funky Delta blues rhythms of her band, from the front door of Pompey's all the way up and on to the stage. Then she finally stepped up to the microphone, throwing back her shoulders and whipped out the words of the song:

"If you was a bee baby, I'd turn myself into the sweetest flower.

"And if you was the rain, Daddy, and me the Mississippi? I'd flood this old Delta 'cause I couldn't keep all of your sweet lovin' all to myself.

"And if you just happened to be the devil. Then, Lawd, Lawd, Lawdy, just help me please.

" 'Cause see, I'd be tryin' to up and sell my soul just to make sure you kept on lovin' up on me.

"I said, Lawd, Lawd, Lawdy, Help, Help, Help me please.

" 'Cause I know I'd be doing so wrong just to keep you lovin' up on me."

Big Johnnie Mae looked like she was feeling that music from head to toe as she stretched out her arms, snapped her jeweled fingers, and moved her hips from side to side. As the lead guitarist stepped forward to pick out his solo, she shifted aside, still dancing, rolling her hips in a sinuous way, and finally shimmying on down to the stage floor. The guitarist looked down at Big Johnnie Mae and smiled. She, in turn, smiled back up at him, pulled that dress up to her knees and rolled her hips some more. All the other musicians stopped playing and just let the lead guitar, accompanied by Big Johnnie Mae's dancing, carry the song.

Now Big Johnnie Mae began to weave her way back up, all the while crooning around the melody, stretching to her full height in front of the microphone. Then the band rose up behind her full and strong, as she reached for a note that sounded like it had started way down deep in the basement and came on upstairs to blow the roof off the joint.

A man sitting only a couple of feet from the stage jumped up and shouted, "Damn, baby. You sho' 'nough is hot tonight! Lawd! What I wouldn't give to be that there micro-ro-phone you holdin' on to right now."

The freckled face man leaned over toward Theophilus and said, "Now, that Negro don't have no sense. 'Cause the way she was movin' down on that flo', any fool would know he need to turn hisself into some wood."

Theophilus could only smile at this observation and raise his tea. He stopped short of nodding his head in agreement. He wasn't so sure he wanted to "turn hisself into some wood" because he wasn't so sure he was man enough to hold all of the woman that was Big Johnnie Mae Carter. Theophilus thought that perhaps he could be the sound system that carried her voice to the ears of her listeners. He sipped his tea and nodded his head at that thought. It would be nothing short of a religious experience to feel her voice coursing through his body and on out to the eager audience. He sipped on his tea some more, bobbing his head to the beat of the next song. The tea felt good, too—cooling him down at the same time that Big Johnnie Mae and the Fabulous Revues were warming up his soul and making him feel almost as good as he had felt at church.

Just as Big Johnnie Mae ended this last song and started up on one with a calmer rhythm, a different woman came toward Theophilus with a plate of food in one hand and a big glass of ice water, a napkin, and silverware in the other.

"You the man who ordered the rib tip sandwich and glass of ice water?" she asked.

He said, "Ummm-hmmm."

She pushed the food out toward him.

"Here, this is yours and you owe me $1.25."

Theophilus took the plate, silverware, and glass of water from her and put them on the bar. He reached back to get his empty tea glass off the bar and then fumbled in his pocket for some money.

Watching him, the woman had to agree with the waitress, who was now stuck helping the bartender fix drinks, that the man in the "silver gray outfit" was sure enough a "big and pretty chocolate man." She tried to steal a better look at his face without his noticing it. She knew that you didn't look at the men coming in here too hard unless you wanted to send them a message you hoped they wanted to answer.

Then he smiled at her, handing over the money while looking her over so thoroughly until she wished she had worn her large cook's apron. It covered a lot of her body but she hated bringing customers their food in that barbecue- and grease-splattered thing. But at least that grimy coverage would have slowed down the speed with which this man's eyes took in her body. She was standing there in a shirt and Bermuda shorts, so her only defense was to narrow her already slanted eyes and give him a nasty look. He wouldn't be the first man to get this look. But he *was* the first one who made her wonder if she had looked at him just a little too mean when she walked back to the kitchen.

Theophilus shrugged off the glare that little woman had given him and turned toward the bar to eat his food.

The sandwich was so thick and juicy he had to eat it with a fork. The tips were tender and dripping in some of the best barbecue sauce he had tasted in a long time. And there was a generous helping of potato salad spread evenly on each slice of bread. The waitress hadn't lied about this sandwich. It did taste good enough to make you "want to do something real bad and nasty."

As he ate, Theophilus found his mind fixed on the image of that mean-acting little woman. She sure was a fine little thing, with that dark-honey-colored skin, thick reddish brown hair held in place with a light blue headband, heart-shaped face, full lips, and those sexy slanted, light brown eyes cutting him in two when he stared at her too hard. And she looked cute in those baby blue Bermuda shorts with her petite, hourglass figure and her backside swinging her own natural, uncontrived rhythm when she walked away from him.

"Umph, umph, umph," he thought to himself. "If that girl didn't have some big pretty legs, I don't know who did."

Just then the waitress came switching back to him to ask if he needed anything else from her. Figuring she was offering more than just another glass of tea, he thought that he had better add a little extra sugar to his smile before he asked a question he knew she wouldn't want to answer.

"Who brought me my food, sweetheart?"

She looked confused and said, "Something wrong with your food?"

"No. I just want to know who was the woman who brought me my food. She didn't look like she was a waitress. And judging from the way she just walked off with my money after I paid her, she didn't act like one, either. I mean, look at you. You're standing here all sweet-like, making sure I'm all right."

"She wasn't nasty-actin' was she?" the waitress asked. She knew Essie Lane was good for giving these men that old nasty, slit-eyed look of hers.

"No, sweetheart, nothing like that. I just want you to tell me who she was."

"That was Essie Lane. She the cook on duty tonight."

"Well, I have to thank a woman who can cook some rib tips like that. Where is she?"

The waitress didn't look too happy about Theophilus wanting to talk to Essie but she said, "She back in the kitchen," and pointed him in that direction.

"Thank you, sweetheart," he said as he gave her a sexy wink and put some money in her hand.

She put her smile back on her face and said, "I just knowed you was the kind of man who really knows what to do with a woman," as Theophilus got up and headed back to the kitchen.

Sighing with regret, she looked down at her tip. The five-dollar bill she was holding in her hand stretched her smile into a big wide grin. Five dollars was a huge tip for a waitress working at Pompey's Rib Joint.

When Theophilus walked into that hot kitchen, Essie was drinking some ice water and stirring a big pot of collard greens. Sensing someone watching her, she turned around, hoping it wasn't that old drunk who kept waving a dollar bill at her every time she came out on the floor. When she saw that it was the good-looking man in silver-gray, she was kind of relieved but also wondering why he was standing in the doorway looking at her like that. Ready to run him out of the kitchen if need be, she put a hand on her hip and looked him dead in the eye.

"What do you want?" she asked.

Theophilus wasn't surprised by the attitude in her voice. At the gut level he knew she was one of those good women who didn't allow for foolishness from a man. And as nasty as she sounded, he liked her voice. It was the kind of voice that could move swiftly from giving a command one dare not disobey, to girlish laughter, to a deep, throaty sigh. The desire to hear that sigh nestled itself quietly and comfortably in the most private, yet-to-be awakened region of his heart.

"I said, what do you want?"

He wanted to smile at her but didn't want to be chased out of this kitchen before he had a chance to meet her. So he decided to put on his "receiving line" face, which seemed to carry him a long way with most folks he greeted after Sunday morning service. He held that look in place as he tried to think of something to say that would match his disarming expression. The best he could come up with was, "Sister, that food was so good, I just had to come back here and humble myself before the chef," with what he truly hoped had a good dose of the preacher in his voice.

He knew better than to say what he was really thinking, which was, "Baby, you so fine, you make me want to say things that can only be whispered in your ear."

Essie just looked at him and said, "The chef, huh," with a frown on her face. "You are talking about a 'chef' in a country place like Pompey's Rib Joint? You must think you in New York City. But you ain't. And since you ain't, get out of my kitchen right now, before somebody gets hurt." She edged over to a small table with a big meat cleaver on it.

Theophilus saw her reach for the meat cleaver and backed away, saying, "Hey, wait a minute, baby," before he could catch himself right.

Looking at him like he was out of his mind, Essie said, "Negro, I know you ain't calling me no baby."

Theophilus moved toward her gingerly, trying to placate her. "Look, girl, I didn't mean you any harm. Your food was good and I just wanted to see you—"

"Wanted to see me? For what? If my food was so good, why didn't your cheap self send me a note about my good food, along with a tip?"

Theophilus didn't even try to defend himself on that one, realizing he had been too distracted to tip her. She was looking at him real hard, meat cleaver firm in her grip.

He tried another tack, extending his hand and saying, "My name is Theophilus—"

"I believe I know your name, Reverend. I thought you looked familiar when I brought you your food. Ain't you that revival preacher who was in Jackson this week?"

Before Theophilus could answer her, she said, "You sure are. And now you back up this way spending up their offering money and thinking you can talk up some little jook joint cook. Man, sometimes you preachers can truly act as bad as the worst street Negroes." She blew a puff of air out of her mouth in disgust, adding, "And I'd be surprised if you ain't a married man to boot."

Theophilus was embarrassed at the mess he had made in his effort to meet this woman. And now he had to convince her that he didn't see her as some "little jook joint cook." But the way she was holding that meat cleaver made him think real carefully before he opened his mouth again.

"I realize that I haven't made much of an impression

on you this evening," he began. "But you have to believe me when I say that I didn't come back here to be disrespectful. I just wanted to meet you. You should call Reverend Murcheson James over at Mount Nebo Gospel United Church and ask him about me. Maybe a good word or two from him will make you feel comfortable enough to see me again."

"Reverend James is my pastor. I'm a member of Mount Nebo."

Theophilus felt like shouting. This woman went to Mount Nebo? Now he knew the Lord was truly on his side. He smiled at her as he said, "You should also know that I'm a single man, all by myself, just hoping to find a good woman."

Essie rolled her eyes at him. "All by yourself? I've never seen a preacher all by himself without a whole bunch of women to choose from. For some reason, women just seem to love preachers. I don't know why."

Theophilus decided to ignore that last comment and said, "Yes, there sure are a lot of women who love preachers and would be glad for one to choose them. But I just told you that I'm looking for a good one."

"And you gonna find her in Pompey's Rib Joint?"

"I'm talking to a good woman right now, right?" Theophilus said, standing over Essie, looking down at her, daring her to differ with him.

Essie knew she was a good woman, one who worked real hard to see that everybody at Pompey's knew it, too. To be sure, good-looking Negro men had crossed her path on many an evening at work. But they all made the fatal error of missing the point—that Essie Lee Lane was not only fine-looking with big sexy legs, she was a woman of fine character who knew she deserved better than what they always wanted to offer her.

"You haven't answered my question."

"What question?"

"I asked you if you were a good woman and you've been standing there staring at me."

Now it was Essie's turn to be embarrassed. She hadn't realized that she was staring at him.

"So, I'm talking to a good woman in the kitchen of one the hottest jook joints in the Delta. Am I not?"

Essie struggled, trying to compose just the right answer to that question. The way he looked her over, head to toe, was jumbling up her thoughts. She frowned. "Why you looking at me like you got X-ray vision? You know that ain't right for no man and especially one claiming to be a preacher."

Theophilus checked his gaze, traveling down to get a fully lighted view of those legs. He wondered if her legs would feel as soft and satiny to his hands as they looked. But he wasn't about to apologize because he couldn't keep his eyes off her. "You know something, Miss—"

"Essie Lee. Essie Lee Lane."

"You know something, Miss Essie Lee Lane. I don't have X-ray vision, truly I don't. But to be perfectly honest, at times like these I sure wish I did." He gave her a smile that started at his eyes and traveled leisurely down to his mouth.

Essie felt flushed looking at him smiling at her like that. Here was a man—a preacher in fact—who told her he wished he had X-ray vision and gave her a look that said volumes about how he would use this gift if he were so blessed with it. She had always been skeptical of ministers—felt that too many of them didn't practice what they preached and had bigheaded notions about themselves. But for some reason, she felt differently about this man, which was disturbing, the more she thought about it.

"What's the matter with you, Miss Essie Lee Lane? You got a thought you don't like?"

Essie couldn't believe he could see through her like that and said, "Nothing wrong, just thinking."

"Just thinking, huh?" Theophilus said with a warm smile that didn't have a trace of freshness in it. "I bet you're thinking you kind of like me and might just let me see you again, right?"

Essie sighed, trying not to let him see that he was getting all up under her skin. She would rather die than so much as breathe a yes in his direction.

"Yes, I bet you're still thinking about me, isn't that right, Miss Essie Lane? And it's bothering you that you want to see this preacher just one more time."

Essie just looked at him as if to say, "Don't flatter yourself." She said, "I ain't troubled about nothing that has anything to do with you. Just because you can see me again—nothing about it that needs extra thought to it. All you'll be doing is what you asked to do, seeing me again."

"Well, well, well, God is truly good. I think nothing short of an act of God would convince Miss Essie Lane to let me—X-ray vision and all—see her again."

Essie blew air out of her mouth and rolled her eyes as if to say "please." She said, "I think no harm could come from you visiting me."

Theophilus guessed correctly that this was about as close to a yes as he was going to get. But with a soft laugh in his voice, he pressed, "So, you're telling me that I can see you again, huh? Is that what you are saying, Miss Essie Lane?"

The slight smile on her lips made him feel certain that he was getting next to her, if only a little.

"Maybe I could see you tomorrow afternoon," he said. "If it's okay with you, I can stop by your house after my visit with Rev. James."

"Yes. Yes," she replied. "You can come by my house tomorrow and eat lunch with me."

His heart swelled with hope.

"With me, my mama, and my Uncle Booker," she continued. "That way you'll know without a doubt that there ain't no good times to be had down here with this little small-town Mississippi girl. Way I figure it, once you're certain about that point, you probably won't want to see me again anyway."

The expression on his face changed. Gone was the heat and in its place was a look she didn't know what to make of. Was it hurt?

He said, "Essie, please know that the only time I am really looking to have, is *more of it* with you. And the only thing I want from you is for you to tell me how to find your house tomorrow."

Chapter Two

JHEOPHILUS SETTLED HIS BILL AT ROSE NEESE'S Boarding House for Negroes and went to visit with Rev. James. He spoke of the revival with warmth and feeling, thanking his mentor for the role he had surely played in getting him the chance to serve as the guest preacher there. But Reverend James couldn't help but notice how the excitement in his voice rose when Theophilus spoke of meeting that fine young woman from his congregation, Essie Lee Lane. He approved of Essie inviting Theophilus to lunch with her mother, Lee Allie, and her Uncle Booker, both of whom he knew well. Being a kind, patient, and extremely observant man, he could see how hard Theophilus was working to stay focused on any topic other than Essie. So he decided to cut their visit short. He knew better than to compete for the attention of a young man whose mind kept straying to his upcoming lunch with a young lady like Essie Lane.

Much as he loved Rev. James, Theophilus was

relieved to be dismissed, for it had taken everything in him not to hop up from his seat and run out to find the Lane house. When he walked up on the small porch and knocked on the screen door, a woman he just knew had to be Essie's mother came and unhooked the latch. She was a nutmeg-colored woman, with thick brown hair that was twisted into an attractive French roll. She bore a strong resemblance to Essie but didn't have her slanted, golden brown eyes. Theophilus did notice, in the most respectful way, of course, that she had Essie's figure and legs.

Lee Allie Lane had been just as anxious for this Rev. Simmons to get to her house as he was to come there. Essie didn't bother with any of the men who came to Pompey's, and she had never shown the slightest interest in a man who was a preacher. So when Essie told her that she invited a minister she met in the kitchen of Pompey's to lunch, Lee Allie was about to bust open with curiosity. There was something mighty special about Rev. Simmons if Essie was allowing him to come to the house, let alone asking him over to eat.

As soon as Lee Allie answered the door, she knew why Essie couldn't resist seeing this preacher again. He was a six-foot-three, coffee-with-no-cream-colored man, with close-cut, coarse black hair framing a handsome face, and dark brown eyes, draped with long, thick black lashes under well-shaped eyebrows. He had a slender nose that flared at the nostrils, well-defined cheekbones, and deep dimples on each side of his face. His full, richly colored lips were accentuated by the well-groomed mustache that stopped right at the corners of his mouth. And from what she could see of him, Lee Allie had the distinct impression that his navy suit, with his starched white shirt and blue, maroon, and silver paisley print tie, hid strong brown arms, a neat waist, long, nicely shaped legs, and one of those backsides that only a Negro man had—it was a backside that made you thank the Lord for making you a Negro woman.

"You must be Rev. Simmons," she said, opening the screen door and waving for him to come in. As he stepped into the house, the comforting scent of fresh-baked rolls went straight up his nose. The pretty room he entered was simple, cozy, and warm, with a soft yellow on the walls, off white sheers at the windows, and plants scattered around, spilling over their bright red, blue, and purple pots. The soft mint green sofa made you want to stretch out on it and read the paper, and the pale blue chair with the matching ottoman was the kind that had "Sunday nap" written all over it. After admiring the room, he extended his hand to Essie's mother.

"Theophilus Simmons from Greater Hope Gospel United Church in Memphis. Your pastor, Rev. James, has known me for years and is my mentor."

Lee Allie gave his hand a firm shake and said, "It is a pleasure to meet you, Rev. Simmons. I am Essie Lee's mother, Mrs. Lee Allie Lane. When she told me and my brother, Booker, that you wanted to come by this afternoon, we both wanted to get a good look at a man who likes to preach and listen to Big Johnnie Mae all in one workin' day."

She motioned for him to sit down in the blue chair and hollered down the hall.

"Booker, come on in the living room, the Reverend just got here and you need to come meet him."

Essie's Uncle Booker walked into the living room finishing a roll and wiped his hands on his pants leg before giving Theophilus a firm, "don't take no mess off a nobody" handshake and motioning for him to sit down.

He looked a lot like his sister in the face and had her coloring. But where she was small, he was stocky and of medium height.

Lee Allie said, "Essie Lee not here yet. Had to go by the store to pick up a few things. She'll be back right shortly, though. Give you, me, and Booker a chance to get acquainted. You pastoring Greater Hope in Memphis? That's a pretty good-sized church for a young pastor like you, Rev. Simmons. How many folks at your church now?"

Theophilus shifted around in the chair and got as comfortable as possible, feeling like he was gearing himself up to face the Inquisition.

"Greater Hope has about 365 members," he said. "I have been there just about a year. And I won't lie to you—pastoring that church has been one of the most difficult challenges I've ever had to face. I've learned a lot. But I stay on my knees, Mrs. Lane, stay on my knees."

Lee Allie opened her mouth again, but before she got a chance to ask Theophilus more about his pastoring, Uncle Booker jumped in.

"Now, Reverend, what I want to know is how you come to preach and swing at Pompey's at the same time? I don't go on about all this thou-cain't-do-anything-if-you-want-to-serve-the-Lord foolishness, but I do think you need to tell me something. This ain't no church business visit. I'll bet some money you sweet on Essie Lee. Am I right, Reverend?"

Theophilus didn't know what to say or even how to say it if he did know. Essie's uncle looked like he could whip his tail if he had a mind to do so.

Uncle Booker, who had been leaning against the front door, now sat down on the couch across from where

Theophilus was sitting. Staring intently at Theophilus, as if to look through him, he said, "Don't you sit there searching for no answers to what I just said. You tell me the truth. Because if you hand me some cockamamie preacher double talk, I'll know it. I'm used to church folk."

"Booker! Rev. Simmons is a minister," Lee Allie said.

"Lee Allie, don't you go and start getting all upset with me. This here preacher went up in Pompey's last night, ordered something to eat, looked my baby-girl niece over, and then came over here the very next day to get a better look at her. Now, he must like the girl to do all of that."

Uncle Booker looked at Theophilus real hard. "Now, son, you have some likin' for my niece, don't you, Reverend?"

"Yes, sir. I saw your niece and wanted to meet her."

"And you liked what you saw, right?"

"Yes, sir. Your niece is a very striking woman."

"Mess. That's just some funky mess, boy. Essie Lee got next to you and you darn well know it. Striking woman, my black behind. Just what you up to, preacher?"

Theophilus respected Uncle Booker's right to look after his niece but he didn't appreciate being treated like some jive-acting, jackleg preacher. He figured he'd better let these people know right now what he was about. He sat up straight in the chair and looked directly at Uncle Booker.

"Mr.—"

"Webb, my last name's Webb."

"Mr. Webb, you're right to think I'm not your regular kind of preacher. Truth is, sometimes I go to places like Pompey's to eat some good food and relax a little without being troubled with church business. You know, I do like being able to talk to folks about more than church. And I like being treated like a regular man instead of always being treated like 'the Pastor.'

"And, sir, when I saw your niece last night, she gave me the impression that she was a good, solid woman. And if you don't mind my being so bold, she is a fine-looking woman, too—so fine in fact, that she held my attention for the rest of the night. So, I came by here today to let her know I was interested in getting to know her. And I knew I needed to meet her family so she'd know I wasn't after her for all the wrong reasons."

This response seemed a little bold to Uncle Booker, who didn't answer but sat weighing what Theophilus had said. Finally he extended his hand. "Son, I'm glad to know that you ain't one of those preachers who so intent on making sure everybody know just how saintly and pure they are. I like that. Lets me know you know you just a man and not some fool who think he got the only connection to the Lord."

Theophilus grabbed Uncle Booker's hand and sighed out loud with relief.

"Mr. Webb, I understand that you need to know what I'm all about. I'm not perfect but I was raised right."

They were interrupted by the sound of Essie pulling at the screen door. She didn't know why her mother waited until the last minute to send her out for kosher dill pickles, big green olives, pickled okra, jalapeño peppers, and potato chips to go with lunch. She thought they had enough to eat, with the fresh-baked turkey stuffed in large, homemade rolls, fresh garden tomatoes, butter lettuce and cucumber salad, and homemade custard ice cream with lemon-flavored tea cakes. But Lee Allie had insisted that these things would make lunch so much better. Essie hoped Theophilus didn't think she was rude for not being there when he arrived.

Theophilus stood up, trying hard to control the big grin stretching across his face when Essie walked into the house.

"Afternoon, Reverend. Hope you haven't been waiting too long."

"No, I haven't been here long."

Lee Allie looked back and forth between the two of them, took the bag of groceries from Essie, handed it to Booker, and said, "Rev. Simmons was telling us a little about his church in Memphis." She turned to Theophilus and asked, "Reverend, how big is your choir? Most solid congregations have good choirs."

Theophilus sat back down. "Mrs. Lane, we have a little over thirty people in our choir, a pianist and organist. One of the first things I did as the new pastor was to appoint a new choir director. Seems like the old one didn't want to sing what the congregation wanted to hear. Lot of folks at Greater Hope love hard-core gospel and they have said that service is so much better now that the choir is rocking the church with some good music. I know I enjoy listening to the choir more now than when I first came as the pastor."

While Theophilus was talking to Lee Allie, he could not stop himself from stealing looks at Essie, who was leaning against the doorway leading to the hall. She was wearing red pants, a red and white horizontal-striped, short-sleeved knit top, and red sneakers. Although the pants showed off her figure well, he sure wished he could have caught another good look at those big legs before he went back to Memphis.

* * *

Later, as Essie and Lee Allie sat in the kitchen, shelling snap beans for supper, Lee Allie said, "Essie, I don't know why you didn't hold more conversation with the Reverend. The whole time he was here, you held up that wall, just sizing him up like you was looking for something wrong with him."

"Mama, I didn't have to look for something to be wrong with him. Whole time he was here, he ran his eyes all over me, head to toe, when he thought nobody was looking."

"Essie Lee, he was looking at you so hard because he likes you, girl. And I hate to tell you this, baby, but a man gone look at you like that when he likes what he sees. Even a good man gone look, baby. He cain't help it 'cause he a man. And the Reverend young, too. So he really gone be looking before he can catch himself. What is he, about twenty-eight or so?"

"Twenty-nine. The revival program said he was twenty-nine."

"Well, like I just said, at twenty-nine, he still young enough for his nature to spill out over his home training when he think nobody's lookin'. And remember, even Booker had a good impression of him. I think the Reverend is a decent man. He sure 'nough a good-lookin' one, too. So the next time he comes, you be sure to give him a chance to talk to you."

"Mama, what makes you think he coming back anytime soon?"

"Because I invited him to be our church's guest preacher for Missions Day," Lee Allie said with a smile on her face. "I called Rev. James and my missionary group. Rev. James said that Rev. Simmons was a fine preacher and that he would come at a price we could afford. So now you'll have a chance to see him again."

Essie rolled her eyes, not wanting her mother to know she was happy that Lee Allie had engineered a reason for Theophilus to return to Charleston.

"Girl, why you rolling your eyes like that? You the one who invited him over here in the first place. Besides, you need to meet somebody and leave Charleston. 'Cause you don't need to stay here."

"Mama, I'm not that crazy about preachers. They can be some worrisome men and wear on your nerves something terrible when you are around them. Some of them can be so greedy—buying big cars, always wanting folk to cook them a whole bunch of food, and then will sit there and practically eat up everything in sight. Remember the last guest preacher who came to Mount Nebo? Ate all of the best pieces of ribs and he didn't even offer Rev. James the last piece. Just snatched it out of the pan and gobbled it up."

Lee Allie interrupted her. "That preacher was greedy, all right, but the problem was that we shouldn't have let Mother Harold convince us to invite him in the first place. Several people knew something about him and didn't care much for his ways. But we just sat back and let Mother Harold have her way again. Should have known better. 'Cause we all knew from the get-go that she wanted him to come just so she could look him over for Saphronia. Lord, if that woman don't wear out my patience looking for some preacher to marry her old stuck-up grandbaby."

She shook her head a few times just thinking about the preacher and Mother Harold.

"But Mama—" Essie began.

"But Mama nothing, Essie Lee. Every preacher ain't like that and you doggone well know that fact is the truth. Rev. James is a good man who loves God and takes his pastoring seriously. And you think Rev. Simmons is okay, too. Otherwise, you sure were some fool to let him come over here to see you. You know, Essie Lee, some preachers really do want to do right."

"And you think Theophilus is a man that wants to do right?"

"Umm hmm. I think *Theophilus*, as you seem to be callin' him now, wants to do right," Lee Allie answered with emphasis on his name.

Essie looked embarrassed. She didn't want her mama reading any more into this situation than she knew she already had. She said, "Well, he'll just have to convince me he is all that you saying he is."

Lee Allie gave Essie a "look" and dismissed that foolishness with a wave of her hand.

Chapter Three

JHEOPHILUS STOOD IN THE PULPIT OF ESSIE'S church exactly one month from the day he met her at Pompey's Rib Joint. Mount Nebo had a small congregation of about 160 members from in and around Charleston on the rolls. Most of them were working folk—domestics, gardeners, farmers, seamstresses, cooks, factory workers—with a sprinkling of those who counted themselves among the middle class (two teachers, the secretary for the Negro undertaker in Oakland, the head janitor over at the white high school, and the assistant head cook over at Ole Miss in Oxford). With its plain, red-brick exterior and simple inner decor, it was a warm and welcoming place that was lovingly cared for by its members—as evidenced by its expertly shingled roof, its manicured lawn, and the flowers planted all around the building, as well as its immaculate interior, which gleamed and smelled of fresh lemon wax.

Theophilus held on to each side of the pulpit podium,

ulders back, looking out on the congre-
t feeling all that confident about his ser-
ed at the folks sitting in the plain, polished
used his attention on a baby girl who looked
like a big chocolate doll in a frilly pink dress and matching bonnet trimmed with pink ribbons. He wondered, as
he watched the father hold her up on his shoulder, what
it would feel like to hold his own baby girl in his arms.
He looked at the baby a few more seconds and shifted
his attention back to his sermon. So far, he had been
quiet this morning—not one whoop, shout, or even the
use of a rhythmic cadence of words to emphasize a point.
And even though he had some reservations about this
sermon, he knew he had captured everybody's attention
with his title, "Lovin' Your Woman like Jesus Loved the
Church."

The inspiration for it had come when he was listening to B.B. King sing "Sweet Sixteen." He loved the
song and the way B.B.'s voice glided up and down the
melody, just as Theophilus imagined his fingers were
gliding up and down the neck of his guitar, Lucille. At
the end of the song, the call and response between B.B.
and the other singers reminded him of a church service.
He wanted to preach a sermon that echoed what
B.B. did in that song. And, while he always prayed that
the Holy Ghost would work through his preaching, to
unite and uplift the congregation, challenge them, and
speak to their hearts—he really did want to impress
Essie Lee Lane.

One or two of the older women had pressed their lips
together when he gave the name of the sermon, making
him a little nervous about starting, but he noticed that
it made the younger women sit up in their seats and
look a lot more attentive. And he became even more en-

couraged when he looked at Essie sitting with her mother and Mrs. Rose Neese, and realized that she was waiting to hear what he had to say.

Theophilus took a sip of water from the glass that was sitting on a table behind him and wiped his forehead and the corners of his mouth with a soft white handkerchief. It was warm in the small sanctuary. He wiped his cheeks and forehead again and unzipped the top of his robe a few inches before he began.

"Now, before I go on, church," he said, his lush baritone voice sending a shiver or two through a few young women in the congregation, "I need to explain myself a bit. See, I don't want to go back to Memphis and wake up in the middle of the night in pain because my ears feeling like they're on fire because you fine folks are discussing how I preached that strange sermon at your church."

Mount Nebo's First Lady, Mrs. Susie James, was sitting on a front-row pew, just a few feet away from the altar. She looked at Theophilus and said, "No need to be frettin' about what you think we gonna say when you gone. Folks at Mount Nebo honest people. We get you told to your face. Now go on and preach!"

A few chuckles circulated around the church because Mrs. Susie James always made it her business to give her own distinct response to Mount Nebo's guest preachers.

Theophilus smiled at Mrs. James. "If the First Lady says hurry up with this sermon, I guess I'd better quit tarrying and give you all a piece of what God inspired to come on into my mind. You see, church, when St. Paul told men to love their wives like Christ loved the church, he left out something."

"And, what did he leave out?" Rev. James asked as he leaned forward in his seat in the pulpit.

"Well, Rev. James," Theophilus said, turning around to look at him. "Paul left out the juice."

"The juice? Well, well, well."

"Yes, Reverend, he left out the juice. And I don't have to tell you that most good stuff like collard greens, pot roast, baked ham, watermelon, peaches, and so forth is not worth too much without the juice. Church, if you leave out the juice, you leave out the best stuff."

Theophilus started getting nervous again when he saw a raised eyebrow on the face of a trustee sitting in the front pew across from Mrs. James. He was looking at him like he wanted to say, "Son, what in the heck you talkin' 'bout?"

He rolled his shoulders again and boldly pressed ahead. "You see, when Paul spoke to us in the Bible, he commanded us men to love our women like Jesus loved the church too dry and neat-like. Now think about it. There is nothing dry and neat-like about love—especially that good kind of loving that is chock-full of passion."

There were a few surprised gasps in the congregation. Mount Nebo had never had a preacher come close to talking about man-woman love, let alone "that good kind of loving that is chock-full of passion."

Rev. James raised his eyebrows and then relaxed them. He had known Theophilus for a few years and had heard him preach more than one controversial sermon in that time. He was confident that Theophilus would deliver a sermon the congregation could use in their daily lives— even if he did shock the socks off of them before he made his point.

Lee Allie nudged Essie and told her to poke Rose Neese in her side so that she could get her attention. The two women looked at each other, behind Essie's back, and said with their eyes, "I don't believe that boy stood there and said that."

"Now, church," Theophilus went on, "you all will have to bear with me. I know this sermon is different and provoking. But you all have to realize that sometimes God pokes at us and the best way to poke is to provoke. So I'm gonna poke and provoke this morning until I finish saying what God is laying heavy on my heart."

He steadied himself at the pulpit podium and continued: "Now, church, real love between a man and a woman ain't all neat and tidy like we *think* St. Paul is talking about in Corinthians. I hope he understood that real love was a whole lot messier than that. Because real passionate love can throw your heart, mind, and body every which way but loose. Gentlemen, you all know that when a woman truly stirs your heart, every part of you goes into a fit and you can almost feel the blood rushing through your veins whenever she is near.

"And you ladies out there—you ladies know that the right man will make you smile all over yourself, light up your faces like sunshine, put some natural blushing on your cheeks, and give you reason to strut all sassy-like when you get to walking. And I know you all know that walk I'm talking about. It's that walk you good Christian men in Mississippi like to sing and talk about when you're not up in church."

Both the women and the men laughed when he said that.

Theophilus wiped his face with the handkerchief again and smiled at the congregation.

He looked right at Essie when he said: "I'm glad to know you all know what I'm talking about with those walks. Even I, a preacher, want to sing some songs a preacher isn't supposed to know about when one of the

brown flowers in this congregation does that good ole
Mississippi walking."

Now Theophilus backed away from the pulpit podium
and moved out front, the Bible in his hand, to make
more direct personal contact with the congregation. He
didn't need the microphone. His voice was strong and
projected easily across the small sanctuary.

"Mount Nebo, I didn't come here to get you all upset
with me. But I have no choice other than to preach from
my heart."

"Then get on with your sermon, son," a man sitting
in one of the middle pews said. "'Cause I'm gone be
gettin' hungry directly and want my soul fed first."

Everybody started laughing and Theophilus relaxed
some more. He did as he was asked.

"Church, I think the reason we men can't figure out
how to love these sweet brown flowers sitting up in this
congregation right, is because we just don't understand
how God could call us to commit ourselves to a higher
level of humanity through our relationships with women.
Sometimes we men get off track and act like these relationships interfere with serving God—like women get
in the way of man and God. But I'm here to tell you
that God didn't mean for that to be so. The passion that
is stirred up between a husband and a wife—if treated
with the respect God intended for us to treat it with—
helps us become filled with a love for the Lord, our
brothers and sisters, ourselves, and life in general, that
makes us better in every way.

"You see, church, this kind of love ignites the senses
and it makes you glad to be alive. And that kind of stuff
flowing through your soul can inspire all sorts of wondrous things. It can make you want to be closer to God.
It can make you want to be closer to people. It can make

you want to stir up life in the people around you. And a lot of you know that it can make you want to create new life—new life like that baby doll sitting over there in her daddy's lap looking all sweet and precious this morning."

Folks in the congregation turned to look at the baby and her daddy as she just cooed and smiled as if she knew that she had helped Theophilus along with his sermon.

Theophilus smiled at her and said, "That's right, sweetie pie, tell us all about how we should be living."

Essie's heart felt warm and tingling as she watched Theophilus talking to the baby from the pulpit. She couldn't help but wonder what kind of father he would be. She imagined he'd be the kind who showered lots of hugs and kisses on his babies—bringing home bagsful of candy they didn't need, just so he could see bright smiles on their faces and hear the squeals of delight in their voices. These thoughts warmed her heart even more and she looked up at the pulpit and gave him a smile that was so sweet and lovely, it made her face light up.

Theophilus saw Essie smiling at him and felt good all over. His voice boomed out, even stronger: "A thinker named Alan Watts wrote in a book about men, women, and nature, that the coming together, the shared passions between a man and woman, was one way of experiencing God. Now don't get me wrong, church. I didn't say *the* way but one way. You all have to remember that. You see, Mr. Watts seemed to believe that passion, or in our case, good loving, was indeed part of the gifts God gave to us—and that this passion was sacred."

The congregation had grown quiet, and Theophilus could tell that they were listening *and* thinking about what he was saying. He now sat down on the altar steps, adjusting his robe around his knees, then leaned forward to give them a mischievous grin. "You all must be thinking that I'm kind of crazy about now," he said. "That's all right, though. Back in the Bible days, folks thought Jesus was kind of touched in the head, too. But, church, you have to realize that dealing with this husband and wife thing is very important—the church is mighty dependent on having a steady supply of married folks with each passing generation. Healthy, happy, sane, and productive folks I might add."

Then he delivered the punch: "But more importantly, *we* are fighting hard in this country for the right to be equal to everybody else in America. And since this fight is important enough for some of our bravest soldiers of the cross to die for, we need to deal with how we act at home. Before we go out to combat the evils of racism, fight the evils of segregation, refuse to yield to the evils of the Klan, wage war against the evils of poverty, and engage in all-out battle against the evils heaped upon us just for being a Negro in America, we need to get right at home.

"Church, I'm sick of the injustices we Negroes heap on one another—especially what we Negro men can do to our own women. We run around this country screaming and hollering for all the world to hear that we're men. Then we come home all puffed up with manly pride and take away the very rights we are demanding for ourselves from our own Negro women and children. Now, church, that's not right. In fact, it's downright ugly. You all hearing me?"

"Yes, Reverend. We hear you," Rev. James said. Encouraged by the chorus of yeses that followed, Theophilus continued: "Have you ever thought, gentlemen, that being a husband means honoring that sweet brown woman you say you love so much? Why not serve that woman who serves you, quiets your stormy passions, and then will endure labor for sixteen hours or more, just so you can walk around this town proud, showing off that new baby boy or girl you helped make to all of your relatives and friends?"

An older woman sitting in the back of the church with five of her grandchildren stood up, raised her hands, and said, "Yes, Lawd. Son, you keep on telling these here mens the truth. I done birthed thirteen babies and I knows what you talkin' 'bout. Part of the life of this here church done come from my loins. Jesus, Sweet Jesus. I done give soldiers to this here war for Negro rights. Yes, Lawd!"

"Thank you, ma'am. I think you have summed up what I've been struggling hard to say all morning. Look here, these beautiful women sitting in this church have sacrificed so much so that we men can be conceived, born, grow, live, prosper, be loved, get love, and it's time that we gave something back. It's time that we built them up so that our children can flourish and become powerful soldiers in God's army for justice and right-eousness."

Theophilus put his hand on the railing and pushed himself upright. He then walked out into the center aisle of the church. Opening his hands to the very attentive congregation, he delivered a quick conclusion, to leave his audience still in the grip of his ideas.

"You know, church, Jesus ate, slept, laughed, cried, played, and even got mad enough to fight. He meant for you to respect and honor those things that make up your life on this earth. And that includes the way you love one another. Jesus intended for us to put some juice in our daily lives. He intended for love to be respectful, pure, rich, passionate, intoxicating—to have some juice. So on this Missions Day Sunday, I ask you all to put some juice in your lives by loving one another in the way the Lord intended you to—as cherished and honored partners in this life on our God's earth."

Theophilus turned back toward the pulpit and sat down. Rev. James leaned over and tapped him on the shoulder, whispering, "Son, your heart sure was being tugged on by the Lord this morning, wasn't it? No matter how hard you fought, He made you say what Mount Nebo *and* you needed to hear."

Theophilus sighed with relief and reached over to shake Rev. James's outstretched hand. The last thing he wanted was for his sermon to offend his host pastor and mentor. Rev. James now took the podium and, raising his hands, motioned for the congregation to stand. Then he beckoned Theophilus to come and stand next to him.

"Church, for some reason the Lord wanted our young Reverend here to talk about husbands and wives and families and friends and how we should be lovin' up on one another. Now I know there were some rough parts to this sermon. But that was because God was workin' on him right in the midst of his preaching. There was something that the Lord wanted all of us, including Rev. Simmons, to hear this morning. You see, God is about love, unconditional, honoring love—love with some juice. And if y'all can't love one another right, especially someone you claim stirs your passions, then what makes you think you gone act right when it's time to enter eternity and to live in love forever with the Lord?

"So, I'm opening the doors of Mount Nebo and I'm making a special appeal to some of you husbands to come on up here and rededicate yourself to the Lord, to dedicate your heart to doing right by your wives and your families. For you see, church, God's love begins in your own heart. It touches the lives of those around you, through you, and it becomes the church when you come together with hearts filled up with His love."

He turned around and addressed the choir.

"Choir, sing, 'Lead Me, Guide Me Along the Way. Lord, if you lead me, I cannot stray. Lord, let me walk this day with Thee. Lead me, O Lord, lead me.'"

The choir members stood and started singing. By the time they got to the second verse, Leroy Dawson, the son of the head of the Trustee Board, had come down to the altar crying and clutching the hand of his fiancée, Pearl. He walked, sobbing, into Rev. James's open arms. Holding Leroy Dawson for a few seconds, Rev. James signaled to his father that both he and his wife should join them at the altar. Pleased that the sermon had touched the younger Dawson's heart, he could only hope that Leroy's witness reached his father and moved him to treat Mrs. Dawson better.

Leroy Dawson let go of Rev. James, shook Theophilus's hand, and grabbed Pearl by the waist. Then turning to face the congregation, he said, "When Rev. Simmons first started this sermon, I thought he was unprepared. But as I watched him struggle to say what the Lord laid on his heart, I realized God was using him to reach someone in this church. And as Rev. Simmons kept talking, I realized that someone was me. You see, church, my Pearl has been on me to treat her right. She has pleaded with me, over and over again, to think about how wonderful our home would be if I did the right thing and married her. I have to ask God now to forgive me for not respecting and honoring you as He intended, Pearl. You are a good woman—you're smart, can cook like my mama, and you're kind and brave.

Now I ask you, church, is there anything that is too good for a woman like my Pearl?"

"No, son. Ain't nothin' too good for a church girl like that," said the lady with the five grandchildren.

Leroy turned to Pearl. "Honey, I'm so sorry I didn't want to listen to you. I love you. And when people come in our home, they're gonna know it is a Holy Ghost home filled with some juice."

Before Reverend James could open his mouth to say, "Let the church say Amen," cries of "Praise the Lord," "Thank you, Jesus," and "Amen" rose from the congregation. Pearl pulled a handkerchief from her purse and wiped her eyes, thankful that God had heard her prayers and opened Leroy's heart. She kissed Leroy on the cheek and gave him a sweet smile. Leroy's mother wiped her eyes, glad that God had answered her own prayers for her son and his future wife, while his father stood by with a sullen expression on his face.

Rev. James laid his hands on the couple and led the congregation in a prayer for them. He then motioned for the choir to sing "Leaning on the Everlasting Arms" and made a gesture for the two young people and the parents to take their seats. He then looked at Theophilus and indicated that they should start the recessional and march to the back of the church.

After giving the benediction, Rev. James directed Theophilus to stand at the back of the sanctuary, where the church members would form a receiving line to greet him. He then excused himself, claiming that he had to help the trustees count the collection money, but in truth, he wanted to check on the dinner Lee Allie's missionary group was setting up downstairs. Already he smelled baked chicken, which he knew would be crispy-tender, brown, and succulent—just sitting in the pan perfectly seasoned with onions, celery, green pepper, salt, pepper, sage, and paprika. And he wanted to see if Rose Neese had contributed a pot of her famous, spicy-hot chitterlings. Other than playing a round of poker with his closest friends, Booker Webb and Pompey Hawkins, chit'lin's were one of Rev. James's few vices. Susie James often joked to her friends at Mount Nebo that if a chit'lin' ever came to life in the form of a woman, she'd be in some deep trouble. Good a man as her Murcheson was, he had never turned down a chit'lin' and he never would.

Theophilus swallowed hard as he stood there waiting for the receiving line to assemble. The first one to reach him was an elderly man, who gave him a sly wink and said, "Reverend, thank you so much for that sermon. I been tryin' to get some of my hardheaded grandsons to love up on they sweet little wives better than they been doin' for years now. *Told* my oldest grandson just the other day, that he wouldn't be so tense and cranky if he was sweeter to that girl he married. *Told* 'im she'd be all over him if he just treated her like she was special and important to 'im, stead of actin' like that po' chile nothin' but a footstool."

Theophilus smiled at the man, who held up the line until he finished what he had to say. "And you know something, son. I'm eighty-seven and I ain't never tense and cranky, 'cause I've always known how to act with my missus. Yes, Lawd. Had a whole lotta juice when I was young and still got a taste of it left in me right now."

Theophilus laughed and marveled at how good this man looked—not a day over seventy. He hoped he had some of that kind of juice left in him when he was eighty-seven.

"I hear you, sir," he said. "I sure enough hear you. I hope the Lord keeps on blessing you like He's been doing all of these years."

The man winked again and thanked Theophilus for his sermon one more time before heading downstairs to eat.

Theophilus kept watching for Essie, who turned up next to last in line. She was wearing a turquoise linen sheath dress that hugged all the right places of her petite, voluptuous figure, with a matching bolero jacket, ivory pumps, and ivory gloves with tiny pink flowers embroidered on the back, and round, turquoise rhinestone earrings with a matching pin. She didn't have on a hat, but her thick, coarse hair was perfectly coiffed in a chin-length flip. When she walked up to Theophilus, he noticed that she was smelling awfully good in what he thought was Chanel No. 19.

When Essie held out a small gloved hand, Theophilus could barely conceal the sultry and non-preacher-like look that spread across his face. He took her hand in his and said, "Sister Lane, Sister Lane. You are adding a little extra sunshine to an already blessed day."

Essie had to admit that he was looking almost regal himself in his robe and black brocade stole with red velvet crosses emblazoned on both sides. Now she was the one who was looking him up and down and had to stop herself—she had never seen a man look that good in his clerical robe.

"Yes, it is a very lovely day, Theophilus," she said.

The woman standing behind her, Mother Laticia Harold, gasped out loud. She had always thought Essie Lane was a fast little number. But to call a pastor by his first name, and at church, was downright shameful.

Essie did her best to ignore Mother Harold's gasp. She smiled at Theophilus again. "You know I was probably the only one in church who wasn't shocked by what you said this morning."

His smile began to fade a tiny bit.

"Don't get me wrong, Theophilus. I liked your sermon. But you do know it was real different, don't you?"

His face began to light up again as he nodded his head yes.

Mother Harold sucked in her breath. She couldn't believe that girl. His sermon was scandalous and she couldn't wait until tomorrow when she was going to march right into Rev. James's office and give him a good piece of her mind about it, too. Some of these folks at Mount Nebo had babies like rabbits and didn't need to hear any foolishness about making more babies they could not afford to have. Mother Harold cleared her throat again and said "Humph" loud enough to be heard across the tiny sanctuary.

Essie, who couldn't ignore her any longer, turned around and said, "Good afternoon, Mother Harold."

She turned back to Theophilus. "Rev. Simmons, this is Mother Laticia Harold, a very important member of our church. Her husband was the late Bishop Rosemond Harold, and her granddaughter, Saphronia McComb, is finishing her master's degree at Jackson State."

Theophilus remembered Bishop Harold, whom he had met years ago when he passed through Richmond and visited his parents' church. Theophilus was a teenager then, but he would never forget how rude Bishop Harold, a light-skinned man with straight brown hair, had been to his dark-skinned father. It had come as a shock to him back then that even a bishop could be color-struck. He had almost forgotten that Bishop Harold was from the Delta.

Theophilus gave Mother Harold a polite smile and said, "It is a pleasure to meet you this morning. I know of your late husband. If my memory serves me right, he was responsible for helping several small missions groups incorporate into sizable churches in rural areas throughout Mississippi."

Mother Harold was impressed. "Rev. Simmons, I am so pleased that you know something about the Bishop," she said. "He was such a great man and you young ministers do nothing to honor his memory."

Theophilus kept the polite smile on his face. He couldn't agree that Bishop Harold had been a great man, so he turned her attention to another subject.

"Mother Harold, Sister Lane mentioned that you have a granddaughter studying at Jackson State University. What is her major?"

Mother Harold looked very proud at the mention of her granddaughter. She said in a crisp, tight-sounding voice, "She is a speech major. Since Saphronia was a young child, she has been interested in studying speech. She wants to teach our children how to speak properly. On several occasions, she has offered to teach a public speaking class here at the church. Isn't that right, Essie?"

Essie just nodded. Saphronia got on her nerves when she put on her phony airs, as if she wasn't living in a little country town just like everybody else who attended Mount Nebo.

Mother Harold wasn't satisfied with the lukewarm nod and said, "Essie, I was speaking to you. You do remember Saphronia's efforts to assist you and several other young women in this church with your speaking problems, don't you?"

Essie narrowed her eyes. "I certainly do remember Saphronia's trying to start that class. And I don't know why she thought we wanted any help from her, since we all talk just fine."

Mother Harold pressed her lips together into a tight, thin line of disapproval. She made a mental note to bring Essie's sharp remark to the attention of Rev. James— not that he would do anything about it. He was so fond of the riffraff in this church.

Theophilus coughed to stifle a laugh. In the short time he had known Essie, he had never heard her talk in such an exact-sounding voice. The social politics of church life never failed to amaze (or amuse) him. But before more sparks started flying between the two women, another one joined them, whom he figured was Mother Harold's speech-teaching granddaughter. He was right.

"Saphronia, dear, this is Rev. Theophilus Simmons. Rev. Simmons, this is my granddaughter, Saphronia Anne McComb."

Saphronia stepped in front of Essie, nudging her aside, and grabbed Theophilus's hand. She was very light-skinned with long, straight brown hair, a thin nose, and thin lips.

"Rev. Simmons," Saphronia said in a voice that sounded like a younger version of her grandmother's. "You cannot imagine how delighted I am to have you as a guest at my church. You have such outstanding credentials and do Mount Nebo a great honor by coming here to preach the word to us today."

"Thank you, Sister McComb. It is good to know that my sermon was appreciated."

Saphronia moved closer to Theophilus. She squeezed his wrist and tossed her head, imitating the white coeds she would see sitting at the lunch and soda counters near Ole Miss in Oxford. They had looked so elegant, laughing and shaking their silky tresses over root beer floats— occupying seats she wouldn't have dared to sit in. She looked over her shoulder at Essie, grateful that her hair wasn't that thick and coarse. Essie could shake her head off before that hair would move.

She started to show off her hair again. But the look in Essie's eyes stopped her in her tracks. She turned her attention back to Theophilus, only to find that the big smile on his face—which was quite unlike the polite expression he had trained on her—was directed at Essie.

At twenty-six, Saphronia was ready to get married, and she was determined to marry a minister with a future as pastor of a large and prominent congregation. Rev. Simmons had everything she was looking for in a husband, with one exception—he was dark-skinned. Even his BA from Blackwell College and his master's degree from the Interdenominational Theological Seminary, down in Atlanta, couldn't overcome that. As handsome as he was, Saphronia did not even want to contemplate what her children would look like if he were their father. He would probably just wipe out her good-skin, good-hair genes, and they would come out as black as he was. Still, there weren't too many pastors around with the education and growing reputation of Rev. Simmons.

Saphronia ran her hands down the sides of her beige silk dress. She had selected this dress because she wanted to look like the future first lady of a church when she met Rev. Theophilus Henry Simmons. Yet, expensive and proper as it was, it made her complexion look washed out and failed to do anything worthwhile for her figure—it was a sharp contrast to Essie's less expensive outfit, which only increased Saphronia's long-standing envy of her.

Theophilus was fully aware by now that Saphronia was trying to impress him with her status as the girl with the most "pedigree" in this little country church. And while he didn't think she was ugly, he was definitely not attracted by her light skin, thin nose, and skimpy lips. But the one thing about her that *did* make him look was her behind. At first, he thought he was seeing things when he noticed those wide, sexy hips sitting on the back of this tight-lipped woman. Saphronia Anne McComb had the kind of behind that would make a Negro man shout, "*Thank you*, Lawd!"

Essie frowned at Theophilus. She didn't like that smile on his face and decided that she wasn't standing there another minute, watching a man who had expressed interest in her ogle another woman's butt.

As she started to walk away, Theophilus reached out to grab her elbow. "Sister Lane, please don't run off like that. I was hoping that you would be able to tell me a little more about your church."

She just looked at him, thinking he could learn more than he ever cared to know about Mount Nebo from Rev. James. And she was about to say so when Saphronia chimed in: "Rev. Simmons, I have written a book on our church's history and can tell you anything you want to know over dinner."

Essie had to close her mouth tight before it dropped wide open. She had seen this "book" of Saphronia's. It was nothing more than a little bitty pamphlet about Mother Harold's financial donations to Mount Nebo over the past ten years.

Theophilus didn't miss the expression on Essie's face. He looked at Saphronia and thought to himself, "Sweetheart, Lord knows you are a piece of work."

Lee Allie looked around the dining room to make sure everything was in order before she went back upstairs to get Theophilus. Dinner couldn't start until the honored guest arrived, and everybody was hungry. She was willing to bet some money that he had been waylaid by Mother Harold and her old stuck-up grandbaby, Saphronia. She would never understand why Mother Harold was so determined to marry Saphronia off to a preacher, when her own marriage to the late Bishop Harold had been stormy to the day he died.

In his heyday, Bishop Harold was as bad and bold with his skirt chasing as Rev. Ernest Brown up in Detroit. Funny thing, though. All of Bishop Harold's women ranged from chocolate to ebony, and most of them didn't go to church—at least not on a regular basis. She knew that had to hurt Mother Harold. She was so light-skinned she almost looked white, stayed up in church, and was proper and tight to the hilt. A shame. But the greater shame was the woman's determination to put the same burden on her granddaughter's shoulders.

Lee Allie was about to walk into the sanctuary when Rev. James stopped her to say, "Sister Lane, just wanted to tell you that I'm glad you asked Rev. Simmons to be our Missions Day speaker. He did a fine job and gave us something to think about."

"Well, Rev. James, I'm glad you approved the request to invite him. Had a feeling when I met Rev. Simmons there was something special about him."

Rev. James nodded his head in agreement and added, "Yeah, you right. He is special. And glad he met Miss Essie. You know that boy gettin' real sweet on your baby girl."

Lee Allie laughed. "Yes, Lord. Kind of thinking that myself. And quiet as it's kept, Miss Essie sweet on him, too. Just too stubborn to admit it."

Rev. James rubbed his chin and grinned. "Well, well, seems like there a little ole love bug runnin' up and down the highway between Memphis and Mississippi."

Lee Allie laughed and pushed at the door leading into the sanctuary.

"Sister Lane, just one more thing."

"And what's that, Rev. James?"

"Where your missionary group putting Rev. Simmons up for the night? I was expectin' to hear from y'all about that a couple of days ago but haven't heard so much as a peep from you ladies."

"He told us he wanted to stay at Rose Neese's place. That's why we haven't bothered you and Mrs. James about accommodations for the Reverend. Plus, Rose lettin' him stay there for free."

Rev. James scratched at the back of his head for a second.

"You know, the Southern Christian Leadership Conference sending some folks in this week to talk with me and some of the other Negro ministers around Charleston about what we're going to do to support the movement in this area. Rev. Simmons helped us out by calling to tell everybody about the meeting. I asked him to because I thought it was too risky to have those calls coming from anywhere around Charleston.

"One of those meetings will be at Rose Neese's, and we'll be having several of our lunches there, too. Might not be the best idea for him to stay there tonight. A few of my preachin' brothers got big mouths and just love to talk about our business with the upstanding white folk who'll listen to them. So I was thinking that Rev. Simmons should stay at Mother Harold's. She has a good reputation with the white folks in this town. They wouldn't expect her to have someone like Rev. Simmons at her house—which is just about true most of the time."

Lee Allie nodded, agreeing with what he was saying. "Then you come with me to talk to Mother Harold. She don't care too much for me and Essie and wouldn't agree to anything coming from me."

But Lee Allie almost changed her mind about asking Mother Harold to help when she saw how Saphronia had wedged herself between Essie and Rev. Simmons. She frowned, thinking to herself, "That sly-cat is just determined some preacher gone up and marry her with that white woman look on her face, clashin' with her big black behind."

She walked up to where they were standing and said more pleasantly than she felt, "Rev. Simmons, everyone is waiting for you to come on downstairs and bless the food so we can eat."

Before Theophilus could answer, Saphronia said quickly, "We have been having the most wonderful conversation about the people Rev. Simmons and I both know in Atlanta and Memphis. The world is so small, wouldn't you agree, Rev. Simmons?"

"That's very nice, Saphronia, but we have to get Rev. Simmons downstairs," Lee Allie said. "It's getting late and he has to be hungry after all of that preachin'." She tugged at the sleeve of his robe. "Now come on, let's get you fed. Wouldn't want you going back up to Memphis complaining about being hungry down here in Charleston."

Theophilus smiled at Lee Allie. "Let me get out of this hot robe and I'll meet you all downstairs." He looked at Essie, who was standing next to her mother. "Where are you sitting?"

"In the back. I'm helping Mama's missionary group serve the food."

"Rev. Simmons, I do believe you will be sitting up front at our table since Grandmother is a prominent church mother," Saphronia said, with a smug look in

Essie's direction. She wanted Essie to know that a jook joint cook didn't have any business trying to compete with her for a man like Theophilus Simmons.

Theophilus looked disappointed, nodded at everyone politely, and went to change.

Meanwhile, Rev. James had found Mother Harold to ask whether she could put up Theophilus for the night, explaining that he did not want him to stay at Neese's Boarding House or any place else that might link him to the Southern Christian Leadership Conference organizers.

Mother Harold secretly thought Rev. James (and Rev. Simmons, for that matter) had no business being involved with those civil rights people, who wanted to mess with what small amount of peace the colored had down here in Mississippi. But Rev. Simmons was a preacher with the right credentials, even if he were too dark, and if he stayed with her, Saphronia would have more time in his company. She had yet to meet a dark-skinned man of the Reverend's stature who would not give anything for an opportunity to court someone like her granddaughter. Even more than Saphronia herself, Laticia Harold was determined that her only grandchild marry a minister.

After making Rev. James stand there waiting on her answer, she finally said, "I would be honored to have Rev. Simmons as my house guest. Bring him to the house after you have finished all of your men's business here at church."

"Thank you, Mother Harold. Sure hope this not too much trouble for you."

"It is not any trouble at all," she replied, setting off to catch up with Saphronia, who had gone downstairs to make sure she got a seat right next to Theophilus.

*   *   *

Theophilus was supposed to go to the Harolds' house right after the church dinner. He changed those plans, however, and went by the Lanes' house first. When he stepped up on the porch, he noticed all the flowers for the first time, especially the soft, pink rose bushes framing the creamy yellow wood house, with its green shutters, porch, and door. He had been so intent on seeing Essie on his last visit that he hadn't paid any attention to the front of the house. He took a deep breath to catch the fragrance of the flowers, and was about to knock when Uncle Booker opened the screen door.

"Evenin', Reverend."

"Good evening, Uncle Booker. I decided to come by and thank Mrs. Lane for inviting me to speak at Mount Nebo before I turned in at the Harolds'."

Uncle Booker was pretty sure that Theophilus really wanted to see Essie Lee and *not* Lee Allie, but decided not to push the issue. He said, "Well, I'm sure Lee Allie will appreciate your thoughtfulness. You go on in. They back in the kitchen talking 'bout church. Seems like from all they been saying, you preached one hell of a sermon this morning. Kind of sorry I missed it."

Uncle Booker pulled his car keys out of his pants pocket and started walking off the porch. He extended his hand toward Theophilus and said, "Be seein' you—and mind your manners in there, if you know what I mean."

Theophilus shook his hand, hoping Uncle Booker did not pick up on the look that crossed his face. He was discovering that Uncle Booker had a special gift for working on his nerves. He walked back to the kitchen and found Essie and her mother sitting at a small red Formica-topped table, sipping on glasses of tea filled with big, juicy-looking slices of lemon. Lee Allie saw him first and got up to give him a big hug. She liked this young man and wanted to make sure that he always felt welcome in her home.

"Reverend, what a nice surprise. Didn't expect to see you this evening. Thought you'd be out at the Harolds' 'bout now, trying to get some rest."

"That was the original plan, Sister Lane. But I wanted to come by here and thank you in person for all of your hospitality. Didn't seem right to me, to leave Charleston without stopping by and thanking you in person."

Even though Theophilus was talking to Lee Allie, his eyes were on Essie. And like Lee Allie had once said, he almost forgot his home training when she stretched out one leg to reveal bare feet and dainty, peach-painted toes. It took him a few seconds to stop his eyes from traveling up her leg to the edge of the same baby blue Bermuda shorts she was wearing when he met her at Pompey's Rib Joint. He forced his eyes away from her legs and smiled at her.

"Good evening, Miss Essie. That tea sure does look refreshing."

She rattled the ice around in her glass as if to say, "It is," adding out loud, "If you want some tea, go get yourself some. Those glasses on the dish rack are clean."

Theophilus looked down at Essie still smiling that smile and watched her as she tried to stare him right back in the eyes without flinching.

"Essie Lee, where is your manners? Get up out of that chair and get this man a glass of tea."

"Oh that's all right, Sister Lane. I don't mind getting it myself," Theophilus said, still smiling at Essie, holding her eyes to his and making her flush from the intensity of the look on his face.

Sensing the electricity flowing between Theophilus and Essie, Lee Allie decided that they needed some time alone. "Theophilus, grab a seat and make yourself comfortable," she said, walking to the kitchen door. "I need to work on my report for Missions Day. Essie Lee good company when she wants to be."

He started to pour himself some tea but changed his mind and reached for a kitchen chair and sat it right next to Essie. "I feel kind of bad about the dinner," he said.

Essie moved her chair away from him a bit. "Why? Didn't you enjoy your dinner?"

"Yes, I did. But not as much as I would have if I could have spent more time with you."

She started smiling at him, then stopped when she remembered that he had spent most of the dinner talking to Saphronia McComb.

He picked up on her change of mood. "Did I say something wrong?"

"What you did was laugh and talk with Saphronia McComb almost the entire time we were at dinner."

"Essie, I'm a preacher. You and I both know that I can't be rude to folks at church, even Saphronia McComb. Comes with the job. Just like being put up for the night at Mother Harold's is part of my job, too. I'd much rather stay at Mrs. Neese's. Believe me, it's a lot of fun over there—can't imagine Mother Harold's house being anything like that."

"Yeah, being at their house will be as bad as you think it will be. I only hope you can handle Miss Saphronia *Anne* being all over you when you get to her house."

He got up, poured himself some tea and leaned against the refrigerator. "Essie, are you trying to tell me that Saphronia will come on to me when I'm at her house?" He shook his head at the thought of it. "Girl, I don't think she has it in her. Her butter barely melted in her mouth at church, and it came off of a hot roll."

Essie cut her eyes at him. "You can laugh if you want to. But Miss Saphronia can be something else when she wants to be."

He started laughing, trying to imagine Saphronia McComb being "something else." "What in the world can that stuck-up Miss It possibly do to me? Look at me. I'm a big man, baby."

Essie shivered. It was the second time he had called her "baby," and the feeling she got when he said that was nothing short of delicious. She said, "Delilah got Sampson good and he was a big, strong man. Don't always take a lot of strength to get to a man."

"Hmmm, don't tell me you're afraid that Miss Saphronia will get me good. Now, why would you be worrying about something like that?"

She looked away from him, thoroughly embarrassed, and started to stammer. "Uhh . . ."

"What's wrong, Essie? Cat got your tongue?" He was thoroughly amused that this tough-talking, knife-waving jook joint cook would almost gag over telling him that she was jealous that he was spending time with Saphronia McComb. He couldn't resist continuing to tease her. "Why won't you answer me, Essie Lee Lane?"

Essie looked like she wanted to crawl under the table. This woman was definitely an original, he thought—cute, sexy, prim, proper, honest, smart, irritating, and funny, very, very funny. It had been a long time since he'd met a woman who tickled him as much as Essie Lane did. He watched her for a few more seconds and thought he should give her some assurance.

"Well, just so you know, I've never been too partial to the Saphronias of this world. They can really work your nerves when they want to."

Essie was annoyed with herself for sighing with

relief. As much as she hated to admit it, she really liked Theophilus. She sneaked another peek at him, trying not to stare at his long legs and the biceps that kept bulging against the short sleeves of his black cotton clerical shirt every time he moved his arms.

Theophilus pretended that he didn't know Essie was checking him out, simply delighted that she was so attracted to him. But the longer he sat there trying not to watch her watching him, the harder it became for him to stay in his chair and not snatch her up in his arms.

Essie was feeling fidgety herself. His eyes were so intense, she felt heat radiating from them. She resisted an urge to fan her face and, to break the heat, got up to put her empty glass in the sink. Looking around for something else to do, she spotted his empty glass sitting on the table, picked it up and rinsed it out, over and over again, hoping to avoid his eyes and to relieve some of the tension that had been building between the two of them ever since he walked into the kitchen.

Theophilus looked at Essie's shapely hips and thought how perfect her behind was. He closed his eyes for a moment, imagining wrapping his hands around her hips, the mere thought heating him up so much that he could no longer bear to sit in his chair. And before he had a chance to think, he had gotten up and stood right behind her at the kitchen sink.

Essie could hardly bear the sensation of Theophilus standing over her. She started to move but stopped when he placed his hands on each side of her, with his palms resting on the rim of the sink, and leaned down and kissed her on the cheek. She trembled from the exquisite warmth of that kiss and then held herself stiff to resist the irrepressible desire to lean back into this sexy, good-smelling man.

Theophilus had hoped the kiss would ease the emotions running every which way inside of him. But it only made him want more. He turned Essie around to face him and cupped her heart-shaped face gently in both his hands.

Essie thought she would melt when she felt his warm palms on her cheeks. Her breath caught in her throat when she felt his fingertips massaging the nape of her neck as he gently kissed her lips. She felt that kiss like a charge running through her body. Never in a million years could she have imagined being so ignited by a kiss—especially a kiss from a man who was a preacher.

Theophilus now drew a deep breath, kissing the corner of her mouth and whispering in a low, sensuous voice, "Essie Lane, Essie Lane," before enfolding her in his arms.

Essie's own arms, of their own accord, wrapped around Theophilus. With her palms just above his waist, she unconsciously caressed the hard muscles in his back through his clerical shirt.

At Essie's touch, Theophilus felt his temperature shoot up. Almost against his will, he pressed her to the sink and kissed her slowly, smoothly, forcefully.

For a moment, Essie got lost in the wonder of the feeling of his body moving against her own. But when a heavy sigh escaped from her lips, it dawned on her that they were moving too fast, way too fast. This was the first time she had ever *kissed* him and the intensity of the feelings running between her and Theophilus scared her. As if breaking some kind of spell, Essie snapped her eyes open and pushed him away from her.

Her push was like a couple of ice cubes dumped down the back of his shirt. "It seems as if we got a bit carried away," he said, raggedly. "I never meant to . . . I . . . just . . . couldn't help myself."

"*We* got carried away?" Essie said indignantly.

Theophilus stepped back and looked at her. He was not about to let her stand there and pin all of that kissing, hugging, and sighing on him. He knew that she had been giving just as good as she had gotten.

"Yes, Essie," he said matter-of-factly. "*We* got carried away—you and me, me and you."

"Well," she said, as if she was trying to dismiss that reality. "You were getting too familiar-acting with me."

Theophilus decided not to push the point. He realized that she was uncomfortable with her own response and that she had little experience with men. Yet she was a deeply passionate woman. Those clothes, the way she put on makeup, and that walk drove him crazy. And, pressed against her, he had sensed a deeper current of desire in her than he had ever dreamed was there. The thought of being the only man ever to know that passion was almost enough to make him want to marry her. Marriage. A shiver ran up his spine that was so strong it made his shoulders twitch.

"What's wrong with you?" Essie asked.

"Felt a shiver."

"Must be your conscience bothering you."

Theophilus leaned against the counter that faced the kitchen sink, folding his arms across his chest and crossing his legs at the ankles.

"I bet you'd just love for me to have a whipped conscience about now. But I don't. And I'll tell you something, Essie. If you think I wanted you, you're right—I definitely wanted you. And it's a good thing your mama is in this house or else I would have been hard pressed not to take this further."

Essie pointed her finger at Theophilus, wagging it back and forth as she said, "And I guess you think that I was just gonna stand there and let you go as far as the high heavens, huh?" She put her hands on her hips, leaned back on those big legs, and was about to say some more when Lee Allie walked into the kitchen.

Essie looked at her mother and clapped her hand to her face, thinking, "Lord, have I just lost my mind? I've been all up on this man, right in my mama's kitchen."

Theophilus, who had heard Lee Allie's bedroom door close when she had first left the kitchen, had been so caught up in kissing Essie that he had forgotten to listen for her return. He didn't want Lee Allie to think that he was trying to disrespect her home. He looked down at himself, grateful for no telltale signs, not realizing that his passion was boldly imprinted, like a great big sign, all across his face.

Lee Allie almost laughed as she watched Essie and Theophilus trying to act all normal and polite. She could have told those two she was definitely born before yesterday and that there was nothing like unnatural silence to alert a mother that hot-and-bothered kissing was going on in her home. Instead she frowned at Essie, whose embarrassment was making her angry at Theophilus.

"Essie Lee, why you huffing and puffing like you gettin' ready to start a fight?"

She looked at Theophilus. "Reverend, you'll have to excuse her."

"I'll do just that, Sister Lane. Essie and I were having a serious discussion and things got heated up a bit while we were talking. Didn't they, Essie?" he said with a smirk that dared her to contradict him.

Essie couldn't believe him. And if she thought she could have gotten away with it, she would have smacked him right upside his head for saying that mess. She rolled her eyes at him and said, "Well . . . I wouldn't go so far as to say it was heated."

Theophilus knew she was worried about her mother but shot her a look, eyes laughing, as if to say, "Guess I got your little tail, didn't I?" He said, "You wouldn't, huh? Well, that's awfully surprising given the passionate way you approached the subject, *Miss* Essie. In fact, I personally thought our discussion was rather stimulating. Didn't you?"

Essie glanced at her mother, praying she wasn't paying too close attention to what he was saying.

But Lee Allie wasn't a bit fooled by their exchange and recognized that Essie was just mad at herself for liking the feel of that man someplace he had no place being—all up on her. She wanted to tell that girl it wasn't a crime to like the feel of a man, if he were the right man and her husband. And Lee Allie felt that at twenty-five, it was high time Essie got interested in a man. All she did was work and save money so that she could move to Chicago or St. Louis and open a dressmaking shop. It had never even dawned on that girl that it would be nice to have a good man to share these dreams with.

As far as Lee Allie was concerned, the man in her kitchen was a good man—and a good man for Essie. She only hoped that her hardheaded child had sense enough to know this herself.

Chapter Four

REV. JAMES PERSONALLY ESCORTED THEOPHILUS to Mother Harold's, out of politeness, but with no intention of staying. Judging by the smile frozen on Mother Harold's face when she answered the doorbell, she was not eager to welcome him either. Still, after ushering them in, she announced, "Rev. Simmons, we will put your things in the guest room, then proceed to the living room for afternoon tea. I hope that you will join us, Rev. James."

Silently begging God's forgiveness, Rev. James cleared his throat and said, "Mother Harold, I'm afraid I will have to pass on your invitation. Lord knows, there a few more sick and shut-in I have to attend to before my day is through."

Theophilus couldn't believe that he was hearing such a baldheaded lie from Rev. James. For the first time he realized that his mentor, like every other preacher, found that certain members of his flock tested his religion. But Mother Harold seemed more relieved than offended by the excuse. With a warm goodbye to Theophilus and a quick nod to Mother Harold, Rev. James put on his hat and quickly made his escape before she could repeat the invitation. When the front door closed, Theophilus was left alone, feeling like he was locked in some place he definitely did not want to be.

"Rev. Simmons, the guest room is this way," Mother Harold said, leading him down the hall to a spacious bedroom decorated in pale beige and mint green. Everything in this room was expensive and tasteful, from the plaid, beige, and mint green armchair, to the mint satin damask bedspread and the matching draperies at the window. It was a fancy room that hinted at long-standing financial comfort but without the welcoming warmth he felt at Mrs. Neese's or the Lanes' sweet little home.

"Rev. Simmons, put your things in the closet. After you wash up, come join us in the living room for dessert and coffee. We also have homemade pound cake, hand-picked strawberries, and fresh whipped cream. Is this suitable to you?"

Theophilus relaxed a little bit and said, "Mmm-mmm. Pound cake and strawberries would sure hit the spot about now."

Mother Harold scowled as if he had just taken something off her dresser and put it in his pocket. He couldn't even begin to figure out what he had done to deserve such a nasty look.

Saphronia, who had appeared in the doorway while they were talking, knew exactly what was wrong. "Rev. Simmons, my grandmother disapproves of slang expressions."

Theophilus was confused. "Huh?" he said.

"Slang, Rev. Simmons. My grandmother hates to hear Negroes use idioms like 'hit the spot'—or say 'Mmm-mmm' or 'Huh.' "

Theophilus looked from Saphronia to her grandmother in disbelief, thinking to himself, "It's gonna be a very long evening."

Theophilus entered the living room just as Mother Harold was setting a large silver tray of desserts on the middle of the coffee table. She motioned for him to sit on a dark red silk Queen Anne chair, settling herself on the opposite red, gold, and ivory striped silk couch. Saphronia fixed Theophilus a healthy helping of pound cake, covered with juicy red strawberries and delicious-looking homemade whipped cream. Her starched white linen dress explained why Mother Harold had wanted to rush Rev. James out of the house. The purpose of this tea was to focus Theophilus's undivided attention on Saphronia.

He couldn't help but notice how different the women looked, even though they were obviously related. Mother Harold was a tiny lady and if you didn't look at her too closely, she could easily be mistaken for a little bitty white woman. Her hair was straight and fine and her skin was very pale, with only a hint of peachy brown in it. Saphronia, though light, had too much color in her skin to pass for anything other than what that behind clearly stated she was. And even though her hair was straight, it was thick and heavy—actually quite lovely, if it were styled in any kind of way.

"Rev. Simmons," Mother Harold said. "I must say that I am curious to know what motivated you to preach that outrageous sermon this morning. I did not approve of it one bit. Your blatant referrals to human passion were unseemly for a minister to have, let alone speak of during a church service."

Was this attack some kind of test? Theophilus wondered. Was he supposed to give a certain kind of answer to prove himself worthy? He took a few sips of his coffee to get his feelings under control. What kind of so-called proper and upstanding hostess would go out of her way to make a guest feel so uncomfortable in her home?

But he did his best to keep his answer measured. "Mother Harold, if Negroes are going to make any real progress in this country, we have to begin by loving ourselves. And that love has to begin in the home where the family is, between a husband and wife, where the family begins. How can the Negro community appreciate itself and believe it deserves the best, if Negroes aren't able to experience an all-abiding, passionate love in their own homes? And if passion helps to bind us to one another, I shouldn't be afraid to preach about it, whether it concerns the deep love we have for a child or the kind that sets off sparks between a man and a woman."

Mother Harold narrowed her eyes at him and took a tiny bite of her cake before saying, "And you attended Blackwell College, Rev. Simmons? Simply amazing. I cannot imagine anyone at Blackwell entertaining this foolish thinking of yours."

Theophilus sat dead still, fighting the impulse to snatch up that hateful little woman and shake her. He said, "A lot of my professors at the seminary thought just like you."

She looked relieved, and that made him even madder.

"Did you attend Blackwell on a scholarship? I run the Blackwell scholarship program here in Charleston and I would never approve one for a colored youngster who echoed your sentiments."

He thought, "I just bet you wouldn't," but said, "I had a partial scholarship and worked to pay for the rest of my education. And you know something? Working that hard taught me a lesson."

"And what is that, Rev. Simmons?"

"That we have to stand up for what we believe in and trust God when storm winds blow over us because of those beliefs. And you know something else, Mother Harold? It is my job as a minister to preach the truth as God wills me to understand it. Where would we be if Peter had shut his mouth when questioned by the Scribes and Pharisees as described in the Book of Acts?"

Mother Harold didn't know quite how to respond to his reference to Peter. But she did know that he needed to be straightened out about his foolishness concerning Negroes and passion.

"Well, young man. You may not like hearing this but I truly resent young people like you who try to undermine all that people like me have worked so hard to accomplish for our race. There is absolutely no reason for us to stay 'field Negroes' by holding on to ways that mark us as overly emotional and animalistic. We must rid ourselves of these low passions that you seem so enamored of if we are ever to become as cultured and civilized as white people. As I always tell Saphronia, we need to act in ways that help white people forget we are colored and originate from the most savage part of the world. We have to help white people see themselves in us beneath this colored skin."

Theophilus sat back in his chair, too outraged to say a word. What was "civilized" about the brutality inflicted on Negroes in this country, after they were dragged off from "savage" Africa? What kind of "culture" would burn a man at a stake shaped like a cross—just to cite one recent horror—and then savagely hack the source of passing on life right off his body?

It had been a long time since he was exposed to such internalized racial self-hatred. He was relieved that even Saphronia had the good sense to look annoyed at her grandmother. He now understood completely why Rev. James considered this home a safe hiding place for Negroes who were involved with the civil rights movement.

"Mother Harold, perhaps we should talk about something else. It would be bad manners on my part to continue this conversation, especially since you have so graciously opened your home to me."

Saphronia, already bored, took advantage of the tension between Theophilus and her grandmother to get him alone.

"Grandmother, I think it would be nice if we finished our coffee on the back porch."

"That is a fine idea, Saphronia. But you two young people will have to go ahead without me." Mother Harold stared meaningfully at Theophilus. "Rev. Simmons, I hope you will conduct yourself properly when you are with Saphronia. She has been raised to expect a man to act like a gentleman when in her company. Do I make myself clear?"

Theophilus was furious at this woman. First, she insulted his sermon, his background, and even his race. Now she was acting like he would go out on that porch and get all on top of her old stuck-up granddaughter. "Mother Harold, I don't have any reason to act in any but the proper way while I am a guest in your home," he declared.

He poured himself a fresh cup of coffee and followed Saphronia to the back porch, thankful to be relieved of the presence of Mother Harold and wishing he didn't have to be bothered with Saphronia, either. He knew from all those little looks she had been sneaking at him that she was interested in more than conversation. He hoped that she wouldn't do anything that would force him to hurt her feelings.

Saphronia motioned for Theophilus to sit down on the porch swing and placed herself only a couple of inches away from him. She yawned and stretched, arching her back and poking out her chest. "Whew, I thought we'd never get away from my grandmother," she said, edging a little closer.

"Sister McComb, your grandmother means well," he said in his best preacher voice, trying to ease away from her, wondering when she found the opportunity to undo the top buttons of her dress so the white lace of her bra peeked out at him.

"I guess she means well, Rev. Simmons, but I do believe that she went a bit too far with you."

Theophilus wondered what she would say to defend her grandmother, but she was headed in another direction. "I must confess that I often wonder what's inside of a man who can think like you do. When we were at church, I noticed that you made all the people you met feel comfortable. In fact, I found you to be especially adept at making the lower-class people in our church feel important."

Saphronia saw the guarded look on his face but mistakenly assumed he was confused.

"Oh, Reverend, what I mean is that you are adept at talking to people who aren't as educated and intelligent as you are—which is an admirable quality."

Theophilus was certain that Saphronia was referring to Essie and he fervently hoped she would not say any more. Because if she did, he was sure that the restraint that had seen him through so far was going to snap.

Unable to draw him into a discussion in which she could bad-mouth Essie Lane, Saphronia decided to tackle her objective more directly. Leaning against Theophilus, so her breasts rubbed his arm, she placed her hand on his thigh. The hard muscle in his leg became tighter.

"Why, Rev. Simmons. I do believe you have just worn yourself out. Your leg muscle is tight and soooo hard," she said seductively, massaging the muscle in his thigh.

Theophilus was shocked at her boldness. When Saphronia's hand started to rise higher, stroking a little too close to the danger zone, he stood up so fast that he accidentally spilled coffee on her dress, marring that pristine white linen. He was about to apologize when he caught her masking an ugly look that was more related to his rejection than to the hot liquid or the brown stain. The look was both angry and filled with contempt. She needed to be taught a good lesson about teasing men and acting like she was God's gift to the Negro race.

Theophilus put his cup down under the swing, and pulling Saphronia to her feet, stood as close to her as he dared.

Saphronia grinned. "I guess this means you do have some interest in me. I was a bit worried that you had become taken with that Essie Lane. But even if you play around with a jook joint cook, I know you have the good sense to want to settle down with a decent woman."

Theophilus swallowed his fury and crooned at Saphronia, in a dangerous voice, words that he hoped would never, ever reach the ears of Essie Lee Lane.

"You know something, Saphronia, decent women aren't dick-teasers. I know you understand that word, because I do, and I'm a preacher. And I understand exactly what you're trying to start here. If I weren't so tired, I'd call up all the good sisters from Mount Nebo's prayer circle and get them over here, so we could lose some of that mess out of your stuck-up butt."

Saphronia looked at him like he was crazy. How dare he speak to her with such vulgarity and presumption? She turned her mouth down and said, in a nasty voice that sounded just like her grandmother's, "Rev. Simmons, what kind of woman do you think I am? How dare you suggest that I would crawl up under any man, just because he had the nerve to ask? Essie Lane might do that," she hissed, "but even if I did, I certainly wouldn't be up under a *Negro* as black as you."

She started to walk away but he was so angry that, without thinking, he grabbed her roughly by the arm. "Saphronia," he said, "I don't know what kind of men you've been around. But I can tell you, girl, that *I* don't have any respect for a woman who plays these games. A woman who's selling it is more decent—at least she's honest about her intentions. As for Essie Lane, I can tell you that she thinks too much of herself to go rubbing up like you do on every preacher she meets."

Saphronia's eyes narrowed into slits so tight that Theophilus doubted that she could see. He loosened his grip on her arm and she snatched it away from him. Her cheeks were flushed a bright pink, and she was furiously blowing steam in and out of her mouth.

"No man has *ever* talked to me like that," she huffed, "and I am going to report you to your bishop for even daring to think about what you just said."

"Girl, you go right ahead and tell on me," Theophilus replied. "And here's something else you can add to your list. You act like you have some kind of prize up under that dress. You think you're so high-class. But what's low-class is you toying with a Negro as black as me because you're sure he wants your old high-yellow stuff. What's low-class is your mean little grandmother thinking that marrying her old bishop gave her the right to be insulting. I'd rather have stayed at Mrs. Neese's and risked facing the Klan than here, putting up with all your snooty low-class mess."

Theophilus didn't wait for her response. Storming into the house, he went straight to his room, closed the door, and sat down on the bed, breathing hard to try to calm his nerves. Those two women had just about run him ragged. If people only knew what preachers went through, they would surely have to stop complaining about them.

Part 2
1962

Chapter Five

WHEN THEOPHILUS CAME BACK TO MEMPHIS from Charleston, he was in love. It was not that eating-up-your-insides, can't-sleep, can't-eat obsession that had consumed him with Glodean Benson. It was a peaceful yet passionate feeling of coming home to himself, and more—something no other woman had ever given Theophilus—of joy. Essie made him feel blessed that he was simply alive and able to love her. And if all of these wondrous feelings didn't keep leading him to contemplate marriage, life would have been absolutely perfect.

His congregation could tell that something had changed in their pastor. Sometimes, when they passed by his study, they heard him whistling what sounded like B.B. King's "Sweet Sixteen." And then there were those days when he came to work looking tired and anxious, as if he had been wrestling with himself (or God) all night over some big, life-changing decision. Then, there were those times when he gazed off into space right in the middle of a conversation, so you had to call his name over and over again to get his attention.

Coral Thomas knew in her gut that a woman was behind all the humming and whistling and starry-eyed looks off into space. When Susie James had first confided the young pastor's troubles, asking Coral to take him under her wing, she had vowed that she would do whatever it took to protect him from Glodean Benson. She knew from Sister Clayton, Glodean's aunt, that she was helping out in the family funeral home in Atlanta and was relieved that she hadn't come back home to Memphis—and Greater Hope—during Reverend Simmons's first year. But there had been times when Theophilus was so heavyhearted that he looked like he was lugging all the bricks and mortar in the church on his shoulders. "Help him, Lord," Coral had prayed. "This young man is in travail. He lonely and his loins on fire. Clear the path, Lord. Make a way out of no way and lead that boy to his wife. Just turn his life around, Lord. Bless him, Lord."

When she prayed she had felt a burning in her heart that told her that the Lord was listening. And now it seemed that, all this time, he had been mapping out the answer to her prayers. She called Susie James to confirm her suspicions and was gratified to learn that Theophilus had been phoning Charleston every Saturday night to get *inspiration* for his sermons from one Miss Essie Lee Lane. And it tickled her no end to hear that during at *least* one of those phone calls, Miss Essie was overheard giving Theophilus a deep sexy laugh.

Coral Thomas now decided that it was her Christian duty to give God a helping hand and bring these two lovebirds together. Since their church district's Annual Conference was to be held that year in Memphis, she urged Theophilus to invite Murcheson and Susie, along with a few "special" church members to attend. Plotting with Susie, she made sure that the "special" delegation included Lee Allie and Essie Lane.

Bishop Jennings assigned Theophilus an important role in the Annual Conference—the responsibility to find accommodations for the out-of-town ministers and their families. With so few hotels and boarding houses open to Negroes, Theophilus planned to ask members of Memphis Gospel United churches to open their homes. Then inspiration struck him—he would require guests to pay their hosts a modest room-and-board fee, which would both compensate the hosts for their trouble and let the guests feel like less of an imposition. The plan won tremendous popular support but logistically it was a nightmare. He was so tired by the time the conference finally started that he prayed he wouldn't fall fast asleep on the floor of the parsonage and miss the whole thing.

Uncle Booker, Essie, Lee Allie, and Mrs. Neese arrived in Memphis on a Friday morning. Coral Thomas had personally offered to host them and had cooked for days to prepare for their visit. As they climbed the porch steps, they were hit with the smell of ham simmering in redeye gravy. Then Coral opened the door, and after welcoming the rest of her guests, grabbed Essie up in a great big hug.

"Ooohh, baby girl," she said. "I sure am glad to meet you."

"Thank you, Mrs. Thomas," Essie said politely, puzzled that she would get such a warm reception. She had no way of knowing that Coral Thomas felt halfway responsible, since she had prayed so hard about it, for Essie meeting Theophilus.

"I've been hearing all about you from Susie James," Coral replied. "And the way I understand things, there a real good-lookin' Memphis preacher who been callin' you lately to get himself a little in-spi-ra-tion for his sermons."

Essie's mouth fell open, and she stared at Lee Allie, who suddenly became interested in the contents of her purse. Clearly her mother had been telling Essie's business at church, and it had now, humiliatingly, spread all the way to Memphis. But before she could scold Lee Allie, Coral said playfully, "What's wrong, Miss Essie? Don't you think you got what it takes to give *yo'* man some inspiration?"

Essie fumed, but saw she wouldn't get much satisfaction when her own mother and godmother, Mrs. Neese, slapped palms and laughed at Coral's remark. Coral Thomas's good humor and outspokenness were engaging—just as long as you weren't her target. Now Coral beckoned them all into the house.

"Y'all come on in, set your things down, and go and get washed up so we can eat this breakfast I been workin' on all morning. My D.S. will catch up with us at church this afternoon. He's working today, but, Booker, he said to tell you he taking you out a little later on."

Uncle Booker started grinning. Rev. James had promised that when Booker got to Memphis, he'd have his old pal D.S. take him to the dog track. Rev. James disapproved of gambling, but he knew that their shared passion for it would unite his two favorite friends. But he warned Booker that D.S. always attended church before going to the track, for he hated to gamble on "an empty stomach"—without giving honor to the Lord first. That was a philosophy Booker could understand and respect.

Coral finished setting the table and motioned for them all to come sit down and eat. As soon as everybody was at the table, mouths watering at the sight of that ham in redeye gravy, grits, scrambled eggs, fried apples, biscuits, homemade sorghum molasses, fresh-squeezed orange juice, and coffee, the doorbell rang. Coral, who had just sat down, hopped up and went to answer the door. She came back and said, "Well, Essie, that man you been inspiring just arrived and looks kind of hungry to me."

Theophilus came in with a warm smile on his face and carrying a large bouquet of fresh flowers.

"Rev. Simmons," Lee Allie said, "I can't begin to tell you how glad we are to see you this morning. Ain't that right, Essie?"

Essie kept quiet, trying to act like he wasn't anybody special, but Theophilus didn't seem to mind. He handed the flowers to Coral Thomas, saying, "Glad to see all of you, too"—while looking straight at Essie.

"This is a nice surprise, Theophilus," she finally said, as calmly as she could. All those phone conversations couldn't prepare her for her overwhelming emotions at seeing him. He was looking so good in his pale blue jersey-knit sports shirt, sharply creased navy blue slacks, and that straw hat cocked up on his head.

"Theophilus, sit down and rest your hat."

Handing his hat to Coral Thomas, he sat down right next to Essie. Coral hung up the hat, then returned, saying, "Theophilus, bless the table."

Theophilus reached out for Essie's and Coral's hands, and, as everybody bowed their heads, prayed: "Dearest

Lord, we are grateful for this morning. A beautiful morning with your saints sitting 'round this table. A bounteous table filled with your precious gifts from the earth. Bless this food and the hands that prepared it. Bless this meal and those who will partake of it. And thank You, for we know that so many are not so blessed as we are to have such a feast before them. In the name of your precious son, Jesus, we thank You, Lord. Amen."

"Whew," Essie said as she pulled her hand out of his. "For a minute there, I thought you were going to break out into a sermon."

Coral looked at her and thought, "That poor girl just don't know *how* to act when that man is around." She said, "Essie Lee, that was a beautiful prayer and it wasn't long at all."

Lee Allie agreed. "Coral, I don't know why Miss Essie thinks it is her duty to give this boy such a hard time about everything."

Theophilus, who was well aware that his nearness made Essie nervous, stuck up for her. "Thank you, but I know Essie. Seems like Essie is always concerned about me doing the right thing. You never let me do wrong, do you, Essie— Ouch!"

She had pinched him hard on the thigh, letting him know that she didn't like his teasing her in front of people—and especially about "doing the right thing." Uncle Booker, who had been studying the two of them, knew from that pinch just how hard Essie had fallen for this man.

Now Coral rescued Essie. "Theophilus, how you been farin' this week? Annual Conferences are a big headache for the folks runnin' it. Lord knows some of them bishops and big shot preachers can wear out the patience of Job."

Theophilus smiled. Mrs. Thomas was never one to bite her tongue. He said, "Between the room-and-board program and other things this week, I have been run just about ragged."

"You runnin' the room-and-board program?" Mrs. Neese asked. "I think it was a good thing you made everybody pay for a place to stay. Just ain't right for ministers to expect folks to put them and their families up for free. Folks be workin' too hard to have to deal with all of that."

"You are absolutely right, Mrs. Neese. That's the very reason why I fought so hard to make these people pay for staying in somebody's home."

Uncle Booker swallowed a piece of his biscuit and said, "Well, I'm glad to hear you making these here preachers do right. You know, some of them is so greedy and spoiled, they expect for plain workin' people to pay for everything, from the grease they put on they nappy heads on down to the soap they use to wash they funky butts."

"Booker, watch your mouth," Mrs. Neese blurted out. "You need to be a little more gentle about preachers with Rev. Simmons here as Essie Lee's guest."

Everyone turned to look at Mrs. Neese, wondering when she got so familiar with Booker. A widow, she was a longtime family friend, but her rebuke implied that she was more than that to Booker. But she revealed no sign, and neither did Booker, who slurped noisily at his coffee. "Aw, hell, son," he said. "I know that *you* all right. When you trying to do the right thing by me and mine, you won't have nothing but support from me."

Theophilus drained his coffee cup, marveling at Uncle Booker's change of heart about him. "Thank you," he said. "And thank you for driving these ladies to the conference."

He stood up, wiped his mouth with a napkin, and patted his stomach, smiling at Coral. "Mrs. Thomas, I tell you, that breakfast was too good for words. I really wish I could stay and let my food settle, but I have some errands to run before the service this afternoon."

Then he held out his hand, saying, "Essie?" She took his hand and let him lead her out of the kitchen, trying to act like she didn't hear the giggles trailing behind her.

Theophilus made sure he was out of earshot of Essie's folks, then said, "I don't think you know how glad I am to see you, girl."

He pulled her chin up and smiled into her eyes. He started to lean down and kiss her, until he remembered that Uncle Booker was only a few feet away. Instead, he said, "Have dinner after service with me, Essie. I would love to take you to Mabel's Kitchen before you leave Memphis."

She smiled shyly back at him. "It would be nice to talk to each other without my family and the whole church staring down our throats."

He nodded in agreement. "So, we eat at Mabel's Kitchen after church?"

"Yeah, Mabel's Kitchen."

He leaned down and kissed her on the cheek and left. Essie could feel the lingering warmth of that kiss when she rejoined the women, who were busy washing the dishes.

"Pastor gone so fast?" Coral said, hands deep in dishwater.

"Yes," Essie said dreamily. "He had to run, but, uhh, he did kind of invite me to eat dinner with him after the service this evening. But he didn't ask me on a date or anything like that, just out to eat."

Lee Allie and Rose Neese looked at each other slyly,

trying not to laugh. "Essie Lee, where he taking you for a *bite* to eat?" Lee Allie asked.

"Some place called Mabel's Kitchen."

"Mabel's Kitchen, Essie?" Coral said. "Baby, I know all about Mabel's Kitchen and I can tell you, it's the nicest Negro restaurant in the city—expensive, too." She got quiet for a few seconds, let that bit of information sink in, and then said, "And, I believe, Miss Lady, it is definitely the kind of place a man takes a woman to when he takes her on a *date*."

This time Lee Allie and Rose started laughing out loud. Rose said, "Well, Coral, I'm with you. I think the good Reverend is taking our baby on a date. What about you, Lee Allie?"

"I'm with y'all. Mabel's Kitchen don't sound like any place *I'd* go just to get a bite to eat."

Essie looked at the three of them and determined that they were not going to get to her with their laughing and sly winks about Theophilus. She sounded a bit more defensive than she wanted to, though, when she said, "Well, Mabel's Kitchen may be fancy and all that, but it certainly didn't sound that way when Theophilus told me about it. Now, can I do something to help clean up, Mrs. Thomas?"

"No, chile, we're almost done. Why don't you go on and get yourself ready, since you got a date to go on after church?"

Tired of their teasing, Essie was glad to leave.

As soon as she was gone, Coral said, "Lord, I hope I didn't hurt her feelings. But don't y'all know, that little gal is just love-struck over that big chocolate preacher of hers. Trying to act like that man don't mean nothing to her—I don't know who she think she trying to fool."

"Herself, Coral," Lee Allie said, shaking her head. "That girl ain't trying to fool nobody but herself."

Chapter Six

THEY DIDN'T LEAVE FOR CHURCH UNTIL CLOSE TO
3:00 because they were waiting on Uncle
Booker to finish dressing. But when he finally
walked into the living room, Rose thought he
looked so handsome in his navy blue pin-striped suit,
starched white shirt, and burgundy silk tie, it was worth
the wait. She smiled at him, and Lee Allie had had to
say, "Booker! Don't you look good? I'm surprised, seeing as you were never a churchgoing man."

Booker just grumbled a bit and herded everybody out
of the house, fussing about being on time after making
them wait on him.

When they arrived at the church, he dropped them
off while he parked, so they could head to the rest room
and get a jump on the pre-service rush. Just before the
service, it would take forever to find a stall or even a
sliver of mirror space, with all of those women pow-
dering and touching up; blotting makeup; combing and
patting their hair; adjusting pastel and brightly colored

hats of all kinds of materials, shapes, and sizes; spraying purse-sized vials of perfume on their necks, cleavages, wrists, legs, thighs, and ankles; and tugging at tight girdles, straightening out twisted garter belts, and trying to relieve the pinch of those confining longline bras.

Essie came out of a stall, washed her hands, and went into the lounge area where there was a long, wide mirror attached to the wall. She touched up her lipstick, blotted her lips with a tissue, and wiped the shine off her face with a red powder sponge. She had made a special dress for the service—a sunset pink, shantung silk shirtwaist, with a wide shawl collar and a low waistline, resting just above the hips, with a full skirt that was accentuated with a soft tulle petticoat. There were pearl buttons down the front of the dress and on the cuffed, elbow-length sleeves. She wore pearl earrings and a dainty pearl bracelet, along with a wide, pleated headband that she had made out of a scrap of material from the dress. In this outfit, Essie was a vision of church fashion perfection—from her thick pageboy hairstyle to the envelope purse tucked neatly under her arm to the matching pearlescent beige, patent leather pumps with tiny bows on the toe.

As they made their way back upstairs, Coral insisted that they stop in the church lobby to find D.S., whom she knew had arrived late. As she searched for him, Essie looked around the lobby, which was full of well-dressed church folk, ministers, and bishops, hoping to pick Theophilus out of the crowd. Finally she spotted him on the other side of the room, talking to Rev. James and another minister who looked to be about his age. A small group of ladies walked up to him and gave him hugs and kisses. She could almost hear him complimenting an older woman—whom he held at arm's length, to get the full effect—on the beautiful white crepe suit with navy trimming on the collar she was wearing.

For a moment Essie wondered if any of the women in this group were his admirers. But as she watched them, she decided that, just like her mother, Mrs. Neese, and Coral Thomas, these were the women who sustained the congregation with their tithes and offerings, care of the pastor, care of the sick and shut-in, care of each other, church dinners, fund-raising events, and maintenance of the church building, along with the parsonage. No, these women were not the pastor's admirers—they were the lifeblood of the church.

Theophilus caught sight of Essie and gave her a smile and a wave. Rev. Eddie Tate, the preacher who was standing between Theophilus and Rev. James, asked, "Who are you waving at?"

He looked across the lobby again and then back at Theophilus with a smile. "Umph. That girl is wearing the daylights out of that dress. Theo, brother, you need to take me on over there so I can get a better look at her and then just shake her mama's hand."

Theophilus's body language suddenly changed from relaxed to stiff and defensive. With a chill in his voice, he said, "I'm not taking you anywhere to shake anybody's hand."

But Eddie wasn't put off. "Now, Theophilus," he said. "Judging from the way you're acting, that can only be Essie Lane—the sweet thing you've been hiding down in Mississippi away from the rest of us."

"That's Essie Lane, all right. But I haven't been hiding her. You don't know her because she doesn't run around in any of these fancy church circles and has little if any interest in being seen at an Annual Conference."

"Well, she's definitely going to be seen at this Annual Conference, Theo. Because a man would have to be blind not to see the legs on that woman."

Theophilus bristled at Eddie's comments about Essie's legs. But Eddie just clasped his shoulder and said good-naturedly, "Relax, man. Don't get all bent out of shape with me because your new woman is so fine. Isn't that the dream of every man—to have a fine woman at his side?"

Theophilus smiled, a little sheepish at his overreaction.

Rev. James, who had been listening to the friends with bemusement, now looked at his watch. "Well," he said, "it's time for me to meet Bishop Jennings in the sanctuary and find out where I am to sit during the service. I lost my seating chart and don't have a clue as to where he put me."

The two young men understood what he meant. Annual Conferences were notorious for sparking rivalries among preachers for the attention of the bishops and prominent pastors. On a few occasions, preachers had even come to blows over being placed in seats too far from the pulpit, limiting their access to a bishop or a highly placed pastor. Bishop Percy Jennings had a lot of power in the denomination, so much of the jockeying would revolve around him. Fortunately, he was a stickler for fairness, which extended even to his seating plans.

No sooner had Rev. James left than Rev. Marcel DeMarcus Brown, the son of Detroit's Rev. Ernest Brown, joined them. Theophilus did not like Marcel Brown or his daddy, preachers who would do just about anything for money and power in the denomination—and, worse, used their status in the church to get women in bed. He had particular disdain for Marcel, who adopted a deep, sexy voice when he preached. And Marcel definitely knew how to use that voice—raising it, lowering it, moaning, groaning, and even growling at all the right points in a sermon. The few times Theophilus had heard him preach, Marcel had given him the impression that he was toying, throughout his sermon, with some woman in the congregation who had momentarily caught his fancy.

"Marcel Brown," Eddie said to break the tense silence. "Surprised to see you at this conference. I always thought Memphis was too far south for a smooth Deetroit boy like yourself."

Marcel shook Eddie's outstretched hand, saying, "Reverend Tate. Kind of surprised to be here myself. But, what the hell— Daddy insisted that I drive my presiding bishop down to Memphis. Said Bishop Giles would grant me a few favors at the Michigan Annual Conference if I came with him. I will be glad to get back to the Motor City, though. Nothing here but a highway that takes me further down to nowhere—Mississippi."

Marcel knew full well how Theophilus felt about him, and the animosity was mutual. He said, "The good Rev. Theophilus Simmons. Why, someone was just telling me what a big hit you were down in Atlanta with some of our dedicated saints. So, how's it going in Memphis?"

It was obvious that Marcel was referring to Glodean, though Theophilus couldn't imagine who had bothered to revive that ancient scandal. But he resented Marcel's insulting effort to imply that they were on the same level, both preachers who would have their way with women. Rather than shake Marcel's hand, he stuck his own in his pocket, saying, "I'm making it, Marcel. But I can't possibly be doing as well as you. Way I hear it, there are a lot of sisters in Detroit who make sure everybody knows just how much they love the pastor."

Marcel adjusted the ruby velvet stole on his black robe and said, "What can I say? I try to make all of my church folk feel happy and blessed. And if I were you, Simmons, I'd count this particular week as filled with happiness and blessings just waiting to be had. Nothing like an Annual Conference to get some of these good sisters all overheated and anxious to do a little extra something for the pastor.

"Take that one," Marcel said, zeroing in on Essie. "My . . . my . . . my. Will you all look at the legs on that girl? Now, that's one I'd like to know better than I know the Bible when this conference is over."

Eddie was getting uncomfortable, knowing how much Marcel was offending Theophilus. He pulled at the sleeve of Marcel's robe and said, "Leave it alone, man. He is working on that."

"Oh, yeah?" Marcel said to Theophilus. "You need to mark off your territory a lot better than you're doing, if you don't want the rest of us preachers prowling around that woman."

Theophilus couldn't say a word. It was taking everything in him not to punch Marcel in the mouth.

In fact, Marcel had already staked his claim on a woman at the conference, Saphronia McComb, who was invited with her grandmother to attend out of respect for the late Bishop Harold. Marcel's father had been pushing him to marry, to curb some of the scandals his womanizing had gotten simmering in the church. As soon as he laid eyes on Saphronia Anne McComb, he recognized how perfectly she fit his father's image of the right kind of wife for him. So he had sought her affections—effortless work, with his light skin, curly black hair, and deep soulful eyes—and set her to blushing whenever he flashed his charming pastor's smile at her.

But Simmons's woman was far more enticing than Saphronia, despite the latter's level of education and status in the church community. He envied Theophilus and decided to walk over and introduce himself to Essie, just to spite him. But he quickly changed his mind when he saw his presiding bishop, Lawson Giles, heading into the lobby, talking to a retired pastor from Grenada, Mississippi. Excusing himself from Theophilus and Eddie, he hurried over to join Bishop Giles.

Theophilus thanked the Lord for helping him hold his temper, as provocative as Marcel had been. Now he decided that he just might do what Marcel suggested, go over and "mark" Essie as his "territory." He walked up to Lee Allie and kissed her on the cheek, complimenting her on the mint green silk suit she was wearing. It was beautifully tailored with a fitted jacket that had a tiny flare where it touched her hips, a Peter Pan collar, a breast pocket with a pale, turquoise silk handkerchief stuck in it, round silver buttons, and a matching straight skirt with a kick pleat. And the suit was polished off with a pillbox hat that was covered with mint green, pale turquoise, and beige chiffon leaves, beige patent leather pumps, and a matching purse.

"Sister Lane, you are looking like a million dollars this afternoon."

Lee Allie smiled and said, "Why, thank you, Theophilus. You know Miss Essie made this suit for me last year as a Christmas present."

Theophilus was impressed. He said, "Essie, you are full of surprises," as his eyes, containing a blend of pride and admiration, swept over her from head to toe. "And I must say that you are looking quite exquisite yourself.

Your dress is very beautiful. Reminds me of a warm sunset. Did you make it?"

Essie smiled at Theophilus, a soft blush highlighting her cheeks. "Yes, I made it and the pattern for it and the pattern for Mama's outfit, too. I make a lot of our clothes."

"Then that explains why you always look so good when I see you."

Just then he heard a cough. He hadn't noticed Eddie coming up alongside him, trying to find a way to meet this Essie Lane. Theophilus gave him a "what are you doing here" look, pretending to be exasperated, but went ahead and did the honors: "Essie, Mrs. Lane, let me introduce you to my good friend, Rev. Eddie Tate. He pastors Mount Zion Gospel United Church in Chicago and came down to Memphis to help me with some of this conference business. We go way back—were roommates when we were at Blackwell College together."

Eddie took Essie's hand and said, "It is such a pleasure to meet you." Then he turned to Lee Allie and took hers saying, "Mrs. Lane, I am pleased to meet you, too."

As soon as Eddie let go of Essie's hand, he felt happy all over. She was a good woman! He had spent time with every kind of Negro woman one could imagine and always told Theophilus that he could smell a good woman fifty miles away. And like Theophilus, he believed that it wasn't holy airs but her sense of self, her fine character, and her love of God that made a woman good. Was she kind? Did she have a sense of humor? Was she fair? Was she shrewd and smart? Could she handle money right? And was she honest and straightforward? These were the qualities found in one of his favorite scriptures in the Bible, Proverbs 31. And they were the ones Eddie always looked for in a woman claiming to be a good one.

Essie smiled demurely at this big, tall yellow man with coarse brown hair and teasing eyes staring out of a boyish face. She looked carefully at his very expensive and superbly cut beige silk suit, knowing he must have searched hard to find the tailor who made it and his ivory clerical shirt, which was of the finest jacquard silk. This man, who was almost two inches taller than Theophilus, was sharp—from his carefully trimmed hair all the way down to the pale silk socks that matched his suit, and those beige alligator shoes he was wearing.

Theophilus began to look annoyed, and Essie realized that she had stared too long at Rev. Tate. Turning away from Eddie, she smiled at Theophilus. He was looking awfully handsome himself, in that charcoal suit, pearl gray shirt, and silk tie and matching handkerchief, with thin amethyst, pearl gray, and charcoal stripes.

Eddie just watched the current of communication flow back and forth between Essie and Theophilus, silently thanking God for bringing what he fervently believed was a good woman into his best friend's life.

Chapter Seven

ESSIE, LEE ALLIE, AND, FINALLY, CORAL AND D.S. Thomas took their seats just as the choir and ministers had taken their places at the back of the church. Theophilus and Eddie were sitting with other guest ministers in a section marked off near the front of the sanctuary. Rev. James and Marcel Brown, who had been asked to represent his father, would march in with the bishops and other prominent pastors.

The steady hum of excited voices circulating around the crowded church quieted down as it came time for the service to begin. The trickle of latecomers hurried to their places, and Glodean Benson, who was in this group, gave one of the male ushers a big, batting-eyes smile as an incentive to find her a seat. Being late was part of her strategy this afternoon, because she wanted to make a special entrance. If there was one thing Glodean Benson could count on, it was commanding everyone's attention when she walked through a church sanctuary.

She was a striking woman, standing five foot six,

with an hourglass figure, milk chocolate skin that was as smooth as satin, smoky brown eyes, and coal black hair that hung down her back past her shoulder blades. But it wasn't her beauty alone that made so many take note when she promenaded down a church aisle. It was her inviting walk that got under their skin.

A regular conference goer, Glodean doted on preachers, and according to the pastor of one Knoxville, Tennessee, church, she delivered on every single thing hinted at in that walk. As he had confided to a handful of ministers at one of the Tennessee/Mississippi District's midwinter meetings, Glodean was as close to heaven on earth as he was going to get. He had said rather wistfully that when he was with her, he felt that he could have lain on her pale pink, perfumed sheets for all eternity. And when a little sweat formed on his forehead at the mere thought of Glodean Benson, he pulled out a handkerchief, stomped his feet, and wiped his face like he had just finished a good sermon.

As Glodean followed the usher to her seat, the enticing scent of her pricy signature perfume wafted behind her. Known for her expensive pink outfits, today she was wearing a pink and gold low-cut lace dress with capped sleeves that molded itself to her body. Her long hair was knotted into a heavy chignon at the nape of her neck—barely visible under a pink silk hat, with a wide brim that curved down toward her face and was trimmed with silk rosebuds. Her beautiful face was adorned only with the dark pink lipstick she always wore on her full, wide lips. And she had on diamond earrings and pink lace gloves, on top of which she wore an array of diamond rings—gifts from pastors over the past years.

All eyes were upon her and she knew it.

While Glodean was walking down the aisle, Essie

nudged Lee Allie and said, "Mama, look at that woman. I can't believe she would hold up the service to carry on like that."

Lee Allie took a good look at Glodean Benson, wondering if all of the woman's brain circuits were fired up right. She glanced over at Coral and saw that she was looking sour. "Coral, you know her? She walkin' up in here actin' like she think she the Queen of Sheba."

"Honey, that there is Glodean Benson. She lives in Atlanta now, but she grew up in my church. And she may think she the Queen of Sheba but she ain't nothin' but a sanctified tramp."

"A what?" Essie asked.

"You know, a woman who only want to sleep with a preacher 'cause she crazy enough to believe that in a preacher's pants there some kind of pipeline to heaven. Cain't meet no decent man 'cause she so fixed on preachers and becoming the first lady of some church. That woman don't believe in dancin', smokin', or drinkin' but she wiggle under those sheets with some preacher every chance she get. Baby, it's a sickness and these mens don't know how to or even want to stop Glodean's goin's on. Sometimes these so-called mens of God sho' do a lot to help out the devil."

"That's a shame, Miss Coral."

"Sure 'nough is, Essie Lee. She just wastin' and usin' herself up on some crazy-thinking foolishness."

"And," Coral thought, "I *still* don't understand how in the world Rev. Simmons got himself all tangled up with that crazy woman."

Marcel stood in the processional line with his friend, Rev. Sonny Washington, watching this woman advertise herself, with pure amusement all over his face. As much as he liked to tomcat his way through churchwomen, he always stayed clear of her kind. So this was the woman who managed to get next to Simmons. What a fool, he thought. Anyone could see that the woman, beautiful as she was, spelled trouble. Then he noticed that Sonny looked like it was taking every bit of his strength not to run down the aisle and grab ahold of that crazy Glodean.

Reverend James was standing right behind Marcel Brown and Sonny Washington. It was clear to him that Glodean Benson wasn't all there, especially watching her like this. What had prompted her to come up from Atlanta and stage a scene at this conference, just when Theophilus was making a place for himself at Greater Hope? He was worried about the effect her entrance was having on Theophilus.

Theophilus sensed Glodean's presence even before he saw her. No wonder Marcel knew about this story. No doubt some folks had been gossiping about it because they knew Glodean would be at this service. He had gotten lulled into thinking that this phase of his life was over, that Glodean wasn't coming back and that he could forget about her threats. Her entrance today made him doubt that she had abandoned her vow to get him. He took out his handkerchief to wipe the sweat off his face.

Eddie leaned over and whispered, "I hope there isn't a showdown between you and Glodean at this conference. If she knows you're seeing Essie, she might want to start some mess. Honestly, man, I don't know how you let yourself get tied up with that."

"All right," Theophilus snapped. "You don't have to keep telling me how much I messed up."

Eddie persisted. "Why did it take you so long to figure out that Glodean was touched in the head? I mean, always having to wear pink should have been your first clue that something was wrong with her."

Theophilus shrugged. The thought that Essie would find out about Glodean filled him with despair. What Essie Lane had done for his heart and soul far surpassed anything Glodean Benson could have ever conceived of doing to his body.

Bishop Jennings got tired of waiting on Glodean to sit down. He scowled at her, and she picked up her pace. But she was still squeezing past the other people sitting on the row when the bishop cleared his throat and began, "The Lord is in His Holy Temple. Let all the earth keep silence before Him."

As soon as he completed the call to worship, the choir started singing a powerful praise song, joined by the congregation and all their esteemed guests. When the choir director was confident that everyone was participating, he signaled to the musicians, who changed the tempo to a faster and bluesier, hard-core gospel beat. Next, he had the soloist step out, got the choir moving to the right rhythm, and led them into a hand-clapping, foot-stomping rendition of the song "Lead Me to Calvary."

Once the soloist got immersed in the feeling of the song, ad-libbing a call-and-response pattern with the choir, the director gave the musicians the sign to push the song up an octave. Now the music got so good that a tiny purple-haired lady stood up, with her patent leather pocketbook hanging off her wrist, daintily grabbed the skirt of her rose satin dress, and danced in the aisle, making sure that her fancy turban hat, wrapped with yards of rose-tinted netting, didn't topple off her head in the process.

When the choir director saw the little purple-haired lady dancing in the spirit, he set the choir rocking from side to side, fueling the excitement of the congregation.

Then with a quick clap, he shut down the melody, letting the congregation, vigorously clapping and stomping, carry the bluesy, syncopated beat. A woman standing at the back of the choir loft raised her arms up in the air, whirled in a complete circle, stomped both feet, and called, "Yeesss! Yeeeesssss LORD! Jeeee-suzzz!" in a shout-scream. And the soloist, who had gotten even more fired up by the shout, started singing a cappella, to the rhythm of the handclaps and stomping feet. She was sounding so good until every time she glided and slid back down a note, a choir member shouted, "Sang! Sang girl, sang!"

As the spiritual heatwave reached a peak, the director brought the choir back in, to sing a cappella with the soloist. Their voices swelled the song for a few bars and then, at another pinnacle, the director brought the musicians back in, one instrument at a time, raising the congregation's temperature a few degrees with each new addition to the music.

The church was so fired up by now that even some of the men had started shouting. One sister got so carried away that she failed to notice that her wig had become askew and was inching its way off her head. The adults watching the wig work its way down just kept clapping and singing, trying to ignore the sight, but for the older children and teenagers sitting in the balcony, away from the immediate scrutiny of their relatives, the suspense was too much to bear. They snickered, poked at each other, and pointed at the woman's head, ducking down behind the balcony pews to laugh out loud whenever that slipshod wig crept another inch.

Three women attendants who were dressed in white uniforms with big lavender lace handkerchiefs pinned on their left shoulders ran over to the woman, who by this time was waving her arms around and preparing to fall out. Right before she fell back across a row of people, two of the attendants grabbed her by the wrists, quickly lifting her up and away. A lady in that pew, wearing a beautiful yellow hat, picked up the wig with an ink pen and gingerly handed it to the third attendant. Two male ushers hurried over to grab the woman by her arms and ankles to carry her out, and the attendant dropped the wig, with half of the elastic worn out of it, onto her chest.

By now the soloist was winding up, and the choir director brought the music and the singing to a quick, dramatic halt. A minister sitting in the front-row pew shouted out, "Praise the Lord! Y'all know y'all praisin' God today. Amen." With hearty handclapping and loud "Praise Gods," the entire congregation joined in.

Bishop Jennings, who had remained seated throughout the song, took the pulpit podium as the last trickle of handclaps and Amens were quieting down. "Choir," he said into the microphone, "I do believe you're trying to sing us right on up to glory. What about you, church?"

A chorus of Amens answered his question.

He then adjusted the sleeves of his robe, revealing more of their purple, velvet horizontal stripes, and continued, "I do believe, Aaa . . . men, that we're going to have some church up in here today and it isn't even Sunday. Did you hear me, church? I *do* believe, Aaa . . . men, that we are about to do some serious worshiping right here on this Friday afternoon. Aaa . . . men."

One of the ministers sitting in the pulpit stood up, waved his arm, and said in quick, choppy phrases, "Yes, Lawd! We having church today. You know something, Bishop? Right now I feel church risin' up in me and fightin' to come out. Yes! Yes! Yes!"

"Thank you, Rev. Eldridge. Like I said, we're having church and this is going to be a blessed day indeed. Aaa . . . men. You know, we come here every year to take care of church business at our magnificent Gospel United Church's Tennessee/Mississippi District's Annual Conference. Thanks be to God Almighty, we have accomplished a lot over the past twelve months. And this new conference year, which begins this June in 1961, has even more blessings in store for this mighty district of the Gospel United Church. For starters, I am pleased to announce that St. Mathews, our host church for this year's conference, held a mortgage burning ceremony earlier this week. Aaa . . . men."

The Bishop looked behind him at the conference's host pastor. "Stand up, Rev. Gant, and let the congregation take a good look at you. Church, say Amen."

St. Mathews's pastor, Rev. Clement Gant, stood up and waved at the congregation.

The Bishop continued, "I also want to thank Rev. Theophilus Simmons for opening up his church, Greater Hope, for our smaller meetings this week. And, how many of you people here today are not from Memphis?"

Many people in the congregation raised their hands.

"Those of you who didn't stay with friends or family, did you find your accommodations pleasant and affordable?"

A lot of people smiled, nodded their heads yes, and said Amen.

"Well, you have Rev. Simmons to thank because he coordinated one of the best room-and-board programs that we've had in years. Aaa . . . men. Church, you know Memphis doesn't have enough Negro hotels to house all of you dressed-up, perfumed people sitting out there in the congregation this afternoon."

Rev. Gant called out, "That's right, Bishop. You know that's right."

"And, you know something, church?" Bishop Jennings went on. "The last time I took a poll, none of these white folks here in Memphis were about to welcome us into their establishments." He stopped to shake his head in disgust. "So, church, I can truly say that I'd rather pay my Negro brothers and sisters good money anyday, than even think about giving one of those mean-spirited hillbillies who don't have the decency to call me a man one red cent. Aaa . . . men. Do you hear me, church?"

Rev. Eldridge stood up again and said, "You tell these folks like it is, Bishop. Yes, Lawd! Yes, Lawd!"

"So, church, you owe a lot to Rev. Simmons." He looked over to where Theophilus was sitting and made a motion for him to get up out of his seat. "Stand up, Rev. Simmons, and let the congregation see you. They need to know who you are. And, church, let's give this fine young man a great big hand because he did a fabulous job for this year's conference. Aaa . . . men."

Theophilus stood up straight and smiled to acknowledge the Bishop's compliment and the clapping congregation. Glodean tilted back her head and stared at him from under her large hat, as a heavy ache of longing, hurt, and anger spread across her chest. Essie, on the other hand, applauded proudly, waving and cheering as she watched Theophilus standing there. She was surprised to find herself imagining what it would feel like to stand next to him, joyful, as he received recognition for his work in the church.

Bishop Jennings had recognized Glodean when she made her grand entrance and now watched as she sat silent and despondent while Theophilus was being praised. He knew that she was the reason Theophilus had nearly turned down his assignment to Greater Hope, and he considered her almost a modern-day version of a temple prostitute. Not that Theophilus was blameless—far from it. He decided at that moment to do a little meddling that would teach the two of them a lesson about the kind of conduct expected of both men and women in the church.

"Don't you go and sit down on me just yet, son," Bishop Jennings told Theophilus.

"Now, church," he said, ignoring Theophilus's obvious discomfort. "I made Rev. Simmons keep standing because there's just one more thing I want to tell you about him. You see, church, this fine young man is a single preacher, and it's high time he got himself his good thang. Aaa . . . men. You hear me, church? I said . . . I *said* this young man needs our help in getting himself a wife—the right kind of wife, the kind of woman his own mama would approve of for him. Aaa . . . men."

He looked over at Theophilus, who was thoroughly embarrassed, and smiled at him.

"Now, I'm going to overstep my bounds a bit and try to help our young pastor out. You upstanding single young ladies sitting out there in the congregation, I want some of you to start baking some peach cobblers and bring them on over to Greater Hope for Rev. Simmons. Aaa . . . men."

By announcing that young Simmons needed a wife, Bishop Jennings hoped that he was putting him on notice—as well as any young lady who set her mind on him—that he was watching and that there were to be no more slipups. Marriage wasn't a foolproof guarantee, but after fear of the wrath of God, it sure was the best deterrent to misbehaving he could think of.

"Didn't you tell me that you liked peach cobblers, Rev. Simmons?"

"No, Bishop," Theophilus said, playing along. "I've always said that I liked blackberry cobblers, especially the ones that are tart and sweet at the same time."

Bishop Jennings chuckled and said, "Ohhh, I'm sooo sorry, Reverend. Don't any of you ladies get all dressed up and sashay over to Greater Hope toting a peach cobbler. Rev. Simmons wants a blackberry cobbler. You must bring him a blackberry cobbler. And you all better make sure that it's right sweet and tart all at the same time. Aaa . . . men."

Rarely had the Bishop seen Theophilus so embarrassed. He was sure that his message was getting through. "Now, Rev. Simmons," he went on. "Do you want any of these fine young ladies to bring you anything else?"

"Well, Bishop, since you asked, some freshly picked collard greens and pot roast would be right nice."

To his credit, the Bishop thought, Simmons was remaining both respectful and dignified, and he admired the young man's effort to be a good sport. He smiled at Theophilus and said, "Rev. Simmons, I guess I should leave you alone. I've given you enough of a hard time this afternoon. But it was my Christian duty. I just don't believe that one of my finest young pastors should be out here serving God alone, without the kind of help-meet who would make an honorable and good first lady. I only want what is best for you, your church, and this district. Aaa . . . men."

Theophilus's whole body relaxed, hearing that he was about to be let off the hook. And he was surprised and grateful to have been called one of the "finest young pastors" by Bishop Percy Jennings. That was a rare compliment indeed. He said, "I thank you, Bishop, for caring enough about me to do your Christian duty right here at the great Annual Conference."

Then he sat down to a hearty round of applause.

Eddie nudged him in the arm and said, "Man, that was tough. I don't know why Bishop Jennings had to put your business all out in the street. And if Glodean wasn't mad at you before, I bet she sure is now."

Theophilus nodded and stared straight ahead, steadfastly avoiding looking at either Essie or Glodean. Bishop Jennings was announcing, "Church, now let us welcome some special guests. Evangelist Elroy Thorn and his Gospel Songbirds are here and they have agreed to render a song from their new album titled *A Soul-Saving Savior Is He*."

A ripple of excited murmurs ran through the congregation as Elroy Thorn and his group made their way up to the front of the church. Elroy Thorn and the Gospel Songbirds was one of the best gospel ensembles in the Tennessee-Mississippi area.

"As they are setting up, I'd like the organist to play 'Great Is Thy Faithfulness.'" He began to hum the melody, and the organist played a few notes until she matched his key. When Bishop Jennings heard the music, he began to sing, "'Great is Thy faithfulness, O God My Father, There is no shadow of turning with Thee, Thou changest not, Thou compassions, they fail not, As Thou has been Thou forever wilt be . . .'"

Then he raised his hands, summoning everyone to stand and sing along with the choir, saying, "I want you all to keep singing as we prepare for our first collection. Now this has been a blessed week indeed and you all need to show your appreciation for all that God has done for you during this Annual Conference. Aaa . . . men. And when you march up to this table, I don't want to hear anything falling into those collection plates. Because if I can hear it, you can keep it. God doesn't like cheapness from His children."

Uncle Booker leaned over and whispered to Rose, "I guess that means I can keep it. He ought to be glad to get whatever he can, seein' that this here congregation filled up with hardworkin' people. And I don't think he need any more money than he already got—especially seein' how he got so much more of it than me."

Rose shushed him as Essie and Lee Allie got up to put money in the collection plate for the group. When they walked back to their seats, Theophilus finally caught Essie's eye and gave her a wink. She smiled warmly, as Glodean stared at Theophilus, narrowing her eyes to let him know she was watching. Eddie nudged him and warned, "Man, Glodean is over there watching you like a hawk. Looks like she is determined to figure out who your new woman is."

Theophilus sighed once more. He did not want to deal with Glodean today—or on any day ever again.

Elroy Thorn now took the microphone. A plain, medium-brown-skinned, portly man in his early forties, he was dressed in a plain black suit with little adornment except the gold watch and large diamond rings on his right hand. He said, "Giving honor to God, I want to thank you, Bishop Jennings, for giving us the opportunity to sing at this great Annual Conference of this mighty, God-filled denomination. The song we've picked out for you is a gospel ballad. I hope and pray it reaches deep down in your soul and helps you know the Lord just a little bit better."

Elroy motioned to his musicians (a pianist, organist, tenor saxophonist, bass guitarist, lead guitarist, and drummer) to start playing. Then the three men and four

women who were the Gospel Songbirds lifted their
voices in the opening chords of Thorn's beautiful
arrangement of "Touch Me Lord Jesus." And when Elroy
Thorn finally joined in, a thrill ran through the church
as his lovely, soothing voice evoked the presence of a
wondrous and mighty God. By the time they finished
the last verse of the song, Theophilus was wiping his
eyes from the intense emotions he was feeling, and even
Eddie Tate, who was always stoic, could not stop the
flow of tears down his cheeks.

Bishop Jennings came back up to the pulpit podium,
dabbing at his eyes with his handkerchief. "Church, if
you didn't feel the Lord stirring your heart after that
song, you just don't know a thing about Jesus. Rev. Thorn,
thank you so much. Let's all show our appreciation for
this good music by standing and giving Evangelist Elroy
Thorn and the Gospel Songbirds another big round of
applause."

Rev. Gant tugged at the back of the Bishop's robe,
handing him a note. A quick grimace flashed across his
face as he read, but he proceeded to tell the congregation, "Church, Rev. Gant has informed me that we are
blessed to have another special guest in our midst. There
was some doubt as to whether he was even going to be
able to make it, but God is great. Our guest is someone
who has served God for longer than many of us have
been alive and who needs no introduction to many of
you out there. He is a faithful servant and one of the
oldest practicing preachers in the entire United States."

A few barely stifled groans escaped from the audience.
The bishop continued: "At the tender age of fourteen, he
became a traveling, itinerant preacher and called many to
Jesus at tent revivals throughout Alabama, Mississippi, and
Louisiana. After marrying, he continued his evangelizing

until the Lord led him to the pastorship of a small church in Lafayette, Louisiana. Years later, he was summoned to Mississippi by the late Bishop Zeebedee L. Carson, Sr., where he pastored churches in Hattiesburg and Grenada. He is now at Solid Rock Gospel United Church in Yazoo City, Mississippi, where he has served as pastor for the past forty-five years. And he says that he intends to stay at Solid Rock until the Lord calls him home. Church, I give you Rev. Roscoe Alexander."

"He can't be gettin' ready to try and preach," said Coral Thomas as Rev. Alexander signaled to several of the younger pastors to help him out of his chair. "He too old."

Rev. Alexander tottered up to the pulpit podium. He was a tall, lanky man with a weatherworn face. He had a thick head of white hair and gray eyes. He put on his glasses and began to fumble with the papers he was holding with one hand, while using the other to adjust his false teeth. Then he began to speak in a strong but scratchy voice: "I don't have a whole lot to say to you this afternoon. But I just wanted to tell you about holdin' up yo' chutch. Hol . . . din' up yo' chutch. You see, you can pray by yo'self, you have to get saved by yo'self, you can even shout quietly in the midnight hour by yo'self, but you cain't go to chutch by yo'self. You need others for that. Others, which include yo' pastors."

Rev. Alexander stopped talking, looked around the church, and cleared his throat. Bishop Jennings handed him a glass of water.

Coral Thomas said, "What kind of sermon is this gonna be? He just standing there movin' those teeth around in his mouth, talkin' 'bout what? This is the craziest thing I've heard of, 'cause I ain't never heard of him giving no decent sermon."

D.S. leaned over to Coral and said, "Coral, why you gettin' so undone 'bout all this? You know them bishops can't insult an old pastor, even though, like you said, he ain't never been able to preach. And he sure ain't gone do anything decent now that he lookin' glory straight in the face."

Rev. Alexander continued, "You see the devil is too busy in chutch. I look 'round this here room and I see all the ladies lookin' like flowers, the gentmins all fined up in they conference suits. But without, withouuuutt!" he shouted. "Without this here building, this here choir, these here preachers, this here chutch, you wouldn't be sittin' here. You'd be all dressed up with nowhere to go. 'Cause the colored chutch is just 'bout everythin' to colored peepes. So whin I sit here and watch you posin' in yo' fine clothes, talkin' durin' service, walkin' in and out of chutch in the middle of the sermon—"

Rev. Alexander stopped suddenly, having spotted a man trying to slip back in church. "See what I'm talkin' 'bout. This here man missed the first part of what I sayed. Son, don't you walk out of chutch no mo' like that—especially durin' one of my sermons.

"Now," he said, and fumbled some more with his papers. "Now, you peepes is blessed and don't even know it. I 'member times back when I had to hold chutch out of my car. Yes, Lawd, I sayed out of my car. Peepes just gathered 'round the car and we had chutch.

"And the missus, Lawd bless her sweet departed soul, the missus sold dranks and sandmidges out of the cooler in the trunk after service. Didn't hear nobody complainin' and everybody left our car happy, sanctified, and full of the Holy Ghost. But y'all? Y'ALL," he yelled. "Y'all ain't satisfied and full of nothin'. You ain't happy 'less you sittin' up in a fancy, fine building you think oughta be good as the ones for the white folks. And some of you won't even come to chutch in the summertime 'less yo' pastor has an air conditioner contraption. That's right, 'less yo' pastor has an air conditioner contraption. You more worried about sweatin' and makin' yo' hair go back up under them wigs and big hats than you are 'bout the Lawd and yo' chutch. Now tell me, peepes. I must ask the answer to the question."

Rev. Alexander paused, gave the people sitting on the front row pews a mean, penetrating stare. "What kinda feeble, cain't-take-the-heat, ungrateful, so-called Christian colored peepes is you anyway?"

He banged on the podium and then stumped around in the pulpit, taking care to add a rickety-rocking-sounding rhythm to the next part of his sermon. "I sayed, what kinda Christian colored peepes is you anyway? Haah. I'll tell you what kind you is. Haah. You is the kind that don't 'preciate yo' chutch. Haah. You hear me, chutch? Haah. You is the kind that don't 'preciate yo' chutch. Haah. And God has made me come here—haah—just to tell you that. That's why I'm here."

He raised his hands, looked up at the ceiling. "Yes, Lawd, that's why I'm here.

"And chutch, you know what the main message the Lawd want you to hear? Chutch, the main message the Lawd want you to hear is that you don't 'preciate yo' chutch and it's TIME TO STOP!" He screamed into the microphone. "TIME TO STOP!

"Time to stop complainin' about the heat when it's hot outside and the cold when it's winter. Haah. Time to stop sassin' and back-talkin' yo' pastor. Haah. Time to stop buyin' fake-haired wigs and cheap corn liquor with yo' tithe money. Haah. Time to 'preciate yo' chutch.

Haah. It's your'en and you got to suppote it. Haah. You got to pay yo' pastors and go to chutch wherever and however it may be. You hear me, chutch? 'Cause I don't hear you. And, if I don't hear ya', I just think you lettin' Satan take over your mind and stoppin' you from hearin' the truth. I . . . I . . . I . . . I aahhhh."

There was a gagging sound, and Rev. Alexander's false teeth popped right out of his mouth. They bounced off the oversized Bible, hit the altar railing, and landed down in front of the altar on the prayer cushions. Rev. Alexander banged his gums together, mumbling like his mouth was full of schoolroom paste, and mopped the drool off his chin with his handkerchief. He seemed not to realize that his teeth had fallen out and that people in the front were whispering about what to do and how to retrieve them as he kept preaching.

Eddie bent his head forward and shook and wiggled his foot, struggling to keep a straight face. Theophilus stuck a piece of peppermint candy into his mouth, and hoped that by sucking it he could keep from laughing out loud. He sneaked a look back at Essie and spotted her walking out of the sanctuary. When Rev. Alexander turned his head, he eased out of church. As soon as Glodean saw him leave, she, too, edged out of her seat and slipped out. Hot on her heels was Coral Thomas, who made her own getaway, determined to head off Glodean before she caught up with Theophilus, whom Coral figured was coming around to meet up with Essie.

The only person who was unaware of all of this movement was Essie. She had crept out of church choking with laughter, to avoid embarrassing herself. She was still giggling about that old fool's teeth when she happened to glance up and found herself staring straight into a pair of sparkling, dark brown eyes.

Together, she and Theophilus burst out laughing. "I don't know what possessed the Bishop to let Rev. Alexander preach," Theophilus said. "Essie, that old man has some sermons that'll make this one sound good. But I have to tell you, those bad-fitting teeth have slipped around plenty during his sermons, but this is the first time I have ever heard of them popping out of his mouth."

"Theophilus," Essie said, giggling. "Those were not teeth. They were 'teefs.' Anything that jump out of your mouth like those things are 'teefs.' Teeth stay in your mouth. And that sermon? Lord, Mama thought she would die. She and Mrs. Neese just started fanning themselves fast-like, trying not to laugh. But when those teeth hit the altar cushions, Mrs. Neese took her fan and started hitting Mama on the shoulder, coughing and laughing."

Theophilus shook his head, imagining what Mrs. Neese must have looked like choking on her laughs and hitting Lee Allie with a church fan. "Essie," he said. "This is one of those Annual Conferences folks will be talking about for a long time."

"You know it. And it was a whole lot of mess going on up in church today. Did you see the woman who strutted in late wearing that pink and gold lace dress? Lord knows she was so hot that I thought that dress was gonna burst into flames. It took her almost five minutes to walk into church and sit herself down. She was sashaying and carrying on so . . ."

Chapter Eight

*A*T THE VERY MOMENT THAT ESSIE WAS SEARCH-
ing for the right words to describe Glodean
Benson, Coral Thomas caught up with
Glodean on the other side of the church. She
said, "Where you think you off to?"

Glodean tipped her head back and a little to the side.
"Why, Miss Coral, don't you mean to say, 'Welcome
back home to Memphis'?"

"You can be all smart and sassy with me if you wants
to. But I know and you know, you out here looking for
the Pastor. Like to broke your neck jumping up to catch
up with him when you saw him walking out of church."

"And what if I did jump up and fly out the church?
The old-tail women's missionary society hasn't passed no
laws that says I can't leave church when the Pastor do."

Coral leaned toward her. "Maybe our old tails
should've passed a whatever just for sly cats like you.
Now, gal, you know you followed that man to find out
who he with. I know that much 'cause I watched you

all during service, looking all around, trying to figure out who it is he supposed to be likin'.'"

Glodean put one hand on her hip, lifting her chin so Coral could see her eyes from up under that big hat. "I heard Theophilus took up with some heifer who came up here out of them Mississippi swamps. Is that why you're all up in my face with some mess?"

Coral pursed her lips like she had something nasty-tasting in her mouth. "For yo' information, Miss Gal, them swamps is down in Louisiana and Florida. And that *heifer*, as you call her, is like my baby girl. I know *all* about you and the Pastor. I been watchin' out, thinkin' you had the dignity and sense enough to stay away from where you ain't wanted. But you ain't worth the Tennessee dirt he sho' wallowed in when he hooked up with your nasty swiggling, trifling self."

Glodean put her hand on her hip. "Coral Thomas, you have some nerve talking to me like that. And if we wasn't at church, I'd smack your old behind for gettin' all up in my face like you doing."

Coral took a step toward Glodean and pushed her face closer to hers. "Glodean Benson, I wish we wasn't outside of this church at the Annual Conference, so that right after you'd smacked me, I could tear up yo' behind for even thinkin' about layin' a finger on me."

Glodean moved away from Coral, a little scared by her force. But Coral moved right back up on her and said, "Don't you know, if that man really want you, honey, ain't nothin' or nobody gone stand 'tween him and you. But you and I both know he don't want you. And from the way I hear it, he made that point mighty clear to you some time ago."

Glodean was hurt by Coral saying that the Pastor didn't want her, but she wasn't about to let some old woman get the best of her, either. She put her tongue behind her front teeth and sucked the air through them, then said nastily, "I'll leave that pitiful thing alone, whoever, naw, whatever she is. 'Cause I know if she need your help holding on to a man, she need all the help she can get. Now I knows the Pastor in the *biblical* way. And I can tell you that I knows him well—what he like, when he like it, and how he like it. And I also knows that if your *baby girl* is capable of making him want to know her, if he ever cry out when he get with her, the only thing she'll hear comin' from his mouth is *my* name. 'Cause you see, Coral Thomas, I doubt very seriously if she can tackle with what I laid on my pastor."

Glodean flicked Coral a wave with her lace-gloved hand, meant to signify that she had just been told off. "So," she said, as she daintily adjusted her hat, "I think this ends our little conversation. And I'd appreciate it if you would move your old, rolled-at-the-knee-stocking-wearing-self out of my way."

Glodean started sashaying away. But Coral wasn't finished with Glodean Benson. She grabbed her arm and pulled her back, forcing Glodean to turn around and face her.

"Gal, you can act all high and mighty with me if you wants to. But yo' butt is, and will continue to be, pitiful. You hear me? Pitiful. And when the day does come for that man to want to cry out anything, he'll be real careful about what he let pass through his lips, 'cause she'll be his wife. Now, I ain't seen the Pastor all up in your face, tryin' to marry you with yo' crazy self."

Coral dropped Glodean's arm. But she was still so mad that practically all the saints in heaven had to hold her back, to stop her from snatching that expensive hat off Glodean and stomping it into the ground. She said, "I need to bless you out some more just because you, with yo' crazy low-down ways, done made me lose my religion right here at church and service ain't even over with yet."

Glodean was so furious at Coral Thomas that she snatched the church door open and stormed back inside just as altar prayer was starting. Pushing people out of her way, she desperately moved toward the altar, hoping against all rational thinking that God would make Theophilus Simmons forget about that Mississippi woman and come to her.

Essie immediately picked up on Theophilus's uneasiness about Glodean and said, "Did I say something wrong?"

He became fidgety and looked away.

"You know her, don't you?"

"Yes," he answered in a tight voice.

"And?" Essie asked.

"And . . . I'll tell you about it during dinner."

"But Theophilus—"

"I'm not discussing it with you here," he interrupted. "Why don't you go back in there and tell your mama that we're leaving for dinner? I'm going to get the car."

Essie did as he said, slipping back into the church to whisper to her mother that she was leaving with Theophilus.

She was gone by the time Coral Thomas got back, still as puffed up with anger as a charging bull.

D.S. looked at her face, raised his eyebrows, and silently asked, "What's wrong with you?"

Coral threw him a look saying, "Too mad to talk now."

D.S. made it clear with his eyes that he expected to get the whole story once they got back home.

Chapter Nine

THEOPHILUS DROVE UP IN HIS 1961 MIDNIGHT blue Buick, parked, then got out and came around to the passenger side so that he could help Essie into the car. When he slid into the driver's seat, he noticed that she was practically clinging to the passenger door.

"Are you planning on jumping out of the car?"

"What do you mean by that?"

"What I mean is that you're sitting on the edge of the seat like you might need to make a quick getaway or something."

"I don't think it looks right for me to sit too close to you in your car."

"Look right?" he said. "Woman, it'll look like we're riding in the car, which we are."

"No, it'll look like I'm your after-service woman."

Theophilus began to pull out slowly, then glanced over at Essie and said, "My what?"

She folded her arms across her chest and said, "You

know. One of those women some preachers sneak off with when they come to these conferences."

"If that is what you think, then stay your little self on over there. And while you're at it," he said, patting the seat irritably, "put your purse right here between us. That way I won't be able to slide you over here by me, in case I forget myself and start acting like the after-service man."

She gave him a "Negro please" look and moved half an inch closer to him.

They rode in silence for the next seven blocks until Theophilus told her, "There's a stop I want to make."

He pulled up in front of a medium-sized church, with a lovely white frame house with brick-red-colored shutters standing next to it.

"This is Greater Hope. And that white house is the parsonage. Just thought you might like to see my church and where I live."

"It's very nice," was all Essie could bring herself to say.

"I like it," Theophilus said, amused by her nervous air, and restarted the car.

They traveled about three miles, and then he turned into a gravel parking lot, alongside what looked like a former warehouse. Over the door was a soft white neon sign that read MABEL'S KITCHEN.

Despite its plain exterior, Essie was surprised to find that inside Mabel's Kitchen was quite elegant. She could see into a dining room that was painted off-white and had silver-trimmed, off-white curtains at all the windows. The tables were draped with soft, off-white linen tablecloths and decorated with silver-bowed clay flowerpots, filled with artificial moss and off-white silk carnations. The high-backed cane chairs that surrounded each table had off-white and silver-striped seat cushions.

"I had no idea Mabel's Kitchen was so fancy," Essie said, looking around the room.

"This dining room is nice but I think you'll like the one upstairs even better."

The second-floor dining room was decorated in gold, black, and ivory. The curtains on the windows were silk, and they matched the gold, black, and ivory striped seat cushions of the same high-backed chairs as downstairs. There were ivory linens on each table, gold-plated silverware, and shiny gold goblets filled with fresh ivory-colored roses. Beside each rose-filled goblet sat two gold candles that gave the tables a warm romantic glow. There was a small dance floor and a stage in this room, on which a Negro combo was playing very softly.

Theophilus took one of Essie's hands and tried not to sway to the music while they waited to be seated. The headwaiter, dressed in a tuxedo, led them to a cozy table near one of the windows. He left them with menus, then returned to fill their gold-rimmed crystal goblets with ice water and to take their order in a small notebook, using a tiny gold pencil that he kept in his tuxedo's breast pocket.

"I'm ready," Essie said. "I would like the small order of baby-back barbecued ribs, with potato salad and collard greens."

"And for your bread, ma'am? We have cornbread muffins, rolls, biscuits, and the evening's house special, which is red-hot bread."

"What's red-hot bread?"

"It's cornbread muffins cooked with onions, fresh-roasted bell peppers, and dried hot peppers. It's hot, but most people say that it is very good."

"Then I'll try it. And I'd like some iced tea with lots of ice and lemons."

The waiter turned to Theophilus. "And you, Reverend?"

"What's the special?"

"Pot roast cooked with carrots, pearl onions, and small red potatoes, with turnip greens and buttered squash."

"That sounds pretty good. I'll have that with the red-hot bread and iced tea, a little ice and no lemons."

When the waiter left them Essie said, "Theophilus, everything about this restaurant is so formal. Why did you bring me to such a fancy place?"

"Because I thought it would be fun. In case you haven't noticed, I can be fun to be with. A lot of women can't imagine a preacher laughing and having a good time, unless of course he is involved in some kind of church activity."

"A lot of women?" Essie said. "Women like that hip-jigglin' woman in the pink dress back at church?"

"Why are you so interested in her?" Theophilus asked with irritation creeping into his voice.

"Because she is one of your old girlfriends."

He was spared from answering by a young woman carrying a gold tray, who left them with two glasses of iced tea, long-handled gold teaspoons, and a crystal bowl full of sliced lemons.

Essie continued, "Theophilus, I timed it—her walk, you know. It took that woman five minutes to walk down the aisle and to her seat. A woman don't sashay through church like that unless she got a reason to. The way you're acting about all this, Theophilus, I think that reason is you. Don't you think you should tell me about her?"

"Essie, I really don't know where to begin," he said, frowning.

"Maybe you should begin where all of this mess first got started."

"Well, I met Glodean Benson when I was in college, before I entered the seminary. Everything between us was just fine until I accepted a dinner invitation at her apartment."

Essie just looked at Theophilus. How "fine" could everything be, if a young woman was bold enough to ask a single man over to her apartment for dinner? Theophilus must have shown some kind of interest in her. But Glodean had given Essie the impression that she was very calculating. Her walk through church this afternoon certainly looked like a well-planned maneuver.

He shifted uncomfortably under her gaze. "You know something, baby, we need to put this to rest. Why would you want to know the gory details of that old relationship?"

Essie cut her eyes at him. "Theophilus, why *wouldn't* I want to know the 'gory details' of y'all's relationship? This thing you had with her was serious—so serious, she made a big to-do in order to get your attention in church this afternoon. She even made the Bishop wait, holding up the processional while we all had to sit there watching her swish herself down the aisle to her seat."

Theophilus tried to stifle Essie with one of the stern looks he gave members of his congregation when he felt they were out of line. Annoyingly, it didn't seem to ruffle her in the least.

"Theophilus, I don't care about you having girlfriends before me," she said. "I've known from the start that women want your attention. Just look at how Saphronia McComb acted with you"—she didn't know the half of it, Theophilus thought—"and she's color-struck. You're a preacher, and I haven't heard of a preacher who didn't have at least a dozen women chasing him down. And Theophilus, I never thought you were some kind of an angel just because you are a preacher. I would never expect or want you to be perfect, either. I know you are a man, subject to the same feelings and desires as any other man. But I did think you had a little more sense than most. What I really can't understand is how you got all tangled up with someone like her. She is fine-looking and all that, but she looked a little touched in the head to me.

"And," Essie said, letting out a deep breath, "more than that, I have a hard time believing that woman's old stuff was so tempting until it made you ignore right to do wrong and forget about your home training, *and* your common sense."

Theophilus started coughing and had to drink some of his tea. He would go to his grave without ever telling Essie just how tempting and good Glodean's "old stuff" truly was. He shivered a bit at that thought. The only way he would go to his grave and not tell Essie something was if she was with him when he died. And the only woman who would be with him on his deathbed would be his wife. He tried to bury that thought. "Look, Essie, I'm not a whorish man but I am a man. And as a man, I do have needs. I know church folk don't want to hear this but sometimes we *all* mess up, even preachers. My spirit is strong but I am still a flesh and blood man. Even as much as we hate it, we sometimes miss it and get ourselves in a position where we are not practicing what we preach. Celibacy is hard, baby, real hard. I only messed up that one time but I messed up bad, baby."

Essie was disgusted that he would dare to hand her some tacky mess like that. She thought about what her mama always said—"A man, even a good one, can sure act like a natural fool over some loose tail." "I'll repeat myself," she said. "Theophilus, you had to know on some level that all of this business with Glodean wasn't right. It should have been clear from the start, that one step in her direction was a step toward disaster."

He sighed with exasperation. "Girl, why do you have to make all of this sound so low-down and nasty? I said—"

She quickly interrupted. "It was nasty, wasn't it? And what happened today just showed you that you can't get away from that. You need to do better, Theophilus, flesh and blood man that you are. You need to stay on your knees over this mess."

Theophilus nodded to acknowledge that Essie was right, recognizing that trying to defend himself would only make matters worse. And what could he say? Even friends like Eddie couldn't understand how he had lost his head over Glodean.

Hadn't he already let this Glodean junk mess him up enough? He didn't want to waste any more of his precious time with Essie talking about her. He took a long sip of his tea and smiled at Essie, taking one of her hands and raising it to his lips. Then, with his thumb, he gently rubbed the spot on the back of her hand that he had kissed.

Essie drew in her breath. That spot on her hand was glowing from his kiss and his touch.

Theophilus closed his eyes, still caressing her hand. He said, "Essie, I am sorry my past showed up at the very moment when I was hoping for a brighter future."

Essie captured his hand between her own.

"You know something, baby," he said softly. "You've had me going since I first laid eyes on you. I think about you all the time. I can hardly write my sermons for wishing I could be with you instead of just hearing your voice over the phone. And, Essie, know this if you don't know anything else—you are, without a doubt, the first woman to ever hold my heart so completely in the palm of her hand."

Essie felt flooded with relief and joy.

Now Theophilus opened her hands, and, covering them with his large dark ones, lightly stroked her palms and wrists. "My heart is in the palm of your hand," he repeated. "You have to know that I want you, Essie."

She closed her eyes, overcome by his words and touch.

"Baby, look at me."

She smiled into his eyes, and he raised her hands, kissing them both. "Essie, what we have is so good," he said. "So good, baby, that I never want to lose it. Lord knows, I want you so close to me that we won't be able to tell where one begins and the other one ends."

Chapter Ten

ESSIE PICKED UP A TINY RIB, DRIPPING WITH HOME-made barbecue sauce, just as a group of ministers from the Annual Conference walked into the upstairs dining room. Theophilus practically missed the taste of the pot roast in his mouth when he saw Glodean Benson with them, hanging on the arm of Rev. Sonny Washington.

One of the ministers in that group excused himself to talk to someone in the room, and three others started arranging with a waiter for the group's tables. The remaining two, Marcel Brown and Sonny Washington, stayed where they were over near the top of the stairs, waiting for Glodean Benson to come out of the ladies' room.

"Will you look at that Negro?" Sonny said, looking down the hall to see if Glodean was coming. "Look at him, sitting over there with that fine woman. What is it about him that gets the women goin', like her and Glodean?"

Marcel shrugged. "Looks like you're the one Glodean

is studying, walking in here with her hanging all over you. It's no secret that she is looking for a preacher to marry her."

Sonny looked at Marcel like he was crazy and said, "Marry her? No. But I do hear that she is supposed to have the best stuff in *all* of Memphis, Tennessee. Besides, I singled out Miss Benson for a few other reasons."

Marcel figured that Sonny was protesting too much. He was about to say so when Sonny added, "Man, I'm with her because I'm doing like ol' Bishop Caruthers said, about getting yourself an informant on your enemies. Ain't nobody like a woman who has been in their beds to get the truth on some of these do-right preachers."

Marcel knew what Sonny was talking about. Bishop Otis Caruthers had told him the exact same thing when he was in Detroit about a month ago. He'd said, "Young Rev. Brown, you need to get yourself a couple of Holy Ghost–filled, unfulfilled sisters in several different churches to keep you informed on the progress of your foes." He had then given him a long hard look, saying, "You're one of those smooth, good-looking, high-yellow Detroit boys. I know you know how to work that avenue, right?"

"There sure do seem to be a lot of them these days," Marcel said. "Simmons and Rev. Murcheson James and even Eddie Tate. High-and-mighties who think God called them just so that they could keep an eye on us. Getting all righteous-minded—motioning and demanding that the churches in their districts file annual reports, showing their budgets, bank statements, receipts, cash, you name it, including the pastor's personal expenditures. They're making themselves the judge and jury on how pastors act, especially with the church-

women. Like Simmons—who ought to cast out the
beam in his own eye, before he goes looking for the
speck in yours or mine."

"Uh-huh," said Sonny, looking at his watch, with a
sour look on his face. "What is taking Glodean so long?
Even a woman don't need that much time to pee. I know
she's in there trying to look her best for that fool sitting over there."

Marcel was surprised at Sonny's bitter tone. "Man, I
didn't even know she saw him—she walked off almost
as soon as we got to the top of the stairs."

"She saw him all right," Sonny said. "Women see
everything—especially a Negro they think they need."

Marcel shifted from one foot to the other a few times,
checking the hall leading toward the women's rest room.

"I'm not standing here waiting on Glodean," he said.
"I trust she will see us just as fast as she saw him." He
headed off with Sonny in the direction of Theophilus's
table, thinking he might lay some Detroit charm on this
little Mississippi girl, just to spite Simmons. Something
he planned on doing in the church lobby before service
started and he was pulled away by Bishop Giles.

When Theophilus saw Marcel Brown and Sonny
Washington coming toward him, he stopped eating,
thinking, "Now what do they want?"

"Good evening, Theophilus, miss," Marcel said slyly
as he let his eyes linger on Essie. He enjoyed the discomfort he was obviously causing Theophilus.

"Evening, Simmons," Sonny said and patted
Theophilus on the shoulder like they were old buddies.
"Rev. Brown and I saw you sitting over here and thought
we should come and introduce ourselves to your lovely
dinner guest."

He turned toward Essie and said, "I am Rev. Sonny

Washington, the pastor of Leewood Gospel United Church in Nashville. And you are?"

Essie didn't like Rev. Washington on sight. He looked like the kind of man who liked to squeeze past women in tight spaces so that he could slip and rub himself up against them. She said, "I am Essie Lane, Rev. Washington. I attend Mount Nebo in Charleston, Mississippi. Rev. Murcheson James is my pastor."

"Yes, I know Rev. James—good man," he said, letting his eyes roll around the contours of her breasts.

She crossed her arms across her chest to protect herself, thinking, "I wonder if Rev. James thinks the same about you, with your nasty self."

Sonny turned back to Theophilus. "And Simmons, I was impressed with the room-and-board program you organized. You'll have to tell me how you did it so that I can do the same when the Annual Conference is held in Nashville next year."

Sonny caught a whiff of freshly sprayed perfume and turned to find Glodean Benson coming behind him.

Theophilus smelled it, too, and looked up—right into Glodean's face. "Why, Rev. Simmons, this is a lovely surprise," Glodean said, with a coy flutter of her eyelashes. Then she leaned toward Essie, extending a pink-lace-gloved hand, making sure to show off all the glittering diamonds on her fingers.

"I am Glodean Benson. I've been working in Atlanta, but Greater Hope is my home church. And Rev. Simmons here has touched me more deeply than any other pastor."

Essie felt like breaking those diamond-studded fingers one by one because Glodean dared say that mess to her. But she kept her cool, pretending to wipe barbecue sauce off her fingers so that Glodean wouldn't want to risk messing up those fancy pink gloves. She refused to shake hands with the woman who had tried to humiliate Theophilus with that scene in church, even if the only one she had shamed was herself.

"I am Essie Lane, Glodean Benson," she said evenly.

Glodean withdrew her hand in silence. Sonny Washington, who looked ready to slap Glodean when she said "touched me more deeply," fidgeted irritably. Theophilus could feel the sweat building up under his collar and hoped that a few wet beads hadn't popped up on his brow, revealing how upset he was. Marcel smirked at Theophilus, thinking, "Glodean really knocked that punk out of his orbit. He looks like he's trying not to mess in his pants."

Composing himself, Theophilus finally said, "I don't want to be rude but my food is getting cold, and I would like to enjoy my meal with Miss Lane before it gets too late. It's nice that you people stopped by to say hello, good to see you, and have a good evening."

"Miss Benson, Rev. Washington," Marcel said smoothly, "we did interrupt Rev. Simmons's meal with his very special guest from Mississippi. We should let him eat. Miss Benson, I'm sure you will have plenty of chances to catch up with your pastor once all these conference people go home."

Sonny Washington was furious, though he knew that Marcel was just trying to needle Theophilus. He was tired of standing there, watching Glodean carry on over Simmons and scrutinize his lady friend. Snatching at Glodean's arm, he excused himself and pulled her away so fast that Marcel had to hurry off to catch up with them.

Theophilus stared at the back of Marcel's pale gray suit, thinking that the three of them hadn't bargained on Essie's cool capacity to put them in their place. For a brief moment it occurred to him that Essie definitely had what was needed in a first lady, especially the first lady of his church. But when he considered what was required for her to become his first lady—marriage—he blinked his eyes to drive away the terrifying thought.

"Now those are some trifling men, and I don't care if they are preachers," Essie was saying.

"Yeah, baby, they are certainly that. But you sure did give them a run for their money, especially Marcel Brown. He has probably never gotten as evil a look from a woman as the one you gave him over his last comment to Glodean Benson. He'll probably have nightmares over that one."

"He deserved it," Essie said, "coming over here trying to start some mess. And that Glodean Benson didn't even have sense enough to see—or care—that he was disrespecting her, too." And she thought to herself, "That crazy woman must have really laid something on Theophilus for him to want to spend more than a second with her."

Theophilus put a big piece of the pot roast in his mouth, closed his eyes, and savored it. "Been waiting for that for what seems like forever," he said.

Essie picked up a rib and pointed it at him, saying, "I just can't get over those men, having the nerve to call themselves preachers. That Rev. Sonny Washington is just nasty, nasty, nasty—and that Marcel, how can he get away with acting like he does?"

Theophilus washed down a forkful of the turnip greens with tea before he answered, "Well, as for Marcel, I think he gets away with so much because Rev. Ernest Brown is his daddy. Plus, he's smooth-talking, light-skinned, and from Detroit. You know how some of these churchwomen can carry on over a high-yellow preacher from a big city like Detroit.

"But Sonny Washington? Frankly, I don't know how

he manages to get away with so much. Just about every church he's pastored loses money, while he keeps up his high living—Cadillacs, silk suits, money for trips to almost every district's Annual Conference, and then some."

"That's ridiculous, Theophilus. Church folk should have better sense than to let a preacher get away with so much mess."

He forked up some more pot roast. "I have those exact same thoughts."

On the drive back to Coral Thomas's house, Essie was so quiet that Theophilus wondered if she was brooding over all of that mess with Glodean. Hoping that some music would get them talking, he turned on the radio, fooling with the dial until he heard a Big Mama Thornton song. He said, "Know something? I love to hear that woman sing. Next to Big Johnnie Mae, Thornton is one of my favorite lady blues singers."

Essie listened to the song a few seconds. "I think I like her a little better than Big Johnnie Mae. Although I have to admit that the last time I heard Big Johnnie Mae at Pompey's, she just about tore that microphone to pieces."

"Yeah, Big Johnnie Mae was so hot that night, until she could have fried some chicken with that singing."

Essie laughed. "She sure could have. I wish Uncle Booker would have heard her that night. He loves Big Johnnie Mae but not as much as he does Howlin' Wolf. Uncle Booker will just about lose his mind over some Howlin' Wolf—has been all over Mississippi trying to be at every place that man is scheduled to sing."

Theophilus chuckled. "Uncle Booker looks like he's into some Howlin' Wolf."

He pulled up in front of Coral Thomas's house and

turned off the motor and headlights, leaving the radio on. Big Mama Thornton was crooning, ". . . Ahhh, got a sweet lil' angel and I love the way he spreads his wings."

Theophilus patted the seat next to him. "Come on over here by me."

Essie moved just a little closer, so he grabbed her hand and gently coaxed her all the way over to his side of the car. She sat up next to him with her hands folded in her lap, as if she was sitting in church. He took one of her hands, surprised by how much comfort it gave him just to touch her. Intertwining his fingers with hers, he leaned over and kissed her on the lips.

Essie wrapped her arms around his neck and pulled him closer to her. Now he enfolded her complete in his embrace, kissing her with so much passion that she could feel heat running through her chest, down to the pit of her stomach, to the center of her thighs, and even to the soles of her feet, making her wiggle her toes in her shoes.

Theophilus whispered, "Hmmmm, baby," in her ear.

Essie took her arms from around his neck and moved a couple of inches away from him. "Seems like when we're alone, we always manage to get all bothered and busy."

Theophilus smiled at her longingly, moving in for another kiss.

"I'd better go in the house, Theophilus," she said.

"Mmmm, hmmm," he said, leaning back against the headrest. He was disappointed but he knew that she was right. Finally he opened his door and walked around to help her out of the car. They walked up to the porch holding hands, moving apart when Coral Thomas answered the doorbell.

"Did y'all have a nice time?"

"Yes. Dinner was real good, Miss Coral."

"I told you Mabel's Kitchen was a real nice dinner place." She pushed open the screen door. "Theophilus, you want to come in for some coffee or iced tea?"

"No, ma'am. I'm going to say good night to Essie and go on home. This has been a long day and I'm beat."

Coral Thomas bid him good night and went back into the house. When they were alone, Theophilus took Essie's hand and kissed the center of her palm. She tried to pull away, but Theophilus held it firmly, enjoying her physical response to his kiss. "Such passion," he thought. With his tongue, he swirled tiny, delicate circles onto her open palm, then drew his lips up the side of her wrist, where he could taste her perfume and feel her pulse pounding. "Ummm, baby," he whispered. "One day we're gonna have to finish this. And when I'm through with you, girl, you'll wonder why it took you so long to get 'busy' with me."

Essie pulled her hand from his and reached up to touch his cheek with her still-moist palm. "Theophilus, I've always given as good as I get in every single thing I do," she said. "And I believe"—her voice lowering and deepening—"that it'll be you, not me, in wonder if there ever comes a time when we get all busy with each other."

Her boldness caught Theophilus by surprise. Flustered, he tried to think of something to say that was as thrillingly seductive and loving as her words. But all he could do was stand there in the softness of the yellow porch light, held captive by those golden brown eyes.

Chapter Eleven

HEOPHILUS SAT IN HIS OVERSIZED, NAVY VELVET pastor's chair, trying hard not to squirm while he listened to Sister Willie Clayton talk at length about the church's anniversary. Her job was to read the Sunday announcements and welcome visitors, both of which she had yet to do. Instead she had taken the liberty of testifying about Cleotis's, her sorry son's, return to church, before she even got around to mentioning that today's service would be a special celebration for Greater Hope.

For months, Sister Clayton had been using the welcome and announcement time to deliver her own little sermons and testimonies—which was his own fault, Theophilus knew. He should have fired Sister Clayton when he first arrived and was reassigning church jobs to better-qualified folks. But he hesitated to fire Sister Clayton partly because she was a financial pillar of the church, owner of a chain of prominent funeral homes, and partly because she was Glodean Benson's aunt. He knew Willie Clayton would be furious with him and then openly blame her dismissal as a petty reprisal on his part concerning Glodean's threats. But this morning he didn't care what anyone thought—he wasn't sitting through another Sunday of this.

To make matters worse, Glodean had chosen today to put in a Sunday morning appearance at Greater Hope for the first time since Theophilus had become pastor. She kept shouting "Amen" whenever Sister Clayton paused for breath, egging her on. Theophilus had heard that Sonny Washington had been censured by the Board of Bishops for poor financial management and transferred back to his home state of North Carolina. He wondered whether that had something to do with Glodean's resurfacing today. Rumor had it that Sonny Washington's conference fling with Glodean was still on, and that she wanted Sonny to "put that uppity Rev. Theophilus Simmons in his place."

He drew strength from looking out at Essie, sitting next to Coral and D.S. Thomas. Though three months had passed since the Annual Conference, this was the first visit they had been able to schedule that didn't include Essie's entire family. It wasn't that Theophilus didn't like her family—he did, a lot—but he longed for the chance to see her alone. She had arrived in Memphis so late last night that, after picking her up at the train station, all he had time to do was give her a chaste peck on the cheek before Coral Thomas whisked her into the house. Back home, he had shared his frustration with Eddie, who was a night owl, on the telephone, only to be told, in no uncertain terms, that marriage would solve all of that. Theophilus had choked on those words, coughing so hard it made tears come into his eyes.

But Eddie had just waited patiently for him to stop

coughing and then said, "You know doggone well you want to marry this woman. Just scared to death, that's all. Think of it this way. If Essie Lane were Mrs. Essie Simmons, you could have whisked her off to your house and *nobody* could say a thing about it."

No wonder he was tired this morning, Theophilus thought. He didn't feel much like preaching. But his congregation, especially the older, tithing members, expected to hear their pastor preach on the church's anniversary. Sister Clayton just kept going on and on, seemingly oblivious to the fact that the entire congregation was growing restless and bored. He bent down, hoping no one could see him shaking his head in disgust. When he sat back up, Essie was looking at him with a big grin on her face, barely able to contain her laughter over this mess. He got control of the answering smile tugging at the corner of his own mouth and shot her a stern look, as if to say, "Girl, you know you ought to be a-shamed of your-self for laughing in church."

Essie tilted her head to the side and wrinkled her nose, as if to reply, "I know but I ain't."

This morning Essie was wearing a baby blue silk sleeveless top with a boatneck front and a V-shaped back, anchored by a matching blue silk bow above a row of rhinestone buttons that stopped where the top grazed the hip of the straight, tailored skirt. She was wearing navy blue pumps with a matching purse, and a wide-brimmed, baby blue silk hat that was pinned on top of a perfectly styled French roll. Her upswept hair was highlighted by silver earrings, and she wore a silver charm bracelet, which made a delightful tinkling sound every time she moved her arm.

In that hat and elegant baby blue suit, Theophilus

thought, Essie seemed every bit the First Lady. He thought to himself, "Now, why did she have to walk her little self up in here, looking like my wife."

Essie's presence wasn't lost on Glodean, who was annoyed to see "that little heifer" sitting up in *her* church on anniversary Sunday, acting as if she belonged there. It had been plain to Glodean at the Annual Conference that she still had the power to work Theophilus's nerves. But today his eyes never strayed from Miss Essie Lee Lane, and he barely seemed to notice Glodean. If there was one thing Glodean Benson couldn't put up with, it was being ignored.

Finally Sister Clayton ran out of steam, and Theophilus gratefully reclaimed the podium. He would trim his sermon a little, he decided, to make up for the time Sister Clayton had wasted and to avoid holding up the church's anniversary dinner at Mabel's Kitchen. And, he had to admit, because then he could be with Essie that much sooner.

Essie stood in the doorway of Mabel's Kitchen waiting for Theophilus. She didn't feel right taking her seat at the head table without him because it was the place usually reserved for the first lady of the church. She considered going to sit with D.S. and Coral Thomas, who had waved when she entered the dining room, but rather than disturb them decided to wait outside on the steps. She was just turning to leave when Theophilus came up behind her and grabbed her around the waist, oblivious to the many pairs of eyes that suddenly locked on to the pastor hugging his woman. Much as Essie loved the feel of Theophilus's hands on her waist, she was embarrassed by this display of affection in front of his congregation. Easing his arms from around her waist, she moved to stand at his side.

"Aaawww, baby, my sermon couldn't have been that bad," he said laughing. "You're acting like—" Theophilus stopped talking when his eyes registered that his whole congregation was staring at them. He stood up straight and tried to look preacherly, as he offered Essie his arm and escorted her to the head table.

Coral Thomas reveled in the sight of Theophilus and Essie together, seeming so deeply in love. She knew that there was nothing more exhilarating than knowing you have found the one that God intended for you, and she truly believed that Essie was her young pastor's other half, the side of himself he was only beginning to discover. Having spotted Glodean at church, Coral only hoped that she had witnessed the romantic gesture Theophilus had just made. Maybe that would convince her that it was time to give him up and leave Greater Hope, taking all of her crazy, pink mess with her.

Glodean *had* seen the hug, as well as the delight on the faces of her own church members, and it hurt her down to the bone. But she steeled herself against that pain and strategized, hiding out in the stall in the ladies' room. When she finally emerged, she knew what to do.

Glodean hovered in the doorway of the dining room, waiting till the timing was just right. Then she strutted into the room, with her head held high, moving like a queen, enjoying the way the conversations ebbed as all eyes turned to her. She was especially gratified by the panicky expression on Theophilus's face when he realized that she was homing in on the head table. He was right to worry, she thought with a secret smile. She was about to turn this little anniversary party all the way out.

She stepped up onto the platform where the pastor's

table stood and approached Theophilus from behind. Then, abruptly, she bent down and threw her arms around him, pressing herself into him and rubbing her breasts across the back of his neck.

"Hello, baby," she said in a husky stage whisper.

Theophilus was so shocked he couldn't move or say a word. Nor could the rest of the congregation, sitting there aghast at her flagrant display. No one could believe that even Glodean Benson would do something this crazy at their church anniversary celebration.

Coral Thomas was outraged. "What the hell is wrong with that crazy, butt-swaying heifer?" she said to D.S. "I'm going up there to tell that hussy a thing a two about herself."

But D.S. caught her by the wrist. "No, Coral, sit down. You can look all you want to but you ain't going up to that table."

"Why not?" she hissed. "Let me go!"

"You got to let Essie stand up to that woman by herself. She the one need to get Glodean straight. 'Cause if she lets Glodean get away with this mess, every fool who gets an inkling for the pastor gone think she got a chance."

Coral saw the wisdom of what D.S. was saying and sat down. "I sure hope that baby girl got it in her," she said.

By now Glodean had shifted her embrace to block out Essie, swinging her hips around so that her behind was staring Essie square in the face.

When Essie had seen Glodean that morning, she vowed that nothing would provoke her into an ugly scene. But this was too much. She thought to herself, "Who does this thang think she is, sticking her big butt all up in my face?"

Ignoring Essie's vibes, Glodean decided to add insult to injury by giving her behind a little self-satisfied wiggle.

"Aww, naw. No way," Essie said under her breath. "That's it!"

Yanking a long, blue topaz pin from her hat, she jabbed it deep into Glodean's behind, so hard that Glodean toppled forward onto the table.

The church members, who had been sitting stunned by the drama playing out at the pastor's table, now burst out laughing at Essie's surprise retaliation. The assistant pastor's wife was so tickled that she got bright red-orange lipstick all over her brand-new yellow gloves as she tried to cover her mouth to stop her discreet little chuckles from deteriorating into flat-out, wide-mouth guffaws.

The shock rushed out of Theophilus, and he sprang into action, catching Essie's arm just as she swung it back to stab Glodean's butt one more time.

"Essie!" he barked.

"Essie, the First Lady of Greater Hope cannot go sticking folks with hat pins when they don't act right!"

Essie was too mad and too fixed on her target to hear Theophilus. She tried to pry her arm out of his firm grip to stick Glodean again.

"I *said*," he stated loudly, with authority in his voice, "the First Lady of Greater Hope cannot go stabbing her members with pins, no matter how they behave!"

As soon as Theophilus stopped talking, his words hit him, and he felt like he was going to faint. He couldn't believe he had just proposed marriage—not once, but twice—to a woman while she was attacking his former girlfriend with a hat pin in front of the entire congregation at his church's anniversary celebration.

Glodean just lay there a few seconds, too distraught to move, her behind and her heart both aching, after hearing Theophilus propose marriage to Essie. At last she managed to pull herself up off the table and strode out of the dining room as fast as she could, shamed by the laughter that wafted after her like her own perfume.

All Essie could do was stare at Theophilus with bewilderment and joy. Had he really just asked her to marry him?

"Hallelujah," Coral Thomas declared to D.S. as the entire room burst into loud applause. "That's the Lord at work. Talk about some mysterious ways. Yes, Lord! Yes, Lord!"

As soon as they could decently get up from their chairs, church members started flocking to the bathrooms, dying to compare notes on the scene they had just witnessed. The most charitable among them made a beeline for the pay phones, out of compassion for the sick and shut-in, to break the news to their sisters and brothers in the Lord who had been unable to see this little shindig with their own eyes.

This was an anniversary celebration no one would ever forget—or be able to top.

Part 3
1963

Chapter Twelve

*J*HEOPHILUS TOOK A LONG SIP OUT OF THE GLASS sitting on the table next to the pastor's chair. He had wondered what would happen if he insisted that the deaconesses put Pepsi in that pitcher instead of the predictable ice water. They would probably fall on their knees, rebuking him and praying for his "backsliding soul" right in front of his face. He had once asked Coral Thomas her opinion, and she had looked at him like he was crazy, saying, "Pastor, did I hear you right? *Pepsi* in the pulpit pitcher? Who ever heard of such a thing?"

So here he was on a warm Memphis Sunday morning in April with only plain old ice water to get him through the service. He looked at his bride sitting in her new spot, the first-row pew, just below his pulpit, raising his temperature a few more degrees in a delectable-looking navy blue dress. Essie had made that dress and bought the white silk hat she was wearing, just for today, her very first Sunday as the official First Lady of Greater

Hope Gospel United Church. It was such a simple and proper little outfit—a soft, cotton voile shirtwaist with no adornment other than the string of pearls she was wearing around her neck. But it looked so good on her that he secretly found it very sexy. He got hot just looking at his first lady. He wiped his face again and started back into the sermon, his rich baritone voice becoming softer and more seductive every time he glanced at his new wife.

Essie couldn't trust those looks her new husband kept stealing at her, looks that had no business coming from his pulpit, especially on her first day as the church's first lady. Before she met Theophilus, she used to wonder why some women got so excited over the sound of the preacher's voice. But she understood now. During their courtship, whenever Theophilus's preaching was packed with fire and passion on a Sunday morning, the hot desire that lingered in his voice on Sunday night used to put Essie on her knees. She had to pray and pray, and keep on praying to hold tight to what she knew was right and resist that man until they said "I do."

This was a fast sermon, moving quickly from what Essie had figured out was Theophilus's everyday teaching-for-living-the-Christian-life phase, to the shouting-all-over-church phase. Today, though, she was so caught up in the sound of his voice that she couldn't have told anyone what he was talking about to save her life. But it must have been good because everybody was right with him, shouting "Amen" and "Praise the Lord" throughout his delivery.

"Ummm . . . and, church . . ." Theophilus said, pausing as Essie shifted in her seat, accidentally exposing the lower part of her thigh. He stopped short for a moment, forgetting where he was, and then recovered himself, throwing her a slick wink that was not missed by a single soul sitting in the sanctuary.

Mr. D.S. Thomas leaned over toward his wife and whispered, "You know something? I think the Pastor got his mind on something other than Jesus."

Coral nodded in agreement. She had told the Pastor he needed to take some time off before coming back to work from his honeymoon. Theophilus was a young man with a strong nature, and it would take him a little extra time to get used to having Essie sleeping next to him every night. And if he had listened to her advice, he wouldn't be standing here messing over that sermon and carrying on like he was.

Theophilus composed himself and mercifully wound up the sermon without any more lapses. By the time the doors of the church were opened and the benediction given, his passion had risen, calmed, and subsided— only to start up all over again when Essie reached him in the receiving line. Wrapping her up in an embrace that was more like a lover's than a pastor's, he kissed her on the lips.

Essie pulled away from him and placed her hand on his cheek, giving him what she hoped was a sweet, "remember we're at church" first lady smile. But he bent down and whispered in her ear, "I wish you were a member of the Pastor's Aide Club because I sure do want some 'aid' when we get home."

Coral and D.S. Thomas, standing behind Essie, watched Theophilus flirt outrageously. It was kind of fun to see a pastor take such obvious delight in his wife. Coral thought to herself how rare it was to see this side of a preacher, because the pastor and the first lady, whether they liked it or not, set the model for married life in the church. What better example could a pastor set for the husbands in his congregation than such an open demonstration of how much he loved *and* desired his wife.

Theophilus kissed Essie on the side of her mouth, telling her to keep the kiss in that spot until later, so he could move the receiving line along. Coral Thomas then stepped up to him, with a big mischievous grin spread across her face, and said, "Now, Theophilus, if I didn't know better, I'd swear you were more inclined to being frisky with your bride than giving us this week's message from the Lord."

Theophilus was mortified to think that, as fresh as he had been with Essie, the congregation had been able to read the feelings between the lines of that sermon.

"Now, see here, D.S. honey," Coral said, winking at her husband, "our young pastor didn't think that us old folks could still hear passion in a man's voice. And don't you just have to wonder what he thinks *really* got some of those good sisters to shouting this morning. I mean, even Sister Clayton was hollering and we all know she full of the devil!"

Coral leaned over toward Theophilus and whispered low enough so she wouldn't be overheard, "So, Pastor, are you and Miss Essie coming to our house for dinner before or after that little bit of 'pastor's aid' you were mentioning? I just need to know what time to put my rolls in the oven."

Essie started laughing. Miss Coral was the only person bold enough to say something that embarrassing to Theophilus. With a twinkle in her eye, she said, "Why don't you answer Miss Coral, Theophilus? What's wrong, cat got your tongue?"

"Well, Miss Coral," Theophilus said, grinning at Essie as he turned the tables on her, "I'll have to call you and tell you what time to put those rolls in the oven. Because frankly, I don't know how long I'll be getting me some of this aid. Ain't that right, baby?

"But first," he added frowning, "I have to meet with Sister Clayton."

Willie Clayton was late, thank God. He had been dreading this encounter, and just thinking about it made his head hurt. Most people had no idea of the extent of a pastor's job—teacher, businessman, counselor, intellectual, friend—and now, what else was he? Community defender? Sister Clayton was furious with him, he knew, but he felt that he had no other choice than to defy her, though it might cost the church the considerable income of her offerings. When she finally arrived, even her knock sounded angry.

"Yes?" he said, and Willie Clayton stomped in.

"Pastor," she demanded. "What is this mess I been hearing about you withdrawing your endorsement of Clayton Funeral Homes for our church members?"

Theophilus hadn't told anyone about his intentions but the family who made the initial complaint against Clayton Funeral Homes. But nothing stayed secret for long at Greater Hope.

"You told the Bobo family that you were going to deal with me," Sister Clayton said, now leaning on his desk, trying to stick her face in his.

"Yes, I told Mrs. Bobo that I would deal with you, Sister Clayton. Everybody in this church knows good and well that the Bobos don't have any money. For the life of me, I can't imagine why you would charge them anything beyond your own costs for burying a stillborn baby, let alone refuse to bargain. They'd be paying out that fee for years."

"I offered the Bobo Family the ten percent discount that is promised every member of Greater Hope for that funeral. Plus, I threw in an extra car at no extra cost, to make sure all of them had a ride to the church and the cemetery. You know how their car don't work. Every time I drive by their house, it's sitting up on a cinder block with a car light stuck up under it."

Theophilus hated to admit it, but Sister Clayton was right about the Bobos and their raggedy car. He didn't think there was ever a time there wasn't a broken-down car sitting up on some cinder blocks in their grassless front yard. But raggedy car or not, the Bobos had the right to be treated with compassion by their own church members. For Sister Clayton to have tried to price-gouge the Bobos was just wrong. She wouldn't miss their little bit of money, not this woman who could afford to buy two fur coats to wear in a city where nobody could even remember the last time it snowed.

"Sister Willie Clayton, you do not have a right to the monopoly of the business of your church members. And I am not sending another soul your way," Theophilus said. "I learned just how outrageous your prices are when I called Mr. Butler of Butler-Caro Funeral Homes to see what he could do for the Bobos. He isn't even a member of our church, and he is doing that funeral for half the cost, even after your ten percent discount. Where is your Christian charity?

"And another thing, Sister Clayton, I simply refuse to encourage *anybody* in this church to buy you another Cadillac, trip to the Bahamas, or new fur coat. You need to know that I have already told the Usher Board to take the Clayton Funeral Homes church fans out of the pews."

Sister Clayton couldn't believe what she was hearing. Greater Hope's members had been patronizing Clayton Funeral Homes since her father first opened the business over forty years ago. People who were grieving didn't shop around, preferring to deal with someone they knew and trusted, so she rarely got complaints about her prices. But if Rev. Simmons started sending people to Butler-Caro, word would get around. She would not only lose Greater Hope's business, which she needed, but also the support of other pastors in the area. She couldn't afford that.

"Rev. Simmons," she said, "you'll regret this—I'm gonna see to it. I wonder how big and bad you'll be when the Triennial Conference rolls around and Greater Hope can't pay its conference fees because your offering box is suffering."

"Keep your offerings, Willie Clayton. This church doesn't need money so bad that I have to be your pimp. And even if it did, I'd rather preach to three people out of the trunk of my car, like Rev. Roscoe Alexander, than be a kept pastor."

Sister Clayton was ready to cuss him out, pastor or not. After all her family's years at Greater Hope, not to mention their financial support, his words were like a slap in the face to her. She was all puffed up and about to let him have it when Essie walked into the office. "That little slit-eyed heifer is part of this!" she thought. "She's the one who drove Glodean out of her home church."

Willie Clayton's eyes locked on a silver-framed wedding picture of Essie and Theophilus. Snatching it up off the desk, she flexed her shoulder, ready to heave it right at Theophilus's head. Essie jumped in front of her and said in a low, deadly sounding voice, "I wish you would," then grabbed her wrist and tried to shake the photo out of Willie's hand.

"Essie!" Theophilus snapped. "Let her go. Let her go

and leave. This is church business. You need to stay out of it."

Essie released her hold on Sister Clayton, shocked that Theophilus would speak to her so sharply and in front of a prominent church member, no less. His outburst also stopped Sister Clayton dead in her tracks, and she loosened her grip on the photo. Essie pried it out of her hand and set it on the desk, then marched out of the office.

Willie Clayton stormed out right behind her, shouting, "Theophilus Simmons, your black behind has made a big mistake this time. You just don't know."

Essie was so mad she walked right past Coral Thomas, who had been waiting to talk to her. Coral had heard the shouting going on in the office and got up to follow Essie, hoping to console her. She said, "I see you getting ready to end this honeymoon, Miss Essie."

Essie started at the sound of Coral's voice, still too consumed with fury to quite catch what she was saying.

Coral repeated, "You gettin' ready to stop being a bride and 'bout to become a bona fide wife, soon as you set that boy straight 'bout his mess. Lord, don't know what gets into him sometimes," she said, shaking her head. "You want me to stay and wait with you until he come out that office?"

"No, I'm okay," Essie said.

Coral understood that she needed time alone so she could calm down before she had to face her husband. She gave Essie a hug and kiss and went to find D.S., whom she had left outside sipping a Pepsi and walking around the church, checking out the building for any problems. Being in construction, he believed it was his Christian duty to keep Greater Hope in tiptop shape.

*   *   *

"Who died and made you bishop, Essie?" Theophilus demanded, huffing and storming around the living room like he was trying to bring the house down on their heads.

"You may run that church but you don't have the last word in running me," she shot back. "You owe me an apology."

"I owe you a what? You're the one who came barging into my office, interrupting an important meeting, and got to tussling with Sister Clayton!"

"Theophilus, I did not know that old witch was still in there. And she was the one who got to tussling—she was about to smash *our* wedding picture!"

"You didn't belong in there, Essie! Willie Clayton was in the middle of threatening to pull out of Greater Hope."

"Theophilus, if you had told me, your wife, why you were meeting with Willie Clayton, I never would have come in that room."

"Why should I tell you church business that doesn't concern you?"

"Because I am your wife, Theophilus. Because we are living one life now, not two. If you rise in the denomination, I rise with you. If you fall, if you wind up out on the street, I do, too. If you fight with Sister Clayton, I am the one who's going to defend you to the churchwomen, who are going to talk to me about it, not you. I am your helpmeet, and all your business is my business."

"The point is, Essie, you should have knocked."

Essie blinked back tears and, raising her eyes to the ceiling, over his shoulder, thought about King David as a young boy facing Goliath. She whispered to herself, "Lord, I need me a slingshot 'bout now."

Theophilus felt outgunned. Whenever Essie felt he was getting the best of her in an argument, she always went over his head and straight to Jesus. Who did this little woman think she was—Queen Esther?

Here his wife was, standing in his living room, having a little talk with Jesus and waiting, literally, for God to straighten him out. The bodacious prayers and faith of Negro women were something. And it wouldn't surprise him one bit, if when they all were in heaven, the Lord would pull out some kind of scroll, and on it would be all of the prayers of Negro women since the day they got off the slave boats on up to this civil rights movement and beyond.

What were the men going to do, then?

"Lord," Theophilus prayed, "I know Essie's gotten the jump on me, coming to You over this one. But I need You to help me, Lord. This marriage bond is *hard,* sometimes almost too hard for me to understand without Your help."

Chapter Thirteen

ARCEL BROWN CLOSED HIS EYES AND LEANED his head forward, letting out a low moan as the soft, cool fingers of his church secretary, Precious Powers, massaged the aches out of his neck. The two of them had been working all morning, shifting money around and straightening up the books. They went through this ritual every month, the week before he met with his Finance Board. And it never failed that Precious, with her astute sense of numbers, found a way to keep his butt out of hot water. It was one of the things he liked about her—and there were very few women he truly liked. He loved his mother but ne didn't like her. And he had a fondness for and admired the accomplishments of his fiancée, Saphronia Anne McComb. But he didn't like her. But Precious Powers? Now, *her*, he liked—and he needed her.

Precious finished massaging his neck and kissed the corner of his mouth. He reached up and, cupping his hand around the back of her head, pulled her closer to him. "Mmmmmmm, girl. Come on 'round this chair and put that big, fine tail of yours in my lap. We still have a few minutes."

Precious, a pretty cocoa-colored woman with large black eyes and a natural, soft blush in her cheeks, smiled and kissed him back. She sat down on Marcel's lap, straddling him, skirt up to her thighs, and placed her honeysuckle-scented arms around his neck. He licked her collarbone, tasting honeysuckle, and breathed in the enticing aroma.

"Ohhh, baby," he crooned.

That made Precious wrap her arms tighter around his neck and bury her head on his shoulder, to hide her silent tears. She was losing Marcel. She loved him, and she couldn't bear the thought of that tight-lipped woman becoming his wife. Marcel kept trying to tell her that being married to Saphronia wouldn't change anything between them. He assured her that she was the one he really wanted to marry, but couldn't because of his father and Bishop Giles. With his career just taking off, they insisted that if he married a woman who was once a stripper, it would mess up any chance he had of ever becoming a bishop. To rise in the church, he needed the right kind of wife—a wife like Saphronia.

"What about Mary Magdalene?" he once asked his father. Indeed, what about Jackie Giles, the Bishop's own wife, who had been a cocktail waitress when he met her? That was different, his father explained. He was already a bishop then, and everybody understood that he had married Jackie out of loneliness and grief, after facing the death of his first wife—a wife who had been the right kind of first lady.

Marcel knew his father's words were jive and hollow because he knew all about Jackie Giles. She wasn't even a decent woman. She had been jumping in and out of Marcel's bed, drawn by his pretty-boy looks, right up until her expensive honeymoon in Barbados with the Bishop and just three days after she got back. Much as she loved putting on first lady airs, Jackie was too young and frisky to stay satisfied with a dried-up old man like Lawson Giles. For Marcel, getting her under those sheets hadn't even been a challenge.

"It's time you took your sweet-smelling self back to work," he told Precious. "You know I'm waiting on Bishop Otis Caruthers."

He tried to nudge her off his lap, but Precious clung to him. "You better get used to interruptions," Marcel said. "Once this church has a first lady, she won't take too kindly to walking in here and finding your legs all up around her husband."

Precious could no longer hide her sniffles.

"Go back to work," Marcel said harshly.

His reference to Saphronia sounded hard, he knew, but he was talking to himself as much as to Precious. To show her he was sorry he had hurt her feelings, he patted her on the head before pushing her off his lap. She was still dabbing at her eyes as she headed back to her office, with the scent of honeysuckle trailing behind her.

She had left not a moment too soon. Minutes later Bishop Caruthers burst into his office, looking so full of hell the devil wouldn't be stupid enough to mess with him.

"Where the hell was your secretary, Marcel? Do you know how long I've been sitting out there?" he bellowed. "Then when she did come waltzing by, she had the nerve to say, 'Just a moment, while I tell the Pastor you're here.' Well, I wasn't about to keep on waiting on Miss—"

"Miss Precious, Miss Precious Powers, Bishop Caruthers," she said from the doorway.

Otis Caruthers stopped and sniffed the air, making it clear that it didn't take a genius to know that a woman had been in the office just moments ago—and that his nose, picking up the honeysuckle scent, told him it was Precious.

"I see you keep your girls real busy, Marcel," he said, looking Precious up and down like she was cheap. "But this one seems too dumb to know when she's keeping a bishop waiting."

"I knowed," Precious said defiantly. "But I was doing my job for the Pastor, just like always."

"You have to be the most loyal church secretary I have ever laid eyes on, Miss—"

"Precious Powers," she repeated. She wasn't afraid of Otis Caruthers, though she knew he terrified Marcel. He had some hold on Marcel, but, much as she snooped, she could never find out what it was. Since she did the books, she knew that it was costing Marcel money.

When Bishop Caruthers saw she wasn't planning to leave the office, he started pacing in agitation, clenching and unclenching his fists as if he wanted to slug her. Precious just smirked at him, looking like she was just praying for him to throw the first punch.

"Miss Powers," Marcel said. "Let's call it a day. I need to talk to the Bishop alone."

Precious looked at him to make sure that he really wanted her to leave, not to stay for moral support and to watch his back. But with his eyes, he signaled to her, "You making this worse, not better."

As soon as the office door closed, Caruthers sat down in one of the two blue, black, and red plaid armchairs facing Marcel's massive mahogany desk. It was a gracious room, with a blue, gold, and ruby red Persian area rug lying on the walnut-stained hardwood floor; subdued sky blue walls decorated with a painting of the church and a large portrait of Marcel; navy blue silk draperies; and the two tree-height plants placed in front of the long, wide windows that overlooked a busy boulevard. Caruthers pulled out a pack of cigarettes, and Marcel pushed a heavy crystal ashtray across the desk to him. It had been a gift from one of his Trustee Board members who refused to smoke outside whenever he came to call on the pastor.

After lighting his cigarette, Caruthers sat back. "Now, your Miss My-Name-is-Miss-Precious-Powers must be one hell of a secretary for you to set back and let her show her tail with a bishop."

In his mind, Marcel begged Precious to forgive him as he said, "Precious is a *real* good secretary, Bishop— a *real* mighty good secretary. And she can type pretty good, too."

Caruthers let out a snort of a laugh. "Well, Reverend, you *and* your daddy always did have a knack for selecting the right women to work for you. And I see you haven't lost your weakness for the ones with big juicy behinds, either."

Marcel, relieved he had scored a few points with Bishop Caruthers, opened his desk drawer and pulled out the bottle of Seagram's he kept hidden in his desk. He opened the sliding panel on the narrow mahogany credenza behind the desk, took out a stack of paper cups, and poured two cups of liquor.

Otis put his cigarette on the edge of the ashtray and reached for the cup with the most liquor in it. "I was about to ask if there was anything, other than Miss Precious, worth having in this office."

"Now, Bishop, it is my duty to please you."

"And you think letting me face off with your secretary was pleasing to me, Marcel?"

Marcel didn't answer that but just asked, "Do you need anything else?"

"Precious Powers would be just what the doctor ordered after a few cups of this stuff."

Marcel swallowed hard and said, "Can't help you there. I'm afraid Precious draws the line at bishops."

Caruthers set his cup on a hand-carved wooden coaster on the desk and leaned back in his chair, letting Marcel sweat a few moments. He was talking about Precious as much to unsettle Marcel as anything else. He knew all about Precious, that disaster-waiting-to-happen with his pending marriage to Saphronia McComb, *and* those secret trysts with Jackie Giles. If Lawson *ever* found out that the son of his favorite pastor put his hands on his wife, there would be hell to pay, both for Marcel *and* his daddy.

"Knowledge is power" was the name of Bishop Otis Caruthers's tune.

"Did Cleotis Clayton contact you?" he asked Marcel.

Marcel poured himself a refill and downed it in three quick gulps. The liquor was strong and made him wince and bite his teeth together, hitting him so hard his eyes burned. "What does Cleotis Clayton have to do with you and me?" he asked. "He said he would endorse my daddy's campaign for bishop if we publicly endorsed the new Clayton funeral home he was opening in Richmond, Virginia, at the Triennial Conference, this year."

Otis sat up in his chair and fingered his cup for a second or two. He said, "Marcel, do you remember me telling you that I knew of someone who wanted to make some extra money as much as we do?"

"Umm, hmm," Marcel said, getting kind of worried. He had a sinking feeling that endorsement from Cleotis

Clayton had some extra strings to it and that Bishop Caruthers was the one pulling them. It looked like Jackie Giles was turning into one overpriced good time, with the price of silence going up.

"Marcel, it's no secret that I am fed up with being on location. The money they throw my way is peanuts and I am constantly at the mercy of tight-fisted jivetimers like Percy Jennings."

Gospel United Church bishops earned a modest base salary from the denomination itself. It was perks that made so many of them fat in the pockets—birthday and anniversary gifts from pastors wanting favors, love offerings taken up at every church they visited, money earned from sitting on various boards in their communities, money earned as guest speakers at churches in and out of their districts, and so much more. Otis Caruthers, as a located bishop, or a bishop who had been suspended by the denomination for questionable behavior, couldn't cash in on any of these perks because they were all connected to presiding over a district.

"I get by on my little odds and ends," Caruthers was saying. He looked meaningfully at Marcel, who now opened his desk drawer. He took out a fat brown envelope stuffed with fives, tens, and twenties and pushed it across the desk to Bishop Caruthers, who let it sit there.

"But, Marcel," he went on, "at this year's Triennial Conference I am determined to get my district back. That's going to take some cash."

Marcel leaned on his elbows and looked straight at Caruthers. "People are afraid to support you," he said. "The daddy and mama of that little teenage girl you tried to pick up raised so much mess that every bishop had to vote to censure you. No one's going to break out of the pack. They're all afraid it will hurt their careers."

"That's where the cash comes in," Caruthers said.

"You mean for payoffs? To buy votes?" Marcel asked. "I cannot begin to imagine what you think will bring in enough money to buy you the votes you'd need to get reinstated to a district. Bishop, there simply isn't that much money floating around this denomination to get you back in."

"Marcel," Caruthers said, "I have always believed that where there's a will, there's a way. And I've been a bishop long enough to know that if you have the right amount of will, you can certainly *buy* yourself a way."

He got an odd, dreamy smile on his face that made Marcel wonder what he was thinking and—not for the first time—if he was right in the head. Every now and then Bishop Caruthers slipped into some spaces that gave him the creeps. After a minute or two Marcel found himself practically yelling, "Bishop!"

Caruthers immediately sat up straight and remembered to give Marcel his attention.

"You're talking about a will and a way. And I know you have the will. But my daddy says that there are people like Percy Jennings who want to bring you back up before this Triennial Conference and petition for your dismissal from the episcopacy. They don't even want you, as my daddy said, to preside over a pissant district out in the swamps of hell."

Venom replaced the grin that had stretched across Otis Caruthers's face only moments earlier. "Who told you that?" he said.

Marcel sat back in his chair rubbing his chin, enjoying being the bearer of bad news. Bishop Caruthers was the one who got all the dirt on everybody else in the denomination.

"Bishop, you're not the only one in this church who can pluck the good grapes off the vine."

"It's preachers like you who put the grapes there in the first place," Caruthers retorted nastily.

He knew the only way Marcel could have been privy to such information was through that ever-tightening connection between his father and Bishop Lawson Giles. Those two wanted to run the whole show, and they were ruthless enough to cut anybody else out, including him. That—and the little hush money it gave him every month—was the reason he had been so happy to learn about Marcel and Jackie Giles. It was a blessing and he intended to make the most of it.

Now Caruthers pushed the envelopeful of money back across the desk to Marcel. "This month's on the house."

"Huh?" Marcel said, confused and growing even more worried.

"The money. You can keep it this month," he told him.

"Why?"

Bishop Caruthers laughed and Marcel felt the hairs on the back of his neck stand straight up.

"If everything goes like I hope it will at the Triennial Conference, you won't have to pay me another dime," he said. "But, Marcel—the next time Cleotis Clayton calls you, be a little more friendly to the man. He is, after all, dropping some serious cash in the pot for your father's campaign for bishop, and he has some big plans for the Triennial Conference. You need to be grateful and quit acting like you doing him a favor just by saying good morning to him."

Marcel almost asked, "What plans?" but caught himself in time. If Bishop Caruthers was cooking up some scheme to get reinstated, he wanted to stay in the dark about it for as long as he could.

But Marcel's blessed ignorance couldn't last. He was soon summoned to Memphis by Otis Caruthers for a meal at Willie Clayton's, and he was told to leave that "snippety-up-in-your-face-Miss-Precious-Powers" at home.

Bishop Otis belched loudly to polish off one of the best meals he had eaten in months. Willie Clayton had outdone herself this evening. She had served baked turkey that was crispy brown on the outside and juicy and tender in all the right places. Cornbread dressing with oysters, collard greens cooked with juicy ham hocks, yam pudding, tossed salad, homemade rolls—and his favorite, ambrosia salad with tiny marshmallows and plenty of chunks of fresh-cut pineapple in it. And the dessert—Otis thought he would hurt himself when he tasted the first morsel of the delectable, four-layer red velvet cake Willie had made especially for him.

Marcel Brown sat next to him, picking at his cake, watching Willie's niece, Glodean Benson, work her charms on Rev. Sonny Washington. Sonny could be mean as a snake, and he had been especially nasty since his censure by the Board of Bishops. But tonight he did seem to be falling even more head over heels for Glodean.

"Can I get you anything else, Bishop?" Willie said.

"Some of that fine cognac you have stashed away would be perfect about now."

Willie Clayton smiled and walked over to the liquor cabinet, pulling out her best glasses and best liquor for Bishop Caruthers.

Otis swirled the liquor around and then inhaled the

fragrance of it before he sipped it. "Sister Clayton, you sure outdid yourself on this meal," he said. "Pour a little more of that good stuff in this glass for your bishop."

He then clinked glasses with Willie's son, Cleotis.

Cleotis had spent the meal outlining his plans for the new funeral home in Richmond, Virginia, which would have an inaugural gala in August during the Gospel United Church's Triennial Conference. Rather than throw a party, Cleotis had come up with a scheme to open the new funeral home to the visiting clergymen at the conference as sort of a club, where they would be free to partake of the vices, such as smoking, drinking, and women, that many liked to indulge in away from home but couldn't pursue publicly in Richmond with their church members and superiors so close at hand.

A stiff admission fee plus hefty charges for services would yield a tidy profit, to be shared by Cleotis, who would use it to finance the funeral home, and by Bishop Caruthers, as well as, to a lesser extent, Marcel and Sonny, who were to recruit patrons for the club. Among the thousands of pastors and bishops in attendance, surely at least several hundred would be willing to pay for the club's services and would be trustworthy enough not to blow the whistle.

The plan was risky, Marcel knew, but it was brilliant, in a perverse way. Looking around the table at his co-conspirators, he thought of the old saying, "The devil always busy in church." It seemed especially apt to him tonight.

Chapter Fourteen

ISTER SIMMONS, I SURE DO WANNA THANK YOU for making all these pretty clothes for my little grandbaby. Chile, she would've been almost naked without them."

Essie put the box of newly made baby clothes in the woman's arms, smiling at her and wishing she wouldn't carry on over her so. Made her uncomfortable.

"Folks keep saying how you can really sew. But Lawd ha' mercy! Lawd, I think you liked to kick the machine in two when you made these clothings."

"I only made two of the dresses. Mrs. Coral Thomas made the rest. I think you should call her and thank her, too. I know she would appreciate hearing from you."

"Naw. Don't need to do all that. Just as happy to talk to my first lady. Lawd, what my folks gone say when they's find out that my pastor's wife made all these here chirren's clothings for my grandbaby."

Essie had to work real hard not to let this woman hear her sigh out loud. Some church members questioned whether it was even proper for the First Lady to start a Sewing Club, but Essie believed that it was doing God's work to make beautiful baby and maternity clothes for unwed mothers and women down on their luck. Eventually she planned to hold classes to teach the women to sew themselves. The Greater Hope Sewing Club was a great necessity in the Negro community, even if some of the women only came to church when they needed something: "Money to turn my lights on." "Food to tide me over to payday." "Change to catch the bus to the doctor." And on and on.

And now, for this one to refuse to call Mrs. Thomas and thank her was almost an insult. Part of the reason, Essie knew, was that she liked getting "special attention" from the First Lady, but part of it was embarrassment, too—shame at accepting charity from a church member she thought of as her equal, one who had the same standing in the church. She sighed. Being a first lady took a lot of gut-level thinking, as well as patience. It carried a heavy responsibility because it was a ministry in itself.

Stifling her annoyance, Essie opened the front door, hoping the woman wouldn't gush anymore. But she wasn't quite through: "Sister Simmons, I just have to thank you one more, no, two more times. Thank you—Thank you. Don't know how I would have clothed my grandbaby without you."

It crossed Essie's mind that the woman might be lingering because she was trying to get up the nerve to ask for money, as well as the clothes. Then she remembered what Rose Neese once told her—that the only way some folks knew how to get love was to beg for things. Saying a firm goodbye, she hugged the woman, then as she closed her door silently asked the Lord to forgive her for being judgmental toward this woman whom He loved just as much as her.

Essie's eyes now fell on her desk, where a large pile of letters had accumulated, all waiting to be answered. Most of them were requests for her to join the various Negro women's groups in the city. At first she had managed to fend them off by claiming that she was a new bride and wanted to be with her husband. But now the requests had started pouring in again and Essie didn't know what to do. She didn't really have the stomach to join any of them, preferring to work with the Greater Hope Sewing Club and to socialize with more down-to-earth pastors' wives, than to get mixed up in all the influence peddling of the city's Negro elite. If she got involved in anything it would be the local chapter of Southern Christian Leadership Conference. She and Theophilus had wanted to join in some of the civil rights protests in Mississippi, but Rev. James and Bishop Jennings had asked them to work from behind the scenes, where they could be more valuable as part of the movement's organizational network than in more visible and active protest activities. But there was still plenty of work to be done—mailings and phone calls about meetings and arranging lodging for protesters passing through Memphis, as well as bake sales to help raise money.

She was just thinking about dumping all those invitations in the trash can when the doorbell rang. To her surprise, Saphronia McComb and her grandmother, Mother Harold, were standing on the porch. Lee Allie had mentioned that the two were coming to town for an Alpha Kappa Alpha sorority reunion.

But they had never set foot in her house in Charleston, and she couldn't imagine what would make them want to visit her in Memphis. As she invited them in, she didn't miss the very large diamond ring on Saphronia's hand, evidence that the rumors of her engagement to Marcel Brown were true. As much as Saphronia got on her nerves, she felt sorry for her—falling in love with a man who was a well-known womanizer and, judging by his daddy's behavior, not likely to change when they were married.

"What brings you all to my neck of the woods?" Essie asked, praying that she had a welcoming expression on her face.

Mother Harold walked into the living room and handed Essie her purse, taking in everything like she was conducting a home inspection, before settling herself on the sofa. Saphronia followed, thinking of some excuse that would enable her to see the rest of Essie's house. She figured that she would have to make a long trip to the bathroom before she left.

"Would you and Saphronia like some refreshments?" Essie asked. "I have tea, lemonade, or Kool-Aid."

Mother Harold wrinkled her nose at the thought of drinking Kool-Aid, and Essie fought back the urge to roll her eyes. Mother Harold always walked around with her nose in the air, acting like she was some rich white lady in *Gone With the Wind*, instead of what she was— a snooty little Negro woman living in a small town in Mississippi most people had never even heard of. She knew goodness well that Mother Harold hated Kool-Aid. She and those other "old high-yellow biddies" in the church felt that Kool-Aid was the drink of what they called "field folk."

"We will have tea with a few sprigs of mint leaves in it," Mother Harold said.

"I only have lemons," Essie replied.

Mother Harold sighed and sucked on her teeth,

looking at Saphronia as if to say, "See, I told you she wouldn't have anything decent in her house."

This time Essie did roll her eyes and just went to get them some tea with lemons. She thought to herself, "I oughta not put any sugar in it. Then it'll be just right for that old nasty-acting sourpuss."

She came back rolling a beautiful mahogany wood tray with tea and some lemon tea cakes she had made yesterday evening for Theophilus, who loved tea cakes. She served both women their tea and tea cakes, then took her favorite seat in the room, a comfortable, deep, and cushiony lavender swivel chair.

"Essie, dear, I know you are wondering what brings us to your home," Mother Harold said.

"Yeah, Mother Harold, you've got that much right."

Mother Harold gave her a mean look and continued, "Since your marriage to Rev. Theophilus Simmons, several ladies' organizations in Memphis have contacted me on your behalf, asking me to serve as the liaison between you and them. It seems that you, Essie dear, have been remiss in responding to their invitations."

As her grandmother spoke, Saphronia kept twirling that big ring, making sure Essie knew it was there. Essie took a deep breath and whispered a prayer for courage. "Mother Harold, I appreciate your help," she said. "But I'm really too busy to join any of those groups."

"Now Essie dear, as I understand it, one of the sororities contacted you, and they were even willing to wait for you to enroll in college to become eligible to pledge. Then, there was the Ladies of Distinction Social Club, filled with the wives of the most prominent colored men in the city. And, you even turned down the Memphis chapter of Class Keys, Inc."

Saphronia kept twisting that glittering engagement

ring around and 'round on her finger, as Mother Harold went on, "Essie, I don't have to tell you that these are distinguished groups of colored women who are trying to help you build a proper social life in this town. No one can just join these organizations. Before you even received the invitations, you were checked out, discussed, and voted on. Most first ladies think that is an honor and would be eager to associate with colored women of this social caliber."

"Well, I'm not most first ladies," Essie said. "Their social caliber doesn't really mean much of anything to me."

Mother Harold was sure that Essie was missing the point. Could the girl really be so obtuse that she had to spell it out? With exasperation in her voice, she said, "Essie, I happen to know that the day your name came up at one club meeting, there was a serious argument. A lot of the women objected to your background. It took real effort to convince them to give you a chance."

Saphronia, who had been silent all this time, stopped playing with her engagement ring and looked at her grandmother like she was crazy. Even she knew better than to insult someone in their own home—especially if that someone was Essie Lane.

Essie got up out of her chair and walked right up to where Mother Harold was sitting.

"That is exactly right, Mother Harold. When I was a jook joint cook, most of those women would not have even formed their mouths to say good morning to me. Now I'm married to a well-respected pastor, and they've suddenly discovered I'm 'worthy' to be in a group with them. But if they didn't want me when I worked for Mr. Pompey, then they sho' don't need me now. And the same goes for you and Saphronia. Now, get out of my house."

Mother Harold looked at Essie with amazement.

"You heard me right," Essie said. "Please leave my house before I throw your old tight-tailed self right out. Mother Harold, you have some nerve, coming up in here trying to tell me how excited I should be because your old stuck-up club ladies decided that I am okay, just because a pastor saw fit to put a wedding ring on my finger. You and your kind always think you better than everybody else. But you ain't."

Essie's eyes shot over to Saphronia. "Girl, you better get her out of my house before I lose my religion."

Saphronia had said that the visit was a bad idea. She had agreed to come along only because she had wanted to show off her ring, to make it clear to Essie and through her, Theophilus, she had done very well for herself. But Essie had hardly even looked at the ring. Now she grabbed her grandmother, gently steering her to the door. When she saw Essie put her hands on her hips, she quickened her pace, practically dragging Mother Harold out of the house and to their car.

Watching them go, Essie's anger ebbed and sadness crept in to replace it. Negroes had enough trouble in their lives—some, like the woman who had picked up the baby clothes, had trouble just keeping food on their tables. But even folks who were relatively comfortable like herself, her mother, Uncle Booker, Rose Neese, and Coral and D.S. Thomas, still had to fight just for their basic rights. Women like Mother Harold could draw all the lines they wanted to between who was worthy and who was not, but all of them were still just plain old coloreds to most white folk. The Klan didn't care if

Mother Harold belonged to every Negro women's club in the South.

Essie felt too restless to get back to her sewing, so she decided to wash her hair. Something about washing her hair always made her feel better when she dealt with some mess. It felt like she was rubbing trouble right out of her brain.

Chapter Fifteen

*S*O WHAT ELSE BEEN GOING ON DOWN AT THE church, son?" Mr. Jarvis, a longtime member of Greater Hope, managed to say in between heavy spasms of coughing that drained his energy. He lay back on his pillows weakly but gestured for Theophilus to stay when he got up to call for the nurse. He reached for Theophilus's hand.

"Now what about that little fast gal you been counseling?" he asked.

"Who?"

"You . . . know . . ." Mr. Jarvis answered.

"Lillian Graves, Jr.?"

"Yeah, little Lillian," Mr. Jarvis said, and drew a breath. "Lord, why did her crazy mama name her Lillian Graves, Jr.? The mama's name ain't no Lillian, it's Flossie Jean.

"Now, Theophilus," he continued. "Ain't nothing wrong with Flossie Jean's baby girl but she fast. Sixteen years old, smoking, drinking cheap liquor, staying out all night with some jive-time twenty-year-old boy who don't half work none, and then have the nerve to cuss out her mama . . ."

Mr. Jarvis sat up a bit. He knew he needed to stay quiet but he wanted to help Theophilus understand what he was dealing with, with some of those fools down at Greater Hope. He had been a part of that church all his life. And at eighty-eight, he knew what was up.

"See," he said, through a haggling cough. "Ahhhh . . . see . . . Theophilus, don't get all caught up in that mess with them peoples. Flossie Jean the one who really the trouble. See, she used to be something else, too. Man in, man out the bedroom. That's all that girl know. That's what the matter with her child. That Lillian."

He started coughing again, so shaken by the spasms that he had tears in his eyes. "This pain like some burning ache, running all which-a-way in my chest," he said, looking at Theophilus through watery eyes. "Reverend, start up a prayer and ask the Lord to give me some real relief . . ."

Theophilus took Mr. Jarvis's other hand in his and started praying. Before he got sick, Mr. Jarvis had been his top deacon in the church. It was he who had taught Theophilus how to minister to the sick and shut-ins, especially the members who were close to death. Seems like Mr. Jarvis had a gift for seeing a brother or sister to the doorway leading them home. Theophilus cleared his throat several times to hold back the tears. He knew Mr. Jarvis didn't have long, and he hated letting him go.

"Lord, this is the first time I have had to lead a prayer with Mr. Jarvis in tow. But this pain in him and this sickness got a hold on him, Lord, and he need for You to make it let go. He needs to be back on his feet, helping to cheer the sick and teaching those You are calling home not to be afraid. Give him the peace, O Lord, that he has brought to so many others. We thank you for your everlasting mercy, O God."

Theophilus expected Mr. Jarvis to say Amen. But Mr. Jarvis was lying back on his pillow with a look of utter contentment on his face. To his surprise, he noticed that Mr. Jarvis's hand was limp and let it go. How could Mr. Jarvis have slipped away from him so quickly and quietly? But then that was so like Mr. Jarvis—looking out for him, not wanting him to be upset or to worry him up to his very last breath on earth. Theophilus pulled a handkerchief out of his breast pocket and wiped the tears that were streaming down his face. He kissed Mr. Jarvis on the forehead and went to get the nurse.

Theophilus pulled up into the driveway of the parsonage and turned the engine off, leaving the radio on. Howlin' Wolf was singing. Mr. Jarvis, like Uncle Booker, loved him some Howlin' Wolf. Always told him that the Wolf was one Negro who could "sang an old man just right." Said he used to play himself some Howlin' Wolf whenever he had a mind to get frisky with the missus. It filled Theophilus with warmth to think about Mr. Jarvis like that, and he hoped he and Essie would feel passion all their lives, just like Mr. and Mrs. Jarvis. That had to be the kind of love the Lord had always intended a man and a woman to have. But when the song ended, it was as if Mr. Jarvis had slipped away on him again. His sorrow crept right back up on him, weighing him down and making his steps heavy as he went into the house.

Essie heard Theophilus's car pull up in the driveway and finished rubbing a mixture of oil and setting lotion into her damp hair. She fluffed it up, then glanced at herself in the mirror, kind of liking the way her hair looked "natural." Recently, some of the civil rights workers had started wearing their hair that way. Unstraightened, her hair was soft and curly, with its reddish gold highlights more prominent, and it framed her face nicely, making her eyes show up even more.

Then she heard Theophilus turn the key in the lock. Something was wrong. His footsteps were slow and labored. She wondered if that had anything to do with Mr. Jarvis, and she hurried out to check on him.

When she bumped into him in the hall, he looked like he was close to tears. But he stepped back and looked at her, saying, "Essie! What have you done to your hair?"

She reached out to him, and he grabbed her, pulling her to him and kissing her forehead. She looked up at his face, wondering about the mood and what had happened with Mr. Jarvis. But she could see that he didn't want to talk right now.

He held her close, and weaving his fingers through her soft natural hair, kissed her lips. Essie could feel the sorrow in him and unconsciously pressed her body closer to his, wrapping a knee up around his thigh. He grabbed her thigh and squeezed it, kissing her and sighing deeply. He whispered, "Those drapes drawn tight in the living room?"

Essie said, "The living room?"

"Yeah, the living room. The bedroom isn't the only place for loving."

"I . . . I . . . just . . ."

Theophilus continued to weave his fingers through her natural hair, softly kissing her eyes. Then, with a tender loving look, he took her hand and led her into the living room, to a comfortable and cozy spot on the floor, between the couch and the coffee table. He sat down and pulled Essie onto his lap, shrugging off his suit coat and fumbling with his shirt and tie. Then he coaxed Essie onto the floor beside him as he unbuckled his pants and, kissing her all the while, removed his socks, undershirt, and shorts.

Essie studied the passion in her husband's face, knowing it had been triggered by the aching in his heart and that he needed this loving for comfort. She started to undress, but Theophilus stopped her and began to unbutton her blouse, slowly and teasingly. He trailed kisses down her neck and chest and stomach. He removed her clothing piece by piece. He stopped to nibble at each expanse of warm flesh he had uncovered. By the time he finished nibbling at her toes and kissed his way back up to her mouth, Essie didn't have a stitch on.

Theophilus gazed into his wife's eyes, telling her "I love you, baby" without saying a word. Essie whispered, "I love you, sugar," in his ear, and he couldn't wait another moment to become one with his beloved wife.

Theophilus reached up and, pulling the quilt off the sofa, wrapped most of it around Essie, who was glowing with the heat of their lovemaking. The sheer ecstasy of it had left them both spent and sleepy.

Half dozing, Theophilus wrapped his arms and legs around Essie and kissed the tip of her ear, murmuring, "Baby."

"Ummm hmmm," she purred, and snuggled closer to him.

"Baby, I was just thinking about your hair and wondering why you don't wear it like that all the time."

"Sugar, you know I can't walk around with a nappy head."

"Why not?"

"Folks at church would have a fit if they saw my hair like this."

"So, let them have a fit. When have you ever worried about what they thought anyway?"

"Well," she sighed. "I've been rocking a few boats at Greater Hope, even today." She told him about Mother Harold's visit, concluding by saying, "I don't need to make matters worse with my hair."

"Aw, Essie, rock the doggone boat. *I* like your hair and that is all that should matter to you. Don't tell me you're afraid to wear it like this."

"Now, when was I ever afraid?" Essie asked, with a chuckle. "Are you daring me?"

"You could call it that," Theophilus said, grinning.

Essie knew that when she stepped up in Greater Hope with a nappy head, all hell would break loose. As she thought whose tongues would be wagging, she started liking the idea of creating a big fuss at church. It would be fun to shake up a few of that old guard.

"I'll take that dare. Deal."

As Theophilus kissed Essie on the forehead to seal the deal, the doorbell rang. He grabbed his watch off the coffee table. It was only 8:30, not too late for a parishioner to come calling with some request. He sighed and started to get up but Essie pushed him back down. "Don't you move. You have had enough for one day. We're not dealing with anybody right now."

"But, baby, what if it's an emergency?"

"This ain't no emergency. If it were, they would have called first, just to make sure you would be ready for them when they got here. No, I'm sure this is about some mess. Never fails—the mess starters always show up in the early morning or late in the evening."

Theophilus leaned back against the couch and started to relax. Essie was right.

"Plus, you're tired, sugar. Walked in this house looking peaked and worn down to the bone."

But whoever it was kept ringing the bell right out of the socket. With a sigh of annoyance, Essie got up and went to put on a robe.

The woman at the door was unfamiliar and looked surprised when Essie answered the door, as if she weren't standing right in her own home. Without even greeting her, the woman walked into the foyer asking, "Where's the Pastor?"

Essie now remembered that the woman worked for Willie Clayton, who had not yet made good on her threat to withdraw from Greater Hope. For the moment, she was thinking she was punishing Theophilus merely by withholding her offerings.

The woman continued looking past Essie like she didn't see her and said, "Pastor available?"

Amazed at her boldness, Essie said, "No, he's not available right now."

"But I saw his car in the driveway, so he must be here."

"Well, he may be here but he ain't available."

The woman now studied Essie more closely and it dawned on her that the First Lady was wearing a robe, probably without a stitch of clothing on underneath it. Essie watched the comprehension build on her face and hoped that her attire was enough to make the woman leave. Unfortunately, it wasn't.

"Sister Clayton sent me over here to give these papers to the Pastor," she said. "Sister Clayton said these papers real important and—"

"Give me the papers," Essie said, holding out her hand. What could be so important that it had to be delivered at 8:30 at night? Whatever was in the papers was sure to make Theophilus mad. It was just like Willie Clayton to give her dirty work to someone else—probably some woman who was stuck on the Pastor and would jump at the chance to see him privately, at home.

The woman just stood there, ignoring her hand.

"I *said* I will take the papers and give them to the Pastor."

Sure enough, the woman looked disappointed. "Well, Sister Clayton told me to put these papers right in the Pastor's hands, and his hands, *only*. So you'll just have to call him because I am not leaving until I do what I came here to do."

Essie had seen some bold women cross her husband's path, but this one was both bold and rude. She moved further into the foyer, as if she meant to push past Essie. A mischievous voice within Essie whispered, "Let her go."

She allowed the woman to elbow her aside and shove her way into the living room. There Theophilus sat, not in a chair, but on the floor, leaning against the couch, draped in a quilt, but obviously just as naked as his wife. The woman blinked hard in disbelief, stammering, "Oh, oh, Rev. Simmons, I needed to give you this but Essie—"

"Who?" Theophilus demanded. "Are you referring to Mrs. Simmons, the First Lady?"

"Well, I—" The woman couldn't bring herself to honor Essie, standing there half naked, with her proper name and title.

"I'm not taking those papers," Theophilus said. "You had a chance to give them to *Miss-us* Simmons"—he

stretched over the syllables—"but that wasn't good
enough for you. So, now you can come to my office
during church business hours like a whole lot of other
folks been doing lately."

He put his hands behind his head and closed his eyes
to show the woman that their conversation was over.

Sister Clayton had warned the woman that the Pastor
wasn't as nice as he seemed. But he had a lot of nerve
trying to throw her out like that.

"You think you bad, don't you, Pastor. Well, keep on
thinking that. Just keep on until the day Sister Clayton
kicks you out of Greater Hope."

Theophilus knew that the threat was idle. The only
one with the authority to remove a pastor in *this* denomination was a bishop. But it didn't surprise him that
Willie Clayton had been telling her people that she was
going to get him kicked out of his pulpit.

For the second time that day, Essie was compelled to
put a troublemaker out of her house. She pointed to the
door, and when the woman didn't move, she said, "If
you don't want to see the heifer in me y'all always talking about come out, you better get going."

As she marched out, the woman stopped to shake the
papers in Essie's face. Essie snatched them out of her
hand, opened the front door, and tossed the papers outside, leaving her to scramble after them as she slammed
the door shut. Then she returned to the living room,
where Theophilus was sitting with his head tipped back
against the couch, with his eyes closed.

She sat down next to him and said, "Theophilus, sugar,
you all right?" She took his hand in hers and rubbed it
comfortingly, as the tears began to creep from under his
closed eyelids.

"Did Mr. Jarvis go home to be with the Lord this evening?"

He nodded yes, putting his head in her lap, and sobbed, telling her how much it hurt that he would never be able to sit and laugh over a Pepsi with Mr. Jarvis anymore.

Essie stroked his hair, thinking that the church was a heavy weight for one man to carry on his shoulders all the time. She sat on the floor holding Theophilus until he fell asleep. Then she put a pillow under his head, covered him up with the quilt, and going into her sewing room, got down on her knees and prayed.

"Lord, the only thing I love more than that man asleep on my living room floor is You. But You know and I know that it's gonna take a whole lot to be the kind of wife You want me to be and the kind of wife he deserves. Help me not to fall short. Teach me, Father, teach me to be the kind of wife You had in mind when You invented wives. Teach me to be the perfect helpmeet. When your son Theophilus is sad, I'm sad, too, Lord. We are one, Father, just as You would have it. I cast all of this pain onto You, Lord, just like the Bible tells me to do. Take this yoke, this burden, and replace it with your peace. Please, Lord, please show me the way to be a good wife."

Chapter Sixteen

ESSIE WAS IN HER SEWING ROOM RIGHT BEFORE SHE left for church, surveying all the unfinished projects hanging on the beautiful purple-painted wooden rack. She loved all colors in the purple family. And there was plenty of it all through the house— lavender, violet, blue violet, magenta, and hot pink. Theophilus always teased her about purple, saying she loved it so much because she was his queen. And the purple item he teased her about the most was a purple-with-shots-of-pink-running-through-it Cadillac convertible, with the white leather interior and whitewall tires that she loved so much.

Essie had never seen a purple car in her life until she spotted it in the window of a car dealership downtown. She kept passing by to look at it, never expecting that a Negro would be welcome in the showroom. Finally one of the salesmen had beckoned her in and personally showed her all of the details of the car. Then one Saturday, she asked if she could test-drive it, knowing full well that such requests were rarely if ever honored for Negroes. But when the salesman surprised her again by agreeing, she returned with Theophilus, who sat in the back with the salesman, talking about the Bible, while Essie drove all over town. She was so happy to drive that exquisite car that she baked the man a sweet potato pie and had Theophilus take it to him the very next day.

And now, for her twenty-seventh birthday, Theophilus shocked her by presenting her with that car. It was an engagement, wedding, birthday, and anniversary present all rolled into one, he told her, adding jokingly, "But I'm sorry, baby—it still didn't cost as much, I'm sure, as that big old diamond ring Saphronia McComb was signifying with and playing the bigshot when she was here, trying to lord it over you."

Essie slid her purple Cadillac into the parking space marked FIRST LADY and pulled to a quick stop, making a little rubber burn, worrying Theophilus over the well-being of those expensive whitewall tires. Her lavender silk suit, accessorized by pale purple sunglasses and a long silver and lavender silk scarf, wrapped loosely around her head and neck, was the perfect look for driving to church in her new Cadillac convertible drop-top.

The first person to see the car was the evening caller Essie had put out of the house a month before. It didn't surprise Essie that she turned on her heel and ran into the church, no doubt carrying the tale straight to Willie Clayton. Essie could well imagine how some folks would carry on about the pastor squandering his money on a purple Cadillac, of all things, for that little slit-eyed, nappy-head heifer he was married to. There had been plenty of sneering, some obvious, some secret, when she showed up last month wearing her hair in a natural. But she got lots of compliments, too.

Whenever they got anything new, some people would get mad, and another faction would get all excited, making a big to-do over how well their pastor and first lady were doing. Those in the mad group always acted like the pastor and first lady had taken money right out of their pockets, and the excited ones seemed to celebrate any new acquisition as their own, as if the pastor and first lady were direct extensions of themselves.

"Umph, umph, umph," Theophilus was saying, holding open the car door. "Baby, what am I going to do with your little fast self this morning?"

Essie just grinned at him. She was feeling real sassy this morning, and as she stepped out of the car, she brushed up against him on purpose.

"Watch yourself. Don't get nothing started you can't finish, now."

Essie laughed at her husband and strutted into church beside him, swinging on his hand not caring who saw her acting "fast." Let those holier-than-thou biddies disapprove of her swinging on her man. One thing she had always done since coming to Greater Hope, as Theophilus's wife, was to let folks see the love and passion, "the juice," flowing between them, just like Theophilus had preached in that sermon that first won her heart at Mount Nebo.

The choir was buzzing today because Mrs. Jarvis was back among them, for the first time since her husband's death. When she moved from the choir to sing, the whole church fell into respectful silence, anticipating her beautiful rendition of the song "I Must Tell Jesus." But she surprised everybody this morning when she sat down at the piano and started singing a song that was the poem she had the pastor read at Mr. Jarvis's funeral. It had been a moving poem, but the melody was so beautiful, folks were moved to tears when Mrs. Jarvis finished the first verse of "Annointed Love."

Theophilus took the pulpit podium during the final strains of the song, directing the organist to keep playing softly after Mrs. Jarvis finished. Then he said, "Church, there ain't nothing the Lord don't know everything about—especially the needs of the human heart. If you believe that, raise your hands high in the air and let the Lord know you need Him. Let the Lord know you want to talk with Him and walk with Him and know that you are His own. Anybody in here this morning need to be with God like that?"

A third of the congregation raised their hands and started praying out loud to God. Caught up in the spirit, Theophilus lifted his own arms high in the air, telling them all, "Church, if you feeling what I'm feeling, you got to give it up to God and start praising Him. Come on! Let's give the Lord shouts of praise up in here!"

Soon the whole congregation was praying and praising, with some speaking in tongues and swaying and calling out "Jesus! Jesus!" Essie had to hold on to the front of her pew, the spirit was running through her so strong. Mrs. Coral Thomas got out in the aisle and started walking back and forth, crying and saying, "Yes, Lord! Yes, Lord!" as D.S. cried and thanked the Lord for his blessings. He kept saying, "I don't know how I would have made it, if you had not brought me through, Jesus." And Theophilus had to hold on to the pulpit, bending over it, acknowledging God's power in his life. The passion, the power of the Holy Ghost were so strong that he set his sermon aside and let the Spirit guide him through the remaining portion of the service.

"Y'all have to know that the Lord don't play after this morning, don't you," he said.

"No," Coral Thomas answered. "The Lord sho' nuff don't play."

"And you know that if God stopped by here this morning, setting off Holy Ghost–filled fire like He did, He means for us to abide by the leading of His spirit."

Mr. D.S. Thomas said, "Yes, Lawd! You talkin' now, boy."

Folks in the congregation started laughing and Theophilus continued, "Now, Lord knows I had a sermon all prepared to preach today. But this morning, the Lord is leading me to open this church up for some testimonies." He tossed the pages of his sermon into the air, back over his shoulders, and just let them scatter on the floor. "Now, church, who has a testimony burning in their heart?"

At first nobody made a move. Theophilus let his eyes roam around the sanctuary, trusting God to let them alight on the person who had the most to say, who just needed a little encouragement from the pastor. Sure enough, when his gaze fell on Mrs. Jarvis, he knew that she had testimony they all needed to hear today. Walking out of the pulpit, he took her by the hand and led her straight to the podium.

Mrs. Jarvis was so full of feeling that she didn't even know if she could get the words out. Sensing her agitation, Theophilus continued to clutch her hand, willing her the courage to begin.

"Giving honor to God and asking all of you to pray my strength," she began, "I want to share with you just what the Lord has done for me. Now there ain't a soul in here who don't know that Jarvis died. And you all know that I always said my Jarvis was a gift from God. That I believed with all of my heart that one of the ways the Lord had blessed me was to let me experience the love of my dear departed husband, Zechariah Jarvis."

Folks in the congregation looked at each other with the same question on their faces and lips: "Mr. Jarvis's name was Zechariah?"

"Jarvis left me to go home. And Lord, Lord, Lord! That thing just about killed me. I been married sixty-five years and I can truly say that each year, from day one to year number sixty-five, were pure joy. Pure blessed joy. And when Jarvis passed on, I thought I would die of a broken heart."

Several of Mrs. Jarvis's close friends nodded, acknowledging how worried they had been and how they had feared, at one point, that she would just shrivel up and die, she was so sad.

"But one night I was laying in bed, face drenched with tears, and I got up and went and sat in Jarvis's favorite chair and just started talking to Jesus. Church, I talked to Jesus like I'm talking to you."

One of the women ushers raised her hands and said, "Chile, that is the *only* way you can really talk to Jesus."

Mrs. Jarvis dropped Theophilus's hand to wipe at the tears that were streaming down her face. Her voice broke when she said, "I was mad at the Lord and told Him that, too. Said, 'Jesus, I know we all have our crosses to bear but this cross is just too much for me. And You said Your burdens were light. Well then, Jesus, if that really is so, why haven't You come through for me and lifted the burden of this pain and sorrow off of my shoulders?' And then, church, you know what I did?

"Church, I got up out that chair and shook my hand

up at the Lord. And I said, 'Jesus, I can't take no more. And, Lord, right now, I don't want to take no more. I can't stand this pain and I want to die. I want You to put me out of my misery and just take me now. Just let the life come out of me and throw this old body down on the floor and let me die.'

"And then, church, I threw my own self on the floor— bumped my head pretty bad, too—and waited to be dead."

The same usher called out, "Chile, you sho' was in some bad shape, throwing your self all on the floor like that."

"Yes, church, I just stayed on that floor like that, waiting to die, hurting so bad, and mad at the Lord. And, church, do you know what my God did? Church, first, the Lord let me sleep. Put me in a deep sleep until the next morning. And when I woke up, the Lord just whispered to me, 'Callie, it ain't your time to go. You had sixty-five years of love, good lovin', and sweet memories. You been blessed with the kind of love I wish all of My children had. Callie, you understand down to the bone what so many only get a glimpse of in their entire lives. Callie, you have a calling while you still here. I want you to teach My children about this kind of love and where it really comes from—Me. All of that love you have for Zechariah got to be shared in this way. And when it get rough, I will comfort you in the way that I know you need comforting.'

"And, church, the Lord gave me that comfort at that very moment. He anointed me and blessed me with the ability to close my eyes and see my sweet Jarvis just like he was sitting right here in front of me. And he gave me a miracle. Made it so I can always close my eyes and hear Jarvis's voice, remember it, just like he standing there when I need to.

"So, church, I stand here today to tell you that God is real. And if you will trust in Him and come to Him with all your troubles, even when you mad at the Lord, He will deliver. He will deliver you. I am a living testimony of that."

She raised her hands high in the air and just started praising God. The spiritual fire radiating from her was so powerful it began to spread out. Theophilus reached out to hug her and felt that fire run all up and down his body, making him cry and thank the Lord for his own blessings. And he wasn't the only one affected—the whole church seemed in tune with the testimony, shouting and praying and crying, sensing the presence of the Lord in their midst.

When the moment finally passed and everyone calmed down, Theophilus dispatched the ushers to collect the morning offering. As they began to circulate through the congregation, he decided it was time to address the gossip that had sprung up the moment Essie had arrived that morning and had spread like wildfire by the time the service began.

"Church, I just want to say something about my wife this morning—about that new purple Cadillac she drove to church. I been hearing little bits and pieces about what you all are thinking and saying and just know in my heart that I need to deal with it before we all leave today.

"First of all, you should know that I bought that car for the First Lady with money I saved from all my extra preaching around Memphis and in Mississippi. Now if I want to work myself like that, while keeping my duties as your pastor, just so I can buy my wife a fancy car, then that is between me, the First Lady, and the Lord. Is that clear, church?"

"Yes, Lord, as clear as a crystal stream in the Bible," one choir member said, drawing chuckles from the congregation.

"But there's another thing I want to tell you today. You've all heard me preach about civil rights, and many of you have contributed to the movement, either on the front lines in Mississippi or in the background here, housing and feeding the workers. That fight is vital, one of the most important struggles in the history of the United States, to win our people the fundamental human right to social and political equality.

"But there is another right we don't talk about as much, and that's the right to economic equality, ensuring that Negroes can lead prosperous lives—and just as importantly, feel worthy to lead prosperous lives. Maybe you're thinking that I sound like Rev. Ike . . ."

Laughter erupted here and there in the church, but most people were listening expectantly.

"That's right. I have to agree with Rev. Ike on those points—I believe that Negroes are entitled to some good living while we are here on God's earth. For Rev. Ike, prosperity might mean six Cadillacs and a twenty-room house, but to me it's more complicated than that. True prosperity means knowing in your heart that God will help you and meet your need whenever and whatever that may be. Of course it's also a good thing when you are in your right mind, being loved, feeling good, eating good food—having spiritual well-being as well as a little more money than just enough to get by. It's good to have a comfortable home, a good woman, a few good suits, a reliable and decent-looking car—"

"Like that purple Cadillac," one of the old men cackled.

"Yes, like that," Theophilus said. "But most of all, to be prosperous, a man needs to have the Lord, not material goods, planted firmly in the center of his heart."

Chapter Seventeen

UGUST 1963 AND THE TRIENNIAL CONFERENCE
rolled around so fast, Essie and Theophilus
found themselves scrambling around at the last
minute, struggling to get ready. It seemed like
their entire church was going, and both of the rented buses
had filled up fast. For Theophilus, the conference would
be a professional and a personal watershed. Sister Willie
Clayton was now waging an all-out war against him—
which couldn't hurt him as long as he had the protection
of Bishop Jennings—but it was hurting Rev. James, his
mentor, who was running for bishop. Willie had invested
a considerable sum to defeat Rev. James and was back-
ing Rev. Ernest Brown, Marcel's father.

With all the trouble that was brewing, Essie and
Theophilus decided to drive down to the conference
alone, in her car, rather than with the Thomases or other
members of the congregation. They needed to pull together their spiritual resources.

One consolation was that the conference was being

held in Theophilus's hometown, Richmond, Virginia. Essie's folks—Lee Allie, Uncle Booker, Mrs. Neese, and Mr. Pompey—along with Mr. D.S. and Mrs. Coral Thomas, were all staying with his mother and father. He couldn't imagine where they would put everybody, but Larnetta, his mother, put his mind at ease. "Baybro, we are country folks. We'll manage just fine. In fact, with good company like Coral, D.S., and Essie's people, I'd say we'll be doing better than just fine."

Essie and Theophilus were going to stay with his sister, Thayline, and her husband, Willis. But they were still an hour away when Theophilus, exhausted from preparing for the conference and from driving most of the way, felt too beat to go another mile. He switched places with Essie, and by the time they reached Thayline's house, he was sound asleep.

Essie turned off the engine and pushed on his shoulder to wake him up. He didn't budge. She pushed on him some more and then poked him with her elbow, catching a relaxed spot on his arm, where his biceps were usually hard and pushing up against the sleeves of his shirt.

"Ouch! Baby? Why you poking me in my arm like that?"

"Wake up, we're at Thay's house."

Hearing the car roll in, Thayline and Willis came out of the house. Willis came down off the porch and started unloading their luggage as Thayline, a female version of her little brother, pulled her housecoat around herself and said, "Baybro, you planning on spending the night in the car? Or can you get out and help us with these bags—half of which I believe belong to you?"

Theophilus didn't say anything to his sister. He didn't like hearing his sister's mouth. Thayline had been getting on him about one thing or another since they were little kids. He sat up, rubbed his chin and moved his jaw muscles around for a few seconds.

Essie opened her door and got out, causing Theophilus, who had been leaning against her, to fall over on the seat.

"Baby, why you let me drop down like that?"

Essie just looked at him, fighting the urge to roll her eyes. "I'm tired and not in the mood to hear any mess from you," she said.

"That's right," Thayline contributed. "The rest of us are tired, just like you, Theophilus."

Finally Theophilus got out of the car, grumbling to himself. "First Essie poking me in my arm and Thay worrying me about some luggage and everybody complaining because they're tired . . ."

He was still annoyed that Essie had poked him so hard and it made him crankier still that she had spoken to him so sharply. He wondered what was eating at her.

The smell of coffee, pancakes, and bacon wafted its way up Essie's nose, luring her out of a heavy slumber into that drifting-in-and-out phase of sleep. At first she couldn't tell if the bacon and pancake smells were real or part of her dreams. But the weight of the brown leg swung casually over her hip let her know that she was awake and those smells were as real as the man lying next to her. The breeze circulating around the room from the open window was chilly. She pulled the spread up over her shoulders.

Theophilus moved around and pulled her into the warm spot between his legs, letting his fingers travel leisurely down her bare arms and the length of her back to rest around the contours of her bottom. A soft sigh escaped from his lips as he pressed her body into his, enjoying the feel of her own soft warmth up next to him. He rolled over on his back and pulled Essie on top of him, making the bed creak loudly from the combined weight of his body and hers.

"What's wrong?" he whispered in her ear when he realized how tense she had become.

"The bed creaks every time you move around."

"And?" he murmured, pulling at the narrow strap of her pale yellow nightgown.

"And someone might hear us."

"Hear what?" he said, his voice half filled with sleep, half filled with desire. "You think somebody might hear me in this room with my wife? Is that what they will hear, Essie?"

"Well . . ." she said kind of hesitantly.

"Well, you worry too much," he said softly, and pulled one of her legs up so that her knee rested on the side of his waist.

Essie relaxed a little and Theophilus pulled the opposite knee up to his waist and whispered, "Is that quiet enough for you?"

When she didn't say anything, he pulled the nightgown up to her waist, slipped his hands inside her underwear and wrapped his hands around her bare bottom. He always wondered why his wife wore panties under such sexy nightgowns—especially those come-up-to-the-waist cotton panties she seemed so fond of sleeping in. He knew that as long as he lived, he would never fully understand the ways and thinking of women.

He was about to ease off her underwear when Thayline yelled from the kitchen. "Baybro! Baby doll! Breakfast almost ready. You two better get up and come eat before your food starts to get cold."

"Shoot," Theophilus growled. His sister had the worst timing of anyone he knew.

Essie pulled away from him and said, "We'll be right there, Thay."

Theophilus sat up in the bed watching Essie get herself straight. He decided that he would take his time so Thay would know he was not happy.

Essie threw his robe over to him, shaking her head at him for sitting there acting like a spoiled brat. She thought to herself, "Now, this is the same man who just told me that he was ready to take over the pastorship of the church in St. Louis, if Bishop Jennings sends him there by the end of this conference. And here he is sitting on the bed with his lips poked out like he's thirteen years old."

Theophilus saw the look on Essie's face and got up and put on his robe. He decided acting funky wasn't such a good idea after all. He wanted to stay on her good side so that he could get a full serving of good loving later.

Essie handed Thayline the last skillet to be washed and then went and pulled the dirty linens off the table. She dropped the napkins on a chair and shook out the tablecloth, dumping crumbs on the blue and yellow linoleum floor.

Thay looked over her shoulder and said, "Baby doll, just put those old things over there in that corner. I'll throw them in the washing machine a little later."

Essie looked around. "Where's your broom?"

"It's over there in the broom closet."

Essie opened the yellow closet door and pulled out a yellow broom with a black rubber handle on it.

"Baby doll, you think you gonna like St. Louis?"

Essie stopped sweeping. There had been a lot of talk lately among Theophilus, Bishop Jennings, and Rev. James about St. Louis, but she didn't know if they were going or not. So much of the decision to send Theophilus to St. Louis depended on whether or not Rev. James was elected bishop at this conference. How would Thay know they were going?

"You sound awfully sure about all of this, Thay," she said. "Know something I don't know?"

"No, just a feeling I got—can't shake it, either. You know how I get those sensations running up and down my spine when something's up."

Thay was famous for those feelings. The last time she had one, Theophilus had proposed to her at that wild anniversary dinner his church held at Mabel's Kitchen. But Essie didn't want Thayline's premonition to be right this time. Garrison Temple in St. Louis had so much in-fighting going on inside its four sacred walls that the current pastor was asking to be moved to another church, any church, anywhere. This was not the kind of church, despite its size and level of prestige, one begged to be appointed to.

"You don't want to go, do you, baby doll?"

Essie didn't say anything, just moved the broom around a little pile of trash.

"You know, baby doll, I thought you'd be relieved to leave Greater Hope. I never thought you'd want to stay at a church where one of the members wouldn't let a soul forget she slept with your husband. What woman would? That Glodean Benson is nothing but a crazy tramp—"

Essie was so quiet that Thayline looked over to check on her. There were heavy tears rolling down Essie's cheeks.

"Me and my big mouth. Baby doll, I didn't mean for that to come out like it did. You know I wouldn't want to say something to hurt you like that."

Essie put the broom against the wall and sat down. "It's not you, Thay. But I wonder what's going on with Theophilus lately. He has been nicer to Glodean, and once or twice I've even heard him talking to her on the telephone, asking her if she was all right. And right before we left for Richmond, I found these in the glove compartment of my new car."

Essie dug down in the pocket of her robe and pulled out a glamorous-looking pair of pink sunglasses with rhinestones sprinkled around the rim. She handed the glasses to Thayline, who also had to acknowledge who they belonged to. No one would wear sunglasses like those except Glodean.

"What else do you know about this, baby doll?" Thayline asked.

"Only," Essie said, blowing her nose, "only that he called me from the church one evening and said not to wait up for him. Had something pressing to take care of—and the next morning, I found these. Thayline, *why* would my husband let *that* woman ride in my car? How—"

"You know for sure she was in the car, baby doll?"

"I'm sure," Essie said. "Her perfume . . . I smelled it as soon as I got in my car."

Thay put her arm around Essie's shoulders and let her cry. She knew she was angry with her brother not for fooling around with that nasty heifer—he couldn't stand her she knew—but for having contact with that thang and not telling Essie why.

"Baby doll, does Baybro know you upset about this?"

"He doesn't even know I found the sunglasses," she confessed.

"Why didn't you ask him? You always speak your mind. Why hold on to some mess like this now?"

"I don't want Theophilus to think that I can't handle Glodean and her mess. You should see how some of the women in our church get all up in his face. They will come up to him and act like I'm not even standing there—grinning and asking for crazy mess like special, private prayer sessions with him at their house. One fool even had the nerve to request a private baptism at her house in her bathtub.

"But Glodean Benson is something else. It's like she got some big secret on Theophilus. Make me feel like she know things about him that I don't even know how to find out, let alone know."

"What kind of things?" Thay asked, getting madder at her brother about this mess. He *knew* better.

"You know, Thay . . . like she know his real love secrets or something. Like she did something to him in bed that nobody else figured out how to do and he liked it a whole lot."

Thayline moved away from Essie and put her hands on her hips. "Now you just hush your mouth and quit talking like that. You hear me, baby doll?"

Essie looked up at Thay, a bit surprised by the harshness in her voice.

"First off, don't you ever let a woman make you think she know more about your husband than you do. And I don't care if the woman was his first wife! You hear me, Essie Lee?"

Essie nodded.

"That thang don't have no direct line into what makes the earth move for Baybro. You better get to remembering that you the only woman who got that kind of power over my brother now. Girl, all you got to do is swing those doll-baby hips a certain way and Baybro get a little sweat on his top lip like he do when he really want something."

Essie laughed through her tears. She had seen that sweat on his lip many times when there was something Theophilus really wanted—be it loving, cake, a piece of fried chicken, or ice water when it was real hot outside.

"I see you know what I'm talking about—thought you did. And if you know that, you make Baybro stop those women from careening around him like that. You give him some hell about it and he'll put a stop to it. Sometimes a man needs a little push in the right direction—even a good one, with a good heart like my baby brother.

"And, baby doll, you get him straight before you move to St. Louis. From what Mother been telling me, that church is filled with some mess out of this world. The two of you gonna have to be on one accord when you get there. And you gone have to walk up in that congregation with an 'I'm the First Lady and don't you people forget it' look written all over your face the very first Sunday you get there."

Essie recognized the wisdom of what Thayline was telling her. She knew she would have to say something to Theophilus but didn't know how or when. She was telling him, though. She wasn't putting up with any mess from Glodean or any other crazy woman anymore.

"How many votes do you think you have coming to you next Friday, Rev. James?"

Murcheson shrugged his shoulders. He was tired. This campaign for bishop was taking its toll on him. He hadn't been all that eager to run for bishop anyway. He was happy at Mount Nebo and there was such nasty politics involved in the race for an episcopal seat, plus the money it took to run a successful campaign for bishop could cost tens of thousands of dollars. Rev. James had seen more than one church go heavily into debt, incurring large second and even third mortgages, just to sponsor the aspirations of one man. He had refused when first asked to run for bishop, and he still refused to put the financial well-being of his church in jeopardy to win an episcopal seat.

But it was this very attitude that made Murcheson James the ideal choice for bishop for many people in the denomination. A lot of folks were fed up with bishops who acted like they owned the Gospel United Church and wanted a preacher elected who would treat the office as sacred. Their strong urging convinced Murcheson James to lay aside his misgivings and ultimately led him to believe that the Lord had called him to run for this office. And it was only this belief that gave him the courage to enter this race and embark upon an aggressive campaign to get elected bishop.

It seemed to Theophilus that Rev. James was taking a long time to answer his question. But then it struck him that they were surrounded by preachers, all of whom probably had big ears and their own allegiances. Rev. James seemed to read his thoughts and said, "Son, why don't we take a stroll around the campus. Be good for both of us after sitting in that hot chapel all morning."

When they were at a decent distance from the other preachers, Rev. James confided, "Theophilus, I think I have 817 delegate votes I can count on."

Theophilus gave a low whistle. "How did you manage that? You only need 925 to win."

"Remember when I went to Atlanta for a meeting with SCLC? Well, I had a long lunch with Bishop Jennings there. He pledged his support and immediately started working for me. Said he was impressed with all my civil rights work and the day-care programs I've been getting started in Mississippi. Also said the Board of Bishops needed a preacher with a good track record for faithfully serving the people—a man like me."

A group of women who were at Virginia Union University for a special pre–Triennial Conference missionary meeting now approached, and when they saw Rev. James, some of them nudged the others, pointing him out as one of the pastors running for bishop. Theophilus was almost surprised that they recognized him, for Rev. James was an extremely modest and unassuming, plain and down-to-earth man, with a keen intellect and a fondness for suits that were just a little bit worn, for comfort. And when he wasn't working at church, he could be found in overalls working his land, happy, content, and talking out loud to the Lord about everything from women and birthing babies to questions about why one seed made a flower and another seed made corn.

A light brown woman with long reddish hair walked right up to Rev. James and extended a pale-lavender-gloved hand toward him. She took a deep breath that made her breasts swell, looked into Rev. James's eyes, and said in a dramatic and breathy voice, "I'm Mae Wilson and I've been trying to meet you during this conference."

Rev. James looked at the woman like she was crazy. He looked her over, not to assess how good she looked—she was light-skinned, long and slender, a marked contrast to his wife, Susie, who was full-figured and brown-skinned—but to better measure her character, or lack of it.

"Mrs.?"

"Miss, Reverend. I must confess that I live the single life because I have not been so blessed as to meet a man like you."

At first Rev. James was taken aback by her boldness. But he quickly recovered his composure and told her, "Miss Wilson, I'm not sure what it is I should be saying to you. But, I *am* sure of this. You need to get out of my face and go spend some time with Jesus. And if you need some extra help with praying, my wife, Susie, is a powerful woman of God and a prayer warrior. She will be more'n happy to pray with and for you."

Mae Wilson's smile froze on her face. She tried to wiggle away from his rebuke, saying, "Uhh, Rev. James, I am late for my next meeting and don't have time to finish this conversation about your wife and prayer."

Rev. James gestured at her departing figure. "I'd bet some of Booker's dog track money, she the kind of woman always got to shout when service get going good. And she a bigger she-devil than some old hoochie-coochie gal out in those streets. And I don't know why some of these women think a man always wanting some old lanky, high-yellow girl. Son, give me a fine chocolate gal like my Susie any night. That woman definitely a handful. And a handful is just what this here old country boy needs."

Theophilus started laughing. They set off walking again.

"You were telling me about Bishop Jennings. What does he have to do with all of these votes?"

"Theophilus, most of the delegates like Percy

Jennings. He's honest, smart, and a good bishop. Plus, as the next senior bishop, he has an enormous amount of power and there are people who want to stay in his favor. All he did was make a few phone calls, and next thing I knew, the pledged votes came rollin' in. Have to tell you, though, when I first started this campaign, thought I'd have to run more than once just to make a dent. But when Percy Jennings got behind me everything fell in place. He definitely wants me over the district for St. Louis and to send you with me as the new pastor for Garrison Temple. Said as big a mess goin' on in St. Louis, Garrison, or if he get his way, Freedom Temple, got what it takes to be a model church in this denomination."

Theophilus stopped walking and faced Rev. James.

"I've been having second thoughts about Garrison Temple. I'm happy in Memphis and not so sure I want to go to St. Louis with all of the mess going on in that church."

"You lyin' through your teeth, boy," Rev. James said as he leaned toward him and continued in a very quiet voice. "I can only wonder how you are so happy pastoring a church with a snake in the grass like Willie Clayton and that there Glodean Benson buggin' you, messin' with Essie, and with the two of them reporting everything to that viper, Sonny Washington, who run and tell that crazy Otis Caruthers everything he know about you.

"Look, I'm your mentor and friend. I'm not leaving you in Memphis and neither is Bishop Jennings. You need to grow and you can't do it at Greater Hope. There some good people there but it was a trainin' ground for something bigger. Whether you know this or not, Theophilus, you got what it takes to be a future force in this denomination. Bishop Jennings grooming you for an episcopal seat, boy."

"And you think sending me to a church where the current pastor was hospitalized for nervous exhaustion is where I will grow into my potential, Rev. James?" Theophilus asked.

"Boy, that man don't have what you got. Nice man, but he can't handle no church that big and complex. I agree with Bishop Jennings. If Garrison gone become Freedom Temple, it will only do so under your leadership. Trust me on this one, son."

It was just like when he was assigned to Greater Hope, Theophilus thought. He believed that the decision was his to make, but it looked like much more powerful hands—the hands of the Master, a power far greater than Rev. James and Bishop Jennings—were pulling the strings. All he could do was go along, praying every step of the way.

Chapter Eighteen

SSIE SAT BACK IN THE COMFORTABLE BLUE COR-
duroy chair and finished stitching up the black,
burgundy, and silver silk cummerbund she had
made for Theophilus's tuxedo. The banquet they
were attending this Friday evening was by special invitation only, and she wanted to make sure he looked his
best. She turned over the cummerbund and examined it
carefully to make sure that every hand-stitched thread
was invisible to the eye. Essie was a superb seamstress
and this cummerbund, along with the matching tie and
handkerchief, would distinguish her husband's tuxedo
from everybody else's. She knew that even though men
acted like they didn't look at each other's clothes, they
did—almost as hard and critically as some women.

Theophilus walked into the bedroom with a big blue
towel wrapped around his waist. He dug around in the
suitcase lying on the bed for a pair of boxer shorts, an
undershirt, and a pair of black silk dress socks. He
splashed on some cologne and selected a pair of black

onyx cuff links that were trimmed with sterling silver and had a tiny garnet nestled in the center of the onyx stone.

Still wearing only her slip, Essie ran a warm iron over the bow tie and cummerbund, then lay them on the bed. She now pulled a pair of silk stockings out of her lavender hosiery bag, and Theophilus stopped dressing to watch her roll the stockings up her shapely legs and hook them to her ivory lace garter belt. She walked over to the garment bag hanging on the door and pulled out her dress. It was champagne silk chiffon, with tiny rhinestones shimmering across a bodice that was cut snugly around the breasts and held up with dainty-looking spaghetti straps. From its Empire waist, it fell to just above the knee and moved softly around the contours of her body when she walked. The finishing touch was its matching, flowing oblong scarf that gave the dress a sophisticated and dramatic flair.

"Baby, you outdid yourself this time," Theophilus said as she stepped into the dress.

She stood up and adjusted the straps on her shoulders. He came around behind her to zip up her dress and planted a soft kiss on the back of her neck, saying, "I sure wish I was pulling this little number down instead of up."

Essie swatted at him and slipped on her champagne satin pumps, dropping the matching purse on the bed.

"Is my lipstick and makeup all right?" she asked.

"Um hmm. But you need to change those earrings."

"Change my earrings? I thought you said these earrings looked good with the dress. I don't have another pair of earrings to wear with this outfit."

"Yes you do," he said, retrieving a small box from

his suitcase and extricating a pair of gold filigree and diamond teardrop earrings.

He placed the earrings in Essie's hand.

"I picked these up right before we left Memphis. Been saving them for something special. You like them?"

Essie's eyes filled up with tears, and she threw the earrings on the floor.

Theophilus was shocked. "Baby, what in the world is your problem? I buy you a gift and you throw it on the floor?"

Without saying a word, Essie walked over to her suitcase. She bent over it, with her back to him, so he couldn't see what she was doing until she turned around to face him wearing a pair of pink—

"Oh Jesus!"

"Don't call on Him. That's all you can say about these glasses, Theophilus?"

". . . Baby . . ."

"Shut up!" she snapped, and, snatching the glasses off her face, threw them on the floor and stomped on them, crying, "Ever since I have been with you, Glodean Benson has been right there with me. Nothing I do can be done without that woman sniffing around my life with my man. And now you go and make it worse by putting . . ."

Essie was so hurt and mad that she couldn't speak for a moment. Theophilus walked over to her and was about to put his arm around her shoulder when she whipped her arm back and slapped him so hard that it made him stumble.

"You put that woman in my car," she finished.

"Baby—"

"You, Reverend Theophilus Henry Simmons, put *that* WOMAN IN MY CAR! . . . How could you?"

"Essie," Theophilus said in his most authoritative, preacher voice. "Sit down and let me tell you what happened. I can't stand to see you upset like this."

He rubbed his cheek, which felt like it was on fire, hoping it wouldn't look all swollen and bruised by the time they got to the banquet. He looked at Essie, wondering where she hid all that strength in her tiny hands.

When Essie refused to budge, Theophilus took her by the arms and forcibly sat her down on the edge of the bed. "Don't you move," he said. "I don't have any more patience. Don't get up off that bed."

She rolled her eyes at him but stayed where she was.

"Essie, I put Glodean in your car to take her to the hospital. I was in the office and she showed up with her lip busted, two black eyes, and a ripped dress."

Essie opened her mouth to say "Sonny Washington" when he continued, "Yeah, Sonny. Always heard he beat on his women. But didn't think he would do it to Glodean—acting like he was so crazy about her."

Essie relaxed some. She thought back to the first time she met Glodean at Mabel's Kitchen. She remembered the look on Sonny Washington's face and thought that he looked like he wanted to hit on her.

Theophilus saw her face relax and sat down next to her and took her hands in his.

"Baby, Sonny been whipping Glodean for a while. She's been hiding it from folks, especially her aunt, Willie Clayton. But this last time, he beat her pretty bad, and right in that alley in the back of the church. And I didn't even hear anything—there was so much noise coming from the men working on the roof. Anyway, from what Glodean told me, Sonny drove into that alley, dragged her out of the car and said, 'I'm gone beat the black off your tail, and right in front of your *pastor.* And if he comes out here to stop me, I will beat the hell out of him, too.' And then he started beating on her, thinking that I would come out there. But since I didn't hear anything, he got more frustrated and threw her down on the ground and walked toward his car.

"She stayed on the ground when he got back in his car, and when she was sure he was gone, she got up and came to my office. I took her straight to the hospital in your car, because it was right out back and she didn't want anyone to see her. I didn't want to, but Glodean needed to see a doctor bad. She must have dropped those glasses on the floor, and I didn't see them. And Essie, as soon as I got her settled at the hospital, I called Mr. D.S. Thomas and told him to come and take her home when the doctor was through with her. That's what happened, baby. It's the honest-to-God truth."

Essie looked Theophilus in the eyes, making sure he knew that she believed him, though she doubted that Glodean, even all beat-up and bleeding, would accidentally leave those glasses in her car. She was crazy, and she was spiteful. But Sonny Washington was downright dangerous, beating a woman like that and expecting to get away with it. This denomination needed some serious changes. No way a man like that had any business running a church.

"Theophilus," Essie said with tears in her eyes, "I don't understand why you kept that from me. Don't you know how much I love you?"

Those words, spoken so softly and with so much emotion, tore through his heart. What was he thinking to believe not telling her would spare her feelings?

"Baby, I am sorry. Didn't want to upset you but—"

"Shhh . . ." Essie said, placing her fingertips to his

lips. "You can't protect me from hurts that come from your church. But you can do your best to be honest with me. Nothing hurts more than to be kept in the dark. Well . . . putting Glodean in my Cadillac, that might hurt more."

Theophilus winced, more from what Essie said than the increasing pain in his cheek. He would need to put an icepack on it before they left.

Chapter Nineteen

THE BANQUET WAS HELD AT RICHMOND'S NEGRO Masonic Hall, which was decorated lavishly with purple and silver ribbon streamers on the walls and windows, purple satin tablecloths with large silver, gold, and white floral arrangements on each table, and a huge purple, silver, and black banner hanging over the stage that read, WELCOME BISHOPS TO THE 1963 TRIENNIAL CONFERENCE OF THE GOSPEL UNITED CHURCH—LARGEST NEGRO CHURCH IN AMERICA!

"Theophilus, you know I love purple, but does every single thing have to be dripping in it?" Essie asked, closing the door to the banquet hall after taking a quick look inside to satisfy her curiosity about this affair.

"I guess it makes sure we never forget that bishops are the linchpins of the denomination."

"Bishops are the linchpins? Seems to me that church folks hold this denomination together, not these purple-loving men."

Theophilus frowned at her. "You behave yourself

tonight, Essie. This room is full of 'purple-loving men' who don't take too kindly to being criticized and especially by a woman."

Essie blew air out of her mouth in disgust. She knew he was right. She adjusted the scarf around her neck and started to walk into the hall when he stopped her, saying, "Just a minute, baby. Wait here for me. I have to use the men's room."

Essie moved out of the entranceway to stand near a long table where two young ministers sat, checking new arrivals' names against the guest list. Overseeing them was a big man, who looked Essie over with harsh disapproval on his face. The invitations had specified that women were to dress all in white, so he figured that lone woman in the lobby wearing a champagne dress had to be someone who didn't belong here. He came and loomed over her, hoping she got the unspoken message to leave.

Essie glared at him for coming up on her, but did not shrink back.

"Mister, is there some problem?" she asked.

"There definitely is a problem," Laymond Johnson said. "Why don't you come over here by the door so I can explain it to you? I don't think you want me to say it in front of these Reverends."

Essie stood her ground. She put one hand on her hip and stared at him defiantly.

"You don't belong in here," he said. "This dinner is for special people and not women like you."

"Women like me?"

"Yeah, women like you who come here to tempt the first godly man they come across for reasons only the ungodly can truly understand."

Essie was appalled. Here was a supposed churchgoing man at a church function talking to her like the old drunk men from Pompey's Rib Joint. She whispered to herself, "Lord, please don't let this devil make me lose my religion at this fancy dinner."

Laymond Johnson heard her prayer and resented being called a devil. He decided right then and there that he was throwing her out of the hall, ignoring the waves of one of the ministers, who was trying to signal him that Essie *was* a special invited guest. He took a quick step toward her.

Essie drew up her pocketbook, ready to take a swing at him.

"Baby? You all right?" Theophilus was on his way back when he spotted his wife poised to beat up a big man with her new purse.

He hurried over, and the big fool turned around to see who was talking, only to discover that it was that young up-and-coming pastor from Memphis, looking real unhappy.

"You know her, Reverend?" he asked, with sarcastic innuendo in his voice.

Theophilus was furious. "Yeah, I know her," he said in a flat, hard voice with the menace of the street in it. "I know her well. I know her as my future babies' mama. And I know she hasn't done a single thing to warrant this mess from you."

He squared off his shoulders, and Essie sucked in her breath when he dropped one shoulder, tilted his head to the side, and flicked his thumb across his nose, looking like he was going to whip up on this man.

"And," Theophilus continued, "I know that if you do not apologize to *my wife*, I will whip your behind right here at this banquet in front of all your bishops. That's what I know."

Essie reached up and tapped Theophilus on the shoulder to distract him. She knew that he must be blind with anger to shout at the man like he was doing, especially at a church function. He would be angry with himself if he completely lost his cool and whipped this man's behind.

He looked down at her, saying, "I'm okay, baby. I'm okay," then turned his attention back to Laymond Johnson.

Laymond didn't want to apologize to this woman but he was scared of this preacher, who, even in that fancy tuxedo, looked like a formidable opponent. If his wife had come here looking like the rest of the ministers' and bishops' wives, they wouldn't be having this problem.

Theophilus repeated, "I am waiting for your apology and will commence to whipping your tail unless I hear it now."

Laymond's face was swollen with resentment. Against his will, he said, "I apologize to you, miss."

"It's Mrs. Simmons," Theophilus said in a tight, nasty voice.

"Mrs. Simmons."

Laymond turned toward Theophilus. "And, I am very sorry, Reverend, for mistaking your wife for the wrong type of woman. I hope you have enough Christian charity in your heart to forgive me."

Theophilus hated to let him off the hook, thinking he deserved to be taught a lesson on how to treat the women in this church. But he said, "I'll do my best," pulling at Essie's arm. "Come on, baby, let's go find our table."

But Essie couldn't resist looking back at that man, and when her eyes fell on his white, fake leather shoes, she whispered, "You nasty, cheap-shoes-wearing thang." The threatening look he gave her, when he was absolutely certain that Theophilus could not see him, told her that he heard what she said.

Theophilus gently pulled Essie along with him, saying, "Let it go, baby."

The huge banquet hall was designed for a big crowd, but to Essie's surprise, there were only little more than a hundred people present. All of the men scattered among the tables were wearing tuxedos, and virtually all the women wore white—white chiffon, white brocade, white satin, white lace, white silk. The women like herself, the ones wearing something other than plain white, were in the extreme minority.

Some of those white gowns were pretty—pretty enough to break the monotony of the sea of white and capture the eye. But most of them lacked color—not color like red, orange, peach, but some character, some sparkle, something that made the woman wearing the dress look good, exciting, and colorful herself. It was no wonder the man in the lobby zeroed in on her. Her dress had such a distinctive quality about it, it was impossible *not* to notice her.

When Theophilus had told Essie that the invitation requested that all the women wear white, she scoffed and said, "I'm wearing whatever I think looks good on me." When he questioned her stubbornness, she asked him if he thought Susie James would walk in the banquet dressed like everybody else. He then raised his hands in surrender.

Tonight, even some of the men had violated the dress code by wearing white, light blue, navy, beige, and even red dinner jackets instead of black tuxedos. And of course, a few of the bishops could not resist wearing their purple clerical shirts with the tuxedos, just to emphasize their elevation above all the other preachers in the hall.

Finally, Rev. James saw Theophilus and Essie and guided Susie over to where they were standing. "Boy, what y'all been doin' out in the lobby all this time? Susie here saw Essie peeking in the door at least twenty minutes ago."

"Essie had a run-in with one of Bishop Caruthers's flunkies while I was in the men's room."

"Rev. James, that nasty man had the nerve to imply that I was one of those temple women," Essie explained.

Rev. James looked confused. "Temple women, Essie?"

"You know, one of those women who are always trying to go with a preacher."

"She means a temple prostitute," Theophilus said, getting angry all over again because he knew Essie was right.

"Well," Susie said in her husky voice. "Ain't no need for us to spend time getting upset over that trashy fool, now is there? We all looking good and might as well try and enjoy this old dry-as-toast banquet as best we can."

Essie had been right about Susie's outfit, which was not white but an exquisite beige and powder puff pink silk brocade evening gown. The tailored coat was beige with pink lapels, pink flaps on the pockets, and pink pearl buttons on the sleeves and down the front of the jacket. Underneath was a sleeveless beige top that rested on the hip of the matching long skirt with a slit up the back. She wore pearlescent pink pumps and a string of pale pink pearls with matching earrings that made her pretty brown skin shimmer, and her wavy brown hair was pulled up into a smooth French roll held together with pale pink, jeweled hairpins that glittered when she moved her head.

"Rev. James, that gown Mrs. James is wearing isn't shortchanging anybody tonight," Theophilus said.

"Sho' ain't. But it should look good, as much as she paid for it."

"Well, it looks like it was worth every penny Mrs. James spent on it," Essie said as she reexamined the gown.

"It certainly is worth every penny I spent on it and this man knows it," said Susie James. "He wanna fuss about my clothes, but don't you know, he want me lookin' good when he take me out of Charleston."

"We need to go sit down. Bishop Jennings is over there waiting for us," Rev. James said, with some impatience in his voice. He and Susie always fussed about her expensive clothes.

But as they were walking to their seats, Essie took a good look at Rev. James. For all his fussing about fancy-pants expensive clothes, he had let Mrs. James dress him in a beige brocade dinner jacket that matched her gown to a tee.

Vivian Jennings, who was sparkling in an incredible ivory bugle-beaded gown, got up and gave both Essie and Theophilus a big hug, enveloping them in a cloud of Joy perfume. She was a beautiful woman, tall and shapely, who looked so much like Nancy Wilson that when she opened her mouth to speak, Essie was always surprised to hear her soft, light tone instead of the Nancy Wilson voice she was expecting.

Bishop Jennings shook Theophilus's hand and then took both of Essie's hands in his, held her at arm's length, and said, "Looks like this little lady plans on putting the rest of our sisters to shame with this dress. I hope you know you're a lucky man, Rev. Simmons.

Just a couple of years ago I was trying to help you find a good woman and look what the good Lord helped you find all by yourself."

Essie tried not to smile because she knew it would make Theophilus mad. Bishop Jennings always teased him about the time he tried to help him find a wife from the pulpit at the Tennessee/Mississippi Annual Conference back in '61.

The bishop and his wife sat down in chairs in the middle of the long banquet table and motioned for everyone to sit close together so they could talk without being overheard. "I invited you good people to this banquet because I want you to get a bird's-eye view of how bishops are really elected in your church," he told them. "You see, this banquet has been held at the Triennial Conference for over twenty years. And, with few exceptions, just about every pastor who has been elected a bishop was introduced at this affair. It has become something of a rite of passage for those who join the ranks of the episcopacy."

"Bishop Jennings, I thought the election of bishops was scheduled for next Friday," Theophilus said. "I mean, how can they select a bishop without the consent of the delegates? Isn't that why we went through so much trouble selecting delegates? To vote for our bishops?"

"Bishops and prominent pastors can influence the selection of bishops, Rev. Simmons, by soliciting pledged votes from delegates long before we come to the Triennial Conference. But the delegates who have not been approached for a pledged vote will most likely vote for the men who tonight have gathered enough pledges for votes to convince everybody that they have what it takes to secure the 925 votes needed to become an elected bishop. Once these men are introduced to this crowd, someone will leave the banquet and report to the delegates who is hot. And once that happens, that election will simply ratify what was done here this evening."

"But—"

"But, Rev. Simmons, this is how *it is,* not how it is *supposed* to be. Just look around this room and think of all the good men in the denomination you know are running for bishop and are not here this evening."

Theophilus looked around the room at who was there. Bishop Jennings was right. With the exception of Rev. James, all the other pastors he thought would make good bishops were absent.

"Then why didn't you invite any of them, Bishop?"

"My political strength rests pretty much within the parameters of my district. Once you travel outside it, you run into another bishop's territory. And unless he is an ally, you can hang up politicking for any support in his district. You see, most of a bishop's power comes from who he can get to support him. Take Rev. Ernest Brown. Lord knows, he has no business trying to be anybody's bishop. But he has that Michigan machine run by Bishop Lawson Giles behind him, and he will be recognized tonight as one of the pastors with enough pledged votes to win an episcopal seat."

"You really think Ernest Brown will win a bishop's seat at this conference?"

"I don't think, Rev. Simmons, I know. Lawson Giles has been grooming Ernest Brown for years—moving him to the right churches, introducing him to the right folks in Detroit and throughout Michigan, and taking him along to any important function in his district. Bishop Giles knows that Ernest wants this so bad, he will uphold everything Lawson does once he gets elected.

And that is a shame, since anything Lawson does is guaranteed to line his pockets at the expense of the denomination."

Bishop Jennings stopped talking because waiters had arrived to serve their dinner. Essie was hungry, so she was disappointed to find that, at this out-of-the-ordinary banquet, the food was the standard fare—baked chicken, string beans, small red potatoes, salad with too much iceberg lettuce and not enough tomatoes, rolls that needed heating, sweet potato pie, iced tea, and coffee. Then there was the long-winded prayer that went on and on and on and on while everybody was waiting to eat, a solo by the most revered soprano at the most prestigious Gospel United Church in the city, comments (mini-sermons for a few) by prominent pastors in the audience, and the soft gospel music played by the Minister of Music at the soloist's church. Everything, as far as Essie was concerned, had that universal church-folk-banquet quality to it. The only thing that distinguished this banquet from any other was the reason they were here—to find out who the bishops wanted to join them in the ranks of the episcopacy.

When the last tables served were finishing dessert, the current senior bishop walked onto the stage. He adjusted the starched white collar of his purple clerical shirt, pulled at the lapels of his black tuxedo, and coughed loudly into the microphone before he hit it and asked the audio man if it was turned on. It didn't seem to matter to him that his coughing blasted across the hall just moments ago.

"Lord, this has been such a blessed evening," he began. "How many of you sitting out there looking all dressed up and pretty would agree with me? Raise your hands if you do."

Everybody raised their hands.

"And you know something, church? There ain't nothing prettier than these lovely little ladies sitting before us all perfumed and silked and satined in their pure white for us tonight. How many of you men out there agree with me? Raise your hands if you do."

The men in the audience obediently raised their hands.

"Well then, now that we know we all looking pretty, let's get down to some real church business. Because, you good people know we're not here just to eat and look pretty, right? You know why we here, don't you? Raise your hands if you do."

Essie said, "If he asks me to raise my hand one more time, I'm throwing my purse at the stage."

Bishop Jennings laughed and said, "No you won't, Miss Lady, because I'm throwing it up there for you."

"Now, the first order of business is to introduce the men sitting in this audience who have, to date, acquired enough votes to convince us that they can win that blessed seat of bishop."

He got quiet and raised his right hand up as a gesture of thanksgiving to God. "Ohhh! What a glorious day it is when a preacher becomes a bishop. Yes, Lord! All the bishops in the audience raise your hands if you agree with me."

All the bishops, with the exception of Bishop Jennings, obediently raised their hands. It never ceased to amaze him how some bishops abused the power of their position. It was as if they wanted to make sure no one ever forgot that they were one of the few men chosen to serve at this high a level in the church. And all of that posturing wasn't even necessary because the men distinguished by those purple clerical shirts and the purple adornments on their robes had incredible power in the denomination—unharnessed and at times even illicit power. Some folks in the church believed that the President of the United States had nothing going for him when compared to the power, privilege, and influence of Negro bishops.

"Now, people," the Senior Bishop announced. "I am going to call out the names of the men sitting in this audience who have the most votes for bishop. As you know, we have a total of sixty men, all stalwart and good pastors, running for the four open seats. And I just want you to know that there would have been only two available seats if God had not called Bishop Walker home and then turned around and told me that it was time to step down. And you know what God said to me, church?"

"I don't want to know—though he's going to tell me anyway," Theophilus said.

"Church, He said, 'Bishop, you been here serving Me for a long time now. And you know at eighty-two you need to step on down and let a younger man do the job.' Now, church, all of you know that I always listen to God and I do everything He tells me to do."

"I wonder if he listens to God before or after he insists on being paid a huge love offering whenever he decides that it's time to visit a church in his district," Bishop Jennings said out loud in disgust before he had a chance to catch himself.

"So you see, good blessed people, the Lord has seen fit that only four of these great men of the Gospel United Church will be the chosen ones out of this group of magnificent candidates for bishop. And now . . ." He looked over at the pianist, scratched his head, and said, "You know, I need something to help me make this announcement. Brother musician, play us a godly march.

This kind of thing happens only once in three years and some pomp and circumstance is in order, don't you think?"

The pianist launched into "The Battle Hymn of the Republic" because it was the Bishop's favorite song.

The Bishop began to move his hands around to the beat of the song, singing off-key and swaying to the pounding rhythms coming from the piano.

Percy Jennings looked up toward the ceiling like he was praying for strength and sustenance to get past this moment.

When the pianist mercifully beat out the very last chords of the song, the Bishop looked back at the audience. "Whew! Yes, Lord! Now that's more like it. Ohhh . . . Jeesusss! A godly song for a godly moment." He raised his right arm up in the air, turned around in a circle and shouted, "Jesus!" an octave higher than his normal speaking voice.

"Now, church, we get to see firsthand the hand of the Almighty God at work. All too often the work of His mighty hand remains invisible to the human eye. But tonight we are blessed with the chance to see God's hand work almost as clearly as we can see our own."

He raised his hands up in the air and waved them around a few times to illustrate his point.

"Now, I am going to call out the top six, ten percent if you will, of our top runners. That way, you will get to see a little variety with regard to the caliber of men running for bishop. So, gentlemen, when I call your name, just come on up to the stage."

"First, with a total of 747 of the needed 925 votes to win, is Rev. Silas Jones of Emmanuel Gospel United Church in Brooklyn, New York."

Rev. Jones walked up to the stage with a sour look

on his face. This was the third time he had run for bishop and he knew as he approached the stage he would have to spend all that time, energy, and money running again. He was getting tired of always being in the bishop's race and never getting far enough to seize the coveted prize. Jones's church was one of the larger congregations in Brooklyn, affording him a very comfortable lifestyle. But becoming a bishop would get him out of the pulpit, improve his social status, and provide him with the kind of power and influence he would never have as a pastor.

"Second, with a total of eight hundred votes, is Rev. Josiah Samuels of Mount Moriah Gospel United Church in Hartford, Connecticut."

Josiah Samuels stepped sprightly to the stage and stood next to Silas Jones. He was excited about the number of votes he had accumulated during this first run for a bishop's seat. Josiah knew he wouldn't win this time and would be happy with a good showing of over six hundred votes. This year's campaign for bishop was merely foundation building for the future when he finally got bored with pastoring and wanted something else to do. He figured that at sixty-two, he had plenty of time to win a bishop's seat and just being a candidate had brought him some unexpected benefits, notably a most enjoyable afternoon with a woman named Mae Wilson while his wife was out shopping with a group of pastors' wives.

"Third is Rev. Willie Williams, with 820 votes, from Long Beach Gospel United Church in Los Angeles, California."

Willie Williams, upon hearing his name called, jumped up from his seat like a contestant in a television game show and shouted, "Praise the Lord, everybody!"

He leaned over and kissed his wife, shook hands with everyone at his table, and proceeded to walk up to the stage and right up to the microphone. He was one of the Senior Bishop's favorite pastors and knew that he would be accorded some privileges the other candidates would not have.

The Bishop patted Rev. Williams on the shoulder and moved aside so that he could speak to the audience.

"Well, church," he said in a raspy voice. "Church, you know God is good to me. And as your bishop I will be good to you. I will uphold all of the tenets of this sacred office, honoring my elder bishops and doing their bidding with all of my heart." He turned to look at the Senior Bishop. "And, Bishop, I know you know I will be the kind of bishop you can count on and I will do you right proud."

"Amen," the Bishop shouted, and stomped his feet and waved his hands high in the air. "Amen!"

Rev. James leaned over and whispered to Bishop Jennings, "That boy ain't even won nothin' yet. How in the world can he stand there carryin' on like that?"

"Because he is one of the two candidates most of the bishops want elected at this conference. I know you have seen them squiring him and the other one around, making sure everyone sees them in the company of all the other bishops."

Rev. James nodded. Williams and Ernest Brown were the only two candidates who had been invited to every single meeting and program that was reserved exclusively for the bishops. They were also the only ones the bishops had openly praised in front of the other pastors and conference delegates. And he could understand why. Williams was, in his opinion, a butt kissing toady who would do all of the other bishops' dirty work when asked.

Ernest Brown, on the other hand, was running on a platform of "God's Tradition." Translation—he would make sure no one got to change a thing.

"Fourth, Rev. Jimmy Thekston, 845 votes, from Burning Bush Gospel United Church in Dallas, Texas."

Jimmy Thekston, sixty, was a big and handsome but thuggish-looking man. There was an air of violence about him, even as he strutted up to the stage in his blue and black brocade dinner jacket, which contrasted well with his pale skin and straight black and silver hair.

Rev. James had the distinct impression, watching Rev. Thekston take his place next to Rev. Williams, that he was being elected to serve as an enforcer for some of the other bishops. And as a bishop, he would have the power to back up his menacing demeanor when faced with pastors who opposed decisions made by the Board of Bishops they believed were questionable and self-serving. Mrs. Thekston, who was trying to force out a smile in support of her husband, was a thin, nervous-acting woman, who Susie believed drank to numb the pain of living with Jimmy Thekston, whom she always referred to as "that man."

"Fifth, Reverend Ernest Brown, Sr., 869 votes, from Samuel Temple Gospel United Church in Detroit, Michigan."

Ernest Brown got out of his seat with a surprised look on his face. He had known that he would be elected bishop at this conference, so being called to the stage wasn't a revelation. What surprised him was the fact that he had not received more votes than all of the other contenders. For the life of him, he could not fathom what pastor sitting in the audience had managed to outdo him.

Ernest was about to walk up to the stage, when he

remembered to plant a kiss on the lips of his wife, giving her the kind of public attention that helped to buy her silence. It was an unspoken agreement between the two of them that she would suffer the heartache over his incessant womanizing in private. And in exchange, he would bestow public rewards on her for being so faithful to her husband.

When he walked onto the stage, loud cheers came from his large entourage of supporters. Theophilus saw Marcel standing up yelling like he was at a football game. "That's my dad, my dad the bishop. Yes! Yes! My dad!" His fiancée, Saphronia Anne McComb, was standing beside him in an expensive white satin gown.

"I still can't get over those two getting together," Theophilus said to Essie.

"Well, get over it, Theophilus, because they are," Essie said, wondering to herself why a woman as stuck-up and proper-acting as Saphronia McComb would want a jive, whorish man like Marcel Brown.

"All right, all right, quiet down, you good Detroit people," the Bishop said with a broad grin. Ernest Brown was his own top choice for bishop. He was a company man, with enough of that Detroit smoothness to cajole whatever he wanted from folks without resorting to the butt-kissing of Willie Williams or the overwhelming forcefulness of Jimmy Thekston. He waited a few more moments for the cheers to die down and said, "For those of you who don't know it, that voice you keep hearing belongs to none other than Rev. Marcel Brown. In fact, young Rev. Brown, why don't you come on up here and stand next to your daddy—let some of that good bishop air just blow all over you and get you ready for your future."

Marcel, a fairer, more slender version of his father,

mounted the stage, decked out in a white dinner jacket, black and white striped bow tie, and matching cummerbund. He waved at the audience, who clapped and cheered for him. He even blew kisses to the ladies—a few giggled—before hugging his father and exchanging hearty handshakes with the other men on the stage.

"I don't believe this crap," Theophilus mumbled out loud, then looked embarrassed when he realized that he was practically in church swearing like that. "Bishop Jennings, please forgive me my manners, I—"

"Theophilus, if it looks like crap, if it sounds like crap, and if it smells like crap, then I'd be inclined to think that it *is* crap."

Rev. James sniffed at the air a couple of times. "Lord knows you right in this case, Bishop Jennings."

The Bishop cleared his throat, to announce the last candidate, the first man who would be elected bishop next Friday. "And, the last of our top six candidates for bishop," he said without enthusiasm, "is Rev. Murcheson James, 915 votes, from Mount Nebo Gospel United Church in Charleston, Mississippi."

Rev. James stood up slowly, looking first at Susie and then at Bishop Jennings, shaking his head in total disbelief. "Bishop, you know you a miracle worker. I am the *last* man they want elected a bishop."

Percy Jennings smiled. He knew Murcheson believed he hadn't made the cut when Willie Williams's name was called, thinking that he had been outvoted. He suspected that Murcheson had been almost relieved to put the business of church politics behind him, and eager to return to his work at Mount Nebo. But God had other plans for him.

When Rev. James walked onto the stage, the Senior Bishop gave him a lukewarm "Congratulations." Rev.

Thekston stared at Murcheson out of the corner of his eye, clenching his fists. Of all the men he could bully, Murcheson James was not one of them.

Willie Williams was vexed. He knew that Murcheson would fight him tooth and nail on anything he believed would hurt the church and its people. Rev. James was a do-gooder who believed all those platitudes about what made for a good preacher. And if he took all that seriously, Williams could only wonder at the extent he would take his vows when he was consecrated as a bishop.

Silas Jones was seething. It was bad enough, once again, he had the least number of pledged votes. But it was a slap in the face to stand in the shadows of an old country boy like Murcheson James.

The most intense hostility came from Ernest Brown, who had counted on being the first one elected a bishop. Here he was pastor of one of the largest churches in Michigan, taking second place to a man who pastored a church with only one-hundred-odd members in a country-bumpkin town like Charleston, Mississippi. When they were finally consecrated as bishops, he was going to make Murcheson James the most miserable man in the denomination.

Otis Caruthers suppressed an urge to pull out a cigarette. He needed one bad after learning that Murcheson James would become the first elected bishop at the conference. Tradition dictated that the pastor with the most pledged votes got to select the location for the bishops' private, preelection celebrations. Unbeknownst to many in the denomination, some of these gatherings were high old times—expensive champagne flowed like water, caviar was passed around like it was tuna fish on crackers, the seasoned bishops shared all kinds of delectable secrets about their escapades with the neophyte bishops—and all felt a common bond, a kinship, a sacred brotherhood that they believed no other men in the denomination could share. And now Murcheson James, a man as straight and upstanding as any pastor could be, would control how this time-honored rite of passage would take place.

With this new development in the bishops' race, Otis knew that he would have to redirect his efforts and find another way to help Cleotis Clayton recruit ministers and bishops for the club he was running out of the new Richmond funeral home. If Ernest were in Murcheson's shoes, everything would be smooth sailing. He would make money and get enough dirt on enough bishops and some select pastors to ensure his reinstatement into his old district before the conference ended. He rubbed his hand back and forth across the edge of the table, trying to think his way around Murcheson and his very powerful crony, Percy Jennings.

The Bishop decided that he would not add to Murcheson's triumph by uttering a single syllable of praise. Eager to move past this unpleasant moment, the Bishop jumped right into the conclusion of the program. It pained him to be passing on the mantle of senior bishop to Percy Jennings, a man he disliked even more than Murcheson James. Jennings had, as one of the old bishops put it, "started off on the right track, until he got all holy, trying to turn the Board of Bishops into a doggone Boy Scout troop."

Jennings's relationship with SCLC and SNCC, his visibility as a civil rights leader in his district, and the money he raised for the Gospel United Church colleges, made it impossible not to select him as the new senior bishop at this particular time. Just about every pastor worth anything was involved with the civil rights movement in some way, but Percy Jennings had been to jail with other SCLC leaders many times and always told folks he would be in jail many more, as long as things were this bad for Negroes in this country. He was a hero to many in the denomination.

Unwilling to so much as congratulate Jennings, the Senior Bishop kept his remarks innocuous and to the point: "I know you good folks know that I am retiring at this conference and stepping down from my position as senior bishop. And in keeping with the tradition of our great denomination and the esteemed Board of Bishops, I will now call forth the new senior bishop, Percy Jennings, to bless these men and call forth a victory for them all. Bishop Jennings, come on up here, son, and do your new job."

Bishop Jennings stood silently at the microphone for a few seconds. His heart ached over this ritual, one that made it virtually impossible for the denomination's best and brightest men to reach positions of power in the church. The corrupt tradition was just too entrenched. But he gave thanks for the small miracles of life. Jennings knew that if he did nothing else for his church, he had put at least one good man in an episcopal seat, and was working hard to have another good one placed at the helm of the church he hoped and prayed would become the church of the future: Garrison—no, Freedom Temple Gospel United Church in St. Louis, Missouri.

Chapter Twenty

THERE WERE SO MANY CARS PARKED NEAR WILLIS and Thay's house that Theophilus was forced to find a parking space a block away, easing his Buick into a tight space.

Thayline opened the door and said, "What took you so long? Everybody here waiting on you two."

"That banquet," Theophilus said. "Did you know that whoever gets elected bishop was practically elected at that banquet? I couldn't believe it." He just shook his head in disgust and then said, "Hey, Eddie Tate here?"

"Yeah, Baybro," Willis said, walking up behind Thayline. "He's back in the kitchen with one of Thay's co-workers who has a booty that is wearing the daylights out of a tight yellow dress."

Thayline rolled her eyes at Willis, who laughed and said, "Honey, don't act like that. You know that girl got a big booty and she wearing that dress right. Now, truth is truth. I can't help that."

Thay knew Willis was right, but she still didn't have to like hearing it.

Willis smiled at Thayline. It made him feel good to know his honey was jealous over him. He put his arms around her waist and pulled her back to him, as Thayline, embarrassed, tried to tug away. But he held on and planted a loud, fat kiss on her cheek. Thayline swatted at the hand he had let slip down on her hip and said, "Boy, you know you need to quit."

Theophilus tried not to smile. It was so rare to see his big sister out of sorts with herself, and his brother-in-law was the only one who had ever been able to derail her. Thayline might boss everybody else around, but that big bad bossiness stopped right at the steel-tipped toe of Willis Bradford's shoe. He took Essie's hand and led her on back to the kitchen where, sure enough, Eddie was deep in conversation with a red-bone woman in a yellow dress.

Eddie turned, grinning at Theophilus and Essie. "Theo, man, I've been waiting on your butt to get here so you could tell me what happened at the banquet."

"Eddie, man, you don't want to know what happened. The election of bishops? Man, it's some bogus mess. The thing is so fixed, we already know who's getting elected on Friday."

"You jiving me. Right, man?"

"No. I know who the four new bishops are—Willie Williams, Jimmy Thekston, Ernest Brown, and Rev. James."

"Rev. James?" Eddie asked with a surprised look on his face. Based on the first three names, he figured that a man of Rev. James's caliber wouldn't play enough dirty politics to compete with that group.

"Yeah, man, Rev. James. Bishop Jennings worked

some kind of miracle, and Rev. James will be the first man to get elected bishop on Friday. And you should have seen the looks on the faces of the other preachers when they found out that he had all those votes. Man, if looks could kill, we would be going to his funeral next week instead of to his consecration into the episcopacy."

"But that's good news, right?"

"Yes and no. Just think about it—even though Rev. James is getting elected a bishop, he is doing so along with Ernest Brown, Willie Williams, and Jimmy Thekston. So I wonder how much he will be able to do as a new bishop, even with Bishop Jennings in his corner."

Eddie looked solemn. "I see what you mean. But how did they get so far with the votes?"

"The bishops have been politicking for months, even years, before this conference to get their boys into one of those four slots. It's almost unbelievable that Bishop Jennings was able to get Rev. James this far. The other preachers who would make good bishops were not there tonight. In fact, they never even had a chance."

"Maaan," Eddie said, shaking his head. "That's messed up."

"My thoughts precisely," Theophilus said bitterly. But then, remembering that Essie and the new woman were standing there, he said, "Eddie, we're ignoring the ladies. Are you going to introduce your lovely friend here?"

Eddie had been so intent on getting the scoop on the banquet, he had almost forgotten about his companion. She was standing over near the icebox, looking at him like she was wondering when he was going to remember that she was still in the kitchen.

"Ahh, yeah, uhhh, this is . . ." Eddie walked over and

said, "Ahh, sweetness, what did you tell me your name was?"

Essie rolled her eyes and tried not to laugh. It was obvious that Eddie was so busy looking at that yellow dress, he had had the nerve to forget the poor woman's name. He was something else.

The woman said, "Sugar, I done told you over and over again that my name is Johnnie, Johnnie Thomas."

Neither Theophilus nor Essie missed Johnnie Thomas's gold tooth, with a star sapphire in it, sitting on the left side of her mouth. Theophilus looked over at Eddie and thought, "Man, you are pure dog tonight. Pure sniffing, barking dog."

Eddie felt kind of bad about forgetting Johnnie's name. He liked her and he didn't want to keep disturbing the easy flow that was building up between them by being trifling about her name. He gave her that big old, bad-boy Eddie Tate grin and said, "People, this here is Johnnie.

"Johnnie, this is Thayline's little brother and my good buddy, Theophilus Simmons. And this little lady . . ." Eddie stopped talking, grabbed both of Essie's hands and pulled her away from Theophilus, saying, "Hey, hey, baby girl. You looking good tonight. Your *hair—baby!* And that dress! The dress is talking to me—talk-ing to me. Lawd, ha mercy!"

Johnnie stopped smiling and ran her tongue over her gold tooth a couple of times. Picking up on her mood— and realizing that he had made a second mistake—Eddie said, "Aww, Johnnie, don't look so sore. This is my buddy's wife. It's just that this dress is so fine, I couldn't help myself."

He let go of Essie's hands and went over and planted a kiss on Johnnie's cheek. "Believe me, Johnnie, as fine as Essie is, she is like my sister. Plus, you see that big Negro standing next to her? Well, he is her husband. And believe me, he'd kick my behind if I thought of her in any other way."

"That's right," Theophilus said. "This Negro is my best friend, but I would definitely put a hurtin' on him if he looked at my baby wrong."

Theophilus now grabbed a kitchen chair, sat down, and pulled Essie on his lap. She adjusted her dress around her knees and straightened the scarf of her dress, which kept slipping off her neck. Theophilus watched Essie fiddle with that bothersome scarf, and then picked up the edge of it and pulled it slowly off her shoulders. He rubbed it across his nostrils, inhaling her perfume, and draped it around his neck, while staring deeply into her eyes. There was no mistaking his desire.

Johnnie picked up on what had just transpired between them and recognized that this woman wasn't the least bit interested in competing with her for Eddie's attention. What woman would be, with her man looking at her like that? Feeling more friendly toward Essie, she said, "Girl, you should take off those pretty shoes and rest your tiny feets. I'll get you and your husband something cold to drink out of the icebox."

"Just get one Pepsi and two glasses, Johnnie," Theophilus said.

Johnnie went to the icebox and got a bottle of Pepsi. She got two glasses off the sink, placed the soda on the table in front of Essie and Theophilus, and poured some for each of them.

Theophilus heard the doorbell ring, along with the voices of his parents, the Thomases, and Essie's folks. Then Uncle Booker appeared in the kitchen doorway. "Why y'all back in the kitchen when the party up front?

Theophilus, you and Eddie know doggone well you need to be enjoying yourselves. Tomorrow morning you gone have to go right back to being preachers. Ain't many chances for you to hang loose and not offend or mislead anybody."

They all followed Booker back to the living room, where Thayline was standing by the hi-fi. She put two fingers in her mouth and gave a loud whistle to get everybody's attention.

"Willis and I am so glad you good folk made it to this party we're throwing for our baby brother and his wife. Now, some of you know that my brother is a pastor out in Memphis. And before your tongues get to wagging, just let me say this. My brother is a good pastor. But sometimes he needs some space just to be. And since I'm his big sister, I'm giving him this space to just be himself without any pressure to act like you all might think a preacher is supposed to act."

She looked at Theophilus and said, "Where, baby doll?"

"Here I am, Thay."

"What song do you two want to hear?"

"Put on 'Green Onions' by Booker T. and the MG's, Thayline," Theophilus said. "My baby loves her some 'Green Onions.'"

Thay looked through the stack of albums.

"Honey, it's in the 45 stack," Willis said.

She found the record and put it on. Theophilus grabbed Essie's hand and pulled her into the middle of the floor as soon as the first beats of that Hammond organ sounded out around the living room. He was smiling and snapping his fingers while Essie stood there looking embarrassed.

Thay said, "You ain't shy, baby doll. Show these folks what you can do."

"You're right, Thayline," Lee Allie said. "Essie Lee ain't shy about dancing. Don't know why she trying to start being like that now. Ain't that right, Booker?" When Uncle Booker didn't answer her, she said, "Booker Webb. Didn't you hear me?"

"Yeah, Booker," Mrs. Neese said. "Why ain't you answering your sister?"

Uncle Booker looked a little sheepish. He gave Rose a grin and said in a low, sexy voice, "I ain't answering that girl 'cause I got somethin' so good and sweet right here in front of me, I can't hardly think straight."

Mrs. Neese lowered her eyes down to the floor. Booker pulled her close and her eyes filled up with tears. Uncle Booker pulled out a handkerchief and slipped it into Rose's hand. "You got it bad for me, don't you, Rose?" She nodded her head, and he said, "Well I got it even worse for you. I been lovin' you a long time now, baby." He lifted her hand to his mouth, kissing it gently.

Lee Allie gave her brother a big smile. It was high time that those two lovebirds let the rest of them in on their big secret—not that anyone had ever been fooled.

Theophilus, meanwhile, was pretending to be impatient with Essie, dancing all smooth and cool in front of her. He said, "Girl, quit stalling and show your man what you know how to do."

Grinning up at her husband, Essie finally started snapping her fingers to the grinding beat of the song, then stretched her arms out to the sides and caught the beat with her hips. Theophilus picked up on Essie's rhythm and swiveled his own hips in a masculine version of her movements. Then the power of the beat gripped Essie and, pulling at the bottom of her dress, she just wiggled her hips on down to the floor.

Theophilus laughed. "Yeah, I *like* that. Do it again, baby."

Essie worked her way back up and then went back down to the floor.

Thay said, "Go on, baby doll. You show that boy how to move, girl."

Willis grabbed Thay's hand. "Come on, honey. Dance with me."

Thay put her arms around Willis's neck and they moved to the beat together, smiling love and friendship into each other's eyes.

When the record stopped, Willis said, with his arms still around Thayline, "Baybro, you pick us another? What you want to hear?"

"How about 'Sweet Sixteen' by B.B. King? Just play me a little B.B. and I'm all right."

Johnnie, who was leaning against Eddie, heard the words "Sweet Sixteen" and said, "Yes! Please play that song. That's my song, too. Ooohh chile! 'Sweet Sixteen' tells my story."

She pulled at Eddie's arm and dragged him out on the floor, throwing her arms around his neck and pressing her hips close to his.

With Johnnie swaying all over him, Eddie looked over her shoulder at Theophilus and just grinned.

Theophilus pulled Essie close, resting his chin on top of her head, enjoying the spongy feel of her thick, natural hair. Essie wrapped her arms around Theophilus's neck and let her body sink into his. She could smell his cologne mingled with sweat from all of that dancing. Even damp and sweaty, she liked the way her sweet husband smelled.

He moved his chin from the top of her head and put his cheek next to hers. He kissed the tip of her ear and whispered, "I want to go to bed" so softly she thought she had missed what he said. She looked up at his face questioningly.

"You heard me right," he said, and started dancing Essie over to the hallway leading to their room. By the time the song ended, they had reached the bedroom door and kept moving to the rhythm. Theophilus pressed Essie against the door and kissed her deeply on the mouth.

"Theophilus, we need to stop carrying on like this out in this hall."

"I kind of like what's going on out in this hall," he said, slipping his hand under her dress and grabbing himself a handful of her thigh. "You know there *ought* to be a law against something this good."

Essie tried to move his hand but he wouldn't let her. Just held on tighter, every time she tried to push it away. When he slid his hand up higher, she said, "Theophilus, open this door and quit this carrying on."

"If I stop carrying on in the hall, can you guarantee there is something better waiting for me in that room?"

Essie giggled. "What do you think?"

He nibbled at her collarbone, just below the hollow of her throat. "I think I want to find out."

They moved into the bedroom, and Theophilus drew Essie to him, kissing her deeply and pulling at the zipper of her dress.

Essie reached around his waist, unhooked his cummerbund, and dropped it on the floor.

He said, "You can work on this shirt if you like."

She smiled at him as she unbuttoned the button at the top of his shirt and worked her way down to the waist of his tuxedo pants.

"And what about these?" she asked in a sultry voice.

He raised his arms up and held them out to the side. "Baby, you the clothes expert. Do what you think is best."

Essie unhooked his pants, unzipped them slowly, and slid them down to the floor. Then, she pushed his shirt off his shoulders. As Theophilus pulled his undershirt over his head, Essie looked him up and down, giggling. He grabbed the back of her head, planting a hot kiss on the corner of her mouth, and said, "What you laughing at?"

"You," she said in between his kisses. "I'm laughing at you in your white shorts, black socks, and shiny black shoes."

He took off his socks and expensive slip-on dress shoes. "Do I look better now?"

"No. But you will if you take off those shorts."

Theophilus gave Essie a sexy grin and ran his tongue slowly across his top lip, which had a layer of sweat on the rim of it. He pulled at the waist of those starched white boxers, glistening against his chocolate skin, and pushed them down. He was simply irresistible with those long muscular legs, that high and well-shaped backside, strong arms with the biceps bulging with the slightest movement, flat and hard stomach rippling with muscles and manhood, hard, deep dark chocolate—and with a bold look on his face.

Now Theophilus reached for Essie's hand, stripped off her dress, unhooking her bra as she placed soft kisses between the muscles on his chest, where his heart was rapidly beating, whispering, "I love you so much," right to his heart.

Breathing heavily, Theophilus slipped his hands inside her silk and lace panties, wrapped them around her bottom and pushed them along with that fancy slip down on the floor. He stood in her embrace, savoring the feel of her bare skin next to his.

His wife felt so good, it made him stumble a bit as he breathed a low "Oooooohhhhhhmmmmmmm" into her ear and walked her back and onto the bed.

Essie moaned softly as she felt the full impact of his weight on her, and kissed the spot where his neck met his shoulder. She pulled him closer, breathing heavily, and softly whispered, "Baby . . ." each time he moved, setting off those tiny ripples that washed over her from head to toe. And just as Theophilus had once told her, she could no longer tell where one of them began and the other one ended.

Theophilus looked into Essie's eyes, trying to find words to express what was flowing through his heart. "Ummm . . . baby," he whispered in a deep, mellow rumble of a voice. "Baby, when God created you from my side, He reached in and took the very best of me, along with the jewels from the deepest, darkest, richest valleys of the Nile to form you, my precious, precious wife."

Chapter Twenty-one

*T*HAYLINE AND WILLIS STOOD AT THE KITCHEN counter, counting out silverware sets. They anticipated a full house—their family, Essie's folks, Baybro's friends, the Jameses, and the Jenningses. The party had been so much fun, and now they were fixing a big breakfast for people they loved. The doorbell rang and Willis went to answer it—walking back into the kitchen with his mother-in-law, Larnetta, following close behind him.

"Where's Baybro and Baby Doll, Thayline?"

"They back there asleep, Mother."

"Asleep?"

Thayline nodded her head yes.

"It's almost 8:30, folks will be here shortly. What time did they go to bed?"

"I don't know. They kind of slipped off sometime during the party."

Larnetta laughed. That boy reminded her so much of his father.

"Well, I'm going back there to get those two love-birds up out of that bed," she said. She walked down the hall and knocked on the bedroom door. "Baybro, Essie! Get up before everybody gets here."

Essie peeked under the cover at Theophilus's naked body and pushed him, making him wake up fast.

"Get up. It's your mother."

Larnetta knocked on the door again.

Essie said, "We'll be right there."

Theophilus groaned. "Give us another hour, Mother."

"Baybro, you get your butt up and get dressed," Larnetta said. "Unless you plan on greeting your bishop naked like you are right now."

Essie was up and dressed in twenty minutes, but it was another half an hour before Theophilus made it into the kitchen, dressed in chocolate-colored pants and a white cotton short-sleeve shirt, looking happy and refreshed. He walked up behind Essie, who was helping Thayline set out the food, and pulled at her shirt, then gave her a fresh pat on her bottom.

She slapped his hand away and said, "Stop."

He turned her toward him, gave her a big smack on the lips, and mouthed the words, "Girl, what did you do to me last night?"

"You two keep going at it like that and you're gonna work up on a baby."

"Aw, come on, Thayline," Theophilus said, and winked at Essie.

Thayline moved her shoulders around a bit to shake off the shiver that was running up and down her back. She said, "Don't come on, Thay-line me, Baybro. You standing over there acting like you pumped up full with a baby."

He dismissed that assessment and squeezed Essie's

bottom a few times "for good measure," as he always liked to tell her.

Thayline, who was putting the last bowl of food out on the table, told Essie, "You better listen to me, baby doll. Baybro got a baby in him just waiting to come out. And if you not careful, you gone slip up with one right at this conference."

Thayline walked to the kitchen door and called everyone to come back and bless the food.

As soon as she turned her back, Theophilus stood with his feet apart, rolling his hips around at Essie, and whispered, "Want some."

Essie whispered back, "You are so nasty."

He winked and murmured, "You like this old nasty boy."

Thayline thought to herself, "They just working up on this baby like nobody's business."

Rev. James leaned back in his folding chair and patted his stomach while twirling a bright yellow toothpick around in his mouth. With all the women back in the kitchen cleaning up, he thought it might be a good time to bring his concerns to the attention of Bishop Jennings. He didn't want to offend him. Percy Jennings was a completely different caliber of man from many who sat on the Board of Bishops, but he was still a bishop. And if there was one certainty about bishops, bishops were like cops—they always stuck together. It didn't matter how wrong another bishop was, the Board of Bishops was a tight fraternity that rarely if ever gave up one of its own.

"Bishop James," Percy Jennings said with a big smile stretching across his face, delighting in calling

Murcheson "Bishop." "Bishop James, you're sitting there after this fine, fine breakfast, looking like you have the weight of the whole world on your shoulders. Relax, you're going to have plenty of time for such contemplation when you join the ranks on Friday evening."

Murcheson moved the toothpick around in his mouth and leveled his eyes on Percy Jennings. Despite his country ways, he was an unusually bright man and few things got past him. He usually figured things out long before most people. He had been seeing some things at this conference that troubled him—things that could not be ignored—and what he'd heard from Booker and Pompey this morning confirmed his suspicions. And he surmised that if he was to be worthy of those purple bishop stripes, he had better let his own bishop know what was going on.

"Bishop—"

"Percy, just plain Percy."

"Percy, somethin's terribly wrong at this conference. I know it has something to do with that Bishop Caruthers."

"You shouldn't be surprised about anything with Otis Caruthers. He's a strange bird, was like that even before he became a bishop."

"Caruthers may be a strange bird," Murcheson said, "but he's also involved in something wrong. You see, Percy, there are these women—"

"Now, you and I both know that some of these church-women don't always act like they are in church when they are at a conference."

"Percy," Murcheson said, closing his eyes and rubbing the bridge of his nose. He didn't even know how to say it without sounding like a fool, but he had to try.

"Percy, this is about more than some silly churchwomen gettin' all dressed up and chasin' down some preachers."

Before Bishop Jennings could answer, Uncle Booker, who had been listening and looked ready to burst, jumped from his seat on the couch and came over to the two men.

"Bishop Jennings, Murcheson is trying to tell you in as nice a way as he can that some of them preachers done got themselves a girl-service thing right here at the conference."

Murcheson looked at Uncle Booker with pure relief all over his face, glad to be rescued from having to figure out the words to explain this whole mess.

Theophilus and Eddie just looked at each other. They knew something had been bothering Rev. James all morning but wrote it off as having to do with the banquet. But a "girl-service thing"? That was something else.

Percy Jennings was shocked. There had always been problems with women and preachers at conferences, but never something purposeful as what they were talking about.

"Mr. Webb, are you telling me that there are working girls here at the conference?"

Uncle Booker sighed loudly. Sometimes these preachers, especially the well-educated and upstanding ones like Bishop Jennings, could be so dense.

"Bishop Jennings, we ain't *tryin'* to tell you nothin'. What we is doing is *telling* you that Bishop Caruthers has a club where he pimp street women for the preachers."

"Mr. Webb—"

"Booker is just fine by me, Bishop Jennings."

"Booker, how do you know that Bishop Caruthers is involved?"

Booker looked over at Pompey and said, "You tell him how we know, since it started with you."

"Bishop," Pompey said, in a low voice that sounded like he was chewing on some food. "I heard a few fools running their big mouths, so I sneaked and followed them. They went over to see Bishop Caruthers about the club."

"But did you actually hear them? How would you know that was their business with Bishop Caruthers?"

"Bishop, has you never seen no thugs doing business on a street corner? Let me tell you something. Thugs is always tryin' to be slick but they will up and display all they business to someone with any interest in what they doing."

"And you are sure the men were preachers?"

"Bishop Jennings, a preacher at a conference is easier to spot than a wino standing in front of a liquor store."

Rev. James started laughing. What Pompey said was so true. Preachers at conferences, Annual and Triennial, could be seen by a blind man.

"Besides, I know Rev. Sonny Washington, and that there pretty-boy preacher from Detroit . . ." Pompey shook his head back and forth trying to remember Marcel Brown's name.

"Theophilus, Eddie—you know the one I'm talkin' 'bout. That boy who gone marry Mother Harold's old spoiled grandbaby."

"Marcel Brown, Mr. Pompey?" Eddie asked.

"Yeah . . . yeah . . . that's the boy. Well, anyway, they the ones. Then, I come and tell Booker."

"That's right," Booker picked up. "So Pompey followed Marcel Brown, and I followed Sonny

Washington. Last night, when y'all was over to the banquet, Sonny Washington went over to the Clayton Funeral Home. That's where the club is."

"Cleotis Clayton's new place?" Theophilus said. He should have known a Clayton was in the middle of this mess. "And here Willie was, testifying a few months back on how he had returned to the church."

"Sure, he come back to the church," Booker said. "He came back lookin' to make a whole heap of money off it.

"So," Uncle Booker demanded, "we told all y'all mens of God"—he waved his arm around the room, pointing to Theophilus, Eddie, Murcheson, and Bishop Jennings—"'bout this devilment happening right up in church. What y'all gone do 'bout it?"

"We're gone need something to back this up," Rev. James said. "All these years I been knowing you, I believe you, Booker and Pompey. But these preachers have a lot to lose. You know they not gone let you go up and say they involved with this club without putting up a good fight. And a mess like this bound to tear apart the denomination."

"That's right," said Theophilus. "All we have so far is an overheard conversation—which Marcel and Sonny can and will deny—a witness who saw them talking to Bishop Caruthers, and a visit by Sonny to the Clayton Funeral Home. That is not a lot to hang such serious charges on."

"You mean, you want proof?" Pompey said. "We can get that."

"How can you prove it?" Eddie asked.

"Eddie Tate," Uncle Booker answered for Pompey. "Now, we all may look like some country Negroes and we just may be some country Negroes. But we got plenty of sense and know-how. Me and Pompey, we is some slick Negroes—always been slick, haven't we, partner?"

Pompey and Booker started laughing and slapping palms with each other.

"Yes, me and Pompey," Booker promised. "We country Negroes gone get you all the proof you need."

Chapter Twenty-two

PRECIOUS POWERS SAT AT THE TINY TABLE IN ONE of the offices at the preachers' club, staring at the record book in front of her. Marcel, who was terrible with numbers, had asked her to make sure the record books were in order, so he could keep up with the money made by the club. Precious was surprised when Cleotis Clayton agreed to Marcel's request to let her go over the books. But even his openness didn't ease the feeling in her gut that there was something up with this agreement—that a lot more money was being made than what was showing up in the books, money Cleotis wasn't splitting with anybody.

She had been sitting at the table for half an hour, trying to force herself to get to work—pushing receipts around, flipping through the record book, and then slamming it shut. Marcel paid her well, but not well enough to make her feel okay about what she heard less than an hour ago. She opened the record book and started adding up the numbers, pounding the keys of the old adding machine so hard she knocked off a sparkling red fake fingernail.

"Shoot! I knew I shouldn't have used that old five-and-dime glue on my nails," she thought, putting her throbbing finger into her mouth—dried, nasty-tasting, cheap fake fingernail glue and all.

Precious continued to suck on her throbbing finger, tasting the bitterness of the glue, and used her pain as the excuse to cry over what she had heard when she had gone to Marcel's hotel room. She was about to knock on the door, just to check on something with him, when she heard him with some hollering, moaning fool who sounded a lot like Bishop Giles's wife, Jackie. And Precious stood there listening long enough to make sure there wasn't any doubt about what was going on.

"You devil, Marcel Brown," she whispered to herself. "How could you mess around on me like that—and right up under my nose? You ain't nothing but a low-down, dirty dawg."

She blew her nose and painfully mentally replayed the sounds she'd heard coming from the room. The worst was hearing, over all Jackie's carrying on, the exact same groan Marcel released when he was with her. That tri-fling, two-timing dog had lied to her, saying that she was the only woman who could make him groan like that. She wiped away another tear, taking care to rub the wet mascara from around her eyes.

"Low-down, dirty dawg," she mumbled again, and started adding the numbers up so fast until she feared that she missed something. She stopped and then started up again at an even faster pace.

"It serves him and them other pimps-in-trainin' right

if I go and mess up these books tonight. That dawg deserves whatever trouble he gets."

Marcel practically pushed Jackie Giles out of the bed, rushed her into her clothes and out of the room. He didn't want to have to linger with her, cuddling up and talking trash just to make her feel like she was special to him. He had already begun to regret their affair, between the payoffs to Otis Caruthers and the funeral home scheme he had gotten roped into. No woman was worth all that, but he was afraid to say no when Jackie Giles showed up at his room. She was one of the most conniving women he had ever met, and the last thing he needed, with everything else that was going on, was trouble with Bishop Lawson Giles.

His daddy had always told him that chasing tail was an art he needed to learn. Said that a man should always be able to discern when the hidden costs outweighed the benefits. How he wished he had not been so hardheaded and listened to his father.

The minute the taillights of Jackie's car disappeared, Marcel ran back over to the club and straight up to the office where he had left Precious working. He desperately hoped that she was so busy with the books that she had not come trying to find him when he was holed up with Jackie.

Precious opened the door, looking delectable in her black pedal pusher pants and sleeveless red shirt. Marcel stared at her a few seconds, resisting the urge to run his hands over her shoulders and then bend down to lick each one, tasting and savoring the silken sweetness of them. It was a shame he had worn himself out with

Jackie Giles because Precious sure did look like she had some awfully good loving in her tonight.

He walked into the room and playfully tugged at the bouncy, curly ponytail she wore high on the top of her head. A few dark tendrils had escaped, making her sweet, round face look adorable. He pulled her over to him, wrapped his arms around her, and kissed her right shoulder. It tasted just like honeysuckle.

"Precious, Precious, Precious. What in the world am I going to do with you, with your fine, sweet, *delicious* self? You know something," he said, unbuttoning a few buttons on her shirt and planting soft kisses on her collarbone. "Right now you taste so good until I think I want the whole meal rather than this little snack."

At any other time Precious would have just melted from the heat of Marcel's inviting kisses. But not tonight. She turned away to make sure she wouldn't betray herself by throwing what she knew about him and that Jackie Giles up in Marcel's face. She had to be real cool and play this one out, with the feeling of her guts in her hands.

So she sighed softly and then took a deep breath and let it out slowly, giving the impression that she was in serious need of his attention. Then she turned back to face Marcel, who had made himself quite comfortable on the couch that was in the room. As much as she hated to admit it, he looked good in that expensive golden brown, jersey knit shirt that hugged every inch of his chest and shoulders. She forced herself to say, "Ooohh, honey-baby, you are looking at me so good-like until you running my temp-ture straight up through the roof," without choking on those words.

She watched him as he shifted around on the couch like he was making room for her, taking note of how carefully he was searching her face and said, "Anything wrong, honey-baby? You know you looking at me like you got something on your mind."

At first Marcel didn't answer. Instead, he put on his cool, seductive smile, and then lowered his voice down to that decibel level that almost always got him what he wanted from a woman.

"Precious baby, what's wrong with *me* is that you are sitting way over there, looking at me with that sweet face, and running up *my* temp-ture."

She let that jive talk settle in her ears and then stretched her body—arching her back, reaching her hands up in the air and then back behind her head, and poking out her pelvis—like she always did when Marcel was getting next to her. She was simply amazed at her own performance.

Marcel decided to lower his lashes down over his eyes—a signal that Precious was getting next to him. Then, coming up behind her, he rubbed her neck with expert hands.

"Precious, I believe you have been working too hard. Your neck is so tense until I don't think this little massage will do the trick." He slid his hand inside her shirt, and rubbed her back. "Ummm, sweet thing, your back is tight, too. I think I should order you to take the rest of the evening off and give this sweet brown body the kind of attention it needs."

Precious couldn't believe this fool could be so bold and cocky! Here he was, rubbing all on her like he hadn't just gotten what had sounded to her like a very, very good piece of tail. She was so mad at Marcel she could have spit tacks right out of her mouth if it wasn't so important to keep up this little game and see how far he would go. She kept her cool, moving her head around like she was enjoying his massage, and leaning her head back so that he could see how much she was enjoying it on her face.

She smiled at him. "Honey-baby, I've got so much to do tonight until I couldn't possibly stop to be with you. I have to balance these books and as much as I hate to say this, you gonna have to take care of me at another time. Okay, honey-baby?"

Marcel smiled, hoping that he looked disappointed enough to hide the relief he felt over this announcement. He was exhausted. Jackie Giles had been all over him, over and over and over again. After that marathon session with her, he didn't even want to think about being all wrapped up with some woman. He gave a low laugh, stroked his chin, and said, "Well, baby, as much as I hate to admit this, you're right. It's going to be hard doing without your loving tonight, but we do need for you to get those books together. I guess I'll just have to go and take a cold shower or two to cool down. Hope I can last through the night. Would hate to have to tip out on you to keep it together until I can get some of your good stuff, baby."

Precious wanted to smack Marcel down on the floor and then kick him in his tail for handing her that mess. She thought to herself, "Humph, that heifer must have wore out his sorry behind. And just look at him standing there, lying and grinning like he is feeling so bad that I got to work tonight. I wonder just who he think he talking to—that tight-lipped woman he engaged to?"

As soon as she thought about Marcel's fiancée, she had to stop herself from grinning at the idea forming in her head.

Marcel kissed Precious on the cheek and walked over to the door. She watched him go with love all over her face, but as soon as she heard his footsteps retreat, she went and got her purse off the bed, digging around in it until her fingers touched a tiny piece of paper. She pulled it out of the bag and immediately went over to the phone, dropped her purse on the floor, and dialed the number of a certain guest suite over at Virginia Union University. When Marcel had the nerve to get all up in her face, playing her for a fool, she realized that the best way to get back at him—to hurt him where it would hurt the most—was to call up his fiancée and tell her *everything*.

Precious laughed softly and thought, "Now if I was one of them trifling women, I would have been all over him. But *this*, this will teach his no-good, low-down, dirty, lying self not to ever up and try and mess with me again."

She removed a big gold hoop earring and put the receiver back up to her ear just in time to hear his fiancée's voice on the line.

"Hello."

The cultured, crisp, and cold sound of Saphronia's voice made her lose her nerve. Precious looked at the telephone, not knowing what to say to her.

"Hello."

Precious hung up the telephone and rubbed her forehead. She had not counted on Marcel's fiancée sounding so intimidating—that woman's voice could have put a freeze on some ice. She sat next to the phone for almost five minutes, trying to work up enough nerve to call her back. Then she realized that Laymond Johnson, Bishop Caruthers's henchman, would be coming by soon to find out how much money was owed him this evening. She couldn't risk having him overhear her talking to that Sapphire woman on the phone.

Precious dialed the number again. This time the hand on the other end snatched the telephone off the hook and the hello was so cold that Precious swore she saw the frost off the woman's breath coming right out of the receiver. She was nervous and said with some hesitancy in her voice. "Uh . . . uh . . . I just called you to inform you that your fiancé is cheating on us."

"I beg your pardon," Saphronia said. Precious sat perfectly still for a few seconds to gather her wits and said one more time, "I sayed that I called you to inform you that your fiancé . . . is . . . cheat-ing . . . on . . . us. Now, did you hear what I just said, Sapphire?"

Saphronia was tired and definitely not in the mood to deal with anybody's foolishness tonight—especially if it had something to do with Marcel and another woman. She thought it best to play dumb and get off the telephone as quickly as she could. She said, "I do not have the slightest idea concerning who you are and what you are talking about. But there is one thing that I know for certain. It is that you are an improper-talking nuisance, who has dialed the wrong telephone number in a moment of extreme confusion."

"Sapphire, wait," Precious insisted, knowing that Saphronia wouldn't pick up the phone if she called again. "Just listen to me a second and don't hang up."

"Why not?" Saphronia snapped, her irritation growing each second she remained in this conversation. "You do not even know me. If I heard you correctly, you are trying to reach someone named Sapphire and my name, slow woman, is Saphronia. Can you say that? Sa-phro-ni-a."

"Shoot," Precious thought, remembering how many times Marcel had stopped to correct her about

Saphronia's name. She was amazed at herself for ever mistaking this stone-cold heifer for a Sapphire.

"Look, Miss McComb. *That* is yo' name, ain't it?"

Saphronia didn't answer but she didn't hang up the telephone, either.

"Uh huh. So now, like I just said, you gone marry Rev. Marcel DeMarcus Brown, right?"

"I applaud you on this one. It appears as if you were able to remember *his* name."

Precious chose to ignore that cut and continued talking.

"Look, just give me a moment to tell you a few things about your man. In fact, me and you needs to talk face-to-face because I just caught his roaming butt red-handed in the act, if you can figure out what I mean by that. You see . . ."

Saphronia chose to ignore *that* cut. Of all the telephone calls she expected to receive at this conference, she never thought she would get one from one of Marcel's disgruntled women. She knew all about Marcel's reputation but assumed that all that womanizing had taken place before their engagement. But this was a woman calling her, mad because she had caught her almost married boyfriend, boss, *and* pastor cheating on *her*.

". . . And, you know Sapphire, I mean, Saphronia," Precious was saying, "I think it is time we got together to put a fix on Marcel's bumpin' 'n' grindin' behind."

Saphronia started laughing, suddenly amused by the absurdity of this entire situation. Marcel had definitely gotten his "bumpin' and grindin'" behind into some hot water when he was caught cheating on this woman. Her voice had a sliver of warmth in it when she said, "Your complaints about Marcel are quite valid. But before we continue with this conversation, I need to at least make sure that I know exactly who it is I am talking to."

Precious sighed with relief—she couldn't believe how hard it had been to get through to this woman. She looked at the clock again and realized that she was running out of time. She lowered her voice and said hurriedly, "I think you already know that it's me, Precious Powers. But, Saphronia, I gotta go right now. I think I hear someone near my room and I don't want anyone to hear me using this phone on my work hours."

Precious got off the phone as soon as she heard Laymond Johnson's heavy footsteps in the hall. She was kind of scared of him and didn't know what he would do if he found out she had called Marcel's fiancée about catching him in bed with another woman. He had some connection to Bishop Otis Caruthers and could mess with her money. She let him knock several times before she went and opened the door. When she finally did, he stood over her sulking in the doorway and looking like he wanted to say something to her about making him wait. She saw him gaze over her shoulder, letting his eyes linger on the couch. She looked up at his face and he gave her that old ugly grin she hated. She thought he had a whole lot of nerve acting like he was expecting something other than what he came for.

Precious went and got Laymond's stuff, put it in a large brown envelope, thrust it in his hands, and practically slammed the door in his face before he could say anything to her. She pressed her ear to the door and then put on the extra lock when she heard his heavy, angry breathing coming from the other side. He took his time leaving and she stayed frozen in that position at the door until she was certain he was gone.

Chapter Twenty-three

APHRONIA SAT BY THE TELEPHONE THINKING about what Precious Powers told her. At first, Saphronia didn't want to hear what Precious Powers had to say, but now she wished that she had not been so terse with her. She wanted to know more. The closer the wedding got, the more unsure she was of Marcel. And she was so torn—all her life, her grandmother had told her that the only way she could be somebody big was to marry a prominent pastor. But now that she was about to achieve that goal, she was coming to question the wisdom of this thing.

She went into the bedroom of their suite and made sure her grandmother was asleep before she got the briefcase Marcel told her to keep safe for him. He had also instructed her not to look inside, saying it was a test to see just how trustworthy she would be when they married. But now, after talking to Precious, she was getting ready to fail this test with flying colors. Saphronia checked on her grandmother again. When she heard a steady stream of snoring, she sat down on the floor and opened Marcel's briefcase.

The first thing she pulled out was a folder containing minutes from the business meetings he had attended at the conference. She dug down in the case some more and touched something that felt thick, soft, and leathery. She opened the case wider and struggled to pull out a fat, red leather address book with a bunch of money stuck in it. Not just dollar bills, either—these were big bills, nothing short of a fifty and mostly hundreds. Saphronia frowned and started to count all of this money. It was a lot, even for a preacher, to have on hand.

She flipped through the book some more and came to a section with the names, telephone numbers, and church names of a number of ministers and bishops whom she had seen at the conference. Next to each name, in a column titled "Type," was a description. Some men had "fair-skinned only" next to their names, while others had specified "long legs a must," or "chocolate delight desired." And there was even one emphatic statement, "no short nappy-headed gals, *please*."

The last three pages had only women's names on them. Saphronia didn't recognize any of those names and wondered if Marcel had affairs with them. At the end of the second page, she saw the name Precious Powers with several numbers next to it, including one that had been hastily scribbled in the book with a pencil.

She lay the red leather address book on the floor and dialed the penciled in number, hanging up at the first ring. What if Marcel was with Precious Powers and answered himself? Saphronia, who had always prided herself on her very proper and distinctive speech, knew that he would recognize her voice if she so much as breathed into that telephone.

"But," she thought, "this woman is angry with Marcel. She would not have him over there after what she found out." Feeling a bit more confident, she dialed the number again and let it ring until someone answered it.

"Hello."

Saphronia recognized the low, deep voice of Precious Powers. Her own throat was almost too dry and tight to let her speak. But she choked out, "Precious, I . . . found . . . your number and . . . I . . ."

"Saphronia, girl. That you, ain't it? You know you shocking me to death calling me like this. I got the feeling when we was talking earlier, you wasn't happy about me calling you."

"No, Precious. I wasn't happy to hear from you. Why would I want to hear, firsthand, that my fiancé is sleeping with not only one but two women?"

"Then why would I call me if your self don't want to know anything?"

Saphronia sighed loud enough to be heard clearly on the other end of the telephone. It was absurd—here she was, a well-respected speech teacher, feeling intimidated by talking with a woman who probably barely finished high school. She said, "I don't think Marcel has been very honest with me about a lot of things. I thought that talking to you would help me think better about all of this—clear my head a bit."

"Well, you need to forget about all of that head-clearing talk. You wasting your time there. Like I said, I think we should fix his sorry behind."

"Huh?"

Precious sighed with exasperation. "Revenge, Saphronia, revenge. Girl, the right kind of revenge could be even better than hearing Marcel groan when he—"

She stopped talking as it occurred to her that she was

talking to Marcel's fiancée. That revenge thing had gotten so good to her until she forgot to watch her mouth.

"Uhh, sorry, Saphronia. I . . . kind of . . ."

Saphronia laughed softly into the phone. She knew exactly what Precious was talking about. She had heard that groan only once when things got a bit out of hand between her and Marcel and she figured out a way to give him some relief without going all the way. That groan had sounded so good when he let it out with her, she couldn't wait until things got out of hand between them again.

"There is no need to apologize to me. I know exactly what you are talking about." She laughed some more and then her voice got breathy when she said, "And Precious, you must agree with me when I say the man has some wonderful kind of a groan."

This time Precious laughed. "Girl, girl, girl! You *sho'* do know what you talking about. I'm telling you. Sometimes, I think that groan can get to me more than some of the other good things that rascal can do to a woman."

"Me, too, Precious. Me, too."

Saphronia was surprised that she was comfortable being this candid with Marcel's girlfriend. She had never talked to anyone like that—never dared to tell a soul about her complex feelings for Marcel. She knew that she must have hit a serious impasse with Marcel to be able to have this conversation with Precious Powers.

"Precious, the idea of revenge is beginning to sound appealing to me. Tell me, just what do you think we should do? You know whatever it is, it has to surpass anything Marcel is capable of doing."

"Girl, you *sho'* is right. And that there is a problem. You know, anytime a preacher working with that crook, Cleotis Clayton, by bringing that jive-timer business for his funeral home ho' club, he'll do just about anything."

Saphronia felt a cold wave of shock run through her chest and down to the pit of her stomach. She thought she heard Precious say that Marcel had something to do with a prostitution service with Cleotis Clayton, of *all* people. Everybody knew Cleotis Clayton was shady, but his mother, Sister Willie Clayton, had only recently testified about his return to the church. Surely she was mistaken about what she thought she heard. But the clear, straightforward tone in Precious's voice let her know that she was not. She started breathing hard into the telephone without even realizing it.

"Saphronia, you all right? You sound like you having a asthma attack or something."

She sat down on the couch and tried to steady her breathing. She was sweating and looked around for something to fan herself with. She found a conference bulletin and waved it vigorously across her face and neck.

"Saphronia, Saphronia, are you okay?"

She calmed down. But as her breathing became normal, she felt bile rising in her throat as she thought of all of those ministers' names and the descriptions of women in Marcel's red leather book. She lay the telephone receiver on the floor and put her head between her knees. When the nausea began to subside, she picked up the telephone and said, "I'm better. Just that I can't really believe what I am hearing."

"Saphronia, believe it. Your fiancé, the Reverend Marcel DeMarcus Brown, is running around this Triennial Conference like he one of the biggest pimps in Richmond. He, Rev. Sonny Washington, and Bishop Otis Caruthers, all working for Cleotis Clayton, and helping that lowlife run a ho' business for a select group of preachers at this conference who have some very deep pockets.

"Saphronia, girl, the only reason I'm in Richmond at

all was because Marcel asked me to come out here and
do the books for what he first told me was some kind of
refreshment club—a place where the ministers could come
get a drink, read the paper, talk, swear, and grab a cigarette away from the eyes of the church folks. Offered me
some good money, too. And I won't lie to you. I wanted
to be with Marcel real bad. But girl, on the first night I
stepped up in here, I knew that something funky was up.
First thing, you know something's wrong when a bunch
of Negroes want to hang out in a funeral home."

Saphronia started laughing. What Precious said was
so true. Negroes just didn't want to socialize in a funeral home.

"I did confront Marcel about this. And you know what
he did? Girl, he started laughing and then patted me on
the head, and told me to keep my nose out of things I
didn't understand."

"Why didn't you go to someone in authority at the
conference and tell them what was going on when you
figured things out?"

"Saphronia," Precious said, resentful of being questioned like that. "Who in the world was I supposed to go
to? Honey, you just don't know who has been to this place
and ordered themselves up a treat. Now tell me, who do
you think could be trusted in the midst of all of this mess?"

Saphronia knew Precious was right. There was no telling
what ministers and bishops were involved in this thing.

"But you didn't have to keep working for them, Precious. You may not be able to do anything to stop it, but
you didn't have to be a part of it."

Precious got real quiet. Saphronia was right. She had
stayed, knowing how wrong she was, for two reasons—
Marcel and the money. She needed the money bad. She
figured Saphronia couldn't understand the first reason.

Saphronia gave the distinct impression of being a tight-lipped priss, who probably held everybody to impossible standards that she, herself, could not keep. And she knew that she had never been in a situation that would help her understand the second one.

Saphronia interrupted her thoughts, saying, "I cannot understand how all of this could happen and in *church*. I don't understand how Marcel could get involved with something like this. And I don't understand how he could do such a horrible thing to me."

"Look, Saphronia," Precious snapped. "This funky mess ain't about what Marcel doing to you. It's about some trifling and greedy men messing over they church and disrespecting they own Negro womens. And your fiancé, a bigtime preacher from Detroit, is trying to sell their souls so that he can have some heaven right here on earth. That's what this is really all about."

Precious was surprised at the vehemence of her anger about this mess. Just a few hours ago, she wanted to be with Marcel. Now she was beginning to wish she had never met him.

Saphronia was hurt and angry. She loved Marcel, but it hurt her deeply that he would ask her to marry him when he didn't even love her—and now this, that he would be mixed up in something definitely immoral and probably illegal. She blew her nose and sniffed. But then she heard her grandmother stirring. If her grandmother caught her on the telephone this late, and crying like this, she would not lose one minute finding out what was wrong.

"Precious, I better go."

"But we haven't figured out what we planning on doing to Marcel. Why don't we meet tomorrow? I'm staying with the woman who cooks the food for the club and I know she'll let us meet at her house."

Saphronia didn't respond to this suggestion because she wasn't so sure she wanted to arrange a meeting at the home of a woman who cooked for a brothel.

"Tee Cole is okay," Precious said, guessing the reason for Saphronia's hesitation. "The only reason she working there is to hold on to her house. She lost her other job and needed some good-paying work real fast."

Saphronia remained silent a few more seconds and finally said, "I guess I'll have to take you on your word. But will I be safe in her neighborhood?"

Precious sighed. She had momentarily forgotten how much of a snob Saphronia was.

"Look, Tee is a good woman and she lives around decent folks. Saphronia, education, money, and where somebody lives don't always tell you who is a decent person and who is not. Look at Marcel—if I used your scale, I'd have to say that he was decent. But we know that ain't so, now don't we?"

Saphronia felt ashamed at the truth of those words. "Precious," she said, "I will come by tomorrow if that is okay with you and that lady. The sooner we get together the better."

"You right. And don't worry, I'll have some kind of plan by tomorrow."

Saphronia smiled to herself. A tiny part of her was looking forward to meeting with Precious, even though she was going to have to tell a gigantic lie to get away from her grandmother. And she didn't doubt that any woman who had the nerve to call a man's fiancée and report that he was two-timing both of them, certainly had the ability to work up a brilliant scheme to get back at him.

Chapter Twenty-four

$\mathcal{S}$USIE JAMES LOOPED HER HAND THROUGH ESSIE'S arm and steered her to a row of seats on the gymnasium floor, with Willis and Thayline following close behind them. Rev. James and Theophilus had met that morning with Booker and Pompey, who had news to fill them in on. Then they would have to race to meet up with Bishop Jennings, who had asked them to march with him in the preelection processional. Any preacher seen in this lineup would be treated as someone who was important enough to keep an eye on.

"Baby doll, you think you gonna get a chance to talk to Baybro before service starts?"

Essie turned around and looked across the gymnasium in search of Theophilus. Like Thayline, she was hoping that either he or Rev. James would find them in enough time to let them know what was going on with this Bishop Caruthers business.

The gymnasium was almost packed to full capacity, though it was only 8:00 and the service wasn't even supposed to start until 9:15. The crowd was looking good, all these well-dressed, good-smelling, smiling, laughing, tall-walking, and proud-to-be-a-part-of-such-a-great-institution Negroes everywhere. The magnificent array of hats on the women's heads alone was something to see. There was one sister standing near them wearing a hat that was so outstanding that she could not help stand out, even in a crowd of more than four thousand people. The hat was made of sheer gold silk, with a silver and gold brocade ribbon around the crisp brim, and a shower of rhinestones on the crown that gave off a rainbow of sparkles every time she moved her head. This sister knew she looked good, as did the four ministers who rushed to hold her folding chair for her when she finally found a seat to her liking.

She spied Eddie and Johnnie Thomas working their way through the crowd, Johnnie's bright red pillbox hat bobbing up and down. She was a good woman, Essie thought, and they all should have known better than to prejudge her. Thayline's friends were bound to be good and decent folks, even if they did have outrageous-looking jeweled teeth in their mouths. Essie watched Eddie catering to Johnnie, making sure she was comfortable and placing his arm protectively around her shoulders so that she wouldn't get cold in that sexy red sleeveless dress she was wearing. This romance looked like it might last, even after this conference ended and Eddie went back home to Chicago.

But there was no sign of Theophilus and Rev. James.

When they had met that morning, Theophilus had been worried that they'd be late for the service, but Rev. James seemed to be focused entirely on the meeting with Booker and Pompey.

"Bishop Jennings asked us to march in the processional," Theophilus reminded him.

"I know. But this is more important. I think Percy would rather I do this first."

Theophilus had to agree—catching and stopping Bishop Caruthers was far more important than walking in a special processional at the Triennial Conference. If they didn't do something about Bishop Caruthers, there might not be much of a denomination to march before anyway. Negro church folk were mighty particular about how much dirt they could tolerate before they began asking themselves if the denomination they belonged to was one led by God or had been infiltrated by the devil. They would run people out of the church in droves— and away from God—if they didn't deal with this mess.

And now, Booker and Pompey's report was every bit as shocking as they feared.

"Murcheson, this ain't just no smokin', drinkin', and gettin'-girls-to-the-preacher thing like I first thought it was," Booker said. "This thing being set up just like any other regular kind of business, even with offices."

Pompey chimed in, "Lawd! Lawd, y'all. It is some real nasty, stanky, skanky, low-down nasty business."

"So like we was sayin', you all need to get off your behinds and do something about it. 'Cause y'all know this devilment ain't right. Preachers!" Booker spat out the word like he was cussing.

Rev. James said gravely, "What I say we should do is get some podium time from Bishop Jennings tomorrow. Then, Theophilus, I want you to get up and tell folks what been goin' on."

Theophilus frowned at Rev. James. "Who said anything about me being the one to go up and expose anybody?"

"I did. I did as your new bishop," Rev. James stated, with a slight grin crossing his face as he recognized how a little bishop's power could come in handy at times.

Theophilus gave him a look that said, "Oh, so it's like that, huh?"

And Rev. James looked right back at him as if to say, "Yes, it is like that."

Theophilus brushed his hand over his forehead. Bishop Jennings or Rev. James were always talking about standing up for what you believed was right, and here they were putting this tremendous burden on *him*.

"Rev. James, I understand where you coming from. But what I don't understand is why I have to be the one to do this thing. Why aren't you going up there to do it?"

"Son," Rev. James said. "Son, the bishops and pastors who got some decency in them believe that you have what it takes to lead this denomination into the next century. Don't you realize that in twenty, thirty years, this church gone be faced with some things we don't even have the sense to begin thinking about right now? You have what it takes to be a bishop in the next century, Theophilus—the right kind of bishop. But you got to cut your teeth on some church mess to get you ready for that responsibility. You hear what I'm trying to tell you, Theophilus?"

Theophilus nodded his head yes and just sighed.

"Now tell me, son," Rev. James asked. "Just what is it you so afraid of?"

Booker and Pompey looked at Theophilus with disappointment. They had long placed him in the category as a man with some "balls."

He took heed of those looks, got quiet for a few seconds, and took a few deep breaths to gain some composure. The last thing he wanted to do was fail those two—not to mention Essie, himself, and God.

"Look," he said, "before I go jumping up on the podium making serious accusations against some of the most powerful men in this church, I need proof—some serious proof—in writing. That's what I thought we were going to be getting this morning."

"No," Booker interrupted. "We said we would get proof. Didn't nobody say a thing about something in writing. You wanted proof that the place exists—which meant that somebody had to go and see it with their own eyes. Now we have done all of that."

Rev. James put his hand on Theophilus's shoulder and said, "Now, son, I know your mama and daddy didn't raise you to let something as shallow as keeping a job stop you from doing the right thing. This here thing is bigger than you being able to pastor that church down in Memphis. It is about righteousness and God and doing right by God's people. You are a pastor and your job as a pastor is to teach, protect, and lead the people God has placed under you to shepherd. You and I both know that one day you will stand before the Almighty and answer to Him concerning how you did your job. And it has been my assumption all along that you, Theophilus, have always been about doing the right thing for your church, your people, and the Lord. Am I right or wrong about you on this?"

Theophilus acknowledged, "You are right, Rev. James."

Rev. James nodded his head as if to say, "I thought that was the case here." He looked straight at Theophilus again and said, "The way I see it, if you don't go up in there and carry out this here plan like we all planned it, whether you have some written proof or not, your church

Chapter Twenty-five

APHRONIA RANG THE DOORBELL AT THE HOUSE of the preachers' club cook, Tee Cole, and a plump, brown-skinned woman answered the door with a warm and welcoming smile.

"Well, a good morning to you, Miss Saphronia Anne McComb."

"Tee?"

Tee pushed opened the screen door and waved her hand, beckoning Saphronia to come inside. With that plain mauve suit, Saphronia looked downright dowdy, Tee thought, and she was holding her body awkwardly, like she was scared.

"Don't no hungry wolves live here, Miss Saphronia Anne McComb."

Saphronia gave her a questioning look.

"I said, don't no hungry wolves live here. Meaning, that we ain't gone eat you up alive if you come up in my house."

Saphronia was embarrassed. Precious had told her not

to worry, and here she was acting just like her grandmother would act with somebody like Tee Cole. She stepped into a small and modest living room that was so clean it almost sparkled.

"Precious back in the kitchen getting a bite to eat. Come on back."

Saphronia followed Tee down the tiny hall into the kitchen, where Precious was sitting at the table munching on a big fluffy biscuit smothered in apple butter and slurping on a delicious-smelling cup of coffee.

"Girl, you need to get yourself one of these biscuits because they is *good*."

Tee said, "Saphronia, you want a biscuit?"

Saphronia nodded her head.

"Want some coffee?"

"Yes, please. Black with a teaspoon of sugar."

Precious looked at her. "You drink your coffee like white folks in the movies, all black without anything to smooth it out?"

Saphronia didn't respond. She took the coffee out of Tee's hand, leaned against the counter, and took a sip, then locked eyes with Precious. Each was trying to figure out what the other had to make Marcel interested in her.

"Y'all gone waste the whole day sizing each other up?" Tee asked, startling them out of their staring contest. Then she commanded Saphronia, "Put down that coffee and stand up straight for a minute."

Saphronia was not used to a woman like Tee ordering her around and she held her place at the counter, stubbornly refusing to so much as move a muscle.

Tee gave her a "you ain't nobody special" look and said, "Girl, ain't nobody asking to borrow your man for the night. I just want to get another good look at you, that's all. Now, will you please stand up straight and turn around for me?"

Saphronia did as she was told and Tee gave her a thorough once-over. Then she said, "Let me help you two out with this situation. Here's what I see: One, a man who out there in the streets running a ho' service and at a funeral home ain't worth nothing. Two, he a jive punk—loving you, Precious, but got no courage to marry you, and Saphronia, trying to marry you 'cause you make him look good. And three, the Negro like big behinds. 'Cause between the two of y'all, there enough butt in this room to supply every little white woman in Richmond with some decent hips. So I say that Rev. Marcel ain't worth all this trouble. Now you two can quit worrying about him and get down to some business."

Looking at Saphronia, she added, "Things have a way of working out for you when you least expect it. All you gotta do is trust in the Lord and then let Him take control over your life. Baby, that man done, done you a favor. Not marrying him is the smartest thing you ever did."

Saphronia tried to hold back her tears. She knew she couldn't marry Marcel, but until now had not made a final decision about it.

Tee headed out into the yard, and Precious got up and rinsed out her coffee cup. Tee was right. They weren't here to compete with each other but to get that low-down dawg Marcel.

"Sit down," she said to Saphronia, who answered with a short sniffle. Then sat down at the table, chin in hand, and said, "I'm all ears."

Precious took a deep breath. She hoped this plan sounded as good now as it had when she first shared it with Tee.

"Saphronia, Marcel likes to run everything. And from what I've seen, he really likes to run you. Probably done started telling you what to wear by now."

Saphronia looked at her indignantly.

"Look, Saphronia, don't get all uppity on me because I'm telling you the truth. Your clothes, as expensive as they are, look like clothes that some man wants you to wear because he don't want nobody looking at you. I'd bet some money that he has made you take stuff back when it looks too good and he know you really like it. And you all ain't even married yet."

Saphronia was surprised at just how much Precious knew about Marcel. They had just had an argument about a dress. It was a beautiful raw silk dress that was such a pale shade of pink, it looked like a blushed shade of white. She had wanted to wear it to that banquet for selecting the new bishops. She looked good in that dress, too, with its wide scooped neckline that showed just a hint of cleavage, capped sleeves, and a perfect fit that showed all the best features of her figure. But when she showed it to Marcel, he told her not to wear it, that it wasn't something *his* fiancée should wear to a Triennial Conference function.

"Saphronia, the way I figure this thing, you the only one who can really get Marcel. I'm the only one who know how to get him. But you the only one who *can* get him."

Saphronia looked a little confused.

"Think about it. You the most controlled part of Marcel's life. Now if you was to go over to that funeral home, just your presence would scare him silly. But if you was to go over there, do something out of control, and embarrass his butt? Girl, that would do it. That would do it good."

"Are you saying that you want me to go to that brothel?"

"No, Saphronia. I don't want you to go to that *brothel*," Precious said in imitation of her voice. "I want you to go over to that *ho' service center* and give that cheating, no-good, lying Negro a heart attack. That's what I want you to do."

Saphronia wasn't so sure she wanted to set foot in a brothel, even if she did like the idea of getting Marcel. "Precious, I know my presence at the brothel would shock Marcel. But how would I ever get in and find him?"

"Girl, that is the best part of the plan. Wait till you see how I'm gonna fix you up. Did you bring what I told you to?"

A delicious feeling of mischief came over Saphronia, who said, "Take a look at the dress I brought. It doesn't look like anything you'd expect me to wear."

When Precious unzipped the peach satin garment bag and pulled out the pale pink dress, her face broke out into a wide grin. "Ooo, girl. This thing looking good. Expensive, too. Did you bring the shoes for it?"

Saphronia dug around in the bottom of the garment bag and pulled out her shoes. They were low-heeled, pale pink satin pumps—and actually quite nice for the dress. But they were a far cry from what Precious had in mind.

"These shoes cute but they ain't gone work."

"What do you mean by, 'They will not work'?" Saphronia demanded in what Precious thought of as her "Miss Anne" voice.

"Look, these shoes have *preacher's wife* written all over them—even though you still in the fiancée stage.

You gone have to get some better shoes than these if you call yourself doing anything worthwhile tonight."

Saphronia got mad and threw the shoes on the floor. "Okay, so my shoes don't work for you. Do you have a better pair I can wear?" she snapped.

Precious rolled her eyes. "Miss Anne, I just might. What size shoe do you wear?"

"Eight."

"Well, see there, our problem has been solved. Tee has some shoes that will be good."

"So, is this all there is to your plan?" Saphronia asked, her voice tight. "I mean, do you honestly think a fancy dress and a pair of high-heeled *shoes* are the key to getting back at Marcel?"

"No, girl, that ain't what I'm saying, but you got to look the part to get to play the part."

She tilted her head and looked at Saphronia real hard. "Your hair. We gotta do something about that."

The horrified look on Saphronia's face made Precious start to laugh. But then she stopped, frowning suddenly.

"What's wrong?" Saphronia demanded.

"Please hush your mouth. I just realized that I don't know what we gonna do about your voice."

Saphronia lifted her eyebrows. "My voice?"

"Yeah. You too proper. You gonna have to talk like you got some street in you and you gonna have to curse, too."

All of a sudden Saphronia's feet started feeling very cold. She didn't want to be *too* successful at this charade. "What if I am so convincing that somebody tries to get me to . . . you know . . . work, Precious?"

"You not going as no ho'," Precious said, with just a touch of exasperation in her voice. "You going as a hostess, food server, or something like that. I do the books for the club, Saphronia, and nothing else. And Tee ain't no ho', neither. All she do is cook food. But you still got to talk right for that place or else your butt won't get steps past the front door."

Tee walked into the room, listening to the two of them going back and forth. "You two standing there fussing like two wet cats. You might as well stop being mad at each other, 'cause ain't nothing wrong with both of you but y'all in love with a trifling man. Saphronia, you knew Marcel would cheat on you, just walked around hoping you was wrong. And, Precious, *you* were wrong to stay with him after he made it clear he was going to marry Saphronia, despite how much he claimed to love you. And plus, he was your boss *and* your pastor. Girl, you had to know that was some kind of mess, right?"

Precious lowered her eyes to the floor and didn't say anything.

"I thought that was the case or at least I certainly hoped so," Tee said, and then looked back at Saphronia.

"Now, Saphronia. I know you take a lot of pride in not talking like the rest of us but Precious is right. You voice is all wrong for what you have to do. And there ain't no sense in half stepping on something like this."

Saphronia nodded her head in resignation. As much as she knew they were right about her voice, she still did not want to walk up in that place talking like the two of them.

"Tee, do you have any shoes that will look good with this dress?" Precious asked.

"Sure do. Got a pair of silver pumps with five-inch heels that'll look real good with that dress. Is that all you need?"

"No. I think Saphronia gone need some kind of wig."

Tee studied Saphronia's face a moment. "My son Junie's girlfriend got the perfect wig. It's red, kind of blond-like but it'll look pretty good on you. Lord knows it don't do nothing for her. I'll call Junie and tell him to bring it when he come over to help me take the dinners over to the club."

The afternoon Saphronia spent with Tee and Precious was the best that she had ever had with other women. Tee fixed them a delicious lunch of fresh pole beans from her garden, cooked with red onions and crispy slices of bacon, salad with fresh home-grown tomatoes, cucumbers, and green onions, and cornbread so light and fluffy it practically melted in your mouth. They talked about everything—men, sex, working, white folks, the civil rights movement—and, of course, they talked about Marcel so bad that Precious swore that his ears were burning off.

Tee lit a cigarette, looked at the clock on the wall, and said as she blew a long stream of smoke out of her mouth, "It's almost 3:30 and I got to pack up dinners to take over to the funeral home for this evening." She took another draw on the cigarette and said to Saphronia, "Girl, you be sure to do some more work on your talkin'. 'Cause right now, chile, the way you sounding up in here is right pitiful."

This time Saphronia laughed and said in her best imitation of Precious and Tee, "Girl, you quit worryin' 'bout me 'n go 'n get those dinners all fixed up."

Precious was so impressed by this she hit the side of the kitchen table and said, "By jaw, I think she done gone and got it," in her best imitation of a crisp British-sounding accent.

Saphronia rolled her eyes. "Precious, it is by *Jove*, I think she's got it."

Tee laughed. "Now, what about that hair?"

"Go get dressed," Precious told Saphronia. "Then we can get to work."

A half hour later, Saphronia returned to the kitchen dressed, perfumed, and barefoot. Her plain face and the straight brown hair hanging down her back were in sharp contrast to the sassy and sophisticated dress she was wearing. She sat down in a chair and Precious draped an old sheet around her shoulders.

"Saphronia, girl, I don't know how I gonna pin all of this long, pretty hair up tight enough to fit under a wig."

She pulled Saphronia's hair away from her face and mixed some Vaseline with a dab of foundation. "Your skin is kind of dry, and this will make it have a nice glow to it."

She began to apply the foundation and Saphronia closed her eyes, completely relaxed under the cool, soothing touch of Precious's soft fingers on her face. Once the foundation was applied to Precious's satisfaction, she put black mascara on Saphronia's lashes, which made her eyes look wider. Then, she put on some pink eye shadow and lined her eyes with a black pencil, smudging some of the liner in the corners of her eyes. She took a big brush and dusted her cheeks with some blush, then finished with a light dusting of face powder to set the makeup in place. Last of all, she took a Q-Tip and lined out the natural shape of Saphronia's lips with a soft pink lipstick, filling it in with feathery strokes so that her thin mouth would look more lush. She stood back and admired her work for a few seconds.

"Saphronia, girl, you know you not as plain as you

first appear to be. All you need to do is wear some makeup and you'll be looking real good. Hold your head back so I can tweeze your eyebrows. I don't know why I didn't do this before I put on all of this makeup."

She touched up the makeup one more time after finishing Saphronia's eyebrows and then began the arduous task of parting her hair and braiding it into sections so that it would fit under the wig. When she was done with Saphronia's hair, she put some hair oil on the wig and started brushing it with a wig brush.

"Girl, get up and turn on that radio. Couldn't figure out what was wrong in here—it's too quiet."

Saphronia, who was enjoying the quiet, turned on the radio sitting on a small table in the corner of the kitchen. A soulful man's voice ran out loud and clear, making Precious move her shoulders like a shiver had just run up and down her spine.

"Ooooh Lawd, chile. What that man can do to me when he sing a song. You familiar with Otis Redding's songs, Saphronia?"

Before she could answer yes or no, Precious continued, saying, "You know something? He sho' do kind of sound like that big, fine preacher from down in Memphis, don't he? You know who I'm talking about?"

"Theophilus Simmons?" Saphronia asked, thinking that Precious was right about his voice. He did sound a bit like the voice on the radio—only she thought that his voice was deeper than the man's voice, more akin to Brook Benton's.

"Yeah, yeah, that's him, Rev. Simmons."

Now Precious put the wig on the crown of Saphronia's head and fit it into place. "Ooohh, girl," she said. "Come on back to Tee's room to see how you look."

Saphronia followed her to Tee's room and went and

stood in front of the large mirror on the dresser. She was transformed. To her surprise, she absolutely adored the way that short, sassy blond wig looked on her.

"I cannot believe how good I look," Saphronia said, and gave Precious a hug.

It was such a warm and appreciative hug that Precious felt a stiff ache in her jaw from trying to fight back her tears. A wave of sadness washed over her heart as she recognized that this was the end, that she would never return to Marcel as his lover, his secretary, a member of his church, or a willing participant in all of the dirty business he was into. How could she have been so dumb as to think this man could help her love herself as a result of him loving her?

Saphronia reached out her hand and gently wiped away the tears that were now flowing down Precious's face. She was deeply touched. No other woman had ever cried with her over shared hurts and sorrows. Even her own mother, who had abandoned her to start a new life in California, hadn't cried when they were reunited at Saphronia's engagement party after a twenty-year estrangement.

"Precious, please don't cry like that over all of this. Look at it this way. If you had not fallen so hard for Marcel, I wouldn't be standing here looking good and feeling brave enough to do something about my life. And if I hadn't gotten engaged to Marcel, you would still be waiting for him to marry you. You deserve better than that. How many women do you think would have had the nerve to come to me and cook up something like this?"

Precious smiled and wiped her face with both hands.

"I guess you right about that, girl. This is probably

one of those 'the Lord works in mysterious ways' kind of things."

Saphronia said, "Probably so," and then turned toward the mirror to look at the wig again. "I'm going to do something with my hair when all of this conference business is finally over with. I've thought about cutting and highlighting my hair for a while, but Marcel always told me that I would look like I worked in a brothel." She shook her head as she said, more to herself than to Precious, "But I guess he should know a lot about what that looks like, huh?"

Precious just listened as Saphronia continued, "And you know what makes me so angry, is that this two-timing rogue didn't even stop and take the time to think that maybe I would have looked better."

Precious took one of Saphronia's hands in both of hers and said with a solemn look on her face, "He *knew* you would look better, just didn't *want* you to look this good."

Saphronia felt a quick stab of anger at the truth of those words.

"Now, Saphronia," Precious said. "There's one more thing we have to talk about. And that is, what you gone do to embarrass Marcel?"

Saphronia shrugged. "What could possibly embarrass that man? You catch him with another other-woman *and* he is helping to run a brothel at a funeral home for preachers attending a Triennial Conference. Now, can you honestly think of something that would embarrass him?"

Precious shook her head and said, "Other than you showing up dressed like this, no. But maybe this ain't something we can plan. When you get there, you're gonna just have to watch and wait and see what to do."

She rubbed her forehead and then snapped her fingers. "Know what, when you get there, don't ask for Marcel. Just give them my employee number, 10, and then go straight to the Sanctuary area."

"The what?"

"The Sanctuary. It's a joke—one of the preachers thought it was funny to call the room where most of them come to the Sanctuary."

Saphronia thought she had heard it all about this club. "Just what goes on in this, this . . . Sanctuary?"

"Depends. It's mostly a waiting area, and the only women who are allowed in there are a few hostesses who get them drinks and food."

Saphronia closed her eyes, hoping that she wasn't going to lose her nerve.

"Precious, you do realize that Marcel is going to be very angry at me when I show up at this place. And once he gets over his shock, he is going to find out who sent me there. Are you sure you are ready for that?"

"Saphronia, I'm not scared of Marcel. I'm kind of scared of that Laymond Johnson, but I'll be ready for him when he figures out that I sent you—because I know that big Negro will figure it out. He's a lay delegate from Bishop Caruthers's old district. He's also on the payroll for the ho' service. And let me tell you, that is one hateful man. Always trying to pat and paw on you like Bishop Caruthers and Sonny Washington. You watch yourself with him. He wears white shoes, and he might be at the door. Try talking a little crazy to confuse him."

"Well, I had better get going," Saphronia said. "Hand me those uncomfortable-looking shoes."

Saphronia slipped the silver pumps on her feet and wobbled from side to side when she stood up and tried to walk. Precious reached out and grabbed her elbow to help her find her balance.

"Saphronia, I didn't know your siddity self couldn't walk in high heels. You know you got to switch your big butt around on these shoes if you want them to let you into the Sanctuary."

"Maybe I can walk slowly," Saphronia said doubtfully.

Tee, who was standing in the doorway quietly admiring the way Saphronia looked, said, "Here's your pocketbook. You left it on the couch." She walked over to Saphronia and examined her carefully. "Miss It, Lord knows when you first walked yourself up in my house, I'd a never thought you could look like this. Chile, you gots to know you looking good."

"Thank you," Saphronia said.

Precious looked her over one last time to make sure that everything was just right and realized that something was missing.

"What's wrong?"

"You don't have on any earrings."

Tee went over to her dresser and rambled through a purple satin jewelry box until she found a pair of crystal beaded clip-ons.

Saphronia put them on her ears and looked at herself in the mirror again. Precious was right. These earrings added the perfect last touch.

Precious frowned again.

Saphronia raised her eyebrows. "Now what's wrong?"

Precious grabbed her purse off the bed and dug around in it until she found her pocketknife.

"You know how to use one of these? Could come in handy if one of them preachers try to get frisky with you."

Saphronia shook her head no. She had never been anywhere where she might need a knife.

"It's pretty simple. See, look at what I'm doing," Precious said, as she grabbed the handle firmly and flicked the knife open and closed. "All you got to do is flick this thing open and whoever it is that is bothering you will leave you alone. None of those preachers would want to have to explain a big cut on them to their wives."

Saphronia took the knife and practiced flicking it open a couple of times. She was surprised that she could learn to use a knife so well after only a few moments of practice.

"Saphronia," Precious said. "When you walk around in that neighborhood, try and look like you belong. Don't you get out of the car looking and acting like some proper Miss It. That's all some of them people gone need to mess with you—you understand?"

Saphronia walked into the living room, put the knife in her purse, turned toward Precious and said in her best new voice, "Okay, Precious, girl, I heard you already."

Precious patted her arm and smiled. "I ought to charge you for all this. I'll be waiting to find out everything that happened, okay?"

Saphronia nodded her head.

"Now, you remember where you supposed to go—the Sanctuary, right?"

"Goodbye, Precious."

"Saphronia?"

"Goodbye, Precious."

"Saphronia, what are you going to do to Marcel?"

"I don't know at this moment. It will come to me once I get there. *Good-bye,* Precious."

"You sure you will think of something?"

"Good-bye, Precious."

Chapter Twenty-six

APHRONIA GRABBED HER PURSE OFF THE SEAT and locked the car. She was putting her keys in her purse when she noticed that the man who had been on the other side of the street had crossed over and was heading in her direction. Trying not to look afraid—remembering Precious's advice about warding off trouble—she managed to smile at the man, who dropped one shoulder down and began to swing his arm, doing that strut that indicated he was going to try and "talk" to her.

Anxious not to offend but wanting to keep her distance, Saphronia smiled again and began to walk away from the car. She tried to switch like Precious had instructed but wobbled in those shoes and had to steady herself by leaning against a tree. She remembered to throw another smile at the man when he said, "Baby girl, baby girl. I sho' do wish I could just turns myself into a pretty pink dress and wraps myself all *o-ver* your fine self. Lawd, ha' mercy!"

She inched away from him and half switched, half

tripped her way down the block toward the Victorian-style funeral home. She wondered if anyone on this quiet street of older homes, a barbershop, a restaurant, and a small dry cleaners knew what was going on just steps away from their own front doors. Walking around to the back of the building, just as Precious had instructed, she tapped three times on the door leading to the screened-in porch.

To her horror, a man wearing white shoes came to the door. That had to be Laymond Johnson. She was tempted to run off as he unhooked the door, but thought to herself, "If I am to get in, I had better be prepared to get past him."

He stood with his face pressed against the opened door, leaving only a narrow space for her to squeeze in past him. She recoiled, and he gave her a curious look, saying, "You must be new here, baby, or you'd know that all you girls have to kind of squeeze by to get in."

Saphronia's cheeks flushed under their soft strokes of brushed-on color.

Laymond laughed right in her face, amused that she didn't want to participate in this ritual. "Now, so that we can get out of this here doorway, you go on and tell me what I need to know to even let you in."

Saphronia stared at him dumbly for a few seconds until she realized that he was asking her for her entry code.

"Uh . . . Mr. Sonny . . . uh . . . I mean Rev. Sonny Washington, he the one that sent me and gave me number 10 and I was told to come on over here and just mingle unless somebody sayed number 10 which he said they wouldn't do tonight, right?"

Laymond had a hard time following her, and she watched him processing all those words. He finally said,

"Precious Powers sick or something? Number 10 the number for the bookkeeper and she the only one we got. And I know you not one of the regular girls 'cause they've all checked in."

He remained silent for a moment, searching her face, looking like he was ready to hurt her if she didn't come up with the right answer.

Saphronia was kind of scared, but she opened her eyes real wide and raised her eyebrows as if to say, "What that got to do with me?"

She looked around the porch like she didn't have the faintest idea where she was, adjusting her bra strap and sucking her teeth like she was extracting a piece of food. And when she said, "You gotta toothpick I could borrow," he relaxed. Most of these ho's were kind of dumb—even the well-dressed ones like this girl—and if she hadn't been sent by Reverend Washington, she would have backed down and tried to leave. He moved back an inch or two, making a little more space for her to come through the door.

"I gonna be real nice to your dumb behind and let you come in here and do whatever you were told to do, if you're capable of remembering that."

"I thinks I 'sposed to serve and stuff like that."

Laymond just looked at her, wondering if she could hold a tray of food right and said, "Yeah, whatever. But I want you to remember something."

"Uh huh, what's that?"

"I want you to remember that the next time you come here to work, you better remember everything you were told, including your work number. I don't stand for no dumb ho's working at *my* establishment. You got that straight?"

Saphronia swallowed hard and forced herself to give

him a toothy grin as she switched and wobbled her way through that tiny space he had allotted for her in the doorway. He had some nerve calling this place *his* establishment, when he was nothing but a lackey for Cleotis Clayton and these preachers. She wondered how many of the women working here really believed that Laymond Johnson was running this place.

The grin and that big old butt swaying up against him made Laymond relax enough to feel that perhaps she was okay after all. He smiled back at her and then reached out and rubbed his hand over the curve of her behind. He liked the first feel so much, he took the liberty of getting another one and said, "Maybe you should think about more'n just serving up some food this evening. That fine-looking behind you got swinging off the back of you is a moneymaker if I ever saw one."

He caught a glimmer of something in her eye that made him feel uneasy, the same kind of look that uppity Precious Powers always gave him. He pointed down the hall and nudged her to get to walking in the direction of the Sanctuary and went to find something to eat.

When he was gone, Saphronia leaned against the wall and fought back the tears that were threatening to spill down her cheeks. She could not believe that man had the audacity to touch her like that. A sob rose up in her throat but stopped cold when she suddenly realized that Laymond had not touched *her* behind, he was patting on a "ho'." Her spirits lifted and she marveled at her own successful subterfuge. With a swell of confidence, she walked to the end of the hall, past two rooms set up for funerals, and knocked boldly on the Sanctuary door. After a brief questioning by some kind of security guard, she was in.

What she saw shocked her. She had expected a room

that looked something like those two parlors she passed in the hall. But this room was so sophisticated that it must have taken months of work to ready for the Triennial Conference.

The walls were painted baby blue, and the molding, doorways, and windowsills were a soft, creamy white. The furniture was an eclectic but tasteful assortment of velvet and silk damask couches and butter-soft leather chairs in various shades of blue. The roomy and comfortable-looking leather armchairs were navy blue, the velvet couch and silk damask love seats were a matching robin's egg blue, and the smaller-looking wood and leather chairs were all upholstered in a rich, jewel-toned turquoise.

There were large crystal vases filled with multicolored bouquets of fresh roses—pink, yellow, ivory, and peach—placed on gleaming mahogany tables that were next to the armchairs and in front of the couches. A sleek, silver-framed mirror adorned the wall behind the long, polished, mahogany bar. The hardwood floor was covered with exquisite tapestry area rugs with navy, ivory, and pale blue running through them, and the velvet draperies, which were closed, were the same baby blue as the soft-colored walls.

The only thing that betrayed the purpose of the room was the mirrors on sections of the ceiling and the wall facing the bar. It was those mirrors that snapped Saphronia back to attention and reminded her that, tasteful or not, this was the reception room for a brothel. Now, for the first time, she noticed the men standing around in front of the mirrored wall, sitting on the couches, and stretched out on the chairs.

She adjusted her purse on her shoulder and walked around the room, hoping to catch a glimpse of Marcel and trying to act as she thought a brothel hostess would behave on the job—swinging her hips and smiling at the men who made eye contact with her. She had just spotted the back of Marcel's head across the large room when she felt the tickling of fingers running from her shoulder to her hand. She jumped and turned to look into the face of a pastor who served at a small church in Detroit. At first she was afraid that he would recognize her, but then she remembered that this man, who liked real fancy-looking women (even his wife always wore busy, ruffled dresses and hats with too much trimming), had never bothered to look her in the face the few times they had met when she visited Marcel's church.

Saphronia smiled at him sweetly and said in her new voice, "Baby, why you runnin' yo' hand down my arm like that? You know you could make me lose my job, temptin' me to take you up in one of them rooms for the en-tire evening."

She started fanning her face with her hand, as if just the thought of being with him was enough to make her hot. The pastor, who Saphronia thought looked like a shriveled-up little laboratory frog, said in a raspy, gravelly voice that sounded like he was up in the pulpit, "And . . . ah . . . ah . . . you know . . . ah . . . I wish you could afford to lose your job ovah me. 'Cause I been lookin' for a blessin' all evening. And I believe goin' up to one of those rooms with you, Laaawwwd, would be more exciting than when Ezekiel saw the wheel way up in de middle of de air."

What a fool, Saphronia thought. He had the nerve to use words from an old Negro spiritual to try to hit on her. She was about to walk away from him in disgust when the man reached out and pulled her close to him, wrapping his arm tightly around her waist. She held her breath when he placed his face a few inches from hers because his breath smelled like whiskey and hog maws.

She looked over his shoulder, trying to find Marcel, and saw a preacher go over to the juke box to play a song. Lavish as the Sanctuary was, Marcel and his cronies were so cheap that they didn't have the decency to provide their club members with free music—and worse, these men were stupid enough to pay for it, too.

The song that began to fill the air was "Just a Closer Walk with Thee" by Evangelist Elroy Thorn, until somebody yelled, "Turn that crap off. We ain't in no church up in here."

Now someone played Big Mama Thornton's "You Ain't Nothing but a Hound Dog," and Saphronia thought that if she could get this pastor to dance, maybe it would get his stinky breath out of her face. "Sweet daddy," she crooned, "why don't us get out on that floor and do some dancing. You know, a little moving around might help to cool me down a bit."

He gave Saphronia a great big grin, said, "Well, Lawd yes, let's dance," and grabbed her even tighter, giving her such a strong whiff of his breath that she could actually tell where the hog maws started and the liquor left off.

She pulled away from him, saying as nicely as she could, "Pastor, this here song got a upbeat sound to it. We'll look silly out on this here floor if we get to dancing all tight and close."

He took a moment to think about what she said and answered, "Ah . . . ah . . . guess you right," and led her to the middle of the floor, right in front of the mirrored wall. All the while, she had been hoping to fake him out because she couldn't dance. But then the pastor asked, "Darling, you do plan on dancing for me, don't you?"

Dance for him? Alone, in front of all these men? She took a deep breath, hoped for the best, and began moving her hips from side to side, with her purse still hanging on her shoulder. Once she got confident with this movement, Saphronia, to her own surprise, began feeling kind of good and feisty all over. She snapped her fingers, gave the pastor a seductive look, swung her shoulders back and forth, and rolled her generous behind around. When she noticed that the pastor had moved back to get a better view of her *and* that she had caught the attention of several ministers, she put her hands on her hips and shook her butt harder, shimmying on down to the floor and staying there, shaking for almost five seconds. When she stood back up, she looked in the mirror and saw Marcel's reflection as he walked toward the small group of preachers, who, by now, had formed a circle around her. "What if he doesn't recognize me?" she thought, but then panicked, thinking, "What if he does?"

"Embarrass him"—that is what Precious had said, and now was the time to do it. When she knew that Marcel was looking at her, Saphronia dropped down on the floor in a squat, put a hand on each knee (still holding her purse up on her shoulder), and rolled her big butt around in the nastiest way she could imagine.

Marcel's first thought when he saw her was that she certainly wasn't a hostess who had been hired and trained by Cleotis. And his suspicion was confirmed when he saw her reddish blond head bobbing up and down in that circle like she was *dancing*, of all things. The women who worked here had all been told a hundred times that dancing, unless specifically ordered by him or Laymond, *was not allowed* in the Sanctuary.

When he first approached the circle of preachers, he couldn't see Saphronia's face. Then, as he glanced in the mirror, the reflection solved the mystery of her identity. Seeing his fiancée shaking her butt for those preachers, he got a sickening feeling high up in his stomach. And when she dropped down on the floor and rolled her butt all around, he thought he was going to mess in his pants. He had never seen Saphronia so much as wiggle her hips. And here she was letting a group of men ogle her as she rolled those hips around like she was sitting on top of a man.

Marcel took a deep breath to calm his nerves, pushed a few preachers aside, and walked into the circle and right up to Saphronia. Quickly surveying the small group to see if there was any recognition of her in their faces, he thanked God no one but he knew who she was. He stood right in front of her and watched the shock spread across her face when she realized that he had seen her— and that he was not going to make a scene and reveal her identity to the other men. Instead, he pulled her up off the floor and over to him, saying softly, slowly, with pure venom in his voice, "I ought to whip your tail good for pulling a stunt like this."

Saphronia pressed even closer to Marcel, putting her arms around his neck, so the ministers thought she was coming on to him. She whispered in his ear, "You do that, and I'll pull this hot wig off of my head so fast it will make your head spin. And then I'll make sure that even the dumbest preacher in this room knows exactly who I am. So there isn't going to be any tail-whipping tonight, Marcel. And there is nothing you can do about what I have just done."

Marcel was stunned, listening to Saphronia. All he could do was grab her arm and pull her out of the room.

As he dragged her to his office, he was silently praying that there wasn't more to this little fiasco than what had already been displayed.

Opening his office door, Marcel shoved Saphronia in and slammed it shut before anyone else came along. Seething, breathing hard, and looking like he was going to burst wide open, he shouted, "What is your problem, stepping up in here looking like a two-dollar whore?"

Saphronia didn't say a word. She just adjusted her purse on her shoulders and put her hands on her hips, with a stubborn "you ain't nobody" look on her face, because he was the one doing wrong, not her.

That look sent Marcel into such a fit of rage that he slapped Saphronia down to the floor. Her face was burning, and she could taste the metallic flavor of blood when she ran her tongue across her lip. She sat up on the floor, with her head spinning and Marcel standing over her, holding his hand, which was throbbing with pain and beginning to swell.

"I asked you a question, Saphronia. You'd better tell me something and you better tell me something *now!*" he yelled.

"And what if I don't?" she said defiantly. "You can beat my butt good if you want to, but you can't make me talk!"

He snatched her up off the floor and grabbed her by the hair, but the wig came off in his hand. That made him even madder. He reached down and, this time, grabbed a fat handful of her real hair, pulling her head back so far it made her neck hurt.

"Okay, you siddity bitch. You had better start talking right now. Because if you don't, I'll put my foot so far up your behind, you'll know what my shoe polish tastes like."

The word *bitch* rang in her ears, and it was *that* evil word that gave her strength she didn't even know she had. She pulled her purse off her shoulder and swung it around, hitting Marcel upside his head so hard that he crumpled over on his side and fell on the floor.

"I am not telling you anything, you low-down, dirty pimp."

Marcel was in shock, the impact of her words hitting him harder than the blow upside his head. He said, voice sounding a shade higher because of the sheer impossibility of this situation, "What did you just say to me, Saphronia?"

"I *said*," she answered evenly, "that you are a low-down, dirty pimp who blasphemes the name of minister and is a disgrace to the Gospel United Church."

"Who the hell do you think you are talking to?"

"You, Marcel DeMarcus Brown. I am talking to *you!* And I know this one thing, you had better quit cursing at me or else—"

"Or else what?" he said nastily, making it clear by the look on his face that he didn't think she was capable of doing anything worth worrying about.

Saphronia stood there filled with rage for a few moments and then said, "Or else this," as she raised her foot and kicked him square in the behind. Before he had a chance to respond, she raised her foot and kicked him again and again. And, when those kicks didn't satisfy her, she jumped on top of him and began to beat him with her purse, hitting him anywhere she thought would hurt. Tears were rushing down her face as she sat on top of Marcel, beating him with every ounce of her strength.

"For the past year I put up with your low-down, cheating self, just walking around acting like I deserved all of that crap you shoveled my way. And Negro, despite all that you have done, you have never even apologized to me. You hear me, *Marcel? Never!* Well," she said, as she grabbed his collar and stared right into his face, "I didn't deserve one iota of the crap you heaped on me and I'm not taking it off of you anymore."

Marcel was speechless. Rarely had anyone had the nerve to confront him on anything. And now his fiancée, a little country girl from Mississippi, was screaming in his face. He tried to shove her off him and give her a taste of the butt-whipping he thought she deserved, but as soon as he moved, she grabbed him by the ears, pinned him down, and began banging his head on the bare wooden floor so hard he saw double. All he could do was pray she would stop, and when he felt like he was about to pass out, started hollering for help.

Laymond Johnson and Cleotis Clayton ran into the room with pistols in their hands. They looked around for a robber and were shocked to see a woman sitting on top of Marcel, beating the living daylights out of him.

Cleotis, who didn't like Marcel, put his gun back in his shoulder holster and then just stood there watching. Laymond, out of loyalty, went over and tried to pull Saphronia off him. But he backed away when she started swinging that purse around.

Cleotis, who now recognized Saphronia, poked Laymond on the shoulder and shook his head no, warning him not to lay a hand on Saphronia. Laymond tried to shove him away but Cleotis stood his ground and now said out loud, "Don't hit her, man."

Laymond tried to shove him again and said, "Get out of my face."

Cleotis pulled at his coat sleeve. "Don't hit that

woman unless you want to end up down on that floor next to Rev. Brown."

Laymond was furious that this scrawny funeral home Negro had the nerve to talk to him like that. He spun around to deal with Cleotis and stuck his face right in the nose of the gun, which Cleotis had taken out again.

"Are you crazy? Put that doggone gun away."

"When you decide to leave Miss McComb alone, I'll put this gun away," Cleotis said.

Laymond wasn't sure he had heard Cleotis right. He looked at Saphronia again and, sure enough, she was definitely Rev. Brown's fiancée. Laymond began to look scared. He had just known something was wrong when he let her in tonight.

"Well, then, you take care of her," he told Cleotis, and beat a hasty retreat.

Cleotis, still holding his gun, held out his free hand to Saphronia. She took it and got up to stand by his side. The sight of the gun made her feel squeamish. It had never even occurred to her that the people involved in this business might have to shoot somebody.

Marcel now stood up, holding the side of his head, his face contorted by anger and throbbing pain.

"You think you have really done something to me, don't you, Saphronia?" he said. "Well, just know this. You haven't done a thing but give me the reason I've been looking for to call off this wedding. Never wanted to marry your big old stuck-up butt in the first place." He laughed, then stopped because his head was hurting. "Did you know that my father and Bishop Giles *made* me pick you over Precious? Huh?"

Tears formed in Saphronia's eyes and started running down her cheeks.

"I see you didn't know that. But now you do," he

said, and spread his hands out like he was saying, "See, you can't have this." He sighed heavily and then gave her a nasty smirk. "Well, *Miss* McComb, hear this. *Because* you have proven yourself unworthy of marrying a pastor of my status, I am now free to go and get the woman I should have asked to marry me in the first place. See, despite your credentials, *Miss* McComb, the woman who has my heart is Precious Powers. So you just did me a favor, baby girl."

Saphronia stopped crying and smiled at Marcel, knowing that the news she was about to deliver was going to wipe that cocky smirk right off of his face. She looked at him for a moment and said, "Who do you think sent me here, Marcel?"

His face got guarded and he said, "What do you mean, *sent* you?"

"Just what I said," Saphronia answered. "Do you honestly think I could pull this off by myself? *Not me*, with my big-old-stuck-up-butt self."

Marcel began to advance on her but she raised that purse up and he backed off.

"Marcel, I don't think you are getting married to anybody anytime soon. You just made it clear you never wanted me. And now I just have to tell you that the woman you want so bad no longer wants you. And she sent me here to get you straight after she heard you in bed with some woman when you were supposed to be with her. So right now, I don't care that you never wanted me. Just telling you that *Precious* doesn't want *you* is enough to ease my pain."

Saphronia watched Marcel digest that information. She didn't care that her face was swollen and hurting, and that she looked a mess, because she had not felt this good since she was five years old and won her first speech contest at church.

Cleotis Clayton started to question her about just how much Precious Powers told her but changed his mind. He had earned all the money he needed to launch the funeral home, and then some. He would be happy to close up shop because he was tired of these preachers, every last one of them.

Chapter Twenty-seven

PRECIOUS EXAMINED SAPHRONIA'S FACE, SHAKING her head in disgust, and held her hand out for the ice pack Mother Harold had just made. She had been furious when she caught Marcel with Jackie Giles. But this? This made her so mad that Tee had to stop her from going to the funeral home and jumping all over Marcel. She couldn't believe he would beat up a woman like this.

Saphronia winced when she put the ice pack on her face, making Mother Harold jump. Despite Mother Harold's dicty ways, Saphronia was everything to her, and it hurt her down to the bone to see her baby hurt. She stroked her granddaughter's hand gently, like she did when she was little, and said, "Dear, is there anything I can do for you?"

Saphronia was about to say no, but something occurred to her. "Yes, Grandmother. There is something you can do for me."

Saphronia sat up slowly, every muscle aching. She

leaned over, her head killing her, and reached under the bed to pull out the red leather book. Precious helped her back in the bed, taking the address book out of her hands. She counted the money in it real fast—over $6,500—and split it between her and Saphronia. Then she scanned the contents of the book, eyes big and round as she read the names of preachers she knew were members of that ho' club. Between Precious's blue record book and Marcel's red leather address book, there was enough evidence to get rid of Marcel, Sonny, and Bishop Caruthers for good.

"Girl, you know this is some low-down funky stuff."

Mother Harold gasped and was about to reprimand Precious for her language when she heard her own granddaughter say, "Girl, I heard that," before they slapped each other's palms.

"So, girl, what you proposing?"

Saphronia put the ice pack on her throbbing head. She said, "Grandmother is taking these books to the session later this morning, and she's going to give them to Rev. James. He will know exactly what to do with them."

Mother Harold opened her mouth to protest but closed it when Saphronia gave her a look she had never seen on her face before. As far as Saphronia was concerned, if she could take a good butt-whipping like a woman, her grandmother was going to be woman enough to put these books in Rev. James's very capable hands.

"Saphronia, dear, do you think this is the right thing to do? I mean, if I understand what is going on, two pastors and a bishop could very well lose their jobs. That is a very serious thing, dear. It takes years for a man to reach those points in a ministerial career. And what you are proposing could take it all away in a matter of minutes."

"That is exactly the point, Grandmother. I want it all taken away in a matter of minutes."

"But, dear, what would have happened if every time someone became upset with your grandfather, they brought him before a Triennial Conference?"

Saphronia sighed and forced herself to sit up straight. Using her own house money, her grandmother had protected her grandfather for years, to pay off a woman who showed up at the house with a big child who looked just like him. He acted like butter would not melt in his mouth, when he was one of the biggest devils around.

"Grandmother, maybe somebody should have called Grandfather on the carpet about all of that mess. Maybe he would have been a better preacher and a better man. He certainly had a lot to offer, but he could stir a lot of trouble, too.

"And as far as Bishop Caruthers, Rev. Washington, and Marcel are concerned, they don't deserve the privilege of being pastors and a bishop in the Gospel United Church. So, Grandmother, whether you like it or not, you are taking those books to Rev. James. You are the only one, of the three of us, who can get in and get into the conference past Marcel, Rev. Washington, the Claytons, and Bishop Caruthers. So I am begging you, Grandmother. Please, help me and do right by your church."

Mother Harold didn't say anything. She reached out her hands to take the books and went to get her purse and hat. As soon as she was out the door, Saphronia and Precious both looked up at the same time and said, "Thank you, Lord."

Chapter Twenty-eight

ESSIE SAT DOWN JUST AS THE ORGANIST STARTED UP a somber march to herald the entrance of the bishops, candidates for bishop, and prominent ministers. This would be the last session before the final vote was cast to elect the new bishops this evening. The first three of the four voting sessions had eliminated all but ten of the sixty candidates. And this was the day the bishops would do their most ferocious politicking to get their choice man into one of those four seats. It was the last day to help or oppose any man you wanted to have a lifetime job of running your church.

The first candidate for bishop in the procession was Ernest Brown, who was marching next to his son. Ernest was stepping boldly and with great pride, like he had already been elected a bishop. But Marcel was dragging and looking battered, as if he had gotten into some kind of brawl. But that wasn't likely, Essie thought. Marcel Brown was too cowardly and stuck on himself to fight somebody straight-up.

Ernest Brown was wearing a pale purple shirt with a matching tie under his robe, forgoing his black clerical shirt for one that would give the impression that he was a shoo-in for a bishop's seat. The sight disgusted Susie James, who was sitting next to Essie. She couldn't understand how men like him always managed to get away with so much dirt. And it was taking too long for them all to march up onto the stage—and not because the processional was so large. It was because they were all marching slowly, to make sure that nobody missed them and who they were walking with. In fact, before the session started, groups of bishops had held court in the gymnasium with the candidate of their choice. A couple of bishops had even taken turns walking around the building with a hand on the shoulder of the man they wanted to occupy one of those four coveted episcopal seats.

Essie looked around the room for Theophilus and was relieved to see him standing with Eddie, Johnnie, and Willis. She was worried about him, and it showed on her face. Lee Allie reached across Susie James and squeezed her hand.

"Essie Lee, Theophilus is gone be just fine."

"I know, Mama. But I hope *he* knows that he's going to be all right."

"He does. Not up in his head, where he running down a list of everything he got to worry about, but deep down in his heart, where he can feel God pulling at him and nudging him to take this stance this morning. Rev. James is right that Theophilus got a whole lot to offer this church. But it ain't gone do nobody a bit of good if he don't learn to stand up for what's right. Just think about what Dr. Martin Luther King, Jr., must be feeling every time he got to face those evil white folks in all those places he go to, to protest for our rights. I'd bet some money that he has been real scared a many a day. And this thing that Theophilus got to do, ain't nowhere close to the danger Dr. King facing just about every single day."

The men finally made it up onto the stage, and Bishop Giles walked to the microphone just as everybody took their seats. He opened the large Bible lying on the podium and turned it to the chapter selected for the morning's scripture reading. But before he had a chance to open his mouth, Bishop Jennings came up over to him.

"Sit down, Lawson," he said.

Bishop Giles looked at Bishop Jennings like he was crazy.

"I said sit down, Lawson. You don't have a right to stand up here in front of all of these people."

Bishop Giles stepped back from the podium and said indignantly to Bishop Jennings, "What do you mean I don't have a right to stand here? I think, Bishop, that you owe me an apology."

"No," Bishop Jennings said slowly, beckoning Theophilus to come up and join him. "No, I don't owe you a thing. Sit down. Rev. Simmons has something to tell us. Rev. Simmons, come up here, because as the *senior* bishop in this denomination, I have just exercised my administrative privilege to take over this session so that I could turn it over to you."

Bishop Giles stepped away from Bishop Jennings. What could Jennings think a junior pastor like Theophilus Simmons had to say that was so important he would break conference protocol on his behalf? He looked over at Ernest Brown to see if he could make any sense out of it, but Ernest just made a face to let him know that he had always thought Percy Jennings was a pain in the butt.

Marcel was reeling from the past twenty-four hours, still mad about Saphronia's performance at the club, worried about the money he had left with her, wondering where Precious Powers was. And now, to make matters worse, Theophilus Simmons was strutting up to the podium looking like he had just come down from a visit on a mountain with God.

He put a hand to his aching head and glanced over at Sonny to see how he was taking all of this. Sonny looked agitated and Marcel's anxiety rose by several degrees when he saw Sonny take out a handkerchief and wipe his face.

The only one who was calm and composed throughout all of this was Otis Caruthers. Unlike the others, he knew without a doubt that all this posturing in front of the pulpit had something to do with the preachers' club. Laymond had called him late last night to tell him about Marcel's fiancée and some unknown preachers who had gotten past their security system. It didn't surprise him that his enemies had found out about the club. He knew his adversaries well enough to know that they were capable of almost anything.

Even though a small part of him worried about the outcome, most of him was amused and eager to see how all this would play out. The danger of being exposed even thrilled him a little. He only regretted that he wasn't at the club when Marcel's siddity fiancée, or that "fabulous hostess girl, all dressed up in a pink dress," as the pastor from Detroit described it, had rolled all around on the floor. Otis would have paid a whole lot of money to see that dance. He couldn't, even in his wildest dreams, imagine what Saphronia Anne McComb looked like doing that dance, and he knew that the look on Marcel's face when he discovered her dancing like that must have been priceless.

Otis unzipped his robe to get a little air, sat back in his seat, and got real comfortable so that he could enjoy the show.

Bishop Jennings had moved aside so that Theophilus could take the podium.

Theophilus was as ready as he would ever be. He knew that what he had to say would be greeted with a mixture of curiosity, shock, and disbelief. He hoped that he would never regret his words when he ran off the list of crimes of the men who had so callously violated the trust of their people and the sanctity of the Negro church. He took a deep breath and looked at Essie, who smiled at him. It was just the inspiration he needed.

He placed a hand on either side of the podium, and began, in as commanding a voice as he could muster.

"Church, it grieves my heart to have to disrupt the order of this service and come to tell you what I have learned. Now, I know that so many of you good people out there are here to help set the course of the church for the next four years. Setting that direction includes selecting the men who will govern our great church, our bishops. I know that not a one of you good, Christian folks came here to support men who, in their need for money, power, and illicit pleasures, would sacrifice the soul of our church.

"Good church folks, since the conference began, two preachers and one bishop have been helping a member of this denomination run a club of ill repute right here in Richmond. And not only that, this business has been thriving because some of our bishops and many of your pastors have patronized it while attending this conference."

Uncle Booker knew how much courage it was taking for Theophilus to put himself on the line. But as he surveyed the room, he could tell that some of the people listening weren't exactly sure what he was talking about. Theophilus was going to have to spell it out in black and white, he thought, and decided to help him to get his message across. He walked to the edge of the stage and said loud enough to be heard by the people in the front rows, "Theophilus, son, you gone have to tell these here folks that Bishop Otis Caruthers, Rev. Sonny Washington, and Rev. Marcel Brown running a ho' house at this here conference. That house of ill repute mess ain't gone pluck nobody's nerve and make 'em mad enough to do something about it."

At that point Marcel Brown lost all restraint. He had enough of Theophilus Simmons to last him a lifetime, and now this old country coot was trying to help Theophilus drive him and his father right into the ground. He wasn't having it. If he and Sonny had to whip Theophilus's butt right up on that stage, so be it. Theophilus wasn't scoring any more points in this denomination—and especially not at his expense.

Marcel and Sonny advanced on the stage, backed up by Willie Williams and the thuggish Jimmy Thekston.

When Theophilus saw them, he unzipped his robe, threw it on the floor, and put up his fists, like he was warming up for a good fight. When Essie saw him drop one shoulder and start dancing in a boxing stance, she cried, "Ohhh Lord," and had to beg forgiveness of a few church mothers nearby.

Rev. James, appalled to see a bunch of preachers getting ready to start a barroom brawl at the General

Conference, stood up and paced in place, trying to think of something that he could do to defuse the situation. Where was Mother Harold? She had called him, saying she had something to help his cause. And when he acted like he didn't know what she was talking about, she said, "Cut the crap, Murcheson. I know it all and you *need* what I have."

Marcel reached out and grabbed Theophilus's starched white collar, winding up for a punch, when Theophilus said, "Man, save that swing. Because if you take it—one, I'll whip your trifling butt, and two, ain't nobody gonna vote for your daddy."

Marcel backed off, as did Sonny, Willie Williams, and James Thekston. The last thing they needed to do was further jeopardize anybody's chances of getting elected bishop by starting a fistfight in front of all of these church folks.

Theophilus went back to the podium, recognizing that the time to mince words had passed, and jumped right into what he had to say. "Look, people. You all need to know what's happening, and I just don't have the luxury of spelling it out to you all nice and churchy-like. Bishop Otis Caruthers, Rev. Sonny Washington, and Rev. Marcel Brown are running a cathouse, a brothel, right up under your noses at this conference."

That quelled the hubbub that had arisen at the prospect of a fistfight. The gymnasium grew so quiet that Theophilus could hear himself breathing. Every eye and ear was on him as he said, "People, these men helped Cleotis Clayton, one of the proprietors of Clayton Funeral Homes out of Memphis, Tennessee, operate this club where some Gospel United preachers and bishops betrayed their office by sinfully consorting with women."

Theophilus looked straight at Marcel when he said, "So, what do you men have to say for yourselves?"

"He has nothing to say to you or to anybody else talking this nonsense," said Ernest Brown. "Look here, young man. Your people have schooled you wrong. While I applaud your bravery and concern for our great church, you are a fool to hurl insults at your brother preachers and even a bishop without one shred of evidence to prove what you say is true."

"He has some evidence all right," Booker said. "I have seen the place and can point out a few of the preachers who was there and sitting right up in this audience."

"That doesn't prove anything," Ernest scoffed. "So a few wayward preachers found their way to a hot spot and decided to go on in. Why, we have been dealing with this sort of thing for almost as long as we have had preachers."

"Oh, there's more to it than that, Ernest," Rev. James said, approaching the stage with the blue record book in one hand and Marcel's red leather address book in the other. It was nothing short of a miracle that Mother Harold had found him and given him these books just when they were most needed.

"Young Rev. Brown, do you recognize this?" Rev. James asked, holding out the red leather book.

Marcel looked at the book with a perfectly contrived, perplexed expression. He shrugged and said, "Don't believe that I do, Rev. James."

"Well that's odd. Because your name is right here in the front of it. Here, come on down and take a better look."

Marcel narrowed his eyes at Rev. James and stayed in his place. Nothing, not even the flames of hell lapping at his feet, would make him admit that this book belonged to him.

Rev. James looked around at the church folks and knew from the looks on their faces that no one believed that Marcel was telling the truth. He held up the blue book, saying, "Ernest"—he opened it—"Ernest, it says right here that you incurred expenses at this club and that your church was to be billed to pay for them. Now, how do you explain all that? I have a copy of your signature right here."

Ernest ran over to Rev. James and jumped up in his face. He said, "That is a bald-faced lie and you know it," loud enough to be heard all over the gymnasium.

A few of the older women held their fans up to their faces and whispered things like, "Chile, he know he courtin' the devil to carry on like that." And, "I always knew he was a big devil—always prancing around here like he got the spirit and all he got is a fit for evil-doing."

Rev. James continued to flip through the pages, prompting Ernest to leap at him, trying to snatch the book out of his hand. But Rev. James dodged his lunge, and Ernest fell flat on his face. Stepping over Ernest, Rev. James presented the book to Bishop Jennings. As Bishop Jennings turned the pages, he said, with disgust, "We don't need to waste another minute talking about this sordid mess. What Rev. Simmons has told you is the truth. Aaa . . . men. Now, some of you sitting out there may not want to hear this truth, and some of you might not want to believe it about the leaders in your church. But accept and believe it you must. Because the lamp of truth is shining down on our church. Aaa . . . men. And I just have to tell you people that the Gospel

United Church is too fine an institution to be desecrated with this filth. Aaa . . . men.

"Church, you need to think long and hard and decide what you want to do about this. You delegates out there, you need to vote right tomorrow. If a preacher's name is in this book, don't make him a bishop. And if a pastor's name is in this book, run him out of his church. Be strong and have the conviction to do right with the Lord. Aaa . . . men."

Folks started jumping up from their seats and running to the stage to see if their pastor's name was in one of those books. Many were not all that surprised by what had transpired this morning—they had been gossiping about their ministers' bad behaviors for years. Maybe, as one lady put it, they had all become so accustomed to the status quo operations of their church that they had lent those no-good preachers a helping hand toward this fall. And perhaps, she had surmised, this is just what everybody needed to get them back on track to doing right in how they served the Lord.

Chapter Twenty-nine

REV. JAMES FORKED UP A BIG MOUTHFUL OF ROSE Neese's chit'lin's, looked up to heaven, smiled, and said, "Thank you, Jesus!"

Theophilus laughed. He had never met anyone who loved chit'lin's as much as Rev. James. He dipped his fork into his own pile of chit'lin's, covered in hot sauce, and tasted them.

"Whew," he said, eyes watering, and reached for his glass of iced tea.

"Now see, Baybro," Thayline said. "I have told you almost all of your life to quit piling all of that hot sauce on your chit'lin's. But do you listen to me? No . . ."

"Honey, let Baybro enjoy his food," Willis chided. "He's only gonna be with us a few more days, and then you'll be moping around the house all sad and lonely for your little brother."

Theophilus looked over and raised an eyebrow at Thayline, who ignored him.

"Don't act like you don't care," Willis said. "Baybro,

it's true. Whenever you and Baby Doll leave, this here woman gets all long in the face and worry me something terrible about when y'all coming back. Don't let all of that fussing and carrying on fool you."

Theophilus smiled at his sister. He knew she loved him dearly but was just too stubborn to admit it out loud. He wiped his mouth and went over to where she was sitting and gave her a big smack on the cheek.

"Boy, stop. You'll have my whole face stinking with your old chit'lin' lips."

He laughed and kissed her again.

Essie smiled. Theophilus and Thayline were something else. They loved each other fiercely, even if they were always fussing and bickering about something.

Theophilus looked around his mother's kitchen at all the folks crowded up in it, savoring the feelings of joy, love, and contentment they brought up, and it seemed to him that he was basking in the miracle of God's love. Some people thought that the only way to feel God was in church, but he knew better. God was everywhere, always there, always a breath away. It could hit you at any moment, like right now, reminding you that one of the many places God can be found is in the love of your family. He wished he had a pen on him so that he could jot down those thoughts for a sermon.

"Baybro, what you think gone happen tomorrow? You know, despite all the action this morning, I didn't get a feeling that y'all accomplished everything you set out to do."

"Me neither," Uncle Booker said to Willis.

"Ernest will not win a bishop's seat at this conference," Bishop Jennings said evenly. "His son will be demoted to serve as an assistant pastor at a prominent church in Detroit. And when things cool down, he'll be moved to a smaller church, and then to a much larger congregation by the time the next Triennial Conference rolls around."

Theophilus shook his head. All this work, stress, and worry for Marcel to chase women at another church.

"You two quit looking so glum. This business we're in is a lot bigger than this mess," Bishop Jennings said. "See, there is your church, then your district and the denomination. But most importantly, there is the business of the Lord. And as long as God is in business, the devil is out there just ready to do some work of his own. This thing we were dealing with this morning was way beyond you and me and a few corrupt preachers. It is a thing, a force, trying to harm the very soul of the church. Those men who started this mess and the ones whose names are in those two books are just pitiful little pawns in a war that outshadows any of us in this room."

"Amen! Preach, Bishop," Rev. James said, in between bites. He had been thinking those thoughts all morning and hoped someone else would see things like he did.

"So," Theophilus said. "So, Bishop, where does that leave all of us?"

Looking at his young pastor struggle against disillusionment with the church, Percy Jennings recognized that this was what it really meant to be the senior bishop. It was about more than overseeing a multimillion-dollar budget and administration of a national organization. It was really about right and wrong, serving the Lord, honor and duty, caring for the folks who made up the church, and preaching the good news of Jesus Christ.

"You know where it leaves you? Son, it leaves you at the altar of God's grace and mercy. Did you really think for one minute that this calling you answered would be easy? No, Theophilus, it is a daily walk to do right, by yourself and those you love as well as by your church. It is a calling to love the church like Jesus did, which brings with it the responsibility to make sure that the Body of Christ, the Church, can stand tall and look the Lord dead in the eye with a righteous heart.

"So before you start getting all discouraged because these men didn't get the just desserts that *you* thought they should have, take stock of why you took this job in the first place. Because, let me tell you, what happened this morning was earthshaking. You didn't feel it all that much because it all came down in a series of tremors, but mark my word, the shake-up happened. And I guarantee you that you will see some surprising things happening tonight when those votes are cast. I have been in this business a while, and I have never ceased to be amazed by watching the hand of God at work."

He turned toward Rev. James.

"Am I right, Bishop?"

"Yes, Lord. You know you got that right, Bishop."

Chapter Thirty

*J*HE GENERAL CONFERENCE ENDED WITH THE blowup Bishop Jennings had predicted. The almost-fight between Theophilus and his adversaries that morning was only a prelude to the monumental battles that raged not only over the selection of bishops but between those pastors who had joined the preachers' club and their irate parishioners. At least forty congregations were anxious to find out who their new bishops would be, so that they could petition them for new pastors. But the first big eruption came with the selection of the bishops. As Bishop Jennings had thought, Ernest Brown didn't win a seat. In fact, he didn't even make a decent showing. And once the church folk smelled blood, they voted down every candidate who was visibly connected with Ernest Brown and the club. Both Jimmy Thekston and Willie Williams were passed over, and men who no one ever expected to win stepped up to fill their vacant seats.

One was another pastor from Michigan, a faithful man

who had long been denied the support of Bishop Lawson Giles, who took all of Ernest's votes. But an even bigger surprise came at the eleventh hour, when there was one seat left and no front-runner to fill it—and so Josiah Samuels won hands down. What amazed Theophilus about Reverend Samuels winning a bishop's seat was that he was one of the first members of the preachers' club. But he reminded himself of Bishop Jennings's words—that the business they were in was a lot bigger than one man's mess.

What bothered Theophilus most was that nothing happened to Otis Caruthers. He would remain a bishop (located or not) and continue to receive a stipend from the denomination. He had not been turned over to the authorities when the Richmond city police started sniffing around the funeral home for evidence of illegal activity, much of which pointed to Bishop Caruthers. All Theophilus could think was that God wanted Otis Caruthers around just to keep them all on their toes, mindful that the devil was still very busy at church.

He leaned over and tied his shoes—Stacy Adams, with all of that fine leather detailing he appreciated—then stood up and went to look at himself in the large mirror inside the closet door. One of the things he liked most about their new house in St. Louis were the mirrors on the doors of the cedar-lined closets. He decided now that he looked pretty good in the black silk gabardine pants and the finely crafted black clerical shirt he was wearing. Good enough to greet his new congregation at Freedom Temple Gospel United Church in the heart of St. Louis's North Side.

He tilted his head to the side, to check his profile from another angle, and then smiled at Essie, still wearing her slip, who caught him at it and gave him a "boy, you know you ought to be a-shamed of yourself" look. He turned around and wrapped her in his arms, making sure to grab a good handful of her butt.

She pushed at him playfully. "Negro, you are too hopeless."

"Maybe so. But I am *your* hopeless Negro."

She laughed and showed him the envelope she had been holding in her hand.

"Who's this from?"

"Saphronia."

"Saphronia? Why would she write us?"

Essie pulled the letter out of the envelope, scanned it a few seconds, and said, "First, she wants to thank us for sending her to Bishop Jennings. Says she loves Atlanta and feels very fortunate to be working under Mrs. Jennings as the speech therapist for her elementary school. Said that she is beginning to feel a lot more like herself."

"I bet she is feeling more like herself because she ditched that clown, Marcel Brown."

Essie shrugged and said, "I guess so."

"That Negro must have been miserable to be with. What else does she say?"

"For starters, that Marcel's ex-girlfriend, Precious Powers, turned in some more of his books, ones that proved how much of the church's money he had mismanaged—something Saphronia wasn't even aware of. Once the bishops got ahold of those books, not even Bishop Giles could save him. So, it seems like he is a bit unemployed."

"And Sonny Washington?"

"He ended up having to marry Glodean Benson after she told him she was pregnant."

Theophilus opened his mouth to say that it had always been his understanding that Glodean couldn't have children.

Essie held up her hand. "I know what you are about to say, but as Saphronia points out, Glodean won't be the first woman to get a man that way. What I can't understand is why she would want that Sonny Washington. I guess we can only pray that when Sonny finds out he was fooled, because she fakes losing the baby or something, he controls that violent temper. That girl is playing with fire."

Theophilus shivered to think that he had once been entangled in that poor woman's crazy mess. All he could do was pray for her.

Essie pulled and tugged at her dress, looking in the long, oval mirror that hung on the pastor's office door. She had made an emerald green shift especially for today, with crystal bugle beading on the capped sleeves and all around the scooped neckline. But already it felt too snug. She asked Theophilus, "Is this dress too tight?"

He took his time looking her over and then smiled that smile, eyes first, then on down to his mouth. "No. It's not too tight, just right. Makes me kind of wish I didn't have to get up in the pulpit this morning. Wish I could sit out in the congregation next to your fine little self and pat you on the knee a couple of times when something in the sermon got to sounding kind of good to me."

"Just my knee?" she teased.

"Yeah, that is, if you plan on sitting next to me in church. Now if you want me to go a little higher . . ."

"You know that you are too nasty for your own good, which is why I am in the condition I am in. I can't even find me something decent to wear for your first Sunday as the new pastor of Freedom Temple. I should have listened to Thayline the very first time she told me you had some . . ."

Essie looked up and then back at Theophilus. "What was it that she said about you at her house?"

"She said that I had a baby packed up in me or something like that. And," he continued, leaning down to wrap his hands gently around her waist and pat her tummy, "I guess she was right."

Essie stepped back, smoothing the dress over her thighs and turning around to check her backside in the mirror.

"Baby, will you leave that dress alone," Theophilus said. "I told you that it's not too tight. You look fine."

His eyes swept over her backside, which was rounder with the baby and even more sexier-looking in that dress. "And if you ask me . . ." he added.

Essie gave him a look that clearly said, "But, I didn't *ask* you."

He ignored her and continued, "Like I said, if you ask me, I don't think a pregnant woman ever looked better in a dress."

He put his arms around her and kissed her on the cheek. His lips had the same warmth and passion as when he kissed her in front of Coral Thomas's house at the end of their first real date.

He said, "Ummmm, thank God some things never change."

There was a knock on the door. Theophilus knew that it was Leroy Dawson, who was doing his training as a minister and had come from Mount Nebo, along with his wife, Pearl, to serve as his assistant pastor.

"Rev. Simmons, do we need to get the processional

started?" he asked. "Folks are getting anxious to see what their new pastor is all about. Seems to me that the buzz around here at Freedom Temple is that they have a pastor with some—"

"Balls. Balls, Rev. Dawson. Your pastor has some balls," Eddie Tate said, grinning into Theophilus's face as he opened the door.

"Man, your butt is a sight for sore eyes. How did you manage to sneak away from your church this morning?"

"Wasn't any problem. Just told my trustees I was coming down to lend you some support. And since you are the denomination's man of the hour, they sent me here with their blessings. Even sent you a little gift for your collection box."

Theophilus took the check, smiling, and then said hello to Johnnie Thomas, who was looking good in an ivory silk suit with a matching pillbox hat. He was still getting used to being a prominent pastor. Seems like ever since the conference, folks were looking to him to be the next new leader in the church. And while all of this attention, along with the gifts and privileges that came with it, was nice, it was at times almost overwhelming. Sometimes he felt as if he would never be able to just relax and be himself as long as folks were so bent on "shouting him up and down," as Essie called it, every chance they got. But he recognized that the old pastor Theophilus Simmons was gone. In his place was a man whose heart was more fixed than ever on answering the call God had on his life, in a way that not only did his denomination proud but that also glorified God.

Theophilus walked over to Rev. James, decked out in a brand-new black robe with very expensive purple silk brocade trimming, and gave his bishop a hearty handshake. He grinned broadly when he said, "Bishop." Rev.

James smiled, took his place next to Theophilus at the head of the processional line, while Essie greeted Susie James with a quick hug, playfully chiding her for being so decked out in a lavender silk suit and matching hat.

Theophilus stepped before his new congregation, confidently trusting God to guide him in molding this church into the kind of congregation that he, Rev. James, and Bishop Jennings felt that all of their churches should be. This church of the future, the one they hoped and prayed would take them into the next millennium, would be where church folk and the not so "churched" folk came for worship, guidance, spiritual development, solace, education and training, as well as to develop strategies to foster the Negro community's growth and progress at all levels. A place where all—children, women, and men—would be welcomed, put to work, and encouraged to reach their fullest potential. A place that was filled with the Lord's presence, where folks would be exposed to the everyday miracle of the love of God. A church that was an evolving, working miracle in itself.

"Our Lord is in this holy temple," Theophilus began. "Let every child, woman, and man be glad in this day and rejoice in the blessings the Lord has seen fit to send our way. Let the church folk say . . ."

"AMEN!"

Reading Group Guide

THEOPHILUS SIMMONS

1. Theophilus's improper relationship with Glodean Benson haunted him for many years, long after the affair was over. How was God's mercy evidenced in Theophilus's life and ministry? **Read 2 Chronicles 7:14; Psalm 41:4-5,12; Jeremiah 3:25; 4:2.**

2. Rev. James reminded Theophilus that the Lord had forgiven him for having an affair with Glodean, yet he continued to live in fear of repercussions. Why do believers often have such a hard time believing that God has forgiven them? **Read Psalm 37:23-24.** How can they break free? **Psalm 103:1-13; Proverbs 28:13.**

3. What was your reaction to Theophilus going to an establishment like Pompey's Rib Joint? Do you think ministers should avoid such places? **Read 1 Thessalonians 5:22; Romans 14:21.** Or do you feel that Theophilus's behavior was entirely acceptable and appropriate? **Read Ecclesiastes 8:15; Matthew 11:19; John 2:1-2.**

4. Theophilus is obviously a very passionate man. How does Theophilus's life and ministry show evidence that he had submitted himself and his passions to godly control? **Read Romans 8:4-6; Galatians 5:16-17;24.**

ESSIE LEE

5. At the beginning of their association with one another, why do you think that Theophilus was so intrigued by Essie, even though she tried to maintain

a façade of disdain for him? **Read Ruth 2:1-10;
Esther 2:17; Song of Songs 4:12; 6:11-13.**

6. Theophilus chose to marry a woman who did not
    fit the mold of the typical pastor's wife of that time.
    How did the Lord use her uniqueness to serve Him
    by supporting her husband and finding her own place
    in ministry? **Read Proverbs 18:22; 31:10-20; Song
    of Songs 6:8-9; Luke 1:5-6.**

7. How did Essie demonstrate confidence in herself
    and her husband's love, despite the fact that other
    women were obviously attracted to her handsome,
    dynamic husband? **Proverbs 31:25-31.** In what
    ways do you think she discovered that being a min-
    ister's wife is a ministry and a special calling of its
    own?

8. Essie had to cope with people who accepted her only
    after she became a pastor's wife. Why do people, in-
    cluding Christians, try to rank the worthiness of human
    beings based on their social standing? **Job 23:18-19;
    Matthew 5:47; Romans 2:11.** Do you think many
    women have wanted to marry a minister in order to
    obtain a higher status in their community?

THE WOMEN

9. Why are many women in the church, like Glodean,
    obsessed with "trapping" a preacher? Why do you
    think men are enticed by such women? **Read
    Proverbs 7:4-27.**

10. Both Precious and Saphronia, feeling betrayed, sought their own revenge against Marcel Brown. Why do some Christians seek revenge instead of turning to the Lord when times get tough? **Read Leviticus 19:18; Judges 16:28.** How should they respond instead? **Read Matthew 5:38-48; Romans 12:19.**

11. Precious was willing to engage in various unsavory acts because she loved Marcel. How could she ever have hoped that their relationship, given its nature, would prosper? Have you ever found yourself going just a little too far to try and hold on to a relationship? **Read Psalm 37:5; Proverbs 16:3.**

12. Saphronia and her grandmother looked down on those whose speech, skin color, or socio-economic status was viewed as less than their own. Do you believe people who think this way ever stop to consider how God feels about their attitude/beliefs? **Read Matthew 25:40; Romans 12:2-10.** How can Black Christians address such behavior within the Black Church?

CHURCH BISHOPS AND PASTORS

13. Marcel Brown referred to men like Murcheson James as "high-and-mighties who think God called them just so that they could keep an eye on" the actions of other ministers. Should more ministers concern themselves with the unsavory actions of fellow clergy? **Read Luke 17:3; 2 Corinthians 2:17; Galatians 6:1.**

14. Why are so many ministers like Marcel Brown, his father Ernest, Sonny Washington, and Bishop Caruthers able to get away with so much mess in the church? **Jeremiah 5:26-28; Matthew 24:5,11,24; Romans 16:17-18.**

15. For a time it seemed as though corrupt leaders like Otis Caruthers, Ernest and Marcel Brown, and the senior bishop, would triumph in their wicked ways. What should our response be when it seems as if the rotten people in the world seem to always get ahead? **Read Job 21:7-16; Psalm 37:7; Habakkuk 3:17-19.**

16. Corruption among certain bishops and pastors was well known, yet tolerated in silence. Why do some good people stand by silently when they know things are not right? **Read Esther 4:14; Psalm 37:14; 39:1-2.**

CONCLUSION

17. *Church Folk* affirms that love, passion, and desire, when properly focused, are acceptable feelings/behaviors for God's people and are part of His blessings to His people. **Read Genesis 24:15-27; Song of Songs.** Why do you think this message has become distorted among some church folk, many of whom believe such behavior is improper for Christians?

18. How does the book's ending demonstrate the spiritual truth that wickedness and evil cannot prevail

over righteousness? **Read Psalm 37:14-15,25; 94:14-15; Proverbs 10:25; 29:16; 2 Peter 2:9.**

19. Many of the problems that afflicted the Black Church during the 1960s (womanizing preachers, classism, color prejudice, women granting sexual favors to ministers) remain today. How can we move beyond these issues instead of tolerating them or accepting them as the norm? **Read Leviticus 26:40-42; Ezekiel 37:8-14; Jeremiah 5:31; 18:6; 1 John 1:9.**

20. How should Christians respond to persons who shun church membership because of corruption with the ranks of its leadership? **Read Acts 5:29; 1 Corinthians 1:12-13; 3:4-11; 1 Peter 4:18.**

CHAPTER 1

"A Little Women's Revolution Right up Here in the Church"

In September 1975, just nine months before Gethsemane Missionary Baptist Church was to celebrate its 100th anniversary, its pastor, Rev. Clydell Forbes, Sr., died. Some church members cried, others immediately started cooking food for the First Lady and her three boys, and Mr. Louis Loomis, one of the senior deacons in the congregation, said out loud what others were secretly thinking: "Why couldn't that cross-eyed, carrying-on stallion of a preacher hang on till the church was 101? If the boy had to up and die, at the very least, he could have had the common decency to get us through the 100th anniversary."

Rev. Forbes was only in his fifties and hadn't even occupied Gethsemane's pulpit all that long; just six years to be exact. No one expected that they'd lose him so soon, and at the worst possible time. A church anniversary without a pastor was equivalent to a pastor standing up to preach without a suit and tie, robe, and handkerchief in his hand—the pastor was that central—and the centennial was the most momentous occasion in Gethsemane's history. The pastor was the one who would appoint and supervise the centennial committees, oversee fund-raising, and most important of all, determine the celebration's theme, developing the sermons to herald and commemorate that special day, the Second Sunday in June.

Now all the planning was brought to a screeching halt until the Forbes family and the church family got through the man's funeral. And it was an ordeal—a long, tearjerking service that became a spectacle when three of his "special interest" women fell out, crying and screaming with grief, and had to be removed by the ushers. Then the congregation pitched in to help his widow pack up the parsonage and get resettled with her children in a new home. So it was some time before Bert Green, the head of the Deacon Board, thought it appropriate to resume business and called a meeting of the church officers to discuss hiring a new pastor.

As they chewed over the list of potential preachers to interview, Bert's wife, Nettie, walked into the room, carrying a tray loaded down with sandwiches, potato salad, pickles and olives, caramel and pineapple-coconut cakes, and sweet potato pies cooked by one of the church's five missionary societies. Bert grabbed himself a thick, juicy, home cooked ham sandwich as his fellow Deacon and Finance Board members heaped their plates high with food. Nettie had gotten an earful of their conversation on her way up from the kitchen, and it hadn't escaped her that the men had quit talking the moment they saw her struggling with that tray in the doorway.

Now they all sat there so self-satisfied, with that "we is in the Upper Room" look on their faces—the same men whose political head-butting had led to the appointment of Clydell Forbes, as spineless and weak a pastor as the church had ever seen. Helping them to their choice of iced tea or fresh coffee, Nettie pressed her lips together, mad enough to want to shake up these smug, never-did-know-how-to-pick-a-good-preacher men.

So she ignored Bert's signals that they were impatient for her to leave. Avoiding his eyes, she asked, as if butter wouldn't melt in her mouth, "So, who's on this list y'all talking about?"

No one seemed to hear her but Mr. Louis Loomis, the oldest member of both boards, who was chewing on the fat from his ham sandwich. He slipped his reading glasses down on the tip of his nose and resumed where he'd left off. "Like I said, some of these here preachers out of our price range."

Bert looked at the paper without acknowledging Nettie, picked up his pen, and asked, "Which ones?"

"Rev. Macy Jones, Rev. David O. Clemson, III, Rev. Joe Joseph, Jr . . ."

Bert started drawing lines through those names until Cleavon Johnson, the head of the Finance Board, stopped him. "Keep Rev. Clemson on the list," he said.

"Why?" Mr. Louis Loomis shot back. He and Cleavon Johnson mixed like oil and water. Cleavon might be a business leader who had grabbed hold of the church's purse strings, but to Mr. Louis Loomis he was still the arrogant punk he used to belt-whoop.

"Because—" Cleavon started to say, then slammed his mouth shut, staring pointedly at Nettie.

Pretending not to notice, Nettie grabbed one of the chairs lined up against the wall, pulled it up to the conference table, and sat down like she belonged there. Then she looked straight at Cleavon and asked, still sounding innocent, "Just what is it that *we're* looking for in *our* new pastor?"

Cleavon Johnson glared at her as if to say, "Woman, you way out of line." His "boys" on the Finance Board coughed and cleared their throats, Bert's cue to get his woman straightened out. But Bert locked eyes with Wendell Cates, who was married to Nettie's sister, Viola, and caught his smirking wink. Bert and Nettie's only child, Bertha Kay, was just like her mama, only Bertha was spoiled rotten and likely as not to create this kind of scene. Though Nettie knew how to behave when she wanted to, her ladylike self-control masked a headstrong streak.

Wendell's expression told Bert, "Your girl on a roll. Let it be." Bert gave Wendell a sly smile that implied, "I hear you," and sat back to watch his wife give Cleavon a good dose of her homespun "medicine."

When it became clear that Bert was not going to chastise his woman, Cleavon decided that he had to intervene. Puffing himself up with his full dignity as head of the Finance Board, he began authoritatively, "Sister Nettie, the senior men of this church, including your husband, have carefully formulated this list based on reliable recommendations . . ."

Nettie stole a glance at Mr. Louis Loomis, but all he did was adjust his glasses and crumple his napkin, as if to say, "My name is Bennett and I ain't in it."

Taking that as approval, she interrupted, "What I'm asking is, who—"

Cleavon tried to cut her off, "You'll meet our choices along with the rest of the congregation—"

"Or rather, what kind of men are being 'formulated' and 'recommended' to be *our* new pastor?" she continued saying, as if he wasn't even talking.

"Sister Nettie," Cleavon scolded, "It's time for you to run along, like a good girl. You have your own proper duties as one of the church's helpmeets. We have ours, and now you are obstructing us from carrying them out." His voice grew stern. "You are not a duly appointed officer of this church and until you are, I think it would be wise, on your part, to let the heads of this Godly house run this house."

Nettie pushed her chair away from the table, rose, and wiped her hands on her apron. Cleavon thought it was a gesture of defeat, that she was accepting his rebuke. But Nettie wasn't retreating. She was retrenching as she stacked the dirty dishes and mustered up her sweetest, most chastised-woman-sounding voice to say, "Brother Cleavon, only the Lord knows what moves you. Only the Lord know what makes you so forceful in what you do and say. But I am thankful that you express yourself so openly. Pray my strength."

As Nettie left, Cleavon nodded self-importantly to the

group, not realizing she had just told him that he was in a class by himself and too dumb to try to keep it to himself.

Bert and Wendell stifled chuckles but felt unsettled by Nettie's exit. She had to be up to something more than needling Cleavon Johnson. The encounter felt ominous, leaving them both with the impression that Nettie was throwing down a gauntlet as a declaration of war.

When Nettie got back to the kitchen, she slammed her tray down on the counter so hard that she almost broke some of the heavy, mint-green glass cups, plates, and saucers that were always in plentiful supply at church.

Her sister Viola jumped up, startled, and Nettie cussed, "I be doggoned and banned from heaven!"

"What's all this banging and ugly talking?" Sylvia Vicks demanded. "Nettie Green, you ain't out in them streets. You up in church. And you just best start remembering that."

"Sylvia, pray my strength, 'cause I am so mad at our men up in that room." Nettie pointed toward the ceiling, shaking her head in disgust. "I mean, they should have learned something worthwhile about hiring a preacher after Rev. Forbes. But they not even talking about character and morals . . ."

She stopped herself—"Forgive me, Jesus, for speaking ill of the dead"—then continued, "Lord only knows how much money they wasted bailing Clydell Forbes out of his women troubles—"

"What 'women troubles,' Nettie Green?" asked

Cleavon's wife, Katie Mae Johnson. "I never heard about the church spending money like that. With Cleavon on the Deacon Board and being head of the Finance Board, I think I would have heard if he was making payoffs to errant women."

"Humph," Sylvia interjected. "Don't know how you missed all that, with the way Rev. Forbes had such a weakness for loose-tail women in booty-clutching dresses—bigger and fatter the booty, the better, I hear. And sad thing, Sister Forbes had a big fat rumpa-seat hangin' off the back of her. Don't know why he wanted all those other women seeing what he had laying up next to him in his own house."

"Y'all, we should not be up in this church, talking all in Sister Forbes's business and up under her clothes like that. It ain't right, and it show ain't Christian."

Viola sighed out loud, raised her hands high in the air, and waved them. "Katie Mae, it's Christian charity to tell the truth about the truth."

"And you should have known something, Katie Mae," Sylvia added, "seeing as Cleavon was the main one in charge of Rev. Forbes's 'errant women' funds. We all keep telling you that man keep too much from you. He your husband, and all he ever tell you is, 'You think and read too much, always working yourself up over some nonsense.' Then he go out in the streets, and when he come home be acting like he just got through passing out the two fish and five loaves of bread to the multitudes."

Katie Mae real quick sneaked and wiped her eyes with the edge of her apron. Sometimes even your best friends didn't truly understand the magnitude of your pain. She sniffed once and put on a brave face before saying, "Aww, Sylvia, you can't judge my Cleavon by your Melvin. Melvin, Sr. tells you pretty much everything and lets you run your house. But in Cleavon's home, the woman is beneath the man. He believe in the strict bible ways."

Sylvia had to stop herself from quoting one of Mr. Louis Loomis's observations about Cleavon's "strict bible ways" mess: "That boy always pontificating about a woman being beneath a man 'cause his tail always so intent on being on top of one."

"Well, it don't matter what Cleavon believe," Nettie said. "The fact is, he used church money to get the reverend out of trouble. But it ain't just the money that makes me so mad—it's our men using they man pride and they man rules, not even God's, to pick our preachers, acting like I committed a sin just by asking them a question. Look at us down here in this hot kitchen, fixing food and washing dishes, while they upstairs eating, talking, laughing, and acting like they the Apostles. This is our church, too. It just ain't right. And I ain't gone stand for it *no more.*"

"But what you propose to do?" Viola asked. "We not on any of those boards. So I don't see how we gone select a preacher."

"That's right," Katie Mae said. "You doing all this big bad talk and you don't even know how to go from A to B."

Nettie took off her apron and closed her eyes, praying for direction. When the inspiration came (she couldn't be sure from where), she snapped her fingers.

"Viola, Sylvia, Katie Mae—here's what we'll do. Our mens thought they could put me in my place. So what we gone use is our women's place to make them do right. We're gone get us a woman's secret weapon."

"What would that be?" Sylvia asked.

"*Who* is more like it—someone who's an expert when it comes to sniffing out a man. Someone who can tell us which one of those preachers on they list is decent. And I know just the secret weapon girl who can help us. My neighbor, Sheba Cochran."

"Sheba Cochran?" Katie Mae snapped. "The heifer with all them baby daddies? That party-hearty club girl used to be one of Cleavon's women!"

For a moment, none of them breathed. Ever since high school, Cleavon had believed he was "fine as wine and every woman's kind," chasing women like his life depended on it. He was still running like a no-good rascal, but Katie Mae continued to defend him. It infuriated her friends, but if Katie Mae wanted to play dumb, they felt obliged to hold their peace.

Now the truth was out.

"I didn't mean to hurt you," Nettie said softly. "And you have a right to be angry."

"Why would you or any other married woman even want to cut your eyes at that thang?"

"Katie Mae, there's something you should know. Cleavon lied to Sheba."

Katie Mae opened her mouth, but Nettie went on before she could speak. "Cleavon met Sheba over in East St. Louis at the Mothership Club. He claimed to be legally separated from you, and she honestly believed his marriage was over. So did I, until I learned he was still spending some nights with you. When I told Sheba, she broke it off. Remember Cleavon's black eye?"

Katie Mae nodded.

"Sheba did that, while she was cussing him out. I've known Sheba since we were kids, Katie Mae. She's never purposefully gone with a married man."

Tears streamed down Katie Mae's face. She was hurt, angry, and convicted in her heart all at the same time. She knew how Cleavon operated. And her grandmother constantly told her, "Baby, just a 'cause you let Cleavon run you, don't mean nobody else will. You better understand that there more folks than not who want to set his tail straight."

Sylvia handed Katie Mae a paper napkin and then gave Nettie the eye, hoping she could think of something to soften the blow she had just delivered. Nettie got the message and went to Katie Mae, taking both of her hands in her own. "I'm so sorry," she said.

When Katie Mae regained her composure, Nettie added, "Please trust me about Sheba. Cleavon picked Clydell Forbes, and he ain't picking our new pastor. But the fact is, none of these mens—including Bert, Wendell, and Melvin, Sr.—have the sense to find a man who can lead the church, bring us together for the anniversary, *and* do right by the womens. It's got to be up to us."

Katie Mae sighed heavily. Nettie was right.

"And for that we need Sheba," Sylvia said.

"Yes," Viola chimed in. "That Sheba knows men like I know my name. If one of these preachers on they list is bad, she'll find him out."

"And if one is a good man?" Katie Mae asked.

"Then she'll know that, too," Nettie answered. "She the one always told me to quit worrying about Bert. Said, with a good man, if you take care of him right, he ain't going nowhere. But with a bad man, ain't nothing you can do. Whatever he looking to find out in the street ain't about you. It's just some of his own mess that he ain't ready to deal with."

Katie Mae sighed again, as if taking her words to heart.

"So, are we agreed?" Viola asked.

They all clasped hands to seal the bargain.

"Now how do we plan to get Sheba next to these preachers?" Sylvia said. "Some of them slick as slick oil and liable to slip from a tight spot. And what if our mens catch her East-St. Louis, love-to-party-self up in church? One of them bound to ask what got Sheba up so early on Sunday morning."

"Hmmm," Nettie said, turning it over in her mind. "I think we'll have to leave it to Sheba to get to the preachers, and we'll each have to find a way to handle our mens ourselves."

"Okay, I can see that part. But Nettie, will Sheba help us?"

"I bet she will. She'll see it as a challenge."

"Wait a minute!" said Katie Mae. "What if Sheba decide she wants to lay up with one of those preachers?" She paused, and her eyes got big and round. "And, what if one of those preachers real lowdown and try to get some from her, when even *she* don't want to give it to him."

"Katie Mae, why you all of a sudden so worried about Sheba Cochran? I thought you said she was nothing but a party-hearty hussy."

"I did. But I don't want to have a hand in her sinful ways."

"You won't. If Sheba will help us, it'll be for her own good reasons. Look, the girl is tough—she's raised four kids alone. I've seen her box down her old men when she needed her child support payments. And do you think preachers are rougher than those mens she meets out in the clubs?"

"Yeah," Viola said, laughing. "If she do want one of those old men, she can have him. That'll be between her, her sheets, that man, and the Lord—and then we'll know for sure that preacher ain't worth a poot."

"Shoot, I say let the chile have her fun," Sylvia agreed. "It'll be worth it to keep some trifling no-good thang out of our pulpit."

Katie Mae closed her eyes and clasped her hands to her chest. She hoped that the Lord would understand and forgive their wayward souls. Still, she didn't see how He could possibly bless this mess.

Sylvia looked over at Katie Mae agonizing and praying over Sheba Cochran, what she needed to pray and agonize over was that no-count, trouble-causing man of hers.

The Publisher's Diary

Dear Faithful Reader,

For many of us there are few things more satisfying than reading a good book. But reading a good book that nourishes your spirit and strengthens your faith provides more than satisfaction—it's a blessing. *Church Folk* by Michelle Andrea Bowen is just such a book!

Thousands of readers have been blessed by the same story I first read and fell in love with several years ago. I am so happy to introduce even more of you to *Church Folk*. Get ready for the hilarious and wonderful story of the southern, and oh-so-fine, young pastor, Theophilus Simmons, and his new, feisty no-nonsense bride, Essie Lee as they attempt to deal with an out of control congregation, denominational politics *and* a new marriage.

Publishers Weekly raved, "Readers will enjoy the rich glimpses into the spirit-filled African-American church of the 1960s, complete with politicking, blackmail [and] colorful dialogue."

Brimming with a realistic dose of traditional African-American church culture, your cup is sure to run over as *Church Folk* serves up lots of laughter, lessons of hope, perseverance, faith, and love.

Be blessed in your reading,

Denise Stinson

About the Author

MICHELE ANDREA BOWEN, a first-time novelist, graduated from the University of North Carolina at Chapel Hill with master's degrees in both history and public health. She lives in North Carolina with her two daughters.

Reading Groups for African American
Christian Women Who Love God and Like to Read.

BE A PART OF THE
GLORY GIRLS
READING GROUPS!

THIS EXCITING BI-MONTHLY BOOK CLUB IS FOR AFRICAN
AMERICAN CHRISTIAN WOMEN SEEKING FELLOWSHIP WITH
OTHER WOMEN WHO ALSO LOVE GOD AND ENJOY READING.

For more information about the GLORY GIRLS
READING CLUB, to connect with an established
club in your area, and/or to become a club leader,
please visit www.glorygirlsread.net.